Pluto Cove

By Arran Forbes

For my A, B, and C

Table of Contents

PART ONE: The Polar Storms   **1**

    Chapter One: Before   3

    Chapter Two: The Early Days   31

    Chapter Three: One Year Later   81

PART TWO: The Birds   **147**

    Chapter Four: In the Middle   149

    Chapter Five: Three Months Later   185

    Chapter Six: Two Months Later   213

PART THREE: The Jökulhlaup   **243**

    Chapter Seven: One Week Later   245

    Chapter Eight: Three Days Later   291

    Chapter Nine: Four Hours Later   305

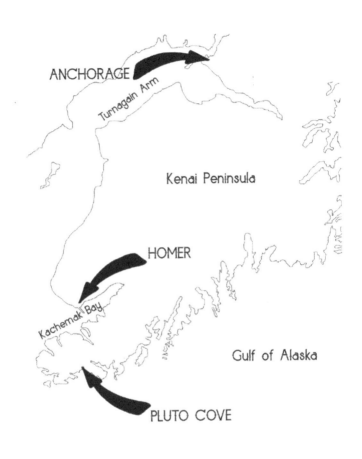

Map of the Kenai Peninsula

PART ONE

THE POLAR STORMS

CHAPTER ONE – *Before*

Callie was six when she disappeared from the blueberry patch. She disappeared from behind me without so much as a tremor in the air she had occupied. If she fell into the creek, there was no call for help. If she tripped into the hollow of a dry and dying tree, there was no gasp as her feet went out from under her. If a mighty animal grabbed her by the neck and dragged her into the forest, there was no huff of a predator or footprint of curling claws ground into the dirt. There was nothing. My little sister was gone.

The day I lost her, the wildfire smoke had turned the blue sky to brown. The air we breathed had the texture of gravel and I tried to pull it back as though it were a curtain I could throw open into another, clear-eyed world. But there was no other world at all. Just this one. My lonely, burning world. I ripped at the empty space in front of me like a person tearing their way through a house in flames. I screamed her name, clearing a coiled path in the smoke with the vibrations of my voice. Not even the birds replied.

Of all the ways to disappear in the Alaskan wilderness, we never considered she had been kidnapped. Grief and hunger leave no room for abstract thinking, let alone an imagination.

HERE'S WHAT I couldn't understand. Her bright orange bucket in the mold of a sandcastle had been full of blueberries, and it also disappeared. Where was her bucket? Of all the possible stories I wrote around her disappearance, none explained why that bucket and her pile of blueberries vanished too. I mentioned this to Mom and Dad, but they didn't seem to care. Or to listen. The frenzy around their grief was too severe.

My own grief was quieter. How can a loss so big and ugly and incomprehensible be reduced to something as simplistic and finite as words or cries? There had already been so much lost. Our big blue house on Manor Avenue. The feeling of fullness after a dinner around our kitchen table. The friends I had known since preschool.

I missed the steady, predictable ringing of the school bells that moved me from one part of my day to the next.

I missed walking Benji around the neighborhood and waving hello to a dozen neighbors whose pets I fed and plants I watered when they took long winter vacations in Arizona.

I missed the smell of old fake leather on the school bus, patched with peeling duct tape, as it jostled on giant wheels down the berms of snow on our unplowed street.

I missed the sound of rain against my bedroom window, dripping from the leak in the gutter just outside; the earthworms flushed out from the ground that Callie and I collected in the folds of our raincoats and fed to the chickens in the yard. Of all the things lost when we fled to Pluto Cove, it was the rain I missed the most. Because of the rain, everything else was gone.

AT FIRST, I HEARD SNIPPETS on the radio when Mom drove me to soccer. Sometimes I would catch a headline on a newspaper in the waiting room of my dentist's office. Ads popped up on my internet searches,

4

ads that proclaimed to know the cause of the drought, or pleas for aid to the hardest hit places. Then Miss Carrew started talking about it in class and assigned reading on the Dust Bowl. I was twelve, I was self-centered, and it wasn't until the world screamed out in one massive, unified fever pitch that I heard the alarm.

It took three years for the drought to penetrate my egocentric world, but I'll condense it for you. Consider it a history lesson.

No one understood why the drought happened the way it did. Meteorologists and climatologists and other kinds of scientists (and many other people with just a *feeling*) posited theories. But no one could explain why the rain slowed and slowed, and all but stopped. The world's mighty waterfalls: Niagara, Victoria, Pu'uka'oku, Kaieteur, Gullfoss – all those great slabs of gushing water – went from churning and boiling natural wonders to ephemeral trickles. Across the planet, drought squeezed dust from dirt like a hand crushing overripe fruit.

Sometimes it rained, somewhere on earth. Clouds rolled in, dark and gravid, wept for a moment, and then dissolved. Some people mapped out the storms, the places where precipitation made landfall, and swore they could predict the next location, swore they could explain why it happened then and there, what behaviors of people or what laylines of the earth crossed at that precise geocoordinate. Some people swore that it was just a phase – as though planet earth were a temperamental child rather than an ancient and ailing being – and that next week, next month, next season, everything would return to normal.

Except that it didn't return to normal.

People flocked to the rivers and lakes and streams like pilgrims to Mecca, storing it in whatever plastic, glass, metal, or rubber containers they could find, and driving it home through record-shattering traffic jams – traffic jams that lasted days, traffic jams through country roads in Montana and Mississippi that had never seen more than a handful of cars in all their existence – because even through the drought, when water hit twenty dollars a gallon, oil was still five.

The oil giants invested $50 billion in groundwater extraction systems to pull water from thousands of feet below the earth's surface, converting their oil drilling rigs into deep water probes. The agriculture giants threw in an equivalent sum for desalination plants to turn salty seawater into fresh water. And the tech giants kicked in an easy nine figures for water treatment systems that could turn sewage into potable water for a city the size of Reno – and then spent another six figures convincing people that the water was safe and drinkable, despite having been flushed down toilets.

But they were too slow – far too slow – in developing the technology. Even confronted with global drought, no one wanted to drink water from a toilet.

Except – and this is a big qualifier – satellite imagery showed there *was* rain. At the North and South Poles. Every wisp of fog, every hopeful gathering of wet, gray clouds, drifted away to the far north or south. And there at the poles those clouds found each other, voltaic, colliding into what reporters called the Super Clouds, and drops of water evaporated from every waterbody and every blade of grass from us in Alaska to my fourth-grade pen pal in Malawi, and those drops whipped and stung and barreled down toward earth in one of the two places no human could ever use it. On some days the images from the space station showed all the green and brown and blue of earth – every inch of coast and ripple of mountains – perfectly visible without cloud cover, with massive swirling black storms at the top and bottom, pulled toward the poles as though by a magnet. It looked like the mitotic cells in biology class, pulling all their DNA and proteins and essential units of life to the very far ends of the cell so that it could split in half. And the world did start to split in half. At least, the world as we knew it.

They called it the Polar Storms.

BEFORE ALL OF THAT – when it was still just an atmospheric oddity, there was just enough rain to make us all say *isn't that weird*. I wandered downstairs after bedtime to find Dad watching late-night TV where the comics cracked jokes about it. A furniture store in midtown hosted gimmicky sales (*One percent off annual interest for every one inch of rain!*), and tourists flocked to all the places typically too socked in by bad weather. The Anchorage airport filled with travelers in search of the perfect view of Denali and the northern lights. Sylvie's family took a vacation to San Francisco, but it was too jammed full of visitors at Fisherman's Wharf – no longer deterred by fog – to be fun. A brochure from a travel agency arrived in our mailbox with a shiny photo showing lines of mountain trekkers snaked up and down the slopes of Everest like streamers at a birthday party, with no storms to impede their ascent.

A team of botanists, never having known a

moment of fame, designed giant satellite dishes of permeable fabric like welwitschia plants to gather moisture from the air. Then they fumbled their way through live interviews on the 24-hour news cycle, for the first time explaining their science to laypeople like us.

Areas that had always been subject to drought, areas with the poorest and most destitute of our species, now dispensed advice to a now-listening globe on how to survive. Our TV saw an explosion of high-level discussions on evaporation, condensation, water cycles, and hydrology. Even my teen beat magazines featured people fetching water atop their heads, wielding well-witching sticks, and holding proud armfuls of drought resistant crops.

On the internet, it was memes of assembled screenshots showing weather forecasts across the world – London, Shenzhen, Lima, Mumbai, Ankara, Toronto, Dar Es Salaam – nothing but blazing yellow sunballs as far into the future as science could see. There was amazement and humor in it because changes like this happen slowly, over geologic time, not all at once. So it couldn't be real. Temperatures were stable – just precipitation patterns were askance. It must be a fluke. Everyone hummed along, falling asleep with the same thought: *tomorrow it will rain*. Or, far worse: *someone out there will figure this out*.

Except Mom. Mom didn't sleep. Mom understood what was happening. Her brain was always on, always looking for the worst possible outcome from even normal events. Before her accident she had been an electrical engineer, and her brain was something quite brilliant and deep and often terrifying. She read about the acidity of the seas, the shutting down of major ocean currents, the new winds that tore around the atmosphere, propelling airplanes across continents at record speeds. She stocked up on canned foods and special drought-resistant seeds and garden bags full of winter clothes from thrift stores.

On Fridays, when Dad had his twelve-hour shifts at the hospital and I played soccer after school, she loaded Callie and all her accumulated goods into the minivan, drove the four hours from Anchorage to the little seaside town of Homer, then boarded a water taxi with Captain Kerry. From Homer it was an hour across Kachemak Bay, past the tiny village of Seldovia, hugging the Kenai Peninsula to stay out of the swell and crash of open water. For another three hours they motored on to the little fjords along the inside passage of the Chugach Islands to the cabin her grandfather had built in his delusions of striking gold in that faraway, lonely, and decidedly gold-free part of the world. She dropped off the food, clothes, and whatever miscellany she had collected – knives, fire starter, first aid kits, blankets, jerry cans of gasoline – then turned right around with Captain Kerry, back to Homer, back into our minivan, and back to Anchorage. Callie was three and a mellow, affable baby. She played with her toes in the backseat, and begged for another trip the moment they pulled into the driveway.

Dad did not fear the drought, at first. *It'll break*, he said, nestled comfortably into his status as a physician and man of self-made wealth. But he did fear for Mom. They tried not to have conversations where I could hear them, but I heard enough. Their conversations in the kitchen I heard from the stairwell. Their conversations in the living room I heard from Callie's playroom in the

9

basement. Their conversations in bed I heard from the guest room. It was in this last place, laying with Benji wrapped up in my arms on a bare mattress – the bed stripped of sheets after Mom packed them up for the cabin – that worry crept into my consciousness. Perhaps Benji sensed it too. He burrowed his nose into my armpit, and I wrapped my arms around his furry torso like a vine growing around a tree.

As a mutt, his fur was both shaggy and bristly. For Christmas, Mom and Dad bought me a dog DNA kit that reported Benji was a combination of twelve different breeds, but the plurality of him was Entlebucher and Bernese Mountain Dog. It showed. His fur was a swirl of black on his back and white on his chest and rust on his legs, with little gray socks at his paws. Having him close to me those nights, as I disentangled the cryptic and tense discussions between my parents, was a salve over the dry and brittle cracks that broke open my world.

"This is not normal behavior, Lisa," Dad said, his voice deep through the walls of the house where I listened, less out of concern than something more like discipline, the way he spoke to me when I told him I had shoveled the driveway but hadn't.

"These are not normal times, Alex," Mom shot back.

"No time is ever a normal time. Every generation of people believes it's the end of the world, that something catastrophic is going to happen. You're turning into one of those people who dig bomb shelters in their backyard and start stockpiling assault rifles."

Mom was quiet. I pictured her pulling at the skin on her wrists, starting straight into space. Dad said she didn't used to be like this. When they met, she was a person of easy laughter and deep sleep. But after her accident, when I was two, she became panicky, anxious. Fireworks on New Years' Eve sent her running into a dark room. The evening news over the radio drained the color from her face. Her psychiatrist encouraged her to do calming, grounding activities, like gardening and chicken rearing. But even that she elevated to neurosis: picking slugs from leaves into the witching hours of the night, documenting the temperature inside the compost pile when the whole city was frozen solid, weighing each year's harvest against the last, and plotting the chickens' egg production in elaborate color graphs.

"You should think about going back on your meds," Dad said, his voice quieter, knowing he waded into treacherous water. I bit into a nail and tore off the tip in a jagged line. "Or make another appointment to talk to Jennifer." Jennifer was Mom's on-again off-again psychiatrist. "It isn't right for Callie and Enna to have to see you like this." My mouth felt dry and I pulled my tongue from where it stuck to my palate.

"Alex," Mom said after a long pause. "I'm not crazy. I'm not. Don't you see? The worst that comes of this is that we have a very well-stocked cabin on the Kenai Peninsula. I'm not hurting anyone. I'm not hurting myself."

"Obsessive behaviors are –" Dad started. Then he thought the better of it and tried a more logical approach. "I know there's a drought, that's obvious. But think about it. Alaska has more freshwater than almost anywhere on earth. All these rivers and lakes, we are in good shape."

"The rain is disappearing, Alex. Do you get that?

Even the rainforest is seeing a seventy percent drop in precipitation, for crying out loud. Even *here*, where it *always* rains, how long has it been now since the last storm? Sure, it might change tomorrow. Or even tonight. But it might not. Everyone is going to start hurting really badly. They're going to be panicking a hell of a lot more than I am." I tightened my grip on Benji in the next room. Mom seldom used bad words. "And up here, in Alaska, yes, we have water. Lots of it. But we are so vulnerable, Alex. We can't grow much food up here. It's too cold. It's too dark. Everything we eat comes from somewhere else. And you really think those people down south are going to let their food get shipped away? That they're going to load up the things they've grown, their vegetables and meats and flour and bread, onto a truck and send it somewhere else? No. Never. All it's going to take is one barge not making it to the port here, one hold-up in the system of a thousand little things that delivers goods up here, and things are going to get very tense. And when – I mean if – *if* that happens, we will have a place to go. And if it doesn't happen, then the cabin will be in great shape for our winter vacation."

I heard her words and understood their truth. Had she been a normal, level-headed mother – like the ones who let us ride in the trunk of their SUV without seatbelts for just one block across the neighborhood, or who sent us out trick-or-treating alone without ruining a costume with a high-visibility reflective vest – I may have believed her. But even in normal times, everything she said came from a place of alarm. So how could I trust her now?

"Lisa, how much more of this are you going to

do? How much longer? You know that highway. You know how deadly it is, how many of my patients through the emergency room come from some idiot taking a corner too fast. Or even the water taxi out there, that shoddy boat. And Captain Kerry isn't the most sober-seeming guy, you know that. What you're doing has risks. Big ones. And you're dragging Callie along every time. It's insane."

Without seeing her, I sensed Mom rubbing her wrists, agitated – like she's wringing the necks of small birds and then snapping them back into place. "You're the one always telling me, Al: life is risky, I worry too much. But now you *want* me to worry about something? But you want that thing to be a car accident instead of a drought?" She dropped her voice, low and dumb, a lame and inflammatory way of mimicking Dad. "*Don't worry so much about Enna going to school, the odds of an active shooter are miniscule.* Or, *don't worry so much about sending Callie to daycare with those kids whose parents have Confederate Flag bumper stickers. You can't let your fears get in the way of living your life.* But now you want to try to scare me? Why would you do that?"

Dad sighed. "It's all about weighing relative risks, you know that…" My cheeks grew hot and I pressed them, one by one, into Benji's cool nose.

"Stop it, Alex. Just stop. I have one responsibility and that's to take care of my daughters. And right now, this is how I can do that. But this *one thing* … I am going to do this *one thing* that feels important to me. I am not a freak. I am not ill. Stop treating me like I am."

It was a combination of words she repeated throughout my childhood. *I am not a freak. I am not ill.* It

13

was a refrain, the chorus to a song that played over and over in her head. Especially when she was having one of her spells. Those times when she could not get out of bed, could not eat, could not get dressed. Could do nothing but wring her wrists, over and over. Dad would allow me to pay a visit to her bedside and she would give me a warm and gentle kiss and tell me she loved me. And I knew she meant it. But that was the end of what she could do. Except later, in private, when she would repeat again to Dad, *I am not a freak. I am not ill.*

"I know you're not," Dad said. As he always did. "I know."

"So just drop it," Mom said.

Dad pulled in a breath, preparing for a rebuttal. I whispered the words into space, willing them to reach his ears and flow from his mouth like I could mime through him from across drywall and earth-tone paints: *No, Lisa. The worst thing of all is that you spend your time driving Callie to Homer and back but miss everything going on in Enna's life. Every soccer game. Every silly attendance award at school. Every time she needs help with her homework and I'm at the ER and she doesn't know where to turn.*

But the air went out of him with no words attached. And that was that.

FOOD PRICES WENT UP. A little, then more. It started with the big meats, like beef, then down to chicken. Then the fruits, so juicy and water-dense. Shelves went bare even in the middle of the grocery store where the dry goods were kept. More kids at school ordered a hot lunch so the pantries at home stayed full. It still seemed temporary. There were signs the Polar Storm was breaking up, ready to float off into a million little clouds and bring rain where it belonged. There were reports of solid, normal rainfalls in places like Panama City and Munich. Even in Anchorage we had some decent downpours that felt familiar and safe – and everyone clung to them like static.

The municipal water system cranked water from faucets like always, though it started charging by the gallon rather than a flat monthly fee. Local governments imposed water rations. Anchorage fell in line out of camaraderie rather than desperate need. We set shower timers to two minutes and stocked up on extra water from a crack in the cliffs outside of town where snow melted through a seep. We built up dishes in the sink and did them all at once in a Rubbermaid tote filled with water drained from our gutters. Mom watered her garden using the old dishwater.

It wasn't because our town had a scarcity of water, but because Alaskans felt proud and needed. There was talk of a pipeline, the longest ever, that would connect us with the rest of the continent, supply our countrymen with water from our massive glaciers and snowfields. We were going to conserve our water so that we could hold up the rest of the country, making Alaska – us, the afterthought tagged to the bottom of maps, a fraction of our true geographic size – relevant. It felt good.

Dad kept us optimistic. Things had changed, but they weren't bad for us. The president got on the radio and the TV and beamed out over every channel, *The strength of our institutions has never been more apparent. In the face of national drought, our industry, economy, and farms are nourished and watered.* I sat at the coffee table with my pre-algebra homework as the applause from congress filled the living room. Dad was not a fan of the man but nodded along as the speech went on.

Even as it intensified over the seasons – even as it crept into my peripheral vision and grew as a threat to my comfortable world – there came a single, startling revelation: things held together for a very long time. *Humans love stability*, Dad said to me one night at tuck-in, though I was too old for tuck-ins. *We cherish our normalcy*, he said. We value the smooth functioning of society more than a few alarmists yelling on the news would have us believe. Hope fed Dad in savory morsels small and large: Chicago and Miami successfully reduced their water consumption by more than eighty percent, California and Arizona led efforts to convert swimming pools into cisterns, and a nationwide push to hand-dig rain catchment troughs to feed public works systems – complete with over 40,000 miles of trench diversions – was complete in less than two weeks.

Sociologists called it the Equal Suffering Contract. So long as everyone suffered equally, people were generally amenable and eager to help. Fire stations and police departments overflowed with volunteers bearing medical supplies and fresh pizza. We conserved and shared. We looked to each other and saw everyone in the same boat. It was akin to human behavior after an earthquake or tornado that levels an entire city – sparing no neighborhood. We rallied and cheered, *We're all in this together.*

Unfortunately, our suffering did not stay equal. Over time, inequalities pierced through our social fabric like the proboscis of a mosquito. First, the puncture holes were small: the feds imposed water rationing in schools, but soon the private schools received more shares than their public equivalents; C-sections for women on public assistance plummeted as hospitals declined to pay extra for the water required to irrigate the cut; and states restricted recreational access to waterbodies by permit-only – with permits costing hundreds of dollars a day. The inequalities grew and grew, until people from the have-nots were gazing through to the other side at the haves, and saw that we were not, in fact, all in this together.

Water became a global status symbol, a scepter for the elite and the lucky. A tech mogul posted a picture of his wife in a crystal pool of fresh water, barely covered by clothing, her hair dripping fat, juicy drops of water, and briefly the internet came crashing down as every registered user inserted themselves to comment – brutally – on the image. Time Magazine reprinted the photo as a cover feature with the headline *Water for All, or Water for the Rich?* I saw it while checking out at the grocery store with Mom. She reached for my hand and clasped it hard, holding her breath as she stared at the magazine cover. I was too old to hold her hand. But I let her anyway.

In Los Angeles, Moscow, Hong Kong, and Cape Town – in the neighborhoods where the houses and yards were the biggest, and the fences the tallest and strongest, and the lion statues guarding the doors the fiercest – looters took to the homes in populist surges. And how did those private security forces respond to the masses? Not with tear gas or rubber bullets or armored tanks. But something so much worse. They drove back the crowds with fire hoses – blasting off thousands of gallons of water, maybe millions – at pressures high enough to peel the bark from a tree.

In Chennai, bandits murdered a dentist while stealing water off a train car he had personally delivered to his home. Riots erupted in Trenton when a homemade pipe bomb knocked down the central water tower. Its water – accumulated over so many precious years of normal rain – gushed down Highway 195 for fifteen miles before trickling to nothing. A protest of 11 million people – the largest human gathering ever recorded – took to the empty lake beds of Guilin, partly in plea to officials and partly in plea to Mother Nature herself, their feet stamping down the earth already cracked and broken open like alligator skin. And, of course, there was the LFR.

After an initial rush for gasoline and toilet paper, Anchorage hummed along, generally unchanged, insulated by geography and culture. But one day a man shot a Salvadoran woman at the grocery store just a mile from our house over an expired sleeve of maple-flavored sausage. It wasn't even during a time of shortage. There were more sleeves of the same past-due sausage right there. She had a baby in her shopping cart, but this guy pulled out a Glock 17 from the seam of his underwear and shot her. Dad wasn't her doctor – Tessa Wong coded for hours before declaring the woman dead – but he assessed the infant, the one from the shopping cart, a ten-month-old girl with a smattering of teeth and unusually thick, wild hair. Like mine had been.

The baby was covered in blood and Dad checked her carefully and cooed at her as she screamed, but determined she was not injured. The blood was not hers. It was her mother's.

It barely registered on the news among the unrest – it wasn't an altercation over water itself, so it didn't fit the bigger story nationally and globally. It seemed more random. But for Dad, it wasn't random. It was part of a pattern spiraling in toward his home, his family. It hit him hard. That night, Mom microwaved him some supper, which he ate without chewing. I listened from the stairwell with my knees pressed into my chest as they whispered in the kitchen.

"I'll start tomorrow," Dad said.

"Okay," Mom said.

"What do you think I should get first? Some antibiotics."

"Some painkillers," Mom added.

"Opioids. Some antihistamines. Antiemetics. Oral rehydration."

"All of the disinfectants and antiseptics you can."

It took me a moment to figure it out. But when I did, the air exploded out of my body. I covered my mouth with a bent knee, dusty and gray from soccer practice on a field where the grass had long ago died. Dad was going to steal medicine from the hospital.

Dad would never steal. Ever. His worst quality was his ceaseless integrity. Whenever I wanted him to relax – to break the speed limit so I could make it to a soccer game on time, or let me watch a PG-13 movie just one year before my thirteenth birthday, or take Benji off his leash when no one else was around – he wouldn't. Dad was the person who tipped waiters on top of automatic gratuity. He stayed up late after long consecutive shifts to read every *Annals of Emergency Medicine*. Dad would not steal from the hospital, from his patients. Never.

And yet.

THE LFR APPEARED in January. That month, the Southeast U.S. saw a little rain, enough to be meaningful, close to what had been normal, but only in very small geographic areas: a neighborhood outside of Atlanta, a cluster of high-end apartments in the middle of Montgomery, and the length of a single residential street in Charlotte. Apparently, the rains were clustered in more affluent areas. People had theories: the rich use more water so there's more localized evaporation there (quickly dismissed by scientists); or, rich neighborhoods do more to preserve their trees and vegetation that trap the moisture (scientists postulated this could be the case); or, it is purely random and only by chance that the rain fell in wealthy areas and with enough data the pattern will fall apart (embraced by scientists).

But then someone on the internet mapped out these rain events and overlaid them on racial demographic data from the most recent census. This person then determined that the rain was concentrated in areas that weren't just wealthy, but white.

Within this dataset, there were a few outliers: rain in Tallahassee over a black neighborhood, squalls in Louisiana bayous, and a few drizzles over the Catawba and Chitimacha Indian Reservations. So, the author of this analysis – who came to be known as Cloudburst – decided that it wasn't just wealthy or white that made it rain, but *American*. True American. Cloudburst then graphed rainfall in an area and plotted it against the number of immigrants in that same area and declared that rain would not fall where immigrants lived.

It was outrageous – dismissed so rapidly that initially no one in the media or meteorology worlds even registered its existence. But then Cloudburst's work started to circulate more and more widely. Those desperately searching for some existential answer to the drought found a simple, concrete rationale that appeared supported by math and data. There began minor agitations for mass deportation of immigrants. At first it only lived on the Internet: on social media and the comment pages of newspaper articles. Every site linked to Cloudburst's data. Bumper stickers appeared: *Cloudburst for President!* There was noise, but no one did anything.

Then, small-town mob a hundred miles from Kansas City calling themselves Let Freedom Rain took it upon themselves to identify a group of fifteen immigrants, kidnap them into the back of a livestock truck, and drive them a hundred miles in the other direction. The mob left their victims with nothing: no shelter, no communication, no food, and certainly no water. LFR live-streamed the encounter on social media and may have been arrested in more normal times. But then a corn field outside of Kansas City experienced fog a few days later. It wasn't technically rain, though moisture did touch upon the earth. *It's just random!* the scientists cried. *It's just a coincidence!* But no one listened. No one cared. It was as good as rain. The drought now had a face, a skin color, a foreign language and undesirable accent. *Remove the immigrants and the rain will come,* they said.

"People just want tribes," Dad said while he and

Mom listened to the radio in the front seat of the minivan. "They want something easy to target, something easy to explain something that's complicated. They'll see that it does nothing, that it doesn't bring rain. They'll see." Mom shook her head. She saw the color of Dad's skin. She had daughters with the last name Martinez. And she never had faith in others. "They'll see reason," he repeated, pleading with himself as much as he was with mom. "They'll see logic."

And, no, it didn't rain any more with the immigrants removed. But that did not stop the rampage. By February, there were twenty LFR offshoots across the country. They seized grocery warehouses once stocked with absurd amounts of food and used them as detention centers for immigrant families. But *detention center* was a generous, evening news-friendly word. Holes opened up in those vast tarry roofs and smoke burned from the openings day and night. Photographs captured entire families entering through the old double-doors of the mega-stores, flanked by armed men on all sides. But no photograph ever showed them going out.

"Call it what it is!" Mom screamed at the radio as on-air pundits speculated wildly as to the nature of these detention centers. She broke her grip on the wheel to rub at the veiny blue skin on her wrists.

Well, Nakiya, the newscaster buzzed on my way home from soccer practice, *if you consider the Minneapolis Detention Center at the former Sam's Club, it appears that there may be an underground tunnel system. Some of the guards seen at that Detention Center were later spotted at the Saint Paul Costco Detention Center but there was no evidence of their transit.*

"It's not a detention center!" Mom howled. A man stopped at the red light next to us turned abruptly at the noise and I sank into the bucket seat, exposing only the top of my scalp.

That's true, David, but you've also seen the photos of the armored vehicles surrounding these detention centers. It's very possible that they are traveling between them simply without aerial photography capturing it. The security around these detention centers seems to rival that of the Pentagon.

"Call it what it is!" Mom shrieked, higher, fiercer, more desperate. I bit my lap in the backseat, clutching my backpack to my chest, willing myself not to see her spasm, not to hear her terror. "It's a concentration camp!" A car horn honked behind us as she delayed at the red light, now green. "It's a concentration camp!"

The government condemned the practice in vague and unconvincing terms but did nothing to stop it. *The priority of our military forces is securing water for the American people*, the President said to reporters on his way to a classified briefing. *Policing of these groups like the LFR is the responsibility of local government.*

My eighth-grade English teacher, Miss Carrew, abandoned our curriculum of abridged Twain, Steinbeck, and Hemingway, and exchanged it for the writing of Eli Wiesel and Anne Frank. "The Germans blamed the Jews for the economy failing. They used them as a scapegoat for bigger problems. When there's a crisis, it's easiest to blame someone else." When she spoke, she looked at me. The color of my skin blazed out of my body like a rash that others feared was contagious. I shrugged my shoulders over my ears, pulling my hoodie over the back of my neck and zipping it all the way up my chest, hoping

23

to pull into myself like a turtle, to cover the part of me I could never change.

Miss Carrew was an athletic, big-hearted woman who was not an immigrant and to whom the LFR had personally done nothing to offend. But one day we walked into class with a banner hanging over the whiteboard:

If you do not speak up for them, who will be left to speak up for you?

The banner hung for four days, until we returned from the weekend. Kids gathered around outside her window, standing on tiptoes to see the damage the principal had already sealed off to those inside: chairs smashed, table overturned, and walls covered in what was later fingerprinted as pig's blood. I stood at the fringe of the crowd, toeing the curb of the parking lot, feigning oblivion, when Miss Carrew emerged from a side door soaked and red from tears. Her hands trembled as she brought a crumpled tissue to her nose, looking at me with veiny eyes. "You could have said something," she said to me. "I was standing up for you, but you won't stand up for yourself." I dug my fingernails into the fabric of my backpack straps and felt the nylon tear under my grip. But I said nothing back.

From then on, a substitute teacher taught our class, and we went back to the Twain, Steinbeck, and Hemingway.

"It's nothing new," Dad assured Mom that evening in the living room while I sat in the kitchen poking at my macaroni and cheese. Mom had made it as a treat to me, sensing my increasing stress. But she mixed frozen peas with the pasta and I didn't have the energy to pick around them. Benji sat at my feet, waiting for the dinner I would reject. "Ancient cultures did this kind of thing all the time: ritualistic sacrifice to control the weather."

Mom shook her head and grabbed at her wrists. "And look how it turned out for them," she said. And the conversation ended.

Each time the LFR opened a new chapter, they hosted a massive rally in the town, launching water bottles into the crowds, firing water cannons from fire trucks, hosting water fountains for children to play in, drenching converts with garden hoses filled with clean, sparkling water in a baptismal rite – all as proof of what would come should their mission prove successful. The water would return.

Often at these loud, groundbreaking, rhetoric-spewing events, it seemed as though the media coverage exceeded the actual attendance. LFR coverage was among the most widely read, listened to, and clicked upon. They were the figurehead of collective madness, the posterchildren of the caveman mentality we all resisted but could feel ourselves giving into.

LFR sects emerged in Eastern Europe – their immigrant targets hailed from the Balkan states. Then the rest of Europe, where the immigrants from North Africa came under attack. In Australia, it was the South Asians. In the Middle East, the Israeli Knesset elected a state comptroller who subscribed to Cloudburst's ideologies and circulated maps of precipitation levels along the Palestinian border that showed preferential rain along the Israeli side. The chairman of the Executive Committee of the Palestine Liberation Organization produced competing maps, showing rain in Palestine, but concentrated along the West Bank. To which Hamas cried foul and generated maps showing rain along the Gaza Strip. But even then, the Middle East reported minimal violence and unrest. Somehow these areas of the world were more immune to the chaos – they knew drought and desertification, having lived it and adapted to it over millennia. Green parts of the world suffered most.

A man claiming to be Cloudburst (though who could ever be sure?) appeared via satellite stream with his face blurred and voice distorted for a live interview with Davis Alistair, a handsome and distinguished TV reporter for the BBC. It went something like this:

Alistair: Many scientists, both demographers and meteorologists, have attempted to reproduce your mapping. But they have found that there is a close-to zero correlation between rainfall and immigrant populations.

Cloudburst: We are using the best data available on the planet and the results do not lie. I would ask to know how many of those so-called demographers and meteorologists are immigrants themselves with a vested interest in the outcome of their analysis.

Alistair: Can you show us this data you are referencing? It does not appear to match what is measured by the National Weather Service.

Cloudburst: I assure you. We are using only the best data.

Alistair: Yes, but what data? What rain gauges? What satellite imagery?

Cloudburst: Only the best rain gauges, and state-of-the-art satellite imagery.

Alistair: But in fact, some of the cities with the biggest LFR raids continue to see the most serious drought. How do you explain this?

Cloudburst: In time, you will see that these cities recover their rainfall proportional the amount of cleansing that was conducted. We cannot expect immediate results and must stay the course.

Alistair: Just, scientifically, how does it follow that rain would stop because a certain group of people are living in an area? How could that possibly correlate to the behavior of clouds?

Cloudburst: There is much of our so-called modern science that cannot explain the workings of God.

Alistair: So, you consider yourself an agent of God?

Cloudburst: The LFR is conducting God's work.

Alistair: What happens to the people you detain in your raids?

Cloudburst: God's work.

When a new chapter opened – each closer to us in Alaska than the last – or another immigrant family went missing from their home, evaporated like steam, Dad buckled a little more. Like a tree branch sagging, slowly unable to support itself, his breath grew ragged and his posture stooped. He never spoke of it to me. Neither did Mom. But my skin was dark. Darker than Callie's. My name was unusual. My hair was black. One day I dug through my mom's purse for a pen and found copies of my birth certificate folded up and sealed in a plastic bag, the city of birth *Anchorage, Alaska, USA* circled in red marker. Proof of my citizenship always tied to her. I rummaged through the clutter of her purse but could not find one for Callie. She didn't need to have a passport. Callie looked like Mom.

Then it was November. And members of the LFR swept both the House and Senate races after ugly, vicious campaigns. The President dropped any pretense, embraced the movement, and praised them for bringing America together under a unified goal of Let Freedom Rain. That evening, from my bedroom window open to the street, I could feel the tingle in the air, the electricity, the heat, of madness.

In the morning we awoke to a black cloud spray-painted on our garage door, a lightning bolt cleaved through the center. The icon of the LFR.

Mom and Dad stood together in the driveway, so small and lonely looking on the street that had always been our home.

"Now?" Mom asked.

"Now," Dad said.

And we loaded up the van, stuffed it to the roof – three chickens and one rooster squawking maniacally at our feet, Benji's head resting upon my lap – and left our home. "Just for a bit," Mom reassured me from the front seat. "Until things settle down."

But it wasn't until things settled down. The world we knew had crumpled, a shift in global order on the magnitude of a change in gravity or plate tectonics – the very things that anchor us to solid ground. We drove away from our sky-blue home that day, from our swingset in the yard, from our bikes piled in the garage, from the tick marks of my and Callie's growth etched on the wall at the bottom of the staircase, with no idea of when we would return.

Driving away in the minivan as my ailing hometown vanished around the bend in the Chugach Mountains, how could I have ever known, that out in that land of endless forest and sea, with each uncertain and strenuous day, you would appear in my life as though fallen like an angel from the smoke-filled sky?

CHAPTER TWO - *The Early Days*

The cabin sat at the head of a small cove where a stream flowed into the ocean. A glacier perched high in the mountains fed the little stream, and from the beach I could see the silky blue white of its ice retreating into the peaks like a cat slinking into the shadows. The melting of the glacier was a steady supply of freshwater for the cabin. But without new snow to build it up, I wondered – without asking out loud – how long that water would last.

But I wondered that about everything. Each time I sharpened our knives I wondered how many more times they could sharpen before crumbling to dust. Each time our cistern sprung a leak I wondered how many more strips of duct tape I could tear before we had only empty rolls of cardboard. Each time I donned a pair of socks I wondered how many more holes they could bear at the toes and heels before coming apart.

The cabin had always been a fixture in our lives. We spent every Christmas and spring break there, plus one month every summer. Great-grandfather Jenkins hewed it from spruce logs, and he and Mom spent long summers modernizing it after her own parents died – installing thick windows, caulking gaps in the wood, building planter boxes for carrots and rhubarb, adding a spacious loft where Callie and I slept. From that loft we stared out a small round porthole up the side of the mountain, thick and wild with evergreen trees. As a little girl, Mom named the mountain behind the cabin Lamplighter Mountain. No map ever called it such, but for us, Lamplighter Mountain was the rock upon which Mom's childhood unfolded.

As a child myself, I had scouted all the cabin's secrets: the concealed door to a hand-dug cellar, the panel next to the sink where the guns hung in a neat row, and Great-grandma's name and Callie's namesake, CALLISTA, carved into the top step of the deck, probably during some spell of prolonged and profound boredom while she waited for her husband to return from another failed exploration for gold.

Wandering the forest with Benji I sometimes stumbled across Great-grandpa's old tools: a pickaxe, a spade, and a handsaw rusted to translucency like dragonfly wings. I found a bald eagle nest in a hemlock up the hill – a yawning and elaborate basket of branches large enough to hold me and my family – a grizzly bear den against a boulder field on the slope opposite the creek, and massive, lush berry patches in small clearings scattered across the lowlands. At night, the howl of wolves and screech of owls echoed in the fjords. On sunny days, whales and seals and sea lions poked their heads up from the green-blue water of the Gulf of Alaska.

Great-grandma Callista named the little cove, Pluto Cove. She said it felt like the very edge of the knowable universe. I felt the same.

The year before the Polar Storms, before the drought, before we left everything behind, Dad took me and Benji on a hike up the Qaneqiraluq River Canyon over Christmas break. He spent nearly a year convincing Mom I was ready for the trek up Lamplighter Mountain, across the ice fields, leaving before dawn the first day, camping overnight in a hand-dug snow cave, and returning after sunset on the second day, lit by headlamps and wielding ice axes to arrest a fall. The trip could only be done in winter, when impassable wetlands froze to solid ground, the bears hibernated, and the noxious Devil's Club and Pushkie lay buried under snow.

For hours we slogged up the Qaneqiraluq Canyon on Pluto Cove's opposite side of Lamplighter Mountain, the sound of unfrozen water rushing underneath our snowshoes, the beams of our headlamps reflected in the vast, untouched snow fields. I thought little of the terrain then, except that I was tired. But later, when the Polar Storms descended, when each day of forecasted rain came and went with only intense, baking sun, I called myself back to those trudging steps up the mountain. The sound of gushing water under ice bridges, the endlessness of the snow piled on rocks and falling from the sky. I ached for it, thirsted for it.

That day, Dad went first to break trail, then me, then Benji following the trench of our tracks. Dad could have hiked that distance alone in a single day, but my legs were short and slow. We ate granola bars as we walked, never stopping for more than a minute to stave off chill. Around the bend of Lamplighter Mountain and just past the treeline he set down his pack. "This is good snow for camp," he said. "Let's dig in."

He was being literal. From his pack he pulled out two collapsible avalanche shovels and started hacking into the snow. I held the shovel but didn't do much. I stared out over the edge of the frozen Qaneqiraluq River, so named for the Alutiiq phrase *mouth of the moon*. During the years when a full moon falls on winter solstice, it rises straight from the mouth of the river; the people who lived this land named it for the phenomenon. From where I stood, the moon rose from the earth's horizon where the Qaneqiraluq River spilled into the immense ocean, casting us in a white light that echoed off the snow.

Once Dad had the opening carved, I crawled inside and hollowed out the cave. After a few hours we were warm and nearly sweating. "Don't sweat," he said. "Stop before you feel yourself start to sweat. It will freeze and take you with it." He lit a single candle under the ventilation tube, and the cave radiated light and warmth as we crawled into our side-by-side sleeping bags. Benji curled himself into me, and I into him.

"This is great, mija," Dad said, using the combined Spanish word for *my daughter*, as he did when feeling sentimental. He stared up at the snowy ceiling. "We are very overdue for a trip like this, just the two of us." And as an aside, "And Benji of course. Your other half."

"Yeah," I said, burrowing my face into Benji's soft fur. I thought of Callie and Mom back at the cabin, curled up with cocoa in front of the fire.

"You know," he continued. "When you were little, after mom's accident, she was in a coma for a really long time. Do you know what a coma is?"

I nodded before I remembered he wasn't looking at me. "Yeah," I said. "Like a sleep she couldn't wake up from."

"Right," he said. "It was a really scary time. Every day that went by it seemed less and less likely she'd ever wake up. So there was a while when I really thought it might just be the two of us, navigating the world

34

together."

"Hmm," I said, unsure of how to reply.

"And I really didn't know if I could do it," he said. "The thought of raising this little kid, all by myself. It really scared me. But then I'd look at you, and those giant brown eyes, just like your Grandma Julienna, and sometimes you'd smile up at me so big like you wanted me to know that we were in this together, that we were a team." He paused, and I could feel him tumbling back into the memory. "And of course, Mom woke up. So it was the three of us again. And then four, once she healed and Callie came along. But I was always so grateful to you for giving me that confidence. And even now I think we make a really good team."

"Yeah, Dad," I said. "Definitely."

Then he spoke to me in the language of his heart, but the language he never fully taught me. "Buenas noches, mija."

"Buenas noches, papí."

In the morning we set out again, stiffer and colder than the day before. We hiked all day and reached the top of the canyon as the last winter light shone gold across the snow drifts. "That's okay," Dad said, seeing my unease at the lateness in the day. "It will be fast on the way down. We already have a trail made, and it's all downhill. You want to see this, trust me."

The canyon narrowed until the rocks disappeared under ice. The glacier. The glacier we could see from the cabin, the one that fed both our little stream and the mighty Qaneqiraluq River. Ice towered over us, as tall as Dad's hospital in Anchorage, falling over in obelisks like the ruins of an ancient civilization. At the top, white snow gave way to gray ice, gave way to swirling bright blue concrete, and under that was flowing water. "The ice is under so much pressure," Dad explained, "that even though it's below freezing, it melts. It's called regelation."

"Wow," I said. But I was merely mimicking the sense of awe in Dad's voice; honestly, I didn't know why something couldn't be frozen and melting at the same time. Why would that be special? It was the next year, when the Polar Storms started, that people started talking about regelation. The clouds were under such immense pressure from the weight of unfallen rain that the frigid temperatures at the North Pole and South Pole weren't enough to make snow. The clouds themselves were so heavy they turned ice into water without applying heat. Those tremendous, calamitous vapors, hovering over the poles, fell as rain, melting the polar ice, making more precipitation, and fueling the cloud all over again.

Dad led me and Benji around the toe of the ice, up to the top of the glacier. I followed him over narrow crevasses and angular horns wondering what could be more interesting or beautiful than the crumbling blue foot of the glacier – but I trusted him and stuck close.

At the top, I could hardly fathom what I saw. The ice broke off into slabs of cliffs, each looming hundreds of feet high, skyscrapers of ice, an amphitheater surrounding us like an ancient, haunted henge.

"This, Enna," Dad said, "is a jökulhlaup."

I rolled my eyes at him. "That's not a word, Dad."

"It is a word," he said, the corners of his eyes smiling over his balaclava. "It's an Icelandic word. This here is a dam made of ice."

I looked at him skeptically.

"See this ice field here?" He gestured toward the massive expanse of snow abutting the glacial cliffs. "Under all this ice, under our very feet, is a massive lake. All this water is churning and swirling and building up under the ice. But the glacier dams it up, holding it back. And someday," his eyes gleamed. "The dam will break, and all this water will explode out in the Qaneqiraluq River all at once. A jökulhlaup."

No eleven-year-old could ever comprehend the scale of the ice or water or river – even Dad in his adulthood and multiple advanced degrees stood in reverence – but there at the top of the mountain, the top of the glacier, in the feeble light of the setting sun, cold creeping its way through the layers of down and wool, into the core of my body, I understood that the jökulhlaup he described was enormous. An event on a geologic scale, a marvel of the physical world, a natural disaster.

"What will happen to the river when the ice dam breaks?" I asked.

"It'll swell up so big it will overflow the sides of the canyon. It will wipe out all the trees and rocks in its path and then flow out into the ocean."

"When is it going to explode?" My eyes blinked rapidly attempting to capture and store this information, this remarkable site.

"Well," Dad started, smiling in the way a boy smiles before obliterating his tower of Legos, "I heard from one of the old miners that it bursts every thirty years. And we are twenty-five years in." His eyes glimmered.

"Will it flood our cabin?" I asked, staring down the side of the mountain, where our cabin lay around the curve of the slope.

"No," Dad said. "Our cabin is on the other side of the spine of Lamplighter Mountain." He gestured toward the pyramidal angle of the mountain, to the place where our cabin sat on the opposite side. "It will be a tremendous amount of water, but not enough to break over that ridge." He paused, taking a deep breath of veneration and humility. "But everything down the Qaneqiraluq River of the jökulhlaup… well that will be wiped as clean as a chalkboard."

And with that, we started our descent down and around the mountain. "Vamos," he said.

WE ARRIVED AT THE CABIN on Wednesday, November 10th, a fact I never forgot because Dad carved it into the wall by the door as though we were prisoners striking down the days of a sentence. Callie was shaking and in tears by the time we pulled the boat up to the gravel bar. but really, she had been in tears since halfway through the drive. I hadn't cried, but my nerves thrummed under my skin like guitar strings.

At a junction in the highway, about two hours from Anchorage, a group of men set up a so-called Security Checkpoint. They parked their trucks into a V-shape, funneling oncoming traffic into a pinch point where we were forced to slow down as they motioned for Dad to roll down his window. They wore light blue hats with embroidered clouds cleaved by lightning.

"Is there a problem, gentlemen?" Dad asked. Mom turned around from the front seat and whispered to us, "Stay quiet".

"No problem, no problem," said a tall man with

broad shoulders and a closely-trimmed beard. The hat cast a shadow over his eyes and a rifle was slung over his left shoulder as casually as a book bag. "We are under orders to stop all traffic coming onto the Peninsula, on account of the food rationing. We're gonna have to ask you to go back to Anchorage."

"Under orders from whom?" my Dad asked.

"That's of no concern to you," the man replied, working his mouth in a way that implied a large wad of chew sat somewhere between his gums and his lips. "You have everything you need in Anchorage, so now just go on back."

Dad did not pause for a moment. "We don't live in Anchorage."

"Oh really?" the man said, craning his head into the vehicle, seeing our packed belongings, Benji squirming between the seats, the pallor of our stony faces. "You sure look like you're from Anchorage." Then he smirked. "If you're from the United States at all, huh?"

"I am a doctor from Homer," Dad said, quickly cutting him off. "I serve the entire Peninsula. We are headed to Ninilchik now so I can keep the clinic running during the crisis. And I, as a matter of fact, *am* under orders. From the Department of Health and Human Services and the Governor."

The man stared at Dad, chewing his lip. "You have some kind of credentials there?"

Dad's wallet was on the dashboard. He pulled his hospital badge from a pocket and held it out the window. "Not that it's any of your business, but yes, I do."

The man inspected the card, turning it over in his fingers as though it may surrender some secret at a different angle. "Doctor Alejandro Martinez, huh?" He said. "They have medical schools down in the *campesino*?" He sniggered. "The *barrio*?"

The tension that seized Dad's body was visible even from my oblique angle in the backseat. But even though the context was new, his response was well-practiced. "University of Washington School of Medicine," he said. His next phrase was aimed at appeasing while conveying power, though I knew it destroyed him to speak out loud. "They admit only the most highly-qualified."

"Now, now," the man said. "I believe you, I believe you. But even if you're a doctor, you could be doing more harm here than good, you follow? We gotta make sure you aren't stopping any rain from coming to our area."

I held back a whimper in the backseat. Right there in front of me, they targeted Dad for his name, for his skin. And I had the same last name, the same skin. Benji put his snout on my lap and nuzzled my leg. I instinctively put my hand to his ears and felt calm.

"The only thing I am stopping," Dad said, "is the spread of infectious disease in our community."

"You're a big talker, aren't ya?" the man asked, gesturing at the other men in identical hats. They saw his wave and moved in unison toward the car like wolves circling a fallen deer. When he spoke again, his voice was bigger, louder, so that the rest of the men could hear him. "I think what we have here are some rain snatchers tryna sneak outta the big city with the rest of the illegals and take over our land down here."

"Momma," I whispered from the backseat. It was

reflexive, it meant nothing, it came out of my lips without my permission the way a cough comes from inhaling smoke. But it did awaken something in her.

"Sir," she said, leaning over the console to see out the driver's window. "I absolutely see your concern. And hopefully with good and attentive folks like you in D.C. we can finally start to turn this thing around." She made a point of flipping her long, light hair. "But as it happens, we are traveling with passports. You can see here that Dr. Martinez, though his name is foreign-sounding, was actually born right here in the USA."

She held her hands up near her face and moved them slowly toward her handbag, maintaining eye contact with the man. I did not know what she intended to do. Dad was not born in the USA. He was born in Guadalajara; we all knew the story of how his mother Julienna fled with him north on her own to escape his father, an abusive drunk. Maybe Mom had a gun in her bag. Maybe she was going to kill someone.

But it was not a gun she pulled out. It was a passport, blue and gold. She passed it across Dad's rigid body and handed it to the man.

He opened it, flipping through the pages, apparently unfamiliar with the document. "The first page," Mom offered. "It lists the place of birth and nationality. As you of course know, a passport is a federal document requiring proof of birth and social security, it's not like a driver's license that can list any old address."

Where had she gotten it? And how much had she paid? I will never know. But that forgery – by listing Norfolk, Virginia as the place of birth– freed us.

The men looked at each other unsure of their next

move. But then one of them spoke. "Ya know, I think I recognize him from taking Marie to the emergency room." He was a chubby, red-faced man who, from behind the curved glass of the car window, appeared wider than he was tall. "He looks familiar."

"You think this spic is a doctor, Joe?" the man at the window asked.

"I dunno," the man named Joe said. He craned his neck to speak into the open window. "You know a Marie Brophy?" he asked Dad.

Dad's eyes flickered. He was sharp, he had the memory of an elephant – but he saw dozens of patients each day in the emergency department. Thousands a year.

"I do," he said solemnly. "Please tell her I hope the doctors over at Alaska Neuro Clinic were able to help her with her back pain."

The man's eyes brightened. "Yeah," he said. "Yeah, I will."

The men exchanged glances. The one at the window handed the passport back. Dad put the van into drive, gave a nod of his head, and drove through the checkpoint as the rest of the men stared us down. There were two stares: the one of ice and hatred for my father the brown man, and the one of lust and thirst for my mother the beautiful white woman. I don't know which was worse.

No one in the car said anything for several minutes. Neither Mom nor Dad gave any indication of stress, relief, or fear though it poured out of them and flooded the space between us like blood from an open wound.

On the other side of the checkpoint, Callie started to cry. Mom reached around and patted her knee. "It's okay, baby. We are fine. Really. Me and Daddy have this under control." But even little Callie knew these words were hollow, readily programmed into any robot.

"Did you really remember a Marie Brophy?" Mom asked in a quiet voice now that the silence was broken.

"No," Dad said.

"Then how–"

"Just a guess," Dad said. "It was just a guess."

THROUGH THE SPRAWLING highway towns of Kenai and Soldotna, past Ninilchik – the place Dad purported to work – and winding through the flat, black swamps of the lower Peninsula we traveled. Rounding over the hill into Homer the mountains appeared over Kachemak Bay like glinting, broken teeth in a wide-open smile. Water sparkled in the late-fall sun, blue and white. Such vistas used to be beautiful – they used to be extraordinary. To come over that corner in clear sun with endless visibility was to step into a heaven few people had known. Except now we would give anything for cloud cover, to drape the view in fog, occlude it by mist. The way it used to be.

In Homer we drove straight to the marina to meet Captain Kerry, but his pier tent was empty. A black swivel chair lay overturned across the greasy floor. Mom asked a passing deckhand, and he shrugged. "Last I heard he flew south. Oregon or something. Lots of people have."

Mom and Dad looked at each other,

communicating telepathically. She motioned to a skiff anchored loosely to a rope off the dock. "Think you could?" Dad asked. She nodded.

"Think she could what?" I asked. But neither of them answered.

"Start loading up the boat, girls," Mom said.

"Whose boat is this?" I asked. Again, neither of them answered. "Are we stealing this boat?" I demanded. Benji clipped at my heels, agitated. The chickens squawked psychotically from the holes punched in their cardboard boxes.

"Just get some bags," Mom said again.

"Mom!" I shouted.

"Listen to your mother," Dad snapped. Dad never snapped. I gave one last look at them, then grabbed a duffel from the trunk and marched it down the dock.

It took Mom all of ninety seconds to hotwire the engine. She opened the engine cover and she saw in all those wires and tubes an order and function and a code that was easily cracked.

"Does it have enough fuel?" I asked, knowing the ride to the cabin was a long one.

"We'll be fine," Mom said, not even checking the gauge. And she steered us away from the dock, the marina, the town, the mainland.

The ride took the better part of eleven hours in the packed skiff, through the choking darkness of a November night. We powered up and over ocean swells, heavy and sluggish. At the bottom of each wave, a spray of water pummeled us and our gear. I sat next to Mom and heard the clicking of her jaw. Each time she sighed in relief at a stretch of mild water, the boat engine shuddered, then revved again to life. I looked at the make, a Honda. Mom can restart it if it fails, I thought. Dad can row us if it fails. Benji is a good swimmer.

Callie sat against Dad's shoulder, shrunken into her lifejacket, her face red and gray and streaked with ocean water and tears. Once we made it to the other side of Kachemak Bay, Mom hugged the boat near the shore and I noted the occasional little cabin with woodsmoke rising from the chimney. Were they doing as we did? Were they making a run for it?

We wound in and out of bays and coves as though weaving ourselves through a blanket. First due west, then around the bend of the Peninsula, and then due south. The cabins and camps became fewer. Then none. And it was only us.

We rounded the corner of the gravel bar that marked the mouth of Pluto Cove. Littering the gravel were the skeletons of spruce trees that had slowly died when an earthquake plunged the land into the ocean and injected saltwater into the roots. Here the water was shallow. The bottom of the boat dragged against the gravel in front of our cabin, too heavy to land on the beach. "Enna, Alex, hop out and fire chain gear onto the beach until I can get the boat up," Mom said.

"I can help too, Momma," Callie whimpered between sniffles.

"No baby, you stay here. Help me look for a good spot."

It wasn't fair, but I couldn't cross Mom when she was this spring loaded. I jumped out of the boat into freezing waist-deep water. Benji followed. My jeans clung to my legs, and my tennis shoes filled with gravel, each step forward a massive labor that sucked the warmth from my body. But I reached for the bags and boxes, one by one. Bear tracks etched deep into strips of sand that glowed in the uninhibited starlight. I stepped into one big enough to swallow my own footprint and rubbed it out with the heel of my shoe.

Eventually the boat rose as the weight lifted, and Mom powered it onto shore. Dad lifted Callie out and held her to his chest, awkward with her bulky life jacket. We trudged up the beach to the wrack line of moss and driftwood, up to the old wooden steps of the cabin. Cold water poured out of the fabric of my pants and gushed around my feet with each step. Mom unlocked the bar across the door and swung it open.

The cabin was dark with ply boards fastened over the windows, but through the beam of Mom's headlight in the door, Dad and I let out a collective gasp.

"Lisa," Dad said. "Oh my god."

Boxes and pallets and overflowing bags covered every wooden plank on the floor. Casting shadows in the headlamp stood towers of canned food, mounds of blankets and towels, a stack of bagged potting soil, a shiny red toolbox the size of my torso, and a new chainsaw still in the box. There was no space anywhere to take a step, let alone to sleep.

"Yeah," Mom said, putting her hands on her hips. "And don't go in the outhouse yet. There's a spool of five thousand feet of fourteen-gauge copper wire in there."

"Momma, I'm hungry," Callie said, tugging at Mom's sopping jacket from the doorway.

Mom gestured at the pallets of canned beans, vegetables, soups, and meats, each stack looming taller than my head. Her headlamp swept light across the scene like spotlights in a theater. "Does any of this look good?" she asked, hoping for a moment of levity or some gratitude for all the food she had stockpiled over the months.

Callie's face fell. "No."

FORTY DAYS EACH YEAR the cabin received no sunlight. We knew this because Great-grandma Callista engraved marks into the front room window where the sun descended on December 1st and did not rise again until January 11th. There were places in Alaska in the north – far north – where the sun did not emerge above the horizon for interminable spells on either end of the winter solstice. But in Pluto Cove, it was because the horizon was high, with mountains on all sides, that the cabin endured a prolonged winter shadow. Feeble light trickled in over the mountaintops like a slow leaking faucet, enough to work outside without headlamps, but not enough to light the cabin.

For this reason, years earlier, Mom had wired the cabin. I was little at the time, but I remember feeling so afraid watching her up on the roof where she installed the photovoltaic panels. Under the awning were sawed down stumps and firewood piles and any fall would have been catastrophic. But she didn't fall. She erected the solar panels, connected them to an array of wires as indecipherable to me as hieroglyphics, and drained the energy of the sun (on the days when it did appear) into a bank of batteries previously in the kitchen, but later moved under Callie's bed.

This battery bank powered four overhead

47

lightbulbs in the cabin: two in the kitchen and two in the main room where we ate, read, and played board games – back when things were normal. They were bare bulbs that emitted a bright and steady light. Sometimes when they were off, I would stare into the darkness of the cabin and wonder how Great-grandma Callista possibly stayed sane for so long. Even at the height of the day it was so dark I could hardly see the shape of my own hand.

Mom also installed two electric outlets in the kitchen, which powered the occasional appliance, a pump for running water from a cistern into the sink, and an electric stovetop for cooking and boiling water. When we arrived that November, she used that outlet to power her cell phone. There was no service at the cabin, but she wanted to keep it fully charged for when she boated hours out into Kachemak Bay to pick up a few bars.

When she did, she let me read the text messages that came in, a lifeline to the world outside Pluto Cove. The messages pinged from neighbors and friends and people whose faces I could still picture and voices I could still hear. They said things like *Natl Guard flew in food and meds. Long lines, but peaceful.* Or *Reports of rain from Nairobi. Not what you'd expect, but hopefully a sign of good things to come!*

In December, there were long texts from the wife of one of Dad's coworkers, Ginny. She was a casual real estate agent, picking up one or two houses every couple of years to stay in the workforce. *They started the H2O pipeline construction, going to connect in McCarthy before crossing border into Canada. Now is the time to buy some property! Going to be a hot market.*

Mom brought this one back to Dad and a rare,

small grin crackled just a moment under the stubble now perpetually adorning his face. "Maybe Ginny has a point?" He asked. "Maybe it's stabilizing enough for the money grabbers to make a business out of it."

But a few weeks after that, the day after Christmas, the tone changed. From Mom's cousin in Michigan: *USA dropped the bomb. THE bomb. Casualties are innumerable.* And from our neighbor, Frankie, closer to home: *City shut off the water. Collecting from the creeks but someone shot a bunch of moose and cleaned the carcasses upstream and water is contaminated.*

Listening to Mom and Dad talk it over, I knew that for every 160-character text message, there were thousands of pages of history being written – more context and consequence than I could wrap my head around. And I was glad for that. I didn't want to understand it. I just wanted to go home.

The last text she let me see was from Corinne, the mom of a boy in my class. She said, *We are heading north. I don't know when we'll be back.*

She got a couple more maybe a week after that one. But the next time she went out with her phone she navigated up and down the Bay for several hours before realizing there was no cell service. Anywhere. She reached her arm as high as it would go, waving the phone into the atmosphere for one small ping of civilization. Higher and higher she reached, up to the tips of her fingers, closer to radio waves, closer to heaven itself… and she dropped the phone over the side of the boat. Without a breath, she watched it vanish into the inky, frigid, endlessly deep Gulf of Alaska. The phone was gone. Not that it mattered. Because the networks were gone, too.

I DRIFTED, DETACHED, THROUGH it all. It didn't
seem totally real, didn't fit with what I understood about
the world and routine and my parents from the last
thirteen years of observing. I felt scared, for sure. I felt
uncertain in my skin and afraid of the dwindling shelves
in the grocery store. But, still, I thought Mom was
overreacting by dragging us to Pluto Cove and had spun
Dad into her web. She was always so worried, always
grinding down the skin at her wrists as she conjured
stories of doom and despair, and it always for nothing. It
would rain any day. Someone would find a way to get
rain down from the poles to the rest of the world. How
hard could it be? There were hoses – surely someone
could just string them together. I even proposed getting
water from the North Pole and not the South Pole,
because then they could use gravity to get it down and
around the curve of the earth. I was a child, remember.
Someone would figure this out – an adult – and this
would just be a blip in my life, a few missed soccer games,
some catch-up with my homework at school.

I clung to Benji each night like driftwood in open
water. His heartbeat was my steady drum, his
companionship my own kind of rain. I missed my friend
Sylvie, my friend since preschool, more than I could put
into words. I hadn't said goodbye to her. Where did she
think I had gone? What was she doing now? I pictured
her going to school normally, watching the empty seat at
my desk, gradually making new friends while I faded
into memory. In the darker hours, I imagined her
trudging up into the dead, icy mountains with her

parents and older brothers, in search of clean water. In the darkest of all hours, I pictured her dad and brothers conscripted into the LFR, hunting for us – the ones who had escaped.

But those thoughts in the dark hours were not mine. Those images of Sylvie suffering in the cold Arctic world were not born of my own mind. They did not come into my brain in my own voice. They were Mom's. They were her nightmares that had taken root in my psyche, her constant worrying and anxiety and what-ifs that laid down tracks in my head that I could not jump.

Even though no one shared details of Mom's accident, it was referenced enough that I knew it accounted for a lot of her behaviors. It happened when I was so young, I didn't know any other version of her. *Be patient,* Dad urged. *After her accident, you know.* But I didn't know. I just trusted. And it had never much bothered me – never struck me as odd that sometimes she could not get herself out of bed, that she continually insisted *I am not a freak, I am not ill* – until the hoarding started.

I was born when Dad was in his third year of medical school and Mom finished her master's in engineering. They weren't ready for a baby and relied on me being a little assistant rather than a little kid. Callie was the child they intended to have – at the right time. But I enjoyed the responsibility, the status, the equal footing with which they treated me. It made me feel important and grown-up. Until we got to the cabin.

Each day, from dusk to dawn, mom and I inventoried the food, sorted foul-smelling second-hand clothes, hauled water, split firewood, beat out rugs, washed towels in the stream, tended to seedlings in the planter boxes, and sealed cracks in the cabin walls. This was not the co-equal footing I had known at home that made me feel grown-up; it was misery. "Just think of it like *Little House on the Prairie*," Mom offered one day. "You used to love those books."

As the winter bore down cold and dry, I went out with Mom to set trap lines in the woods. I learned to skin marmots and rabbits across a boulder slab with a collapsible knife I kept clipped to my belt loop. It was never enough, the small, sinewy animals we caught. Many nights around the little round table in the cabin Mom and Dad simply watched me and Callie eat, or split a can of diced carrots while making sure the two of us cleaned the plate of the chewy, acrid meat of a marten. There was a lot of food in the cellar – canned vegetables and beans, fruit in syrup cups, spam, peanut butter, bags of dry oatmeal, a dozen sacks of rice and flour. Watching them voluntarily starve, I knew that no matter how many times Mom said *We're just here for a bit, just until things settle down*, she had no idea how long we would be there, how long it would take for things to settle down, because she wanted that food to last and last and last.

Sometimes Mom and I had better luck motoring out on the stolen boat and casting nets into the ocean. Benji rode the bow, wind whipping his long ears like the battle ropes in gym class. For all the remoteness, all the wilderness, all the immense distance between us and civilization, it was staggering the amount of trash we pulled in from the net. Plastic grocery bags and bottle caps and six-pack rings. Each haul contained more and more jellyfish, sticky and translucent. But sometimes there was rockfish and lingcod, enough for a meal. In a way, those big, warm fish were worse than the strained canned peas or unleavened bread Mom cooked on the stove. In the fullness of my belly as I sucked down their rendered fat came a familiarity, a yearning for food so acute it physically hurt: Thanksgiving dinners, neighborhood potlucks, Thai takeout nights, and Sunday morning brunches. I wrapped my arms around my abdomen, trying to squeeze away the empty space where memories of those meals lived.

What I craved even more than catching fish on that boat was a glimpse of the mainland across the Peninsula – civilization. I sat, statue-like, on the aluminum bench, gazing out at the long line of the subcontinent, considering whether I could simply steal the boat one night and go back to Homer with Benji, hitchhike to Anchorage, just up and go home.

For as much responsibility my parents had given me at home, I had failed to see all the ways they also let me be a kid – until that was taken away. I'd had playdates and sleepovers, after school clubs and birthday parties, an iPad with colorful, meaningless games, long, lazy days with nothing but fantasy books and cartoons and drawing at the kitchen table. There was none of that here. And I could not fathom that it had also been robbed from all my friends back home. Surely it was only me.

So what, a nuclear bomb had gone off? The childhood world was small and insulated and shockproof. Obviously, Margot was still going to ballet class on Mondays and Wednesdays. Obviously, Sofia was still working on her Claymation project for Mister Yestes' class. Obviously, Grace was still kicking her soccer ball into the side of her garage. And Sylvie. No person in the world had I trusted more than Sylvie, and now she was gone. The world, or some version of it, was going on without me, just across the water.

Things were bad on the mainland. I could understand that. But to me, nothing could be worse than being forcibly outcast by my parents. I knew it was selfish and nearsighted – even an undeveloped brain could see that – but it overwhelmed me.

In our rush to unload our minivan into the stolen skiff back at the mainland, somehow a soccer ball rolling around in the trunk found its way into a duffel bag and out to the cabin. Any moment not spent working or reading up in the loft to keep my brain awake and alive, I kicked the soccer ball into a large boulder near the mouth of the creek. I etched a bullseye on a flat face of the rock with a crumbling piece of slate and aimed for it over and over. The ball bounced erratically off rocks and around the beach gravel, and I used every ounce of flustered, agitated energy chasing the ball and kicking it back into the boulder. Benji jumped and nipped at my heels, and I could barely admit to myself that there was some actual, authentic joy in hitting the bullseye. It felt familiar, and it served no purpose but having fun.

Then, one night, the cold encircled us like a massive and muscular tail that lashed across the earth. I went out to kick the soccer ball after a long afternoon bushwhacking with Mom up Lamplighter Mountain, hunting ptarmigan. The day's cold had left the skin hard and brittle. I delivered a swift kick to the center and hit the bullseye square in the middle. The ball let out a great POP and deflated into a shapeless mound of synthetic leather.

"No!" I screamed. "No!"

Mom and Dad came running down from the cabin, fearing a bear or rockslide or some nameless, faceless danger that now haunted us every moment of every day. But instead they found me sobbing over the remnants of the ball, Benji full of worry and squeezing his way through my arms to lick my cheek.

Their relief at seeing that it was only a ball made them less sympathetic to the magnitude of my loss. "Maybe some duct tape…" I whimpered. "Maybe I can duct tape it and reinflate it…"

"Baby," Mom said, with a hand on my shoulder. "We really can't spare any duct tape for that. It's one of our most useful things here."

So I just cried into Benji's back on the beach, which he gladly obliged, and they ambled back up the hill to the cabin, feeling it was best to leave me alone in my silly little grief.

In the days that followed I did what was needed but did it sullenly and quietly. Mom and Dad asked me if I was okay. And I wanted to tell them *No, of course not, what a dumb question.* But I could never get the words out. Their voices made me too angry, and the concerned looks on their faces were too irritating. I couldn't give them the fulfillment of knowing what was in my head. I thought it could be nice to keep a journal, to write down what I could not say. But Mom took my school notebook out of my backpack because – of all the millions of things she had packed out to the cabin – she forgot paper. She insisted she needed mine to keep notes about the weather, vegetable gardening, and tide times. So I stayed trapped inside my head, enormously lonely and a little bit hungry.

TIME COLLAPSED INTO itself out there in the cabin like the globe of a sinking hot air balloon. Dad's calendar on the wall kept us anchored to linear time, but the days swirled and pooled at my feet, each indistinguishable from the last. Without rain, even the seasons blended together – defined now by temperature gradients rather than snow, light and dark rather than plant growth and bird migrations.

"Time moves slower at the top of a mountain and faster at the bottom of a mountain," Callie announced to me one afternoon when I took a break inside to warm my hands. She had a book on her lap by a scientist called Richard Feynman. I took one glance and saw she was simply looking at the pictures.

"No, Callie," I said, tired and resentful of her quiet life in the warmth of the cabin. "Time is the same everywhere."

"No, it's not," she said. "Gravity pulls it down."

"Callie, that doesn't make any sense. Gravity is for things like bowling balls and feathers. Stop making things up."

"I'm not making things up," she insisted. "It's beautiful. We should walk to the top of the mountain to be where time moves slower."

I rolled my eyes at her and went outside to help Mom tighten the laundry line across two spruce trees.

Teenagers! So narrow-minded. Two years later, having nearly run out of books to read, I picked up this same one, *Six Easy Pieces: The Essentials of Physics*, and learned that not only did time move faster at lower elevations, but that my tiny sister was a brilliant mind trapped in the body of a little girl – trying to get my attention. Although I did not understand relative time, I was living it. The tenses – past, present, and future – lost all meaning or relevance. All were rewritten by memory, undone by the drumbeat of human history, or just completely unknowable. My thoughts passed between Pluto Cove and the blue house on Manor Avenue as seamlessly as the ripples of a fallen stone. I lived in the moments before fully waking when I did not remember where I was or how I had gotten there. With my eyes closed against the pillow and my arms wrapped around Benji, I could be home where I belonged. When Mom told me about all the things the Polar Storms had caused – the wars and the famine and the false gods – it wasn't the detached recollections of a history book but the scribbled writings of a diary in real time.

I wished I could reach out and bend time like a wet willow branch, bringing myself back to Callie. I would tell her she was right about time being a function of gravity, and then we would walk to the very top of the mountain where our minutes together would count for more.

THERE WAS A DAY in the winter – some otherwise meaningless day in the vast and undefinable winter – when Mom and I went out in the skiff to a small cove in full view of the mainland peninsula. The water spread out around us still as glass; with a spoon I might have shattered it like crème brûlée. She dropped anchor while I pulled the net out from under the bench and found it frozen into a tangled mess. I growled under my breath, wishing there was someone else to blame but myself, knowing I was the last one to put it away. I started in on the knots but kept losing my gaze to the peninsula. My fingers tripped over each other and snagged in the nylon. My hands numbed from handling the frozen rope and soon I was crying hot and angry tears into the net, pulling haphazardly at loose ends that thawed under the heat of my fit, gritting my teeth *come on come on, come on* before I threw the net to the bottom of the boat and stomped on it.

When I looked up, Mom stared at me. Her face was slapped with red, a burning of cold, sun, and wind. "Enna," she said. "Are you okay?"

"I'm fine!" I shouted, bending over to pick up the net and fix it for real.

"Okay," she started, slowly, as though testing the water in a bathtub. "But I know that things are really crazy right now."

This was the most enormous understatement and I refused to dignify it with a response. Instead I buried my attention in the net.

"And you're thirteen now, there are a lot of changes going on in your body, too."

This was explosive. An eruption started at the pit of my stomach and crested up and out of my throat, down my shoulders, out through my fingers. I threw the net down again. "Mom! Are you seriously trying to talk to me about puberty right now?"

She stammered, aware of the landmines she passed, but perhaps wanting to take advantage of having me captive in the boat, unable to escape. "Honey, it's true, though. You have no idea the kinds of things that happen in your body when you start to turn into a woman, and the things that happen in your brain when you start to feel attractions–"

"Oh my god, I cannot believe you!" I shouted. "You know there is literally no one else within, like, a thousand miles of here. I am literally completely alone in the world, and you are wanting to sit me down and have *The Talk*. You are unbelievable." I sat down with a huff and pretended she wasn't there as I disentangled the knot.

She was quiet for a long time. She leaned over the edge of the skiff and dipped her fingers in the ocean, tracing circles into the still lens of the water. It must have frozen her fingers solid, but she didn't seem to mind. Her breath came out in slow and even puffs. When she finally spoke it was quiet, and she did not look at me.

"I cannot imagine what you are going through. I really can't. Sometimes I think of how hard this is for me, but really it's nothing compared to how hard it is for you." In spite of myself, my shoulders softened at her words. "For me, I feel like everyone in the world who I need is right here. You and Dad and Callie. You are my universe. But it's different for you. You had this huge, big, open world back in Anchorage. I can't imagine how much you must miss that."

I resisted it, but I cried. Not angry-crying, but the kind of crying when I was a kid and skinned my knee, but I wouldn't cry until I had made it to Mom and she had me wrapped up in her arms and it felt safe to acknowledge how much it hurt.

I pulled at the knots, starting to make some progress, starting to feel the static in my head quiet down.

Without meaning to, I spoke. "Sometimes I think it might be nice if we talked about home. Or about how things used to be."

"Do you feel like you can't?" Mom asked.

I shrugged. "No one has ever said that I can't. But, yeah, it feels like we're just supposed to forget everything from before. And not make each other sad with memories."

She nodded. "I know what you mean." She took a breath. "We actually don't have to ride this far out to fish, you know. I just like getting a glimpse of the mainland. Seeing it over there, it makes me feel connected to something. And I keep hoping that one of these days I'll see something, or there will be some kind of sign, that it's okay to go home. That it's safe." The boat rocked in a frigid gust of wind and she waited for it to settle. "You know what I really miss from home? That brown chair in the living room. The one by the window. The heating vent was right next to it, and I could prop up my feet and they'd just melt under the warm air coming up. Listening to the rain coming down off the leaves on the birch tree outside. I loved that. I wish I had made time to do it more, to just sit there and enjoy it."

To my surprise, I smiled. I knew the chair, knew the vent. Rather than devastate me, the memory warmed me.

"What do you miss?" Mom asked cautiously, knowing she may be triggering a landslide.

There were so many things. I missed making cookies with Sylvie but eating only the dough. I missed listening to music and looking up lyrics on the Internet. I missed the taste of fresh orange slices during halftime at my soccer games. The privacy of my own bedroom. The sound of the hallways at school as they overflowed with my peers bustling from one classroom to the next. I missed walking to the bus stop in the rain but refusing to wear a sensible coat because it was bulky and I didn't like the way it looked. But there was just one thing I missed the most, the thing we all missed, the source of all our madness and loss and agony: "I miss the rain. Why won't it rain? Why won't it just rain? Why is this happening? Why can't you stop this?" I plunged my freezing fingers into Benji's fur and instead of recoiling at my chill, he pressed himself into me.

"No one knows," Mom said, her voice so thick with sadness I could have grabbed it out the air and lathered it on my hands.

As much as I wanted to spread around my own misery, seeing my mom that way did nothing but make it worse. I knew she wanted to change things, that she would have disassembled a mountain rock by rock or cut off her own fingers and toes if it would make the rain come, if it would make a world that was good and safe and stable for me and Callie. But there was nothing she could do. Nothing more than what she had already done. Most of my life she fought these demons inside her head, and now they had manifested in real and physical ways and the only option on the table was running away. So I swallowed every last drop of my bitterness and forced out words to spare her some helplessness. I spoonfed her a small piece of hope the way I used to feed Callie smashed sweet potatoes. "I miss school, too."

And at this, did she lighten. A child knows how to navigate the emotional ecosystem of their parents. By this statement, she was proud of me, and by extension, proud of herself for raising me. "I understand," she said. "That brain of yours is a big one. It gets hungry, I bet."

I nodded. We were quiet for a while, letting the boat rock in the waves. I distracted myself by brushing out Benji's fur though he had no knots.

"Well, you know," she said, blowing warm air onto her hands. "We are kind of lame, and just your parents, but you can learn a lot from Dad. He's one of the most brilliant people I've ever met. And if you ever want to learn anything from me, I know a little bit more than just all this backcountry stuff your Great-Grandpa Jenkins taught me."

"Electricity," I said, thinking of all her afternoons spent on the roof tinkering with the solar panels, and evenings in the cabin spent manipulating wires on light fixtures. She never talked openly about being an electrical engineer for an oil exploration company, about how she designed power stations for floating drill platforms. Most of the time I thought she glossed over these details because they happened before Callie and I were born and, therefore, were irrelevant. In moments of clarity, though, I could see that she didn't speak of them because they brought her pain. It was Dad who remembered aloud most often, sharing memories as though to redeem Mom during her spells of apparent madness. *She used to be magnificent*, he seemed to say, wanting me to believe it. *She's worth believing in*.

"Electricity," she repeated, turning the word over in her mind like a beach stone. "My head is stuffed with it."

"I'd like to learn electricity," I said, convincing

myself of it, moving from a place of manipulating her into a better mood to genuinely believing I might feel better with something to challenge me. "I don't really understand it. Or, like, what power is at all."

"Oh," Mom said, seemingly astounded that I had approached a topic she could speak to with authority. "Yes, I know electricity." She paused. "When we get back to the cabin, would you want me to show you how the solar panels work?"

"Yeah," I said, feeling a slight, distant prickle of something that took me a moment to register as anticipation. It had been so long. "That would be great."

"You got it," she said.

"Okay," I said. As I readied to cast the net into the ocean, another question bubbled up inside me. "Actually, could we start now? With the boat engine?"

"Of course," she said, stepping across the bench and removing the plastic cover from the motor. "Now, what you need to know first is how electrons behave."

WE WERE NOT THE ONLY inhabitants of Pluto Cove. A bear, too, called it his home. In the mornings we awakened to his tracks stenciled across the sandbars where he could walk unencumbered by bushes and brush. Whether from the drought or the sudden arrival of vulnerable chickens, this bear would not hibernate. There were nights when Benji barked maniacally at the door, then jumped onto the back of the couch to bark at the window, then jumped down and went back to barking at the door. The bear was a skittish bear. Each time Mom threw open the door, shotgun cocked, he was gone.

Callie and I caught the first glimpse of him one

afternoon while I was filleting salmon on the porch. Callie collected their bright orange egg sacs, passing their soft, oily shells through her fingers before dropping them into a Mason jar. "Don't pop them," I scolded. "That'll ruin them."

"But they look like bubbles," she said. "They are so beautiful." I was about to grab them from her when we heard a shaking of branches and the soft but throaty grunts of an animal that lumbered when it walked. I put an arm across Callie and pulled her toward me.

"Stay quiet," I whispered. I knew this was not the indicated approach. Bears run from loud noises, waving arms, even screams. But I wanted to see him. It felt safe enough on the porch. Could he even climb stairs?

Yes.

His fur shined and rippled like scales in the sun. It was a light honey brown with streaks down his shoulder blades like melted caramel. His eyes were little dark beads that could barely see a thing, but his nose was long and wide. He sniffed his way across the ground, following our footsteps, toward the salmon. He wasn't big as grizzlies go – but his size was still an arresting, terrifying thing. He opened his mouth into a yawn, and his teeth carved through the air like bayonets. Callie whimpered into my sweater. But I was paralyzed, mesmerized. For all the fears that plagued us at Pluto Cove, they were ambiguous. Nameless. Long-term, amorphous threats like hunger or loneliness. But this was acute, real. My skin prickled and my heart quickened. It was bewitching.

But then he moved toward the porch. He put a paw up on the first step. And I snapped out of it.

"Hey!" I shouted. "Hey bear!" I released my grip on Callie and threw my hands into the air, waving them high. The sound and movement startled him. He had not realized we were there. "Hey bear!" I yelled, louder than I intended, and the words came from the top of my windpipe and sounded more like a scream than a hard, assertive shout. He didn't like this one bit. He stumbled backward off the first step and took off in a wobbly trot back into the woods. Benji tore down from the hillside where he had been chasing rabbits. Mom and Dad came running from the beach where they had been tinkering with the boat engine. But the bear was gone. I stood on the porch, Callie at my side, with an enormous grin.

"A bear?" Mom gasped. "*The* bear?"

"Yeah," I said. "He's gone now."

"What'd he look like?" Mom said, whipping her neck around in hopes of catching a glimpse.

"Brown bear," I said.

"What else?" Mom demanded.

What else was there? It was a brown bear. I could have described the fine color of his coat, the way it undulated across the massive muscles of his back. I could have described the whiteness and length of his teeth, or the drops of moisture on his nose. But I didn't want to. It felt private, personal. Something I had shared with this beast that I would not give away. But Callie interjected.

"He had a really big butt," she said.

"What?" Mom asked, puzzled.

"His butt," Callie repeated. "When he walked away his butt was big and round like a peach."

It took Mom and Dad a moment because the act was so foreign, so stuck in their throats after all had that passed – but they started to laugh.

"Like a peach?" Dad repeated. "Like a little Georgia peach?"

"No," Callie corrected. "Like a *gigantic* Georgia Peach."

And they doubled over and laughed even harder. It came out of them in rasps and squeaks, like a bike tire turning for the first time after rusting to the axel.

We named him George. He was never far away, but always easy to scare off. He was restless and skittish. I didn't mind him, and Callie adored him. Over time, Mom grew to hate him. Our chickens had successfully multiplied themselves, but he killed half in a tear of feathers and eggshells. He robbed from our traplines. He punctured holes in our tarp. He rooted through the garden boxes. But every time there came an opportunity to shoot him, some noise – usually Benji – frightened him away.

Mom was obsessed with George. She walked the banks of the creek to find tufts of his fur snarled into branches and collected them in fistfuls. She used them to stuff her pillow. "Keep your enemies close," she said.

Dad shook his head.

"I'm not crazy," Mom said.

"I know," Dad said.

THEY ASKED LITTLE of Callie. She was young and particularly clumsy. Before the Polar Storms, Mom took her to an occupational therapist to practice basic motor skills. For a long time, I teased her over holding markers in her fists rather than her fingers – or the way she dropped so many dinner plates that Mom switched to plastic. But then it became clear that something was wrong, something more than just being young or having butterfingers. Dad started using the words *cerebral palsy.* So I stopped.

She spent her days at the cabin playing with dolls and pretending to read the enormous stacks of moldy, musty books that accumulated out there over the last sixty years. Sometimes she was so engrossed in the pages of those great bound books that she gave the impression of actually reading. But she was only four. It wasn't possible.

Still, though, she resented the idleness. "I want to help," she said. "I want to help." But to have her help was worse – would take more time, more corrections, more wasted effort in tasks that were essential to survival. So Mom gave her an assignment with an official name: The Fire Keeper. She sat in the cabin monitoring the fire. If it appeared to be getting low, she was to find Mom or Dad and report to them the exact words, "Sergeant, the fire has dwindled. Please report to duty." Mom made her practice the line over and over, to her utter delight. It made her feel important. Necessary.

She was born on a school day. Third grade. Dad showed up in the middle of my gym class with a smile on his face so large it seemed to swallow his face. He was like an independent light source standing there, motioning for me, handing me what he thought would be the best news I had ever received. "She's here!" he called out, embarrassing me. "Your sister is here!"

My gym teacher, Mister Fam, walked over to Dad and shook his hand warmly, almost aggressively. "Congrats, man," he said. "Heather is due in a couple weeks. The girls will be almost the same age. What a blessed day."

We had been in the middle of shark tag and I was reluctant to leave. But both men stood there grinning like llamas, and I didn't want my classmates to see.

In the van he buckled me into my seat, even though I hadn't needed help with that for years. "It all happened so fast," he said. "I was at work and your mom called that she was at home feeling a little funky. I told her to make an appointment with her OB, and the next thing I knew I got a call that she was already in the hospital just on the floor above me!" His voice was light and fast like bird wings.

I remember the blue tile of the hospital hallway. The creamy doors with dry-erase boards in the center, the balloons that bobbed around from the nurse station countertops and in the hands of other visitors. I held Dad's hand as we walked down the hallway. You never know when something happens for the last time. I know now was the last time I ever reached for Dad's hand.

She was smaller than I thought possible. Her eyes were sealed shut like a kitten's. Dad brought her to me wrapped up in a blanket with rainbow hot air balloons on the fabric, and I had the feeling of never having held anything so fragile. He beamed. He radiated. Mom was out of the room getting something fixed up, but he didn't seem worried. He took several hundred photos of me holding Callie for the first time, but not one ever made it to print. In them, my face is tense, fearful, unconvinced. I had never longed for a sibling. I understood my privileged position with my parents, and now it was compromised. And whatever was laying in my arms was clearly nothing I could ever be friends with, ever have a relationship with. I had Benji. He was all the companionship I needed.

Callie inhabited her own world. She was the precious baby while I was the nine-year-old with aching limbs that never stopped growing, never stayed in the same set of clothes for more than a couple months, who fomented body odor while she smelled of sweet baby soaps and sugary milk. Callie, with her light porcelain skin, was a delicate creature pieced of gossamer wings. And I? I looked tougher than I was, more mature than I was, and sometimes it felt like my parents forgot that I needed help, too.

I did my part. I carried my weight. That was my role. But she was not an equal, not a playmate, just a nuisance. I rarely had friends over because she was young and annoying and always spilling sticky things. It was easier at other people's houses where siblings were closer to our own age, and we could play together and chase each other and tease one another. Callie was tender, precious, even shy. Especially around me.

Mom said it was because Callie worshipped me, and one does not speak needlessly in front of an idol. I thought she just didn't know how to talk. How much language should a four-year-old have? Maybe her clumsiness made her shy, or maybe it affected her speech. I had no idea.

At home in Anchorage we had separate rooms, separate schedules, entirely separate existences. She had not started kindergarten, and I was nearly done with middle school. We knew little about each other. In fact, the only meaningful time we spent together was during family trips to the cabin. And this was no exception. But now our quarters were impossibly close, our beds an arm's distance away from each other, the steepness of Lamplighter Mountain and the ferocity of the ocean boxing us into the same postage stamp of land on Pluto Cove. And she started to talk to me a little here and there. Mostly at night as we lay in bed, staring out the porthole window up at the sky.

One night George woke us while pawing at the storm door into the cellar. Even vacuum sealed and boiled in glass jars and aluminum cans, he could smell the food that beckoned there. Benji barked him away with the ferocity of an animal twenty times his size. Mom leapt from bed and threw open the porch door. The metal of her shotgun clanged against the doorframe.

"Is he gone?" Dad asked sleepily from below our loft.

"Yeah," Mom sighed. "He took off." I heard the irritation in her voice even half-asleep. She wanted so badly to shoot that bear. She talked about it often. The meat, the bones, the hide. More than anything, she wanted the knowledge that she could. That she was the apex predator of Pluto Cove.

The chickens clucked and the rooster crowed for hours after that. Callie and I lay awake, unable to fall back asleep.

"Do you think there's anybody else out there?" She asked.

Her question surprised me. That she spoke at all, and that she had such big, scary thoughts.

"Yes," I said. "Definitely. Mom just wanted us to come out here to wait for people to sort things out. That's all."

She was quiet for a moment. "I don't know," she said. "It still hasn't really rained. How long can people go without rain?" She was whispering to not disturb Mom and Dad below us, but it added a chill to her words.

"People are really resourceful, Callie," I said. "There are scientists and engineers and stuff working on it. They'll figure it out."

Although I knew her silence more than I knew her voice, her stillness spoke that my words were of no comfort. And that scared me – they were the only words that comforted me.

"Do you ever think sometimes that we are the luckiest people on earth?"

Though it was dark, my eyes went wide. Such a thought had been the furthest thing from my mind. It would never, ever spontaneously occur to me.

"Not even a little bit," I said. "That's insane."

"I don't know," she said again. "We have a cabin to go to. Do other people have a cabin to go to? And Daddy is a doctor and Mommy is an engineer. They can do anything. What about Paulie's dad who shakes all the time and can't walk? Do you think they are okay? And our cabin has water from a glacier. I think other people need rain for water if they don't have glaciers. Sometimes I think about how lucky we are, and it makes me so sad."

My heart sat heavy in my chest, and I could not disentangle the reasons. I felt guilty that, as the sister tasking with being wiser and more mature, I lacked the same gratitude or depth of thought. And there was also a profound sadness that Callie, a little girl, had to navigate a world so drenched in sorrow and chaos. After so many years of silence, this is how she chose now to speak. I wanted to cross over the little gap between our beds and hold her. But I had never done such a thing and had no idea how to initiate the move, how to put my arms on her, what she would feel like. What if she pulled away? So I did nothing.

"I don't think we are lucky," I said simply, disappointed by my response.

"What about the *Little Match Girl?*" Callie asked. In my empty silence she continued. "The story about the little girl out on the street all alone, trying to sell matches but the matches are the only thing to keep her warm, so she burns them. And she sees happy things when she burns them. She was so poor. We have never needed to burn matches to stay warm or to sell matches so we can eat."

"Callie–" I started, frustrated. We had always been comfortable, but I was often irritated by the way Mom and Dad spent money. Other friends with doctor parents lived in bigger homes, drove nicer cars, took fancier and more exotic vacations than a boat to an isolated cove twice a year. Those kids got ten-dollar bills from the tooth fairy and had second homes in warm places. I understood that Dad sent a lot of money to his half-sister in Texas and extended family in Guadalajara, but it didn't seem fair. But how could I say that to Callie? "Did Mom read you that story?"

"No," she replied. "I read it. There's a copy downstairs."

"No, you didn't," I sighed. "Don't tell tall tales."

"I'm not," she insisted. "I just think about her a lot. The match girl. And why do we get to be here safe with our parents when other little kids aren't?"

I dug deep into my exhausted brain. "In math class, Miss Tischler talked about something like this once." I said, trying to offer something. "When we were talking about probabilities. Do you know what that means?" I heard rustling that could have been her nodding or shaking her head. I did not know and pressed on – more to assure myself than her. "She said that when someone hits a golf ball, the golf ball flies through the air and lands on a blade of grass. Of all the millions of blades of grass on a golf course, it lands on just a few. And if those blades of grass could talk, they would be like *Oh my god, it was us! What are the odds! We are so lucky!* But the truth is that the golf ball had to land somewhere. And when it happens to be you it feels really special and really lucky, but if it weren't you, you wouldn't even know." I could feel I had lost her. She was thinking now about talking blades of grass. But still, I needed to hear the words. "I think that you feel lucky because this is what you have. And if you had something else you would feel lucky for that. Like, if Dad were a farmer and we could grow a ton of food. Or if we lived in Hawaii and it was warm all the time and easy to get around. Or if we lived in a little neighborhood or town where everyone worked together to get water and food and not have to do it alone. This is just one way to be lucky, but we aren't the only people who are lucky."

"Or if someone had magic," she said. "They would be really lucky. They could just make rain, or make food, or make friends to be around."

I sighed. She had not appreciated how excellent a speech I had delivered. "There's no such thing as magic,

73

Callie."

"Yes, there is," she said defensively. "There is such a thing as magic."

"Okay," I said sarcastically.

"Don't!" She whined, using the voice she took when she wasn't taken seriously. "There really is."

"What magic have you ever seen, Callie?" I demanded.

"Sometimes I make magic," she said.

"Uh-huh," I dismissed, rolling over on my pillow, bored now with the conversation.

"I really do," she insisted. "I have magic with batteries."

"That's not magic," I said. "That's electricity."

"No," she said. "I make batteries work. Really."

"No, you don't."

"Then how else do batteries work?"

Here I was lost. I had no idea how batteries worked, even though a whole stack of them were piled under Callie's bed. I made a note to ask Mom later, then tell Callie as though I had known all along. "It's electricity," I said simply.

"Then I have electricity magic," she said.

"Whatever, Callie," I said. "Go to sleep now."

"I can't. The chickens are still acting crazy."

"I know," I said. "Just try."

"Do you believe me, Enna?" she asked, so earnestly I felt there was only one possible response.

"Sure, Callie. Yeah. You have electricity magic."

And a few minutes later I heard the heavy, steady breathing of her asleep.

WINTER FELL HARD. Some years it crept in, slowly infiltrating all the nooks and crannies until one day I realized that the same block of ice had been barnacled into the wheel wells of Dad's car for eight weeks, so filthy and crusty it looked like rock. Other winters the snow came on so gently it was almost tender, the way it fell light and bright and coated the ground, like textured glass, and slowly piled up until it reached the bottom of windowsills.

But not this first winter at Pluto Cove.

The weather was chilly at first, but not extreme. There were some afternoons with blasts of fast, stinging, freezing rain. Not snow, not hail, just daggers of rain trapped between the two. It never lasted long, just minutes on its way north, never enough to nourish anything or resuscitate the dead. It dumped and then left. But that water was precious. It needed to be trapped, saved, harnessed. It was Dad's work to dig a water basin.

I wondered why we needed a water basin, with the creek right there. But in the months leading up our escape, as the LFR built ranks and took over towns, it became the duty of every able-bodied man in America to dig a water basin. The President called them Patriot Trenches, and they lined the fronts and backs of every home, apartment complex, and state capitol building in the country. Dad dug one in our yard, moved by the spirit and camaraderie of it all. Maybe it was silly to dig a basin at the cabin, but it was reflex. It was the only sure physical act of water storage we knew. If the creek mysteriously dried up with the rain, we would still have the basin.

He started next to the creek, moving out

smoothed stones and packed gravel one shovelful at a time. But the ground there was too loose; water seeped right down. So he went up the slope of the mountain to a flat spot and dug past the moss and fluff of fallen leaves, to a layer of gray silt. I thought it was clay at first, the way it packed in my hands and let itself be molded. But Mom corrected me. "That's silt," she said. "Not as good as clay. But it will have to do."

Dad transformed before our eyes from a doctor to a miner, filthy and crusty and broad-shouldered. He hauled silt from the side of the mountain down to the hand-dug hole at the bottom of the creek. Day after day he excavated a pool, piling up rocks too big to trap water, and packing down the silt into a hard pan. The pool would collect runoff from the creek and capture any precious rain that fell from the sky.

All other tasks, the millions of tasks that needed doing, were suspended. "We got lucky that it's December but the ground is still warm," Mom said. I stiffened at her use of the word lucky. "He has to finish before the ground freezes."

It scared me, seeing Dad this way. He was, by definition, a man of intensity, of singular focus. But this was a mania. He became an animal bound to the subfloors of the earth, a gopher or vole. The hole grew so deep he disappeared into it entirely. But it was never big enough. There was never enough silt to keep water he trapped from simply washing into the ground.

Meanwhile, Mom and I inventoried the food, using precious pieces of paper from my notebook, a relic of my former life, to list all the canned goods and dry goods and perishable goods. Then we ranked them by their expiration dates and moved those to the front of the cellar. The ones with a longer shelf-life we moved to the back.

We reinforced the enclosure around the chickens about twenty times, piling downed trees around them like Lincoln Logs – as though it would ever be enough to keep out George and the wolves who howled across the mountains in the night. When an eagle took up a perch in a spruce tree overlooking the coop, we added logs to the top as well. The threats came from all directions.

We tried to learn to distinguish between an egg with a chick and an egg with a yolk. We scrutinized the eggs, shook them, held them against the sun. But we still cracked so many eggs into the pan only to find the small body of a baby bird.

The days leading into the first winter hardened us, but there was no scarcity. Not yet. We had enough. Benji chewed up fish bones and licked gristle from the pots and pans. Mom even spared me the worst of the tasks – the most dehumanizing and disgusting of all possible tasks – mucking the outhouse and chicken coop. Sewage.

"It will compost," she said. "After a while you will hold this in your hands and never believe that it was waste. It will help us grow things." But I did not hear her. I did not allow myself to hear her. I grew up in a clean, warm home with objects collected solely for their beauty and comfort: flower vases and oil paintings and bookends carved from dark wood into elephants. Faucets that I could flip on and have endless filtered water at any temperature I desired. Toilets that flushed, and trucks that came to our driveway and hauled away the filthy things.

No longer.

Then, overnight, what mildness had graced us that winter, vanished. A storm came from the Gulf. A mighty and raging storm, something from a book that begins with castaway sailors. Winds ripped off the cove with so much energy they screamed as they hit the mountain like banshees heralding death. Trees toppled around us like pillars in a crumbling city. We could only pray none fell on the cabin. Waves reached out of the water and crashed up onto the shore like drowning hands clawing for mercy. The sound of water convinced me that the storm brought rain. But it had not. The sea level rose and rose until it appeared it may touch the steps of our porch.

It never did, but it did reach our water basin.

Just like that, his long, backbreaking days spent digging, not eating, coughing out dust from dried out dirt, losing the lines on his face to grit and gunk, were obliterated. Washed out to sea. Replaced with the greatest enemy in our time of drought: saltwater.

He didn't want to, he fought it as hard as he could. But he cried. He wept onto Mom's shoulder, and she held him in close. Callie and I watched, terrified and unmoving. In the soft light of our single bulb, Mom took one hand off his hair and motioned for us to come. In broken, uncertain movements, they wrapped me into their embrace, a tangle of arms of different shades, my head pressed into Dad's back, strong and trembling. Benji put his paws upon my shoulders, and he felt, too, that this was a time for mourning.

When we woke up the next day, the world was

frozen. Ocean spray hung suspended from tree branches like diamond necklaces. Rocks along the beach were smooth and shiny as ivory under the ice. Water particles in the air condensed and anchored themselves to the side of the cabin, crusted across our windows.

It would be many months of relentless winter before the ground thawed and Dad could dig again.

CHAPTER THREE - *One Year Later*

A peculiar thing happens to the forest in a drought. Whereas before the Polar Storms, the air sat dense and fragrant, trapped in between the trunks of trees, curled about the forest floor like a sleeping cat, now it buzzed, it tingled. Almost unbearably light and hollow. Whereas before, walking through the forest was squishing on moss – wearing boots even in sunshine because the earth was so rich and sodden – now each footfall cracked and snapped like walking over a pile of matchsticks. Each broken step was the sound of being followed, chased, by an unseen enemy. Vibrant green leaves turned the color of dirty dishwater and fell limp on their branches. Mud turned to dust. Pollen turned to dust. Moss crumbled like fossils and turned to dust. Spruce needles and alder leaves turned to dust. Everything turned to dust. And the dust blew around and around, into our mouths, into our eyes, getting caught in our hair, in between our teeth. Even in the winter.

And here's the great irony of it all. When it did rain – those small bursts of rain that erupted from the sky and then disappeared as quickly as they arrived – a fraction of what was needed, of what the forest depended upon – the world was too dry to receive it. The ground was hard and packed. Rain hit the surface and slid away.

I remember our yard at home as the Polar Storms set in, watching the leaves of the big birch tree outside my window turn brown in July – not the orange and red of fall, but the sepia of illness and surrender. And each evening – the summer before imposed water rations – I watered the birch tree, hoping to revive it, to have it hang on just one more season when I believed the rain would come and all this would end.

But the ground was dead, and dead things cannot drink.

The water from the backyard hose pooled and swirled until it found a channel, until it gathered up and flowed away, until it hit the pavement and disappeared into an echoey storm drain where it washed out to the ocean. So even when it did rain, even when someone came along with a watering can, even if a hose was set right atop it and allowed to run free, it did nothing. "Water finds itself," Mom had said. "The negative electrons in one molecule grip to the positive charge in another. It clings to itself." Water does not disperse or soak without the help of healthy plants to ease its tension. Water moves fast. Water finds the downhill leading to the creek that leads to the river that leads to the ocean. To saltwater. And where there is no downhill, water carves it out.

Each one of those rain bursts, those teases of precipitation, was a psychological torture. Maybe this one would last, we thought. Maybe this one will be the one that marks the end. Maybe this one will be normal. But it never was. It rained for moment, and then it moved north, gone.

I remember waking up at home one morning with my heart pounding outside my body from the excitement, the joy. I heard the rain outside, drumming on the rooftop. I ran downstairs to tell Mom and Dad, to share this great joy of a rain that was hard and lasting. But when I reached the kitchen, I saw Mom cooking bacon. Its drops of grease popped over the pan, making the sound of rain on a roof. There was no rain at all.

Once a bug flew into the windshield of Mom's car. She turned on the windshield wipers to flick it away, and I hadn't recognized the music of their swish swish swish across the glass until I remembered how long it had been since she used them.

Sometimes, when it was cloudy, I stared out the window, wondering if maybe it was that gentle sheeting of rain that is so soft and so persistent it doesn't even look like rain until you step outside and feel it. I remembered how it used to rain so passionately that the view outside would flicker, popping in and out of frame like ticker tape.

I cared that the trees were dying. I cared that birds dropped from the sky and fish washed up dead on dry creekbeds. I cared that plains of caribou collapsed with fur hung limp from their starved bodies. But more than anything, I cared about my world staying the same. About my school bus route and my class schedule and my friends at the lunch table and my chart of chores hanging on the refrigerator. And it was clear that no matter how remote the impacts of the drought may have been in the beginning, each one crept closer and closer into the tiny chamber of my life.

In the end, the drought became everything. We came to Pluto Cove. And there was no one around, no familiarity with our former lives, no comforts or pleasures or things just-for-fun. Movie theaters, trampolines, museums, monkey bars. And even though we had given everything up, every drop of ourselves, the drought persisted. No matter how much we changed, the drought did not.

Mom and I trapped a rabbit in a snare, and the rabbit was starving, but she and I carved it up anyway. George had lurked around the cabin for months now and snatched healthier animals from their snares, seizing his free meals. But even he had left this rabbit, not worth his effort. I hated it all. The letting of the thick, dehydrated blood, the skinning of muscle without any fat, the gutting of intestines that had already curled in on themselves, self-digesting, the glassy stare of two coal black eyes.

"This rabbit was sick," I said, running my fingers through the patchy, malnourished fur. "It's not fair."

"What part isn't fair?" Mom asked, barely registering my question, all too accustomed to my words, knowing that none of this was fair, as she tugged a string of muscle from its bony attachment.

"We came out here to escape the drought," I said. "But we just went deeper into it. We are just going to kill sick and starving animals like this until we're one, too."

Mom stopped. She turned the knife in her hand, contemplating it. She looked up at me. "Enna, we are not out here to escape the drought."

I shook my head. "Of course we are. There is no other reason to be out here."

She cast her eyes toward the bones of the unlucky animal. "There is no escaping the drought. Not anywhere in the world, you know that."

"Except the North Pole," I said, with some snark that I did not intend.

"Sure," Mom offered. "But no one can live there."

"So why did we come here then? What was the point in leaving everything behind? In being lonely all the time, in struggling all the time?" A sadness crept into my voice that I could not fight. "It seems like maybe it's raining a little more often, maybe the drought it going to end and we can go home." Now my voice simply broke.

"Enna," she said, peeling off her gloves and putting her hand on mine. "We are here to run away from people. Not drought."

"People?" I asked, wiping my nose with the back of my sleeve.

"People," she repeated. "The drought would've been okay if it was only drought. There were a lot of solutions out there, there was the pipeline and the desalination plants and reclamation ... our lifestyles would have changed, but our lives themselves could have stayed the same. But for some people, when they feel scarcity, when they feel there's not enough to go around, they lose all sense. They go crazy. They get violent."

"Do you mean the LFR?" I asked. The letters had been so ubiquitous, everywhere on television and the Internet, inescapable. To hear them in my mouth was a surprise, like resurrecting a sunken ship from the bottom of the sea.

"Yes," Mom said.

I couldn't quite grasp this. The timing of our escape coincided with the LFR sweep of congress, but Mom had done so much before that: stocking the cabin, hoarding canned foods, ordering Arctic seed packets online, losing sleep every night thinking about how we all used to complain about the rain and stay inside because of the rain and now she would do anything in the world to just bring it back.

The drought was big and bearing down on

everyone. It was the clear and present danger. The LFR was just fringe. They were radicals, they were a small band of extremists in vulnerable areas. How could they possibly exert more power than our own climate? But Mom, maybe mindreading, went on.

"The LFR is just one example. When humans feel under threat, they default to an us-versus-them mentality. They find people who feel like them and resolve to hate all others. It's primal. It's animal. And it was taking over out there," she gestured out to the water, to the vague notion of a mainland beyond. "People were kidnapping each other, killing each other, over things that had nothing to do with the rain."

The effect of her words came over me like a slowly rising tide. "But, Mom," I said. "That means that even if the rain comes back…"

She looked at me with a sadness in her eyes, blunted by how fully she had accepted this reality. "Even if the rain comes back it might not be safe," she confirmed. "And the thing about our family–" she paused, turning over her words and deciding there was nothing worth keeping from me. "The thing about our family is that even though we are one family, and closer than anything, there are some of us with light skin and some of us with dark skin. And so no matter who is in charge or who is in power, someone in our family will be seen as the enemy."

What was there for me to say? If we weren't climate refugees but political refugees, then no amount of falling rain could signal that it was safe to return home. And if our fear was not drought and hunger and fire, but people themselves, was there any world beyond Pluto

Cove that could ever feel safe?

WE SOMETIMES SAW A PLANE fly overhead or the speck of a motorized boat skipping across the water in the distance. But these sightings became further and fewer in between. Eventually just sailboats traversed the Gulf by wind power. And before long, there was no indication of human activity anywhere.

Mom and Dad debated whether to go out looking for other people. I eavesdropped in the loft when they thought I was sleeping. "They could be violent, or greedy, and come after our supplies," Mom said, audibly wringing her wrists.

"Or they could be in need of help, and would we be able to share our supplies," Dad added.

In October, nearly a year into our escape, Mom went out in the skiff for a reconnaissance trip around the far corner of the Chugach Islands. There, against the water, was an old miner's cabin owned by an elderly couple, Daisy and Dennis, once friendly with our great-grandfather. Of all possible populations, this couple would be the most benign. Or, simply, Mom could overpower them if needed. She carried a shotgun and bear mace.

Before she left, she hugged me and Callie, long and desperate, and placed both of her hands on Dad's face before kissing him. Callie shook in Mom's arms and ran straight into Dad's after Mom disappeared in the skiff into the frozen mist. They had waited for a calm and windless day; today the water fell flat and gray against the horizon like an ironed sheet.

Dad assured us everything would be fine, but he

did not look us in the eyes. Why wasn't it him who left? He said he couldn't drive the boat – but why didn't Mom just teach him? It was just a small skiff with a single outboard motor. Even I was proficient by now.

We anticipated she would be gone for several days. I encouraged Callie to come inside but she refused. Instead, she sat at the mouth of the cove, stacking flat stones into small towers before they collapsed. I needed to refill the small cistern next to the cabin – a laborious task of hauling water, bucket by bucket, from the creek – but found my shoulders lacked the strength to move. So I walked down to the beach and sat with Callie, helping her find good stones for tower-building and throwing the occasional stick into the water for Benji.

But Mom was gone only a few hours. Callie and Benji heard it at the same time, their ears perking in unison: the boat motor. As it drew closer, the stillness of the air cast the sound about wildly, rattling the boulders on the mountainsides. Callie pushed herself up so quickly she nearly toppled over and sprinted full speed to the tideline, tripping over icy rocks and skinning her knees more than once. Even in the excitement, I reflexively thought of the thread it would take to mend her pants. Thread that was running out.

Mom waved from the boat, motioning for us to climb on board. "Get on the boat!" She shouted. "Get on the boat!"

"Lisa, what's going on?" Dad shouted back, wading ankle-deep into the water as she approached.

She landed the boat on the gravel. "They're sick, Alex. Or Dennis is. I think Daisy is already gone. He needs you. Come on!"

Dad looked back at us on the beach. "Do we all have to go?"

"We can't leave them here," she said, frantic to turn back to the water.

Dad looked at us and then back to her. "Come on," he said, gesturing us toward the boat. Benji leapt in and took his usual position curled up under the stern bench. "I'll grab my kit. You girls get on." Mom cinched our life jackets tight, squeezing the air from my lungs. I loosened the straps when she turned to do Callie's. "It's a long ride," she said. "Stick together to stay warm."

For two hours we skipped over the silky, fast water until Mom slowed into a deeply set cove framed by once-mighty spruce trees, now blood-red from beetle kill. Their cabin loomed, massive. It stood on pilings high above the beach, with glinting windows facing the water. Dennis' family had successfully operated a palladium mine in the area, – the cabin showed. Our own great-grandfather was not spiritually captivated enough by palladium and squandered his dreams and resources on looking for gold instead. "Wow," Callie whispered, whether for the size of the cabin or for simply seeing something other than the narrow confines of Pluto Cove.

"Stay here girls," Mom called out as she pulled the boat into a dock. "It's bad in there." She and Dad ran down the planks and up the beach, impervious to their slippery surfaces, his pack full of medical supplies banging against his back with each step.

Callie and I looked at each other. "Wanna play rock paper scissors?" she asked.

"Not really," I said, motioning for Benji to jump onto the bench so I could lean my head against his back. I stared up at the sky. It was monochrome. Gray. It had been for weeks. Up above that flat and implacable cloud was a whole atmosphere of gases and moisture and wind currents that people once thought they understood, but in the Polar Storms realized they knew nothing.

They were gone a long time. The dock was sheltered from wind, but there was no escaping the cold. In our rush we had not properly dressed down, and I traced the numbness blooming from the tips of my fingers and toes. With each exhale I manipulated my mouth and tongue to make my breath come out in shapes like I saw in a movie once. Callie curled into the fetal position under life jackets on the floor of the boat.

I hoped so badly to find someone alive – someone new with a different face and a different backstory. Someone to inject us with hope and possibility. I imagined Daisy and Dennis brought along a grandson or granddaughter – a friend for me. Maybe they had a dog for Benji. I imagined Dennis might come back to our cabin, wrapped in blankets, and we would nurse him back to health. He would tell me stories. Stories I had never heard before. Songs I did not know. His strength would return, and when he filleted fish there wouldn't be a lick of red flesh left on the spine. Then one day he would remember he had a radio, and Mom would fix it up. We would call out into the world, huddled by the fire awaiting a response, and a response would come.

This long and tumbling and juvenile narrative eddied around my head, my skin alive with hope. Again, I was just a child.

But when Mom and Dad finally emerged, walking toward the dock, they each carried boxes. Big boxes. Their faces were grim, eyes laced crimson, mouths set in wire-thin lines. I understood the situation without them saying anything: Daisy and Dennis were dead, and Mom and Dad were looting the cabin. I wanted to be sick.

In third grade, Dad took me to the grocery store to give Mom time alone with baby Callie. While standing with him in the checkout line, I saw the most beautiful magazine cover of a dog sled team running across an open river under the northern lights. In their silhouettes below the green and purple of the aurora, their legs leapt and tongues wagged in pure joy for the run, the land, and the instinct to race. My heart quickened and my fingers tingled. I wanted that magazine. I needed something so beautiful. But Dad was irritated at me for being too loud with my bouncy ball when the baby was trying to sleep; he would never indulge me a gift right then.

Without any real thought, I snatched the magazine from the rack and tucked it into the warm space between my t-shirt and down jacket. He paid for the groceries and we walked toward the door. This was it. I was home-free, just me and the magazine with the huskies. Then, at the second set of sliding doors, a hand grabbed my shoulder. Hard. "Excuse me, little girl," a rough voice said.

He took me and Dad to a small, windowless office next to the pharmacy. I remember the wiry orange of his mustache as he sat in his chair: judge, jury, and executioner. I sweat and cried. The wall behind him was blank. No photos, posters, or OSHA handouts. Just a thinly painted white that spoke of nothing. He wanted to call the police. He *really* wanted to call the police. Dad talked him out of it, insisting I was a little girl whose lesson had been learned.

But the lesson learned was yet to come. Later that evening I finished a time-telling worksheet at the little desk in my room when I heard Mom and Dad talking under my window. Dad was shoveling the walkway, and Mom paced the driveway with Callie strapped to her chest under an oversized jacket. She did that those days – paced the driveway with the baby. She said it was for the fresh air and movement. But she never crossed the threshold of the driveway. Something about leaving the bubble of our home and yard frightened her. I cracked my window just an inch, enough to blast me with the cold winter air and enough to overhear their conversation from under the sill.

"She's acting out because of the baby," Mom said, patting Callie's rump under the layers of clothes enclosing them both. I hung my head, both to hide from view, and as a reflex to being misunderstood. I just wanted something beautiful. Those dogs under the aurora. Nothing else. Was it so bad to want something beautiful?

"That's not the point," Dad replied, digging his shovel a little too hard into the snow. It scraped the bare concrete underneath. "She can't be so reckless. She has to know that people are going to come down harder on her."

Mom nodded, though I didn't know why. "You think that's what was going on?"

"At least in part. This bogus shop cop said to her, *We don't steal things in this country. We have laws.* Do you know how hard it was to keep myself together?"

"I can imagine," Mom answered.

"So how do I have that conversation with her?"

Dad asked. "She's eight years old. But she has to know. For her to steal is a thousand times worse than for a little blonde girl to steal."

"Yeah," Mom mused, digging the toe of her boot into a snow berm. "I guess you learned that the hard way."

"Six months locked up," Dad said, pausing and leaning over the shovel. "Six months. That can't happen to Enna. I won't let it. I want her to know what is right and what is wrong, and to never cross that line. Other people can. Her friends, even. But she can't."

I don't know how Mom replied because I moved away from the window. When Dad came upstairs to have a Conversation with me, I jumped into my bed and pretended to sleep at the sound of his footsteps. We never returned to the topic. We did not need to. I heard what I needed to hear. There was a right and a wrong. Some people could toe that line. We could not.

Watching Mom and Dad carry necessities and valuables from the cabin brought me back to the windowsill. To that winter evening, to the feeling of that beautiful and glossy magazine close to my skin. To the way Dad wouldn't even let me feed ducks in the park because it was against the rules. How he made me stick to the designated trails so I wouldn't trample mountain vegetation if I took a shortcut. How he wore cleaned, pressed button-up shirts to work every morning even though he changed into scrubs as soon as he got there. And it filled me with a swift-moving fire that burned out the boredom and antipathy, that overwhelmed any intended projection of being sullen and withdrawn.

"Are you serious?" I demanded, standing up in

the boat so quickly I lost my balance. This was not a young relative who could be my friend, not a new dog to play with, not a kindly old man with a radio. These were my own parents becoming the ruthless pillagers and robbers from whom we had fled. "You're stealing from them?"

"Enna, they're gone," Mom said, expressionless. "Dad did everything he could."

"Did he?" I interrogated. "Did he really? Or did you just want to make out like bandits with their things like the LFR??"

"Shut your mouth!" Dad shouted. Dad never shouted. There were so many qualities about him I assumed he didn't have; but they were only dormant. "Don't you ever accuse me of that!"

"Just ignore her, Alex," Mom said, dropping a box into the boat at my feet where it sent the shudder of vibrating aluminum up my back. "She's being a brat. Don't listen to her."

Callie wept from her perch on the boat. "What happened, Daddy? Did they die?"

Dad set his box down and knelt on the dock to face her. "Yes, sweetie. They died."

"How?" Callie asked, shivering.

"I think it was a germ called botulism," he answered tenderly.

"Are we gonna get the germ?" Callie asked, drawing upon her small knowledge of microbiology.

"No, sweetie. No. It's a germ that lives in fish, but we cook our fish really, really well. We won't get it."

She nodded. I threw up my hands. "But you guys are seriously taking their stuff? They just died in there.

There are dead bodies in there! We're supposed to be the good guys!"

Mom kicked her foot against the dock railing and recoiled at the pain. She reflexively grabbed her wrists and started churning them like a butter pole. "This isn't a time for righteousness, Enna. They're gone. It's awful. It's beyond awful. But you need to quit it with the teenage-angst."

"You're taking things that aren't yours!" I yelled. It came from somewhere deep in my belly, something burning and hot. Something that only stayed quiet when I believed that we were the innocents, the underdogs, the protagonists in a world filled with ugly and violent and greedy hearts. Somehow, I could stomach the demise of law and order on the national and global scale – but the rules and structure that governed my own family were far more sacrosanct. Their obliteration went beyond the looting of a cabin, and hit me deep in the solar plexus, where my trust and sense of duty lay.

Mom's voice turned low and cold. "Enna, I'm very glad that Dad and I did such a good job of instilling a sense of right and wrong in you. But this is survival. And I won't let my daughter make me feel guilty about me trying to keep her alive."

"But you–"

"No," Dad said, cutting me off. "No more. This is awful for us, Enna. You will not make it worse. Do you understand me?"

And with that he lifted his box and set it into the boat. Mom did the same. They each went back for one more load – canned foods, tools, building supplies, toiletries, utensils, and the sorts of things that make up a home. Someone else's home. I hated it. It felt cursed. Daisy and Dennis were people I had never met, but they were casualties of this drought. It could have been us. It could still be us.

And who then would pack up the things we carried, the things we valued, the things that made up this wild and lonely existence? How would our bodies lay in an empty and looted cabin for all eternity if the rain never came to wash us away?

MOM MADE MORE TRIPS over the next few days. Dad wondered about moving us out to their cabin, for some combination of it being haunted and surrounded by cliffs with no workable land or freshwater source, Mom talked him out of it. I tried not to think about the bodies inside.

Each night, she and Dad discussed how they might uninstall and transport Dennis' beefy diesel generator, drawing up diagrams in the dirt using sticks of pulleys and sleds and rafts. Ultimately, they realized that there was no safe way to do it without hurting someone or sinking the boat. So instead Mom dissected it, gutting the machine for parts and reassembling a stream-powered version of it at Pluto Cove.

"Electrons are incredibly unstable. They jump around like crazy, always looking for a better place to be. More than anything, they want to be with protons," she said, stepping over a drawing of an atom she had sketched in the gravel to reach for a screwdriver. "They'll take great leaps to be with a positive charge. And to make power, we have to capture the energy in those leaps." I held the blades of a ceiling fan while she connected it to the rotor she had harvested from Dennis' generator. Mom gave me physics lessons to ease my mind. My world was so small, yet my thoughts were so enormous. It helped hearing about the impatience, the agitation, the unrest of unruly electrons that always wanted to be somewhere else, that never wanted to be alone.

"We're going to put the fan into the stream," she explained. "It'll be like a windmill, but instead of turning in the wind where it's harder for me to access, it'll turn in the current of the water when the creek runs. This shaft will turn, which will make the rotor turn. Inside the rotor are magnets with opposite charges. That's going to make the electrons jump around like crazy, which will then flow through this copper wire." She pointed to the enormous spool of copper wire once stored in our outhouse when the cabin itself overflowed. "And the wire will go up to the batteries to store electricity for when we need it."

All my life I was delicate around Mom. *Her accident, her accident.* All my life she was anxious and forgetful and quick to apologize. There were times – weeks at a time – when she stayed in bed for reasons not explained to me except that her illness was not contagious. But out there in the wild, she was a different person. It was as though her anxiety had simply been without an outlet back in Anchorage, and so it spun uselessly around her head, generating static and noise. But at the cabin it had a purpose. It served her. I hadn't understood the extent to which Great-grandpa Jenkins had taught her about life in the bush – or appreciated how much she had mastered as a girl.

Though Dad insisted she was a gifted engineer,

his words lacked evidence until I watched her use shredded aluminum cans to adjust the torque in a squirrel-cage rotor so that she could better modulate the electromagnetic field around the axis. She was our boss, and we were her lackeys, but our faith in her was complete. Even Dad – who in our lives had always been the most educated, the breadwinner – simply carried out Mom's ideas. He barely contained his glee when one of us sustained even a small, meaningless injury like a splinter or a scrape and he could put his own skills to use. And it was hard for me to reconcile, but somewhere in the middle of all his stress and worry and hunger, he was proud of Mom. Even though their bellies rumbled while they watched me and Callie eat, some happiness endured between them.

Of all she did that first year at Pluto Cove to improve our station, one feat stands above the rest. Somehow, Mom extracted those giant ocean-front windows from Dennis and Daisy's cabin, one by one, and transported them across open ocean. And with them, she and Dad spent that spring constructing a greenhouse. South facing, made of thick and crystal-clear glass covered with a tin roof from Dennis' woodshed. I stood in it, between the windows, and felt transported to another place, another hemisphere. The air outside needled at us with increasing cold, but the inside of this greenhouse stayed warm. And more than warm, it was wet. It sucked moisture from the ground and condensed it on the walls like a steam room. The air inside was thick and gooey and passed through our lungs smooth as syrup.

Above the door, Mom allowed me to carve the words "In Memory: Daisy and Dennis." In that greenhouse, Mom's little seed packets of kale, cabbage, carrots, chard, beans, peas, and beets exploded into a garden that was more jungle than agriculture. The freshness of the food – not salted and pressurized from a can – gave us life in a way we forgot had been lost.

As the greenhouse came to life, we sprinkled the roots with salmon blood, and, as time went on, compost from the plant cuttings and chicken manure. On many nights, George prowled around the structure, walking curious circles and even once standing upon his hindquarters and putting his paws on the glass. We left his dirty prints there, each one as wide as my head, a souvenir of his visit. A reminder of our place in the chain of things. And a talisman for Mom against her great ursine enemy.

The dry and arid ground upon which she built the greenhouse slowly healed itself; each watering and each new root that took hold a defibrillation, bringing circulation back to just a speck of earth in a suffering world. Mom wired a single light bulb into the ceiling, and even on stormy days the warmth from that incandescent bulb was enough to strip my coat off at the door and go to work in short sleeves.

We let some plants go to seed – and though it seemed impossible – they yielded more plants. Each day going out to harvest or trellis or transplant, I first touched my fingers to the names carved above the door. Dennis and Daisy. And I saw the food that we made from their glass and the light that we made from their generator and the strength that rippled up in Mom as she combed through their lifetime of possessions even as she became skinny and taut. In carving up their home, we had convinced ourselves we were the good guys. I hoped we were right.

BEFORE THE NOOSE tightened around the global neck and we made the move to Pluto Cove, the descent into acceptance of drought was slow and bumbled and full of denial. I overheard Dad at one of his work parties comment to another doctor, "It's like that patient who learns they have cancer, but instead of taking a deep breath and crying, he peels off his gown and goes outside to smoke a cigarette."

In the space of the dark, interminable days at the Cove, Mom tried to explain it to me. She was interested in what I had gleaned – which little facts and fears made it through the filters of my child mind.

The water got carved up in all sorts of ways once people realized it was scarce, she said. Lakes were easiest, of course, with their defined boundaries and tendency to occupy a single space. Rivers were harder, as they passed through multiple properties, townships, states, or even countries. But nothing was as hard to stake or claim as groundwater – the aquifers.

In the beginning there was a sense that municipalities would supply water to residents. As the drought grew, states took on that burden. They invested in small, almost quaint, reverse-osmosis systems. But drinking water was only one concern and relatively mild against what really annihilated the supply: agriculture. Local water availability became an issue of national food security. And eventually, federal governments stepped in with their access to labs and scientists and radical technologies – but most of all they used their armies, weapons, and engines of war.

Alaska was a natural place for water mining: it was enormous, wet, and fell within the borders of the United States. But there were two problems. First, even though part of the country, Alaska was terribly, miserably far away. Engineers dreamed up a pipeline – one that was flexible and soft like intestines, but made of a combination of hydrogels and glass fibers that were impact-resistant as steel – that would traverse Canada. But Canada saw no reason to permit a project that did not advance their own water claims. The second problem was that the Alaskan Governor had been approached early in the drought by the Chinese Minister of Foreign Affairs regarding Lake Iliamna – the largest lake in Alaska, the third largest in the nation, roughly the size of former Connecticut. In one stroke of his pen, the Governor sold all state-owned lands and freshwater rights to the lake to China.

The sale was a one-time windfall to the State of Alaska, which the Governor then used to prop up an oil exploration company in which his brother-in-law had a controlling stake. To assuage his constituents, the Governor cut a dividend check to each resident representing a fraction of the sale. For some, this money was enough. For most, no amount of bought wealth could ease the loss of Lake Iliamna to a foreign government. Despite the societal uproar in Alaska over the deal – from Native tribes and environmentalists to the libertarians and isolationists – there was little talk of it down south. News in Alaska seldom made it that far. It had been apparent to Alaskans for years that rainfall was on the downward swing. But no one cared that much. Not until the drought settled in a bit deeper and all eyes swiveled

101

to the colossal freshwater reserves up north.

When news broke nationally about the Lake Iliamna sale, the anger was directed toward Alaskans more generally. We accepted the dirty money. We didn't stop the Governor. The feds threatened to overturn the sale, but China presented a copy of the contract, which stipulated this would be an act of war. No lake seemed worth that.

So, while different options were weighed for how to extract water from Alaska, the high-density population centers of the East Coast felt too much strain to wait. There were dozens of attempts to seed rain, but like every other rain, it simply blew north and came down thousands of miles from the silver iodide cannon. The East Coast relief effort was a highly classified engagement named Operation Drip Drop. Under the cover of darkness, navigating up through the rocky veils of Canada's fjords, the American Navy sailed a flotilla of aircraft carriers to the northwest coast of Greenland. Docked in narrow inlets along Baffin Bay, crews of men using spiderwebs of explosives blew off chunks of glacier ice for transport to New York. Of course, the Indigenous peoples in the area noticed the explosions immediately. But what really sunk the operation – quite literally – was the journey back to the naval docks. The ice, as ice does, melted. No one had factored this into the operation. The ice had been balanced on the ships, arranged around the metacenters of the aircraft carriers. But water does not hold formation, and it slished and sloshed and poured over the edges and capsized three ships whose personnel were then rescued by the Royal Canadian Navy.

It was estimated Operation Drip Drop cost

upward of $3 billion, with not a single drop of potable water in return. But someone in an office somewhere thought *what could go wrong,* and in moments of confusion and uncertainty, humans entertain absurd ideas. The US Navy was the laughingstock of the world. The President punted to the Commander, who, while wearing his full-dress uniform on national TV, attempted a casual brushoff: *There are no bad ideas in brainstorming*. It was an embarrassment, but some comedic relief at a time sorely lacking.

The comedy did not last. The southwest states were engulfed in a perpetual state of emergency. The Ogallala Aquifer – stretching under eight states and representing one of the world's biggest basins of nonrenewable groundwater – drained out like a bathtub. Homesteaders served by wells turned on their taps and silt poured into their sinks. City dwellers served by municipal water turned on their taps to air sputtering like bicycle pumps. The local governments started twelve-hour water restrictions except for essential infrastructure. Under the Las Vegas Strip, a sinkhole collapsed into the void space where water used hold up the land. The Stratosphere Casino toppled like a house of sticks by the big bad wolf; and though sirens blasted advance warning of the collapse, the joke – if one can call it that – was that a handful of hunkered over men and kyphotic women pulled handles on the slot machines until the very end.

Still, the order of things persevered. Like traffic in a power outage, people were generally deliberate and considerate, protective of order and equity. Volunteers resurrected railroad lines largely dormant since the days of manifest destiny, and they filled massive tank cars with potable water, dispensing it along the whistle stops. People became inventive, clever, and cautious. Again, there was a sentiment that this could not possibly last. The climate changes on the order of millennia, not seasons. We just had to wait it out.

Then there was the *Entamoeba histolytica* outbreak in South Dakota that followed the rail line from Rapid City to Pierre to Brookings. The bug was a deadly protozoon that contaminated a water shipment and left a trail of dysentery-like deaths along its path of travel. Like so many diseases, the very young, the very old, and the infirm were hit the hardest. An estimated 4,000 people died over the course of 32 days.

From then on, no one trusted the rail delivery.

Anthropologists teamed with cartographers to map human migrations as water dwindled. Thick black lines marked the movement of people from the Midatlantic toward the Great Lakes. People in Idaho and eastern Oregon coalesced around the Columbia River. Those in the desert southwest relocated to the Mississippi watersheds. It was in this chaos, of course – this diaspora and dissolution of community and culture – that the LFR took hold. *American water for American people*, they declared. And, lacking other options, what could anyone do but believe them?

Even the great hydropower reservoirs of Southeast Alaska, representing some of the rainiest places on earth, dipped and then dropped and then dried. While these places maintained massive flowing aquifers below the ground, it left many communities along the coast without electric power. I first noticed these places, as they were close to home. I took it as incontrovertible fact that places like Juneau, Sitka, and Ketchikan would always be shrouded in rain clouds, always wet and cold. But these realities quickly changed.

The media didn't care so much about these places. The great energy-producing reservoirs grabbing the headlines were Krasnoyarsk in Russia, Guri in Venezuela, or Itaipu that straddled Brazil and Paraguay, leading to a massive and rapid invasion into the latter by the former. It was a ninety-minute war, and to Brazil went the spoils of water. Water for consumption, irrigation, hygiene, electricity, and power.

But all of this was Out There – the Before Pluto Cove. Mom and I reflected upon it out at the cabin, tried to contextualize our existence with what lay beyond the Gulf.

"It wasn't just the water," Mom said one afternoon while we baited shrimp pots. "It was energy. Those lake reservoirs are like batteries," Mom said. "All that backed up water is potential energy waiting to be released. If you can harness that energy into turbines, you can create electricity. That's what Brazil wanted when they invaded Asunción." She wasted no opportunity to bring electrophysics into any discussion. It wasn't just her teaching me; it was how she made sense of the world.

The concept of batteries baffled me. She explained that chemical reactions inside a battery causes a buildup of electrons at the negative side, the anode. Much in the way water from a reservoir builds up at a dam. But electrons do not want to be built up – they want to be with opposite charges. As the electrons travel through the battery, they create a current and generate power. But as they do this, they change the chemical properties of the battery so that it cannot be used forever. They eventually run out. "The reservoir runs dry," Mom said.

"Will our batteries run dry?" I asked.

She gave me a crinkled look. "We'll do everything we can," she said, her lips pursed off to one side.

What I didn't realize was that, over a year into our duress at Pluto Cove, our batteries had already run dry. Bone dry. The sunlight reaching our solar panels was too sparse to run all winter. The little turbine in the creek froze solid from December to February. The double-As in our headlamps and flashlights expired months earlier. But still, they worked. I flipped the light switch, turned on the water pump, ignited the heating element to cook our food, watched the blinking red light of the smoke detector on the ceiling of the cabin. There was no accounting for our electricity use. But I didn't think about that, in the way I never reflected on the myriad conveniences in my old life. And for all I learned about the movement of electrons and the storage of energy, I never truly considered its scarcity until Mom left and took it all with her.

WE HAD ONE MIRROR at the cabin, a little disc embedded into the belly of a ceramic owl. It was art, not utility. But by way of a reflective surface, it was all we had. I took it up to the loft and made a nightly ritual of inspecting myself frame-by-frame, holding it out wide and in close to gauge my angles, hair, and skin.

The small LED light illuminating mine and Callie's beds cast a hideous whitish glow, throwing shadows across my face that I hoped were not there in daylight. Hairs sprouted from my upper lip; pimples mounded across my forehead. My skin erupted in eczema, thirsting for moisture to hydrate and heal. My jeans fit snugger across the hips. When I pressed my hands down on my waist there was now a shelf of bone where before had been only straight lines.

At the same time, my pants grew short in the ankles. Dad remarked upon this fact one evening meal. "Look at that height!" He yelped in delight, pulling down at the hem of my pants that hovered at my shins. "That's a sure sign of solid nutrition. That's one tall young woman in front of me."

At this, I threw my fork down onto my dinner plate and ran up to the loft, which was less satisfying than storming up the stairs at home. I couldn't stomp up a ladder. From upstairs I heard him ask Mom, "What? What did I say?"

Dad was tall. Quite tall. I looked like Dad, and I did not want to look like Dad. Mom was small with light skin and cornsilk hair. Callie was her spitting image. But so many times at school functions or soccer tournaments or even random grocery store errands, people asked Mom if she had adopted me. My skin was dark like Dad's, hair black like Dad's, and nose flat like Dad's. He told me once – thinking it funny – that in the animal kingdom the first born had a biological imperative to look like the father so that the father did not eat the baby. The way I looked at him blared how unfunny this was. He never repeated it.

It wasn't that looking like Dad made me feel masculine. It was that it made me feel like a second-class citizen. Dad taught me that life was harder for people with dark skin, people who look different. I grew up hearing about the patients he attempted to treat who turned him away, even in emergencies, because they did not trust him to be their doctor; stories about those who mistook him for custodial staff; his frustrations at being passed over for chair positions even with his seniority.

"It never matters to anyone that I grew up in this country," he told me when I was nine, in the car driving home from a soccer game he had missed after working late. He didn't usually disclose the details of his day to me – he saved that for Mom – but that day, the words spilled out of him, their weight and speed too powerful to barricade. Mom had been laid up in bed for days, and his usual grasp on his thoughts had lost its tread contact with the road.

"I coded on him for 41 minutes," Dad said, his fingers white from their grip on the steering wheel. I had gleaned from years of listening in on conversations that coded meant Dad had done CPR. "And it worked. It worked." He shook his head in disbelief. "You should have seen the heart rhythms on this guy. It's a miracle. And then he's awake, he's lying there, looking up at me. He's in an emergency room, he was clinically dead, and what is it that he says under his oxygen mask?"

I sat behind Dad in the bucket seat of the minivan but could see his eyes flare in the rearview mirror. "He said '*Get this spic off of me*.'" I hadn't heard the word much, but it was one of those definitions I didn't need to know – the tone, the feeling of the word, said everything. "'*Get this spic off of me*.'" He repeated, quieter this time.

I clutched my soccer ball. "I'm sorry, Dad," I muttered, not sure what else I could say. I was cross that he had missed my soccer game, but I really did feel sorry for him.

108

He softened and looked back at me through the rearview mirror with eyes suggesting he had forgotten I was there. "Oh, I'm sorry, honey. I shouldn't have told you that story. I'm sorry."

"It's okay," I said. Not because it was okay, but because that's simply what one said.

He sighed. "It's hard sometimes, Enna. I guess I feel like you should know that. You gotta be tough. You gotta be sure of yourself. Because everyone else is going to second guess you. Going to think you're less than. Because you look like you come from a different place."

"I'm a fourth generation Alaskan," I chirped, repeating a fact Mom taught me about her side of the family, a fact that impressed a great number of people. Most non-Native people living in Alaska were new. Like Dad.

"You are," he said affirmatively. "You are, and it's amazing. But you are also Mexican. And I hope you think that's pretty cool, too."

I nodded passively, staring out the window. I didn't think it was cool, but I wasn't going to show Dad that. He meant for his talks to empower me, but too often they filled me with shame. Instead of making me feel confident, they internalized in me a bigotry that made me feel weak, defeated, and inferior.

"If you even knew half of what your Grandma Julienna went through to get to this country, and how hard she worked once she was here…" his eyes misted over, as they usually did when he spoke of his mom. She had died of liver cancer shortly after Callie was born. Dad thought it was from tetrachloroethylene exposure at the dry cleaners where she worked. "You come from a family of very determined, very strong people, Enna. From both sides. People are always going to think you're tough because you're Alaskan and half your family homesteaded here. But what they might not understand is how tough you are because you're Mexican. Things are just going to be a little more uphill for you. But I know you are ready for it." He looked back at me in the rearview mirror. "Estás lista, ¿sì mija?"

"Sì, papì," I said.

But I wasn't ready, and I never had been. I hid my skin. I lightened it with foundation from Mom's make-up bag. I stayed out of the sun. Now, at the far reaches of the world, away from anyone who cared about my complexion, it gripped me tenfold. In that little owl mirror I only saw more and more of Dad staring back at me. I saw the faces of the LFR gazing down at me through the tinted windows of the minivan. It terrified me.

I pulled a pair of tweezers from a first aid kit and spent my evenings plucking hairs above my lip and down the sides of my ears. One night, I noticed hair under my arms, so I started picking those, and repeated the same with the coarse hairs that replaced the soft downy ones on my legs.

Callie stared at me every night, transfixed, quiet. One night she spoke. "Why do you care?" She asked.

Her question startled me. Callie was meek, never so brazen. She didn't ask *Why are you doing that?* She asked: *why do you care*? It was judgmental, accusatory. She was getting older, bolder. And no longer was I the mysterious older sister who flitted around to social gatherings or took turns driving the family van on empty roads– I was just a person with a constant presence, who had no secrets, no hidden life separate from hers.

"Why do *you* care?" I asked. "Stay out of my business."

"There's no one here. It doesn't matter what you look like."

What she said was true, and I burned up inside for it. "It matters to me, okay? Leave me alone."

"I can't," she said. "There's nowhere for me to go."

I stared into the owl mirror next to the light and furiously plucked at my eyebrows, which only grew bushier and more linear when what I wanted were the slight, curved eyebrows that Mom had. "Just shut up, Callie." I had never spoken to her like that.

She sighed and rolled over in her bed, her back to me. "No one is going to notice you. I think we are the last people on earth."

Now, more than under the guise of self-improvement, I plucked my eyebrows out of spite. To prove to her that I believed people lived out there, that I had reason to take care of myself, to care about my appearance. That we were here out of an abundance of caution, not because it was all that was left.

Because just a few weeks later – sixteen months into our tenure at Pluto Cove – Callie learned that she was wrong. We were far from the last people on earth.

WE DOUBTED OUR EYES at first. It didn't seem possible.

"Is that a *ship*?" Mom asked, standing on the beach with her hand covering her brow to shield the crystalline April sunlight glinting off the water. The earth

111

turned on its axis, bringing us closer to the sun, but the air remained frigid and cutting.

"It looks like a Viking ship," Dad said. "What in the world…"

It was a massive wooden ship, something from a storybook about pirates. It loomed far from us, making its size all the more impressive and confounding. As it rounded the shallows around the islands, we saw, fuzzy at first but then more clearly by the shadows and ripples, that it was powered by a dozen oars on either side, each long as a flagpole.

"Alex," Mom said, with a steeliness to her voice.

"Yes," he answered, as though she had asked a question they had rehearsed. "Enna, go into the cabin. Put out the fire. Quickly, please."

He and Mom moved in concert to clear the big, colorful things staked on the beach – the blue tarp, an old red drum – hauling them into the trees for cover. It was pointless. Anyone on the water would clearly see a settlement in the cove. Over time, we had created an oasis-like habitat around the cabin with our careful watering of berry bushes, the garden, the rhubarb patch, the potato hills, and trees that held the slopes intact. The rest of the hillside faded to a bilious brown for want of water. Only this little patch of land received attention and care.

I grabbed a bucket of water and heaved it inside where Callie looked up, bewildered, from pretending to read *The Giver*. I opened the iron door to the woodstove and doused the coals. They steamed and hissed, sending a puff of vapor up the chimney. But it squelched nothing. The smoke continued rolling out and up into the sky, a

112

beacon, for nearly an hour.

The ship passed our inlet without stopping, around the bend of Pluto Cove to the other side of Lamplighter Mountain.

The next day was cold, bitterly cold, a cold that sound cuts through like a stone sinking in water, and we heard them. First the thwack of axes, then the thud of hammers. They were in the distance, but how far from us exactly – we did not know.

In the following days, Mom's breath came shallow and quiet, as though the very sound of her heartbeat might mask impending danger. Dad's shoulders clenched around his ears, flexed, as though at any moment he would whip around, his arms swinging. They took turns keeping vigil at night, one awake by the door with a gun. George sniffed around one night, and Dad let loose a fury of yelling and jumping so great that it was weeks before he wandered back again. They did not say anything out loud, did not acknowledge the fundamental tilt of our situation, but Callie and I could read it as though it were painted in red across their foreheads.

I should have felt scared. Of all the dangers lurking in the woods, humans were the ones to fear the most. But the sighting of the ship did little to change my inner landscape. I continued with my chores, I scrutinized the way I fit into clothes, and I plucked unwanted hairs.

But Callie was terrified. "Are they bad people, Daddy?" she asked at dinner.

"We don't know, honey. They are probably totally fine," he said.

"Then why have we stopped keeping a fire going during the day?" she probed. "Is it because we're afraid someone might see the smoke?"

He bit his lower lip. "Just saving some firewood. That's all. It's almost springtime."

She was unconvinced. One night she gathered her dolls and hauled them down the ladder to sleep with Mom while Dad kept night watch.

Up in the loft, alone, I should have felt elated. Precious moments of solitude were all I craved. But suddenly there in the dark, without the pulse of her little body, I felt alone. So I, with Benji, scrambled down the ladder in a semi-controlled fall and climbed into bed with the two of them. Mom wrapped her arms around both of us, Callie in the middle. And though the innate concern and panic she tended to like a flower garden was tangible in her touch, a relaxation came over her as she held us. I felt her muscles go heavy and soft and I fell into them like warm sheets from the dryer.

FOR A WHILE nothing happened. Daylight returned, but spring resisted. The cold snapped around like a rope pulled too tight before bursting apart, seeping through cracks in the cabin logs and settling like fog at our feet. We stuffed every crevice in the greenhouse with pieces of plastic from our trash heap to insulate from the wicked cold. On the coldest of days, when sounds whipped through the air, violent as rawhide on wood, we heard them working on the other side of the mountain, the distant booms of hammers, axes, and guns.

For seventeen months we had been the only known, living people within a hundred square miles. To have others occupy that space disconcerted Mom to the point of madness. There was no terror as great as another human. So how was it now to live in massive, pulsing cities like Houston or Kinshasa where the only ecology was human malevolence? We had once been so connected, so aware of the world and its inhabitants. Now we knew only that these places once existed. Did they still?

They came on a windy day. We anticipated, the way they used sails, that they would wait for the wind. I saw them first, the bow of a boat rounding the corner of Pluto Cove – a smaller boat, holding only nine or ten people, not the massive one in which they had travelled from wherever it was they had come.

I dropped the splitting maul and ran up the hill to the greenhouse where Mom and Dad tended to the seedlings. "They're here," I called breathlessly through the door before running back down to shore. I should have stayed behind and waited or gone into the cabin to hide. But I didn't. I ran to the tideline and watched them approach, slicing through the water with coordinated oars. A man stood at the front, gazing out like a bow figurehead, Washington crossing the Delaware.

He put his eyes on me and my skin went cold. "You here all alone, little lady?" he called from the boat as the rowers maneuvered it to shore.

He was tall, very tall, with thick, wild hair that was dark but streaked with white as though he had been struck by lightning. His face was almost a perfect square, as were his shoulders. But the furs adorning his body made him seem more animal than man. Atop his head was a lynx, mouth open and teeth bared, plastic eyes glaring green in mid-attack. A jacket, grizzly bear, sat heavy and thick from his chest to his knees. It was not the mellow honey color of George, but a dark brown, ragged, flecked with red. The tops of his boots met the bottom of his coat and were lined with the ruff of wolf tails. For a moment I reminded myself: this was not how humans typically looked. Could he be some sort of god, riding atop the bow of the boat, covered in the hides of apex predators, enormous and unflinching? He was something from an ancient myth.

"You speak English?" he said, suddenly in an impatient growl suited to his clothing, hopping off the boat as it ran aground, the figurehead come to life. Benji stood by my side, and I kept one hand upon his head, feeling his steadiness permeate my skin, circulate through my body, keeping me upright when suddenly it became hard to stand. I stammered, "Y-y-ye–" all but forgetting how to speak to another human, when I heard my parents' footsteps.

Seeing the adults emerge from the forest behind me, he eased and broke into a wide and gleaming smile. "Hello, my fellow escapists," he said, his voice clear and deep, loud as a kick drum.

Mom and Dad did not return the smile. They were just as startled to see another human, though they had anticipated his arrival for weeks. They each carried bear mace under their coats and handguns in their waistbands.

"Hello," Dad called out, summoning a strength and volume out-of-practice from his years commanding an emergency room. "Who are you?"

"I could ask the same of you," the man said, walking up to Dad and extending a hand. Both men wanted to stay on the offensive, to be the one asking questions and not answering. The handshake went on two beats too long, and I knew they squeezed with all their might.

Visually, there was no contest. Though the man was about the same height as my dad, or even a little shorter, he compensated in overall *bigness*. Side by side, Dad looked like a broom next to a refrigerator. Dad's pants and jacket were worn and ripped, filthy and hanging off him in clumps where the insulation sagged and stuck. But this bear man dressed specially for the occasion – bear skins and wolf pelts are not how a person dresses day to day, but how a person adorns himself for ceremony, to impress, and to intimidate.

They separated hands but stared at each other wordlessly. Dad's face was granite, the other man continued smiling. Though they did not move, it reminded me of two dogs circling each other, locked in eye contact. Perhaps bolstered by his obvious physical advantage and apparent superior health, the man ceded to speaking first.

"The name is Bird. Danny Bird."

My eyebrows shot up and I hoped no one noticed. Danny Bird? An absurd name for a Herculean person.

"And these here are my brothers. Johnny and Keith." He motioned back toward the boat where two very large (though not *as* large) men stood at the bow with their arms crossed, each wearing light colored bear furs. Their ceremonial dress stopped there. Atop their heads were baggy beanies bearing the logo of a formerly popular California surfing outfit. On their feet were mismatched boots with obvious tears that wrecked the waterproofing. But their faces – from under the shadows

117

of their hats and whipping of their long hair in the sea wind – their faces were melted like candle wax. Or, rather, half of each face – Johnny's left side of his face, and Keith's right side of his face – were burned beyond recognition of human form, with no space for the corner of a mouth, no tone for the arch of a cheek, no hollow for an eyeball but instead a patch of striated skin pulled down like duct tape. A ruler-straight line split their faces from burned and healthy, like the edge of a mask. These were symmetrical, intentional burns, that, combined, made the two halves of one monster.

"Your turn," Danny Bird said, almost daringly, though the smile never left his face.

"I'm Alex," Dad said. "And this is my wife, Lisa."

"And the girl?" Danny asked, pointing to me.

"That's my daughter," Dad said.

"Your daughter got a name?"

"Yes," he answered simply, volunteering nothing.

Danny Bird smirked. His smile broke. "Not much by way of manners, eh, Alex?"

"Who are the other men?" Dad asked, looking quickly past the mutilated faces of Keith and Johnny, toward the six men still sitting in the boat. I had barely registered them before, too absorbed in the giganticness and animality of Danny Bird, and the matching puzzle pieces of his brothers' faces. The other men were small, quite small. Maybe they weren't even men, I thought. Some could have been teenagers. They wore drab, old clothing, wholly insufficient to protect them from winter. Their exposed skin looked dark. My stomach corkscrewed as I assessed the color of their bare hands and cheeks. My tone, or darker. Surely that was no coincidence.

The rowers kept their gazes down at the hull of the boat, averting their eyes. I scoured their faces for a clue when one suddenly looked up and straight at me. His eyes were bright and green as spring grass, the color of how things used to be, his hair dark and shaggy under a knit hat. There was a pleading in his eyes, a desperation, and it plunged into me cold and sharp. I saw through his sun chapped skin and frostnip scars, that he was very, very young.

My fingers tightened around Benji's fur, and he squirmed under my grip, releasing my eye contact with the boy.

"Ah, those are just my helpers," Danny Bird said, waving them off dismissively. "Part of my crew."

"Where does your crew come from?" Dad asked.

Danny Bird laughed. "You sure do ask a lot of questions! How about me, for a turn? How long have you been here?"

"Over a year," Dad said.

Danny Bird whistled. "A year, eh? Pretty impressive. What're you, Mexican? Didn't think you type would know how to survive out here for a night, let alone a whole year."

There it was. The knife into Dad's side.

Dad crossed his arms over his chest and seemingly grew six inches. Danny Bird was bigger, but Dad stood taller and used his height to look down upon the lynx hat with it burning eyes.

The message landed on its recipient. "Oh, come on, then," Danny Bird said, laughing. "Can't take a joke?"

I was eight when Dad taught me people conceal

their prejudices behind humor. I was at a swim lesson and the instructor, a high school senior with highlights in his hair, looked me up and down and blurted, "You don't need even need lessons! Must have been hard to swim across that River at the border." Tears brimmed over my eyes, and he immediately backtracked. "A joke! It was just a joke! Chill out!" I told Dad about it at dinner. He dropped his fork on the plate with a clang. "Listen to me, Enna," he said. "You never, ever let someone make a punchline out of you. There is nothing funny about marginalizing a person. Ever." And that was the end of my swim lessons.

Danny Bird's words struck something deep and primal in Dad. But we were outnumbered and in no position to speak candidly. Dad ground his teeth, looking for words to reaffirm himself without jeopardizing us. Such words did not exist.

"I was born in Norfolk, Georgia," Dad said. "I have the documentation to prove it."

My heart stopped. Dad said the wrong place. His fake passport listed Norfolk, Virginia. I wasn't sure a Norfolk, Georgia existed. The information hadn't been solicited – he just volunteered it to sound legitimate. But hung himself in doing so.

Danny Bird opened his mouth quizzically, ready to reply. But then, from the trees up the hill: "Mommy? Daddy?"

Danny Bird's eyes brightened. "Another little one? How many of those do you have back there?"

"Go back inside, baby," Mom called out. But it was too late. Callie was halfway to the beach.

"Is there someone here?" She rubbed her eyes,

disbelieving. Then, seeing the snarling lynx atop Danny Bird's head, she gasped and ran into the space between Mom's body and right arm, grabbing her around the waist. Standing off to the side, not involved but still so close, I wished I had the same cover. Benji sat alert, attentive, somehow knowing this was not the time to nip at heels or beg with a throwing stick.

"A whole little family back there," Danny Bird marveled disingenuously. "Doing pretty well for yourselves. What all do you have in that cabin?" He craned his neck toward our cabin in the gap of the spruce trees. "I'm gonna go take a look."

"That won't be necessary," Dad said, stepping in front of him so that their chests nearly touched. At the sudden move, both brothers jumped down from the bow of the boat, striding over to Danny Bird's side.

"Now, now," Danny Bird said. "We live on two sides of the same mountain, Alex. How about a little neighborliness? I just wanna see your cabin up there. What kinda supplies you got. And maybe your food. Your weapons. You know," he said with a smile. "The basic stuff."

He was scoping us, ready to loot everything we had. And he didn't care to hide it.

"Mister Bird," Mom said, startling me with her interjection. "With all due respect, our presence here can be an asset to you."

His jaw set tight as he swiveled to look at her, as though having to look at a woman was something displeasing, even disgusting, to him. "And why on earth would that be?"

"Alex is a physician," she said. "An emergency

121

room doctor. He can help you – any of you – if you get hurt. And out here," she gestured to the ocean and up Lamplighter Mountain. "It's only a matter of time."

Everyone paused. Danny Bird chewed with nothing in his mouth, mulling it over. "Johnny!" He called, without looking away from Mom. Johnny stepped forward, scowling down at me with his one blinking eye. "Johnny, show 'em your cut."

Johnny peeled the leather glove off his right hand and unwound a scrap of fabric. Under it was a gash about three inches long traversing his palm. It oozed, red and angry.

Dad took a breath, weighing his options. Mom nudged his back with the hand not gripping Callie. He stepped toward Johnny. "It's infected," Dad said. "But the edges are clean. I can stitch this."

"Then do it," Danny Bird said. There was no more lightness, real or feigned, in his voice.

Dad looked at Mom. She nodded. He walked up to the cabin for his supplies, tortured by the thought of leaving the three of us behind.

"You. Little girl," Danny Bird said, jutting his chin at Callie. "What's your name?"

Callie moved behind Mom. Only her eyes peered out.

"Oh, now," Danny Bird said, the same sinister smile finding its way back to his face. "I'm not so scary, am I? Look," he said, reaching into the pocket of his bear coat and fishing around. "Look, a toy." He held out a headlamp dangling from an elastic band.

Callie looked up at mom. Mom whispered, ever so softly, "You're okay, baby."

"Battery went out," Danny Bird said. "Not like I can buy new ones out here, so it's as good as garbage."

Callie emerged cautiously from behind the coat and reached out her hand. Danny Bird dropped it into her fingers. And the light flicked on, bright and steady.

"Huh," Danny Bird said, screwing up his face. "That thing was dead as a doornail."

"Do you want it back?" Callie said, holding it far away from her body.

"Yes," he said, grabbing it from her. The light went out. "What the hell…" he muttered, flipping the toggle back and forth, unable to ignite it again.

Dad returned with his kit. He cleaned and sutured Johnny's hand there on the beach with Danny Bird standing watch, gazing over the procedure as though he suspected Dad simply posed as a doctor. But there was something comforting, even tragic, about the swiftness and smoothness of his motions, one hand looping and crossing over the other as though he were weaving a basket and not sewing together two pieces of skin.

He missed it. His face had an easy expression, the muscle memory resurfacing at the tips of his fingers. Every time one of us had a cut, even a little one, he wanted to stitch it. Every time we rolled an ankle or sprained a wrist, he wanted to splint it. He missed it, this detailed and profound way in which he contributed to the former world.

"It should heal up fine," Dad said as he bandaged the hand. "But you have to keep it clean. Try to keep it out of that glove," he said, motioning toward the grimy, grease-stained glove from which Johnny had pulled his injured hand. Dusk came fast now, and the glove was a

123

vague shadow on the gravel beach.

Danny Bird nodded, gruff. "You got any medicine if it gets infected?"

Dad shook his head. "Just this topical stuff I used before stitching." It was an enormous, brightly shining lie. A whole box full of pharmacy samples sat in the cellar. I looked at Danny Bird, convinced he would know. With all the fur, it was hard to believe he couldn't just sniff it out.

"We'll take that," he said, snapping the bacitracin out of Dad's hand. "You understand."

We did understand. There was a hierarchy, and Danny Bird was the crest. Dad said nothing. We had more tubes in storage, but it was a big loss. Another irreplaceable thing, gone.

"Well, folks," Danny Bird said, straightening his posture. "We'll be getting back to camp now. The dark comes quick." The three Birds turned from us and boarded the boat. The rowers scrambled for their oars, attentive and terrified as the trio returned. "But you'll be seeing more of us," he added. "Never know when the need for a doctor will arise."

Part of me loosened. He was going to let us be. Maybe he really believed Mom that it was useful to have a physician. Maybe, in the vast tangled web of things that could go wrong in our lives at Pluto Cove, this one small thing could go right.

But then he reached into his coat, to a pocket just inside the opening. Mom and Dad reflexively pulled me and Callie behind them, forming a wall of adult bodies. A wall that, in spirit, was as impenetrable and powerful as any material on earth; but that, in reality, was soft, fleshy, vulnerable.

I saw from the gap in Mom's coat sleeves that he held a semi-automatic handgun. He rotated it in front of his face, staring at it, contemplating it. "It's important to remember, though," he said, turning the weapon side to side. "That there's a natural order to things. The strong and the powerful will always win. Even over a hotshot doctor. This is *my* land."

And with that he twirled, fast, toward our skiff anchored in the cove and fired six rounds into the hull and engine compartment, piercing the aluminum. Mom gasped. The boat – the small, dinky, stolen boat that was our only line to the mainland, our access to the fish that kept us alive – shuddered and wheezed as it took on water.

Benji barked and yelped, throwing his front paws down on the ground, ready to be our protector, our barrier to this danger. "Benji," I whispered desperately, crouching between Dad's knees to reach out for my dog. "Benji, hush."

Johnny Bird smirked. "A year out here and you haven't eaten that little rat," he said looking at Benji with his one glimmering eye. "Only a matter of time."

My stomach dropped to the bottom of my pelvis, and with its swift descent was a matching rise in my throat like the upward push of mercury in a thermometer. Not my Benji, not my dog. "Benji," I whispered again. "Come, come." He gave a long look at the men before turning back to me, obedient. I grabbed onto him and buried myself into his body, desperate to disappear into his fur.

Danny Bird watched in disgust. "Well," he said,

taking one last scope of the cove and casually swinging the gun, pausing for a fraction of a second aimed at each of our heads. So fast we could have imagined it. But too accurate to be coincidence. To remind us that he could. "*Hasta luego*, as I think you would say," he growled as he tucked the gun back into his coat, snapping his fingers such that each man in the boat rowed in unison. From my view behind Mom I sought out the green-eyed one. I swear, he was looking at me too.

"Oh," Danny Bird said, turning to look at us one more time. "You can have this piece of shit," and he launched the broken headlamp from the departing boat onto the gravel at Dad's feet.

A minute passed. Then two. No one moved. The boat made its way slowly out of the cove, into the darkening sky.

"Is it safe, Daddy?" Callie asked from her grip behind his legs.

"It's safe, sweetie," he said, knowing full well that it was not and never would be again.

She emerged from her hiding place and picked up the headlamp. She reached with her short fingers, grabbing with all five because her pincer grasp had never fully developed, and the light flicked on, strong and bright in the dusk, casting her little face and braided hair in shadow. From across the water, Danny Bird watched it all.

THOUGH WE'D HAD lean days – days when the meat off the chickens was too tough to chew, days when the shrimp pots came up with only bottle caps and jellyfish, days when the chard leaves were too small to pick and it was too wrenching to open a dwindling, brightly labeled can in the cellar – there had never been a day when we did not eat. Until the days after the Birds.

The four of us piled into Mom and Dad's bed. They took the outsides and Callie and I curled between their bodies, Benji at our feet, his snout buried deep into the blankets. We did not dare light a fire, though it did not matter now. We did not dare to venture outside, though it did not matter now. We did not dare to make a noise beyond the shallow, frightened gasps of our breath, though it did not matter at all because there was no place to hide.

I might have done something different – done anything at all – had Mom or Dad signaled it was okay. That Mom lacked a plan – that she did not buzz around the cabin and shed, or pull together wires for a new project, or crack ice out of the creek to melt on the fire, or muck out the chicken coop to warm up the compost pile – unnerved me more than Danny Bird himself. It transported me to a time at our actual house, our actual lives, when Mom got into bed and never got out. Paralyzed. Helpless.

For as much we anguished while hiding in Pluto Cove, there was a sense of protection, a sphere over our lives insulating us from the actual world. We had written our own narrative, with no additional authors or footnotes. Our story was ours alone to write, even if it was a grim one. But Danny Bird came upon our shore and seized that story from us. Our fates became entangled in him, his moods, his hunger, and his prejudice.

Callie stayed on Mom's side. I could not bear the inanimacy of her body, the stiffness of her muscles, the entropy of her mind. I stayed next to Dad, who stared straight up at the ceiling, one arm around my shoulders as I rested into his armpit, and the other arm crossed over his body like half a corpse. His eyes were wide. He did not blink. His mind was alive, firecracking. No matter which problem he tackled first – the loss of our boat, Mom's crippling anxiety, the presence of armed, human enemies – he got nowhere.

I fell asleep at some point that night. Callie did, too. The two of us also slept through the next day in some combination of hunger and an unwillingness to open our eyes. When I awoke the next evening, the light already gone from outside the window, Mom and Dad sat at the kitchen table with the LED between them, casting a harsh pale light over their stony faces.

"They were slaves," Mom said, her voice a whisper pulled tightly as a harp string. "Those boys rowing the boat."

"I know," Dad whispered back, kneading his eyes with the palms of his hands.

"Where did they come from?" She asked, rubbing her wrists so hard I heard her skin abrading from across the cabin. "Where did he find them? They were just kids, weren't they? Where are their parents?"

It was the sort of question cycling she used to do all the time around the kitchen table at home. *What if someone comes into Enna's school? What if she's in PE and there's nowhere to shelter? Where is she going to go if a shooter comes in through the cafeteria doors? Has the principal thought about that?* They spun out of her head like miniature tornados, as though somewhere in her she hoped there was an answer, and that answer would resolve the hypotheticals that consumed her. But there were never answers. Dad knew that.

"I don't know," he said.

"We have to get out of here," Mom said. "We need to pack up. I can caulk the holes in the boat. Rewire the engine. We can leave tonight. They won't see us in the dark."

"Lisa," Dad said, putting a hand over hers to quiet the wrist wringing. "Lisa," he repeated as though her name alone would help pull her from the undertow of her thoughts and deliver her upon solid land.

She nodded. Then she cried. Softly, trying not to wake us. "It will never be seaworthy again," she said. "Alex. Maybe I can fix it enough so that I can go out to fish, but it will never be able to hold all of us. It will never be able to make it across open water."

"I know," he said.

"Then how will we ever get out of here, Alex? How can we make it out to the mainland if we don't have a boat? We always had a way back. We were just looking for a sign that it was going to be safe. Now we don't. We don't. We–"

"Lisa," Dad interrupted, his voice a bit stronger than maybe he intended. He turned in his chair toward us in the bed. I screwed my eyes shut, feigning sleep, but he couldn't see me in the darkness of our corner. "These aren't things we have to decide right now. We have time to figure this out. I know it feels really urgent, but I don't think it is. I think they are going to leave us alone. You made our case. We are an asset."

Mom shook her head, putting her unanchored wrist onto her lap and pressing the skin into the cotton of

129

her pants. She needed the sensory stimulation, but with Dad holding one hand – always begging her to stop with the tics – she sought it another way. "For how long, though?" she said. "How long can you sewing people up be more valuable to him that this land, this cabin, the greenhouse, the solar panels, the batteries, our tools? It's only a matter of time."

"But we have time," Dad said. "Nothing needs to be decided tonight. Nothing at all."

Something came over Mom at that moment and she sat up straight, her face rapt and alight. "We could walk."

"I'm sorry?" Dad asked.

"We can walk out," she said. "This isn't an island. It's a peninsula. We don't need a boat. We can walk."

"Lisa," Dad said, his voice soft and patient. "Lisa, that's over a hundred miles with no road, no trail, over some of the roughest terrain on earth. It's virtually impassable."

"I bet we could do it," Mom said earnestly. "I bet we could. If the conditions were right. If it were springtime, and the ground was frozen but there was enough daylight. If we packed out enough supplies. If we–"

"Okay, okay," Dad ceded, still kind, but audibly exhausted. "Right. Sure. We can walk. But to what? We don't know what's out there. And it's springtime right now. We are not walking anywhere right now, you understand that, right?"

"Of course I understand that, Alex," she said, irritated. "You think I don't understand that? But we need options. Don't *you* understand that? Maybe what's out there isn't as bad as what we left. Maybe the people left out there aren't like Danny Bird. Maybe they've started to work out solutions and cooperate instead of offing each other." I winced.

Dad mulled over his next words. "I just think it's important to remember that you might always think it's safer somewhere else. You were like that at home. Never convinced that where we were at a given time was the right place to be. It's a big reason we are out here…" he trailed off. He had crossed a line.

Mom shot to standing, knocking over her chair. I brought the edge of the blanket closer to my face. "You think we're all out here because of *me*?!" She spat. "A year and a half of daily agony, always panicking about food, not having the girls in school or having any kind of a normal life at all? And you want to blame *me?*" She squeezed her wrists like they were something to be choked and killed.

"Lisa–"

"Don't rewrite history, Alex. We made this decision together. That was not my anxiety that brought us out there, it was reality. It was the LFR. It was trying to save *you* and *Enna*." My breath shook in my throat like the wind through leaves. It was me. The darker one. My fault. "And now, when I make even the slightest whisper of changing our situation it's back to the old doctor-slash-preacher Alex who knows what's best for me and knows his wife is crazy and he is the freaking saintly voice of reason that all of us would be doomed without!"

"Lisa, shush!" Dad exclaimed, turning again to check on us. Callie scooted herself into my body, burying her face into the side of my arm. The blinking of her

131

eyelashes – very much awake – brushed the skin above my elbow. But they were consumed in their own world. It took little on our part to pretend to sleep. "The girls are asleep. You can't wake them up and scare them."

She stood across the living room, such a small, tight space we inhabited, her arms crossed at her chest, wrists pressed into her armpits. "Again, Alex? Just accusing me of being hysterical. You can't use this against me. You can't disqualify what I have to say because you think my brain doesn't work as well as yours."

"Will you stop?" he said, pulling at his hair. "Just stop. You know that is not what I think. It has *never* been what I think. Back at home, yeah, I just wanted to make sure you were getting the support you needed. But I never didn't take you seriously. I think you know that. You just want to be angry at me because things are out of your – our – control right now. You know how strong you've been since we came to Pluto Cove? How tough and resourceful and brilliant? We would be dead without you. You think that's lost on me? On the girls?"

Her shoulders visibly softened. Neither of them said anything for a while.

"If you think we are getting close to the time when we should leave here," Dad eventually continued, "then that's a discussion we should start to have. It will take a lot of time. And we don't know what we'll find on the other side. It'll be a huge gamble. But we can't stay here forever. We can't get old out here. The girls can't turn into adults out here. At some point, we gotta go back. If Danny Bird landing on the Cove is our sign from the universe that it's time to do that, then let's have that conversation."

Mom nodded. She made no movement toward him or the table where he sat, but she released her wrists from their traps in her armpits. "Maybe in the fall," she said. "Before the next winter comes, but after freeze-up. But before the light disappears. The timing would have to be perfect."

"A lot of things would have to be perfect," Dad said absently. Then, sensing the purposelessness of those words he added, "Maybe in the fall."

"Are you just placating me?" Mom said tensely.

"No," Dad said. "I'm not."

"I'm not a freak," she said. "I'm not ill."

"I know," he said. "I know that."

At some point they both made their way back to the bed, enclosing me and Callie as Dad reached across us to put an arm on Mom. Could it be true? that the end of our time at Pluto Cove was drawing near? What lay ahead was a month-long journey through pathless wilds overflowing with dangers both seen and unseen. A simple twisted ankle could spell the end for someone on land so remote and lonely as the peninsula stretching between us the road system. Starvation. Predators. Cliffs and ravines. Brush so thick it could blind. Poisonous plants masquerading as edible. Dozens of miles with no streams bearing drinkable water. But if we made it to the other side, an entire world awaited. A dangerous world, maybe. But maybe not.

It wasn't optimism in me – that upswell of hope. It was delirium. A wish for the community who would welcome us as we staggered out of the forest. There were people out there. They, too, would be hard-bitten and ragged from living in this new world of water shortages, atom bombs, and food riots – but they would welcome us. There would be livestock. Hardy fruit trees. Unread books still intact at the spines. Music. Open spaces unencumbered by the ocean on one side and mountain cliffs on the other. There would be children, teenagers, peers. Dad would treat whatever ailments had accumulated in them over the seasons and Mom would dazzle them with her electrical genius and light up their worlds, literally. We would reminisce and laugh about the day the four of us stumbled out of the wilderness and into this new civilization. Perhaps we would enshrine the day with a yearly celebration. Together we would pool our resources and our knowledge and be better off than we could ever be alone.

That wasn't optimism at all. It was naivete. You've heard enough now to know that.

And, of course, none of that would come to pass. That fall, as Mom and Dad readied us for the colossal expedition through the mountains out of Pluto Cove, Callie disappeared.

ANOTHER DAY AND NIGHT passed before Callie and I made a meaningful exit from the bed. We ran through the cold to the outhouse as needed. I emerged from the covers to let Benji outside and back in as he required. But otherwise, I stayed with Callie and Mom.

The previous autumn, Mom baited the end of the gravel spit with salmon carcasses – typically a death wish to draw bears from the woods – but she needed to attract birds for their feathers. We were coming into the second winter at Pluto Cove and the blankets she had packed thinned, their down collapsed or drifted away from microtears in the stitches. Maybe she was trying to bait George, too. How she hated that bear.

She caught several birds with a long-handled net, conserving her bullets. But the rest she shot as they circled the fish and swooped in for scraps. Up to that point, she had never asked me to slaughter our chickens; she understood my closeness and attachment to them, so she did it herself. But this was a massacre, and she needed help.

She taught me to let out their blood with a swift cut across the throat that popped as the knife released thick tendons encircling the neck. I sobbed the entire afternoon as feathers floated around the air, as though we were in a pillow fight and not a genocide. At one point, Mom tried and failed to stifle a laugh as I sniffled, dramatically, in my angst – but instead inhaled a clump of raven down. Then I spent fifteen minutes coughing it up while screaming at her that it wasn't funny.

Awful as that day had been, the exercise paid off. We stuffed our blankets with the gray feathers of gulls and the inky feathers of crows. The meat was atrocious – barely edible – but meat nonetheless. Benji happily scarfed what we could not palate. Those feathers stuffed into our blankets made our winter nights bearable, survivable. Staying in bed with Callie and Mom – and Dad as he came and went, trying to maintain the order of things as we slept away our despair, hoping to wake up and find that Danny Bird and the shot-up boat was just a fever dream – was a siren song of warmth, pulling us into the deep, dark sea of sleep.

But Dad decided enough was enough. He rousted us from bed. "You need to eat," he said. "You need to do your arithmetic."

"I'm not hungry," I said. "And who cares if I can do math."

He ripped the downy blanket off me. "You *are* hungry," he said. "And I, your father, care. Out of bed, now."

He prepared some oatmeal. Plain. We long ago finished the cinnamon. But the mush was animating. It descended into my throat in warm, soupy clumps and with it a bit of color returned to the earth. He scrawled out some algebra on the inside cover of a short novel, and I picked my way through the equations, not making a show of it, but maybe a little glad to have my brain pulled from the loops it ran while lying in bed.

If we ever made it out of Pluto Cove, if I ever set foot again in a classroom, how I would fare? My reading comprehension was good – I was sure of that. I had consumed most of the books in the musty and mildewed Pluto Cove library, that toppling pile of books that Great-grandma Callista accumulated in the Gold Rush days, through to grandma Samantha (or, Granny Sammy as we called her despite never knowing her), to Mom's books, and to ours. Mom joked that books were the only decoration in that old cabin, but there was nothing more colorful or interesting that could have lined the walls.

In that first year and a half I had made my way through the Old and New Testaments, the Secret Garden, the History of Standard Oil, the Joy of Cooking, the Second Edition Big Book for Alcoholics Anonymous, and the complete sets of Sue Grafton, Stephen King, Roald Dahl, the Boxcar Children, Harry Potter, and the Hitchhiker's Guide to the Galaxy. Anything I did not understand, Mom and Dad explained to me. At home, I heard a lot of *We'll tell you when you're older*, or, *You're not ready to know the answer to that yet*. But at Pluto Cove, there was nothing left to shield from me.

As for math, Mom and Dad wrote out equations on the blank inside covers of the books, our best source of paper. Neither of them knew what sort of math a 14-year-old learned. They agreed it was more than multiplication but less than calculus. I suggested geometry. Both gave a slight wince. Neither of them retained enough memory of geometry to teach it. They scribbled out a few right triangles and gave me the formula for Pythagorean's Theorem, but it made no sense as to why that would work or why it mattered. Without a calculator most square roots were impossible anyway. So I stopped.

But for what I lacked in math, I made up for in science. I could describe in exquisite detail the structure of an atom and the behavior of the basic elements: hydrogen, oxygen, carbon, and nitrogen. I could explain the way energy was generated and stored by the attraction of particles, either statically by accumulation, or dynamically as a current. I could tell you that our solar panels were made of a silicon semiconductor, an element that forms a lattice, and that half the silicone was doped with phosphorous and half with boron, so that electrons tore off when the structure got hit with photons from the sun. I knew that the electrons flowed from the phosphorous side to the boron side, creating a current. And from the electric field came voltage. And from a combination of current and voltage, came our power.

And, whether or not it was part of any ninth-grade curriculum, I could perfectly dissect a rabbit kidney and identify the cortex, medulla, and the major and minor calyces. I could take that same rabbit and differentiate between the upper, middle, and lower lobes of its lungs and separate the bronchus from the bronchiole. And in that same poor rabbit, I could show Dad the four chambers of its tiny heart and map out to him how blood flowed into the right side for passage to the lungs for oxygen, then into the left for distribution to the entire body. I could even distinguish the pulmonary artery from the coronary artery. Then I fed the heart to Benji.

Mom and Dad's expertise intersected in physiology. Maybe it was how they both lit up, came alive, huddled together over the paper or dirt where they sketched out the flow of charges and currents through the body – the way they could simultaneously interrupt or say the same words at the same time – but it was my favorite of all. In physiology, electricity pulsed in the human body. It was a language they shared.

In the clumps of my pillow, I would trace out a neuron and map its action potential. Here it was at rest, negative relative to the exterior of the cell, -70 millivolts. But then here comes an impulse, a positive charge. The electrochemistry of the inside of the cell shoots up to -55 millivolts at a speed many times the blink of an eye. It's so small – this change of 15 millivolts – it should be meaningless. But instead it buzzes opens the sodium ion-gated channels, and positive charge floods inside the cell. The positive charge surges forward, opening more sodium gates, turning it more and more positive, barreling down the length of the nerve like an out of control train … but then here comes the potassium channels, opening fast, and potassium pours out of the cell, taking its positive charge with it until the change in polarity reaches the axon terminal where neurotransmitters are ejected and the cell returns to -70 millivolts. It was terribly exciting. I played it out over and over like a little kid playing with race cars.

Every thought in my brain, every choke in my throat, every dreadful bite from our 500-pound stash of rice, every feeling of cold or hunger or loneliness was only that: changes in polarity, the movement of positively-charged ions in and out of my cell membranes, the irresistibility of charges to rush toward their opposites, and their manic infatuation with each other. But then here is the steady control of the fastidious anatomical gatekeepers, maintaining the order of all things even at only one atom wide.

Things were a little easier if I just thought of them that way.

I finished my oatmeal and took another bowl. There were never seconds of anything at Pluto Cove, but a three day fast warranted exception. I solved Dad's algebra equations (too easy) and started reading the book he wrote them in: *The Little Prince*. A children's book, well below my reading level, but a salve to my mind. One of Mom's favorites.

Later, I would need to bundle up and harvest ice from the creek. While I melted and warmed the ice on the woodstove, I would turn over the rocks we kept near the cabin foundation and dig out insects to feed to the chickens. Later, when the water was warm, I would dunk our filthy clothing into the basin and wring out the dust, sweat, oils, and grime. Then I would hang the clothes on the clothesline where the fabric would freeze into stiff cardboard caricatures of shirts and socks. Later, in the evening, I would plait willow fibers for lashing into ropes. Later, in the following days, I would repeat a combination of those tasks and a thousand others. It was a pioneer's work, a survivor's work, work that was real and critical and that most people on earth at that moment were not fortunate enough to do.

But in that moment, reading *The Little Prince* with a belly crying out for more oatmeal, Benji licking the serving spoon at my feet, Mom and Callie still entombed under the covers, I did not feel like a pioneer, or a survivor, or anyone at all. I was the Little Prince's lamplighter, burning and extinguishing the same flame 1,440 times a day, with never a moment to rest, to contemplate, or to find meaning. I was blind, beholden, with no room on my little planet for anyone else.

DAD FOUND TWO EIGHT-OUNCE tubes of epoxy stored in the touring kit of the skiff. It was not enough to patch the bullet holes that pierced both sides of the hull and the engine compartment, but it was a start. "It'll be like skin grafting," Dad said to me, reading the directions on the tube at the breakfast table. "Not so bad."

"When's the last time you skin grafted?" I asked out of genuine curiosity – but the tone of my voice was snarky. It didn't strike me as a procedure done in an emergency room.

He nodded, then immediately shook his head. "Yeah." He said. "A while."

Although Callie had slid out of bed following Dad's bribes of cuddling and playing board games, Mom stayed. After reaching their soft agreement to hike out of

Pluto Cove at the turn of the season, she fell back into her place of darkness, of paralysis. It was not new behavior to me – but I had not witnessed it out here. There was no door to her bedroom to close, no privacy to speak of. As she slept and shuddered her way through the days, we watched mere feet away. Powerless.

"Wanna get up, Mama?" Callie asked one morning, offering a bowl of oatmeal to the lump of body under the covers. "Breakfast is warm." Dad and I watched from the table, wondering if we should intervene on Callie's behalf, or if Mom might react to the plea.

There was no movement, no sign of life from the pile of blankets. Callie pressed in again. "Mama, breakfast time," she said in a sing-song voice. Still, nothing. Now, desperately. "Mama, here–" and she forced the bowl of oatmeal into the blankets where Mom recoiled from the sudden touch. The bowl tumbled into the sheets, spilling the soupy mix across the bed.

Whether from guilt at making such a mess or longing for her mother who had seemingly vanished into a fleshy shell, Callie burst into tears. Big, hot, sour tears. I stood up and went to her, wrapping her in my arms. "It's okay, Cal," I whispered. "It's okay, I'll clean up the sheets. It's not that bad of a mess." Though it really was quite a bad mess. "Don't worry about it."

But my comfort only made her wail harder. "There is no quick comfort for emotions like these," she choked between her cries.

"What?" I said absently, the combination of words too strange from a child to sound meaningful. I presumed them gibberish – utter nonsense – without realizing until months later she quoted from *The Giver*.

I tried to carry her away from Mom, but she craned and angled her body to keep herself near the bed, watching the bed, wanting any sign of life. I couldn't maintain a grip on her squirming, so I set her back down. She crawled into the bed, straight over the oatmeal, spreading it around the sheets and working it down into the mattress itself, all over her clothes. "Mama," she wailed. "Mama. To gain control of some things you must let go of others." She thought this book was what Mom needed. *The Giver*.

Mom was in there, breathing, but could not rally herself. When this happened at home, we walked away from it. Let her sort it out or let her medications kick in or whatever she needed. But here we could not insulate ourselves from her pain.

"Callie," Dad said, walking to the bed and pulling Callie's body out of the blankets. He, too, had not understood her recall of the book. "Callie, it's okay, baby." Callie squirmed less in Dad's arms than she had in mine. "Mama is just kind of on a trip right now. She's not really here even though she looks like she's here. But she will be back." He raised his voice so that Mom had to hear him. "She will be back really soon because we need her. We really need her. So now," he said even louder, speaking to Mom even though it was Callie whom he faced. "Now we are going to go out to the boat and try to repair the holes. I have this epoxy here that I have never used. But I am going to give it a try and fix the boat because we need the boat."

The blankets shifted.

He went on. "I get one shot at this. Hopefully I can mix this epoxy correctly." And he turned and walked out the door with Callie.

I took a deep breath. The cabin was a mess. The walls were more pressed in and cramped than ever. Dishes littered the sink basin. Muddy footprints crisscrossed the worn wooden floors. Empty aluminum cans licked clean by Benji overflowed near the table. The soot in the woodstove was a cancerous mass spilling out onto the hearth. And oatmeal was smeared all over the bed, Callie, and Mom.

I dipped a rag into the warm water atop the stove and started scrubbing the blankets. I could not pull off the sheets with Mom on top of them, so I tried working around her. Occasionally my hand bumped into her back or I accidentally scrubbed the tips of her hair. She couldn't even acknowledge that. I scrubbed harder. It did nothing but rub the oatmeal deeper into the bed. I wiped the same spot again and again, jagged, rough, and angry. My heart rate climbed. Still she did not move. A small hole appeared in the thin sheet where I rubbed too hard. There was no good way to repair that hole – it would only grow and grow, and soon the entire sheet would be a gaping mouth that served no purpose and was just one more thing gone from a world where it could not be replaced.

I threw down the rag, right onto Mom's body. "You know what," I said. "If you want to sleep in oatmeal, go for it." I stood up straight and pulled an oversized winter coat tight around my waist. "I'm gonna go help Dad with the boat. We will probably mess it up. Too bad the one person we trust the most can't even acknowledge her daughter bringing her breakfast in bed." And I left the cabin.

Down at the water, Dad held Callie in his lap next to the beached boat. They stared out at the ocean. The sky was a blend of orange, pink, and red as the rising sun sat on the brink of the horizon. The air held a blade to my skin. I sat down next to them. "I don't know what epoxy is," I said.

"I don't really either," Dad said.

We sat for a moment in silence, listening to the waves lap against the ice-slicked shore. "Do you think we'll be okay without a boat?" I asked. "If we can't go out and fish?"

He adjusted Callie on his lap so that he could face me. He struggled with how to answer, how to be honest, how to treat me like the adult I was forced to become too quickly. "I don't know, Enna," he said, his voice soft and afraid. "We eat a lot of fish."

I nodded, full of terror that boiled up and out of my chest like a pot of water forgotten on the stove. But I also needed to hear that truth. "Maybe we can fish more off the shore," I offered.

"Maybe," he said, turning his gaze back to the sunrise. Callie nestled so deeply into him she nearly disappeared into his coat.

"When do you think Danny Bird will be back?" I asked. I was asking questions like Mom: questions no person could answer, casting out blindly for any measure of support or reassurance.

Dad shook his head and took a deep breath – then we heard it. The gunshot.

It echoed clear and sharp through the cold morning air. A single shot, the piercing crack of a 12-gauge barrel. It bounced off the mountainsides around us and rang through our ears over and over and over again.

It was one sound, a sound I knew well, a sound that swept my feet out from under me and whisked me away. But not to a place up the mountain hunting ptarmigan. Not to a place of target practice at the range outside Anchorage. Not to the meadow of deer with the slow, limping baby who I intentionally missed. That shot took me to when I was six years old and I came home on the bus to a quiet house. The sound of that gunshot took me to that day when I figured Mom was upstairs in bed because she had been in one of her dark places. The sound of that gunshot was the sound of my heartbeat when I opened the door to the bathroom and found her slumped against the cabinet under the sink, frothing at the mouth, breathing but barely. The sound of that gunshot was my own screams *Mama! Mama! Wake up!* but she wouldn't wake up. It was the sound of running for the phone and not remembering my own address for the dispatcher. It was the sound of being scooped into the arms of a paramedic, and having a blanket put over my shoulders until Dad came running down a long hospital hallway.

In the sound of that gunshot, every organ dropped out of my body and sat suspended in space. Thoughts evacuated my head like people stumbling from their homes after a powerful earthquake, wandering the streets, stunned. The only movement in my body was the involuntary twitching of my legs that begged, *Run, run away, run for help, run for anything, just get out.* My mind was both wild and blank, desperate and vacant. Callie screamed and threw her arms around Dad's neck. He reached and grabbed me in a single pull, throwing me behind his body. "Lisa!" he cried at the top of his lungs, barreling out of his chest like a charging animal.

"Dad," I whimpered. "Dad, was that Mom….?" My eyes went bone dry and blistered. I knew. She had either been shot by Danny Bird, who had never actually left the cove and was hunting us. Or she had done again what she did when I was six. But this time there were no pills at her disposal. Only guns.

Like ticker tape behind my eyes, the last thing I said to her spun around and around in my head: *Too bad the person we trust the most…*

I pressed my face into Dad's down jacket and screamed and screamed and screamed. The fabric of his coat absorbed my sound but I felt the screams rattle around inside his rib cage, knocking his heart around like a bell. Next to me Callie sobbed, "Mommy! Mommy! Mommy!"

He was paralyzed. If it was Danny Bird with the gun we should run. We should hide. But if it was Mom having done the unthinkable, then there was no physical threat and only the worst sadness known in the human story. Either way, there was no point in moving. Either way, our lives and our hearts and our souls were gone.

But then.

Mom walked down the hill, the shotgun cradled in her arms like an infant. It gleamed, massive and sturdy against her small and shaking body. The three of us took off toward her in a tear, ignoring any sense that we might be running toward danger. It was Mom. She was alive.

"It was George," she said as we reached her, throwing our arms around her, tangling ourselves around her and each other, sobbing and sick. "I shot him."

PART TWO

THE BIRDS

CHAPTER FOUR – *The Middle*

The boat was gone. I had never felt a stuckness so complete. One side of my world was rocky mountains and cliffs, and the other side of my world was deep and salty water. Up to that point, I could access the ocean. I could go out with Mom and change my vantage, change my scenery, look back on Pluto Cove from the water and see its small, finite, pitiful totality. I could get some perspective on the size of our lives relative to the wilderness, relative to the ocean – both of which were so unfathomably big. And in this view staring back at the cabin, I found some meaning. Some context.

But no more. Mom patched the bullet holes and did her best to repair the engine. But it was no sturdier than a dinghy. She forbade me from boating with her. It was too risky. I didn't understand why it was an acceptable risk to her but not me. But when I asked, she grew agitated and distressed – nearly pulling her hands off their anchors to her wrists – so I stopped.

I explored back into the mountains more, telling Mom and Dad I was scouting for berry patches when really, I was scouting a trail to lead up and out of the cove. I carried two cans of bear mace, a machete, and a whistle around my neck. Benji followed my every step, happy, eager, and ready. George was gone, dissolved into our stomachs, and it would be a while before another bear seized his territory. Aside from grizzlies, the only real threat I minded was the Birds. And if they arrived, then nothing I carried would make any difference. So I walked confidently, purposefully, slashing away at dry and brittle brush to blaze a trail. Two attempts led to sheer cliffs, another to an avalanche chute. The third seemed so promising, until it dead-ended at one of Great-grandpa's collapsed mining tunnels. I kept trying.

The winter finally broke apart in our hands, crumbling away at the edges and giving way to fair weather. I avoided the cabin as much I could. It felt toxic inside. There was a layer of filth that could never be fully cleaned, a smell no open window could air, a heaviness after Mom's episode I could never scrub away. I would have slept outside if my parents let me. But the only place to sleep was the beach, and that's where an invading boat would land.

So instead, I stayed outside long into each night, sitting with Benji on the rocks. The sunlight accelerated each day, and I willed wakefulness until the last lick of light disappeared. Soon that would be impossible; there would never be a darkness beyond twilight. Our plants in the greenhouse would explode under the assault of sunlight. Our minds would bend and warp around the light. Our sense of time would distort like a curved mirror. But in so many ways, it already had. There was a tautness now to our daily lives, a physical tension between us and within the cove where there had not been before.

I watched the moonrise one night in mid-May. I saw its glow before I saw its shape; silver and sparkling over the eastern mountains while the sun still cast a bruised yellow and purple light from the west. It was a full moon. Had I been in contact with the radio or Internet or a chatty friend, I might have known that it was a perigee moon: the point at which the moon is closest to the earth in its orbit. I had seen the full moon what felt like a thousand times since arriving at Pluto Cove, but tonight's was a spectacle. It swallowed the mountaintops as it emerged from the horizon, looming larger than any celestial feature I had ever seen. It was textured and mottled like animal fur. It dangled in front of me, glowing, as might an ornament on an extravagant Christmas tree. Despite myself – despite knowing full well how ridiculous – I reached out my hand. For a moment, I thought I could touch it. Maybe that wouldn't be the craziest thing in the world. Maybe it really was that close.

My hand swept nothing but the cool evening air. And I felt a fool.

There is a narrow window for stargazing in this part of the world. Much of the year is dark, yes, but far too cold to sit outside and idly watch the sky. And, for the fleeting part of the year when one might be outside without contracting a cold-related disease, it is simply too bright in the sky to see stars. I was inside that window of between-seasons and pulled my coat up to my chin against the nudge of the wind but otherwise felt the soft relief of air that is easily inhaled and warmed by the chest, of lips that do not chatter, of ears that do not burn at the tips and lobes.

A bright, iridescent star that must have been a planet hung suspended in the velvet sky, a single glittering teardrop. Jupiter? Venus? Surely not Pluto. I learned as a little kid that Pluto was not even a planet anymore. Dad brought home a magazine with Pluto on the cover, its odd swirl of blue and brown, with the white ear in the middle of a disfigured face. He read to me that although Pluto orbited the sun, it was no longer a planet because it wasn't gravitationally dominant. He said the scientists called it "clearing the neighborhood" because its gravity wasn't strong enough to force out other astral bodies. It wasn't enough of an astronomical bully to warrant planet status. *Poor Pluto,* I thought then. It didn't belong in any category. Like me, my skin, my hair, my culture, my language.

How fitting, I thought, looking out at the moon over Pluto Cove. Great-Grandma Callista named the cove after Pluto because it felt like the furthest landmark within the knowable universe. Now it wasn't even that. It was a nothing place, an in-between place, an ice dwarf unworthy of any meaningful classification. Not even strong enough to compel away competing orbits as the Birds built up around Lamplight Mountain's center of gravity.

But staring at the moon – that massive, faraway satellite that looked like a snow-covered planet to which we might jump and start over in a new life – was akin to being out in the boat, staring out at the ocean, being overwhelmed by a sense of smallness and meagerness that dulled the pain of loneliness. It washed over me with the sense that, even if our lives had the worst possible endings, it was just a part of the story being told. That no matter what, there would still be room for joy and love and unabashed, incomprehensible beauty.

MOM HAD PACKED us so much, yet it could never be enough. She had honed her packing skills on everything from day hikes to holiday vacations, for settings from hotels to rented RVs to tents anchored in high winds and pelting rain. But how do you pack for entire years of a person's life? Four people's lives? And when two of those people are constantly growing, changing, expanding?

Shoes were the first to go. After a few months at Pluto Cove, they grew tight at my toes. I cut open the fabric to relieve the pressure, which worked until my toes grew out and over the lip of the rubber sole, like a tree root breaking through pavement. So I started wearing Mom's shoes. But Callie had no way to level-up. At first, she also cut the ends off her shoes, allowing her toes to spill over the edge. But then her feet grew too wide, even with the Velcro straps fully released, so she cut those open too. Soon she just had the rubber sole and pieces of the fabric lashed together with willow reed in a deformed Roman sandal.

But that failed. So she abandoned shoes all together. Everywhere she went around Pluto Cove she went barefoot. Up the hillside of dirt and roots and prickly plants and loose rock, along the beach of angular gravel, standing on the cabin porch with splinters and exposed nailheads. Her feet became tough as leather, hard but pliable, gummy and wrinkled.

Dad begged her to wear shoes, any shoes, any kind of protection over her feet at all – he knew the sorts of injuries and germs that could cross through one's foot – but didn't have a choice in the matter. He couldn't run out to the store and get her new shoes, or log-in to his computer and order more online. He asked Mom when Callie was immunized against tetanus. She wracked her memory. "Not since she was a baby, I think."

"Then it'll only be good for a couple more years.

153

Those vaccines have a lifespan." Dad said, pulling down the skin under his eyes, looking older than he was. Even the antibodies circulating in our blood had an expiration date.

And then the soap started to run out, even as Mom cut it thinner and thinner with water. On a cloudy day that yielded no rain, I doubled over with my first period and saw the panic in Mom's eyes as she combed through the box of toiletries with only a handful of tampons and no pads. Our toothbrushes lost their bristles and our pillows lost their plump. We squeezed the toothpaste tubes down to the last smear but still one of Dad's teeth turned brown with rot. While of sound mind, he walked Mom through tooth extraction, the precise angle from which to pull, the amount of torque needed to minimize the root exposure, how to pack the hollow hole with gauze. Once she could repeat it back to him in a clear and confident tone, he took a small handful of painkillers and wasted himself on the pills while she set to work.

While our hygiene deteriorated, matches posed a bigger problem. Little Callie maintained the fire while the rest of us worked outside with the animals, the water, the plants, and the wires. Whereas at first, she had been directed to find Mom or Dad when the fire ran down, she later gained the cherished responsibility of reviving it herself. She took to it with a passion. She developed a knack for building up kindling into a log cabin, starting a neat little flame in the center, and sensing the moment when it needed more fuel or a little bit of breath to keep it going. The fire was her purview; it gave her purpose and pride.

One day, during a cold snap in early summer, she

wandered out of the cabin to where Mom and I replaced nesting material for the chickens with dried twigs and leaves. "Mom, where are the matches?"

"What do you mean, honey? They're right where they always are." Mom replied, nudging aside a friendly hen. "By the woodstove."

"Those are out," Callie said. "Where are the others?"

Now Mom stood up straight, staring down at Callie with a gaze that toggled between fury and fear. "Callie, there were five boxes of one thousand matches each. That was all our matches. What do you mean they're gone?"

Callie's face went pale. "I... I..."

Mom turned on her heel and ran to the cabin, as though going quickly could mitigate this disaster. I followed behind and watched from the open doorway as she grabbed a sturdy red box, shaking it side to side and up and down, willing a match to fall from some stuck corner. "Oh, no," she whispered.

She dropped to her knees and opened the metal door to the stove, finding only cold ash. There was not even the smallest ember to kindle or revive in the way ancient men carried fire in smoldering leaves as they traversed continents.

"How did this happen?" Mom asked into the empty stove, her voice going up into the chimney. "There were so many matches. There were so many."

"I'm sorry, Mom," Callie sobbed from behind me, gripping my leg. "I was the Little Match Girl. I'm sorry."

She told me later, up in the loft, that she liked letting the fires die completely – sometimes several times a day – so that she could build it up anew. Constructing the little kindling cabin, engineering it just right, was her favorite task. In building the towers of twigs, her palsied hands were pliable, obedient. She could not butter toast, but she could construct a tiny city of sticks and then watch it turn to intense, twinkling light. She pretended she was the Little Match Girl from the story, thinking of some happy memory each time she lit the phosphorous red edge. She just assumed there were more. Why would she think otherwise?

I registered then that she was still so young. All she had known were grocery stores, drug stores, and hardware stores. Where those failed, there was the Internet and neighbors. Mom and Dad did everything to help us feel like there was enough, but it was her turn to realize we were in constant peril of running out.

IF DAD'S CALENDAR by the door was right, the Birds returned on solstice. That day in June was a hot one, hazy, the air so dry my fingers cracked and bled as I scraped root maggot larvae off the stems of our cabbage. How had the maggots found us so far away from anything else? It was a common grievance as the Polar Storms set in – these pests that flourished in the new conditions. In Kentucky, a woman snapped a picture of a wasp nest as big as a school bus. In fact, she parked a school bus next to it as a point of comparison. Tuna fisheries in the Gulf of Thailand pulled up only sticky, translucent jellyfish. In Alaska, the spruce bark beetle multiplied a million times over and mowed down trees with their shiny jaws. People lamented, *Why can't the good species thrive?* The honeybees, the songbirds, the trout all suffered and perished. It was pests who loved this new world.

Mom spotted their boat, the small one, rounding the corner of the Cove. "Alex," she called in a matter-of-fact voice. By their coordinated response – the grabbing and hiding of guns, the positioning of Callie in the loft, the leashing of Benji to the porch – they had rehearsed this many times. There was no surprise in their arrival.

The boat made a smooth landing on the shore, navigating easily through the heat and high-pressure air. Mom and Dad directed me into the cabin with Callie, and I pretended to leave, but at the last moment ducked into a canopy of collapsed spruce branches, wilted and gray in the shape of an umbrella. I could see Danny Bird perfectly. Mom and Dad's backs stood to me, but a child can read so much more of a parent than simply a face.

Danny Bird stepped from the boat while it was still in motion, absorbing the momentum into his stride as though he disembarked an escalator. He wore the same bear coat, wolf pelts, and lynx hat. He must have been very hot. But such was the price of his prestige and prominence. To be the half-man and half-monster.

"Here we are," Danny Bird said, his voice dull and cold. In the spring he had been sing-song, mocking. That would not be the interaction this time.

"Hello," Dad said, lowering his voice. Mom stood behind him.

"I have an injured crew member," Danny Bird said. "He needs medical attention immediately."

"Okay," Dad said.

"Okay?!" Danny Bird exploded. "You don't *okay* me. I *own* you. Go get your supplies. Now. And get that daughter of yours. You're both coming to the compound."

I couldn't see Dad's face, but he didn't miss a beat. In the hospital, everyone wanted everything fast. He was accustomed to people pushing him around in emergencies – at the expense of planning and forethought.

"Hold on a moment," Dad said, putting his hands up in the universal *slow down*. "Hold on. Even in emergencies we have to get our heads around things. What happened to this crew member?"

"I can explain that to you on the boat," Danny Bird growled. "Get your goddamn kit and your goddamn daughter." His eyes were furious slits on his face, the lynx eyes open wide and doing the looking for him.

"I will get my kit," Dad said. "But I am not bringing my child."

"You will," Danny Bird said. "We let you stay out here as a matter of serving *us*. Now you will do as you are told, or we have no reason to keep you around."

Mom's hand crept up Dad's back and gripped the fabric of his shirt. She turned to him and whispered something. He looked at her, then walked up to the cabin to fetch his supplies. She turned to Danny Bird and confronted him alone. I trembled. She had been changed these last few months. Easier to scare, faster to provoke. Now she stared that fear straight in its merciless eyes. Alone.

"You have to tell us why you need our daughter," she said, her voice hard but fragile. "We can refuse, and you can kill us. The loss of one of us is the loss of all of us." I held my hand over my mouth to keep the sounds in. What I would give to have Benji to hold.

Here Danny Bird retrieved his smile – his thin, snarling, sinister smile. "A man by himself is a man you cannot predict," he said. "A man with his child is a man you can control. Send the little one."

"No," Mom said. Her body settled deeper into the gravel, as though she were anchoring herself to the ground. "She is six-years-old. She has no place anywhere near your home."

The smile evaporated from Danny Bird's face. He ground his teeth together in what appeared to be both anger and contemplation. He was in a negotiation. Even though Mom had taken away his threat of death, there were cards far worse yet in play.

"The darker one then," he said.

Dad's footsteps returned down the beach.

"Okay," Mom said.

Every cell in my body congealed, as though previously I had a warm, thick lava of life circulating through me and it hardened instantly to stone. She was sending me. Because I was older? He hadn't called me the older one. He called me the darker one. There was no world in which Callie could leave Mom. No world in which Callie could board that boat and sail to their compound, even with Dad there. If it was anyone, it was going to be me. But why did it have to be one of us at all?

Mom whispered to Dad as he returned. I could not hear her. But I heard his response, "No," he cried. It was not a statement. It was a plea. "No, she can't," he said. "I go alone."

There was some inaudible discussion between the two of them. Their whispers came hoarse and low, desperate and sad. Somewhere in the middle of it, my own legs stood up and walked out from under the tree. "I'm here," I said.

Mom spun around and threw me an infuriated look for eavesdropping. But that look quickly melted to pure anguish. "Baby," she whispered.

"I'll be with Dad the whole time," I said. "It's fine." Whether I believed myself, I did not know. I trusted Dad. If there was anyone in the world I trusted, it was Dad. But I had seen enough to know there were many forces in the world against which he was powerless.

The reality was that – since the Birds' arrival three months prior, since squeezing through the LFR checkpoint on the highway twenty months prior, since the drought edged its way into our lives years before that – I had not known safety since I was a kid writing letters to Santa or leaving my tooth under my pillow. Each new location changed the shape of our danger, but never eliminated it. I looked at Dad. He stood tall and strong, with eyes that howled his wish to change our situation, control this narrative, and bring us back to the life he dreamed of and worked for. I felt bad for him. He was as subject to the whims of the universe and humanity as I was, but he had the responsibility to act like he wasn't.

"Pat 'em," Danny Bird said, turning to Johnny and Keith.

They both strode from the boat to us in five easy steps. Keith grabbed Dad and roughed him up and down his sleeves and pant legs. He pulled a snub nose revolver from the back of Dad's jeans and pocketed it for himself. "You have no need for this," Keith said.

Johnny Bird came for me. The skin on his burned

face curled and rippled like the edges of paper in a fire.

"Don't touch her!" Mom screamed.

Johnny Bird gave a little laugh and grabbed my left thigh, stroking it. I went rigid, frozen. I had no weapon on me. But his touch was apocalyptic. No longer was I a human person, but a stuffed thing, something soft and yielding, powerless to his hands.

"I said get off of her!" Mom yelled, lunging toward me. Danny Bird stepped in front of her and brought his C7 rifle over his shoulder, whipping the buttstock into the side of her head. She crumpled like tissue paper onto the beach but was down only a moment before trying to push herself up. Keith restrained Dad who thrashed in his arms.

"Lisa!" He shouted.

"I'm okay," she gasped. "I'm okay."

And Johnny Bird, waiting a moment for Mom to gather herself so that she could see it all transpire, moved his hands up my thighs, and – bringing his teeth next to my ear, breathing heavy and wet into my skin, the smell of the charred plastic of his scars choking and wicked – grabbed me between the legs.

I wanted to cry out. I wanted to crumple as Mom had. But I couldn't. I had to stand there, upright and strong, and show everyone I was no pawn.

"Get in the boat," Danny Bird barked. "If he dies waiting, it'll be on you."

Keith released Dad, and he rushed toward Mom, hauling her up from the ground. They swallowed each other in a fierce and desperate hug. Fear shone in their eyes. But more than that, there was love. There was no fear without it.

Then Mom turned to me, "Baby," she said. "My baby." I looked at her, breathing slow and steady to still my body, to broadcast to her that everything was alright, that I would be fine. "I love you so much." She wept as Johnny Bird pulled her away. I did not care, I stepped in and put my arms around her, tugging against Johnny. I now stood over her, taller than her.

"Everything is going to be okay. It's like that *Llama Llama* book Callie used to make us read a hundred times a day," I pulled back as Johnny yanked her arms.

She smiled weakly at me, knowing. "*Mama llama is always near,*" she said.

"*Even if I'm not right here,*" we said in unison as Johnny threw her to the ground like a discarded fast-food wrapper, hustling me toward the boat.

"You are my heart," she called to me. "I love you."

"I love you," I said, wondering why, if I was her heart, she sent me away.

Dad and I walked toward the boat with Danny Bird closing in behind us. I twisted back for one last look at Mom, at Pluto Cove, a glimpse of Callie in the window, of Benji tied to his tree. But all I could see was the thick red fur of Danny Bird's bear coat

I LOOKED FOR the green-eyed boy. Six men – or, rather, boys on the brink of becoming men – rowed the boat swiftly out of the cove. They were mechanical, automated. None acknowledged Dad or me. No turning of heads, no shifting in their seats, not so much as a scratch on the cheek or rub of an eye.

"Faster!" Danny Bird shouted, smacking the top

of one boy's head with the back of his hand. "Faster, you idiots!"

There was a small space at the stern where Danny Bird directed. As the boat glided out of the cove, I tried to angle myself to see to see Mom – whom I knew would stand at the lip of the water for as long as her own body and Callie and mother nature would allow. She would stand there until Callie cried of hunger, her own body crippled in thirst, or until the tide rose and swallowed her whole.

But I could not see her. Without a word, Danny Bird stood before me and brought a cloth over my head, an old shirt, and cinched it tight at the back. The world was dark, gone. "Dad!" I screamed.

"Danny Bird," Dad said, as a blindfold came over him as well. "Is this really necessary?"

"Yes," he said. "Of course it is."

I scooted closer to Dad, zipping up the space between our bodies.

The blindfold was filthy and smelled of sweat, grease, rot, and vomit. I gagged inside it, choking on the smell as though it were a tangible thing.

"It's alright, mija," Dad whispered. "I've got you, okay?"

"Sì, papì," I said, blinking furiously, pushing back tears borne of fright and foul odor. I could have cried. No one would have seen it under the mask. But if I started, I could never reign it back.

How long did we row? I cannot really say. How does one measure time without seeing the passage of distance or the movement of light? It felt like a long time, too long a time, though I knew the distance fell within

163

what sound could travel across the mountain. We heard them from time to time. Their hammers, their guns. Mom and Dad speculated they set up camp at the mouth of the Qaneqiraluq River. Back when Pluto Cove was a retreat for us and not a shelter, we sometimes boated over to the river where it had carved a wide, flat beach with perfect stones for skipping. The river that came from the glacial jökulhlaup at the top of Lamplighter Mountain. I tried to trace those former journeys against our current path, but we could have been going anywhere.

When we stopped, it was not the jarring, scraping arrival of a boat onto land. It was a soft stop, and the boat rocked as people climbed out and pulled ropes. "Get 'em out," Danny Bird growled. Someone grabbed me by the arm and pulled me to standing. I immediately collapsed under the unsteadiness of the deck.

"Dad!" I shrieked, unable to right myself as a mess of arms grabbed at my torso. "Dad!"

"I'm here, mija" he called. "Estoy aquì."

Someone – or multiple people – hauled me up and escorted me in jolts to the side of the boat where they lifted me over the hull. I was on a solid platform. I could feel that. It was a dock. Wherever we were had a dock.

They marched me off the dock and onto the familiar grooves of a gravel beach. "Where are you, Dad?" I called out.

His voice came from close by. "I'm right in front of you, mija. Estoy aquì."

Light strained, muddy against the old fibers of the shirt. A whole sighted world was just beyond its grime. In that darkness, I swirled with panic. My breath filled the void space in the shirt, hot and afraid. Each inhale came faster and shallower than the last. I snapped my neck around and around like Benji shedding a collar, wanting to throw the shirt off my head. But men pinned my arms down on both sides, and it did nothing but spiral me deeper into my own frenzy.

"Dad…" I called out, but my voice shook and was too weak to overcome the sound of so many footsteps on gravel.

"Step," said a voice. A strange voice. It was a voice trying to sound harsher than it was, older than it was. I looked toward the source but saw nothing. What did he say? What did he want? "Step!" he commanded again.

With this, he dug deeper into my arm and yanked my body up. I tripped over a wooden step and then understood – we were on steps. I put one foot uncertainly in front of the other, feeling my way up the staircase the way one navigates to the kitchen in the middle of the night.

A door opened. I was pushed inside. The door closed and the shirt was ripped from my head.

I sucked down big, greedy gulps of air. My eyes strained against the sudden light of the room. Keith Bird stood in front of me, his face the mangled mirror of his brother's, pulling off Dad's blindfold. Dad, too, blinked hard and cast around the room looking for me. "Amor," he said, the relief and tenderness falling from his mouth like boulders tumbling down a mountain.

"He was shot," Keith Bird said, pushing Dad toward a table in the middle of the room. "An accident."

I gasped. There, in the middle of the room, was a wooden table with a single light bulb suspended above it.

On the table was a boy lying still as a gravestone. Without seeing his face, I knew it was the green-eyed boy. His right shoulder dripped blood so dark it was black. It pooled on the wood and slipped over the edge, slick and viscous as oil. "Oh my god," I whimpered. "Oh my god. Dad, is he … is he…?"

But at that moment the boy took a sharp, ripping breath and arched his back clear off the table, a fish gasping for water. Dad crossed the room in two steps and looked down at the body clinging to life. I stood near the door, too scared to approach death, afraid that his next spasm on the table might pull me down too.

Dad slid the backpack off his shoulders and rummaged through it. "Mija," he said. "You need to help me."

I was frozen, stuck to the wall like the splatter of a fly. My eyes fixated on the limp hand of the boy, a hand with no shape or muscle. It was gelatinous, his fingers spread out over the side of the table like spilled jam.

Dad looked up to see if I had moved. "Mija, I need you." He found what he needed from the pack: a plastic case of syringes, all different lengths and widths, with the inside cover lined by needles of different gauges. He pulled the biggest syringe and the longest, most terrifying needle – like a car antenna – and popped them together while rubbing vigorously with an alcohol swab. "Hold this," he said to me, his face glowing under the incandescent bulb.

I took several trembling steps toward him, keeping his body between me and the boy. I reached out and grabbed the syringe, every part of me shaking. Dad reached into his bag and pulled out a pair of scissors. He cut off the boy's bloody shirt and pulled it open like the cover of a book, exposing a skinny bronze torso, each rib articulated under the skin, the points of his hips jutting from his pelvis like icebergs in open water. Dad reached back to me and grabbed the syringe and in one swift, impossibly fast movement he plunged the needle into the boy's chest.

I screamed, leaping backward. Even Keith Bird gave a startled step back. Dad was calm, measured. He did not register our shock. He kept his attention on the boy, drawing the plunger back until it was simply an open syringe with a hollow needle descending into the boy's chest.

Then Dad bent down and placed his mouth over the syringe barrel and drew in a long breath, then coughed it out to the side as forcefully as he could, expelling every last molecule of air before going back to the syringe to inhale again. He did this over and over. It didn't make sense – he was taking air *out* of the boy, not doing CPR to put air in. But he did it so deliberately, so rhythmically, I did not doubt him. And nor, it seemed, did Keith Bird. He watched next to me, saying nothing, the unmarred side of his face contorted into a look of horror and sickness. For just a moment, the minor beast of Keith Bird was quiet and still. Human. From the tatters of his jeans, a pistol winked from his waistband.

And then, as Dad coughed up a lungful of air, the boy gave a squirm on the table. His hand wiggled, then flexed. He was coming to life. His sudden wheezes pierced the room, sounds of air moving fast and cold into his body. His eyes opened wide, the green glinting even in profile.

"Hello," Dad said in a voice clear and kind, bringing himself face to face with the boy. "My name is Dr. Alex Martinez. I am going to help you."

WE WERE IN a storage shed, spacious but stuffed to the ceiling with boxes, crates, and bags of provisions. Cracks in the walls gaped into open air; this was no structure suited for habitation. Someone hewed it in rush. Judging by the light seeping in through the roof, any amount of rain – however meager – would leak onto the floorboards, already warped and jacked. A thin wall separated our room from another, where a soft but steady whooshing, almost a vibration, emanated at our feet. With the boy breathing, I had time to take inventory of our lot.

"It's a pneumothorax," Dad said, turning toward me. "His lung collapsed."

"But why did you suck air out of him?" I asked. "Don't you need to put air in?"

He turned back to the boy and answered me while continuing his exam. "When a lung collapses, air gets trapped in the cavity between the lung and the chest wall, and the lung can't inflate. I had to pull the air out between that space so the lung could expand." He stood up straight and turned to Keith, intent and stern. "How did he get shot?"

Keith put his hands on his hips and rolled his shoulders back, resenting the shift in authority. The pale side of his face still had a tinge of green, but he appeared relieved that Dad's body blocked his view of the boy. "Dunno," he said. "He was out hunting and one'a the other guys thought he was a deer or somethin'."

"What kind of a gun?" Dad asked.

168

"Why do you care?" Keith challenged.

"It matters enormously with regards to the injury," he said, pulling latex gloves from his backpack.

"Dunno," Keith said again. "We got a lotta guns out here," he said, smiling cruelly.

"I don't have the tools here," Dad said. "The injury is too severe." The boy flinched on the table.

"He's our best hunter," Keith said. "Danny said under no circumstances is he to die. You understand that?"

Dad pulled at the dressings haphazardly stuffed into the boy's wound, saturated and sticky with blood. "Keith," he said. "I am going to need you to don a pair of gloves and come over here to apply pressure to the subclavian artery."

"Huh?" Keith asked, startled, shifting uneasily to the right as though the weight of his scar listed him to one side like a sinking boat.

"The bullet seems to have grazed the subclavian artery. I need you to pinch it shut while I look at what other damage is here. Otherwise he's going to keep bleeding too heavily."

Keith swallowed hard. Even his shuttered eye seemed to twitch. He took a few steps toward the boy on the table. "Here," Dad said, peeling the gauze like the skin of an orange. "Once you get your gloves, I'll need you to pinch here, right where you can see the pulse."

I could not yet see what Keith saw, but it sent a profound shiver through his core. He pulled away from the body as though it were electrified and tripped on one of his own shoes. "That there is for a professional," he said. "That's best left to you. That's why we have you here."

"I'm going to need an –" Dad started.

"Here," Keith said, kicking over a large cardboard box from the corner. "Maybe this'll help. You do your thing." And he turned and lunged for the door. I heard him taking great swigs of air on the other side.

Dad stuffed the dressing back into the wound and patted the boy on his arm. "Mija," he said, turning toward me. "I need you. He needs you."

I held my breath and moved toward the table. "Put on some gloves and put pressure on this dressing," Dad directed. He opened the box that Keith kicked over. "Good lord," he whispered. He pulled out unopened packages of butterfly bandages and roller gauze, tourniquets, catheters, instant cold packs, bulb suctions, forceps, scissors, clamps, probing rods, and surgical blades. There was even dentistry equipment. Mouth mirrors and torque wrenches. He pulled out a pad of lined paper – what Mom would have done for such a treasure – and read from the letterhead *Nanwalek Clinic*.

"Nanwalek?" I said, startled to hear the name of a small Alutiiq village across the water from Homer, my hand shaking as it pinned the dressing where the boy's clavicle met his chest. "How?"

"I don't know," Dad said as he palpated the boy's foot for a vein and stuck the needle on his first try. From a splinter on the cabin wall he hung a yellow IV bag and set the clamp to a slow drip. "They must have looted the place."

Dad was somehow both excruciatingly slow and meticulous in laying out the instruments – but also so swift one might have thought he did this all the time:

repair a gun wound to the upper chest in a dimly lit cabin with an uneven floor and supplies plundered from a small community health center. Watching him, my shaking steadied and my breathing slowed. His calm and confidence began to overtake my fear and uncertainty. Keith Bird, that tough and wild animal, did not have the stomach for this. But I did.

There was no measuring the passage of time in that cabin. Through cracks in the walls and ceiling, the solstice sun cast never-ending shadows upon the boy. I reflexively thought of how a cabin so shoddily constructed would surely start to leak, of how many buckets would be needed under the roof to catch the drips of rain – until I remembered that it did not rain.

"For a bullet wound," Dad commented from under his surgical mask. "It could not have been more perfect."

"What do you mean?" I asked, not sure how this was possible. He had already collapsed a lung and was bleeding out more fluids than it appeared his small body could hold.

"Whatever gun they were using must have been poorly maintained," Dad said. "Rusted or something. It was a very slow bullet. Even though there's no exit wound and it stopped at his scapula, it barely tumbled around. It only grazed his subclavian artery but didn't sever it. Another millimeter and he might've bled out. Or lost his arm. It was to the right side, so it missed his heart. There are all sorts of ways this could have been much, much worse."

I nodded and looked at the boy. As Dad probed the wound, he moaned and wheezed. The left side of his body jerked and flopped, and his head thrashed. But he did not open his eyes. "He's in pain, Dad," I said, stating the desperately obvious but hoping that if I said it out loud a solution would materialize. Dad left all the narcotics back at Pluto Cove; he would never let anyone know but us, he would never use them on anyone but us. *You can control entire armies,* he once told me *with little white pills that promise escape from pain.*

"I know," he said, his lips tight. "There's nothing I can do for that. This is battlefield medicine."

And then the boy spoke. Just a whisper, quiet as rabbit hops over snow. "María," he said. "María."

Dad and I looked at each other. "Talk to him," Dad motioned. "Let him know he's not alone."

I stood across from Dad on the boy's uninjured side. "Hello," I said, placing a gloved hand on his left arm.

"María," he repeated, a little stronger.

"My name is Enna," I said softly next to his ear. From the depths of his injury and pain, my voice awoke something inside him. His head spun in my direction and his eyes flew open. He looked squarely at me, his green eyes blazing like the wilderness. His skin, drained of color, was a light brown that magnified the green like sun under glass.

"María Luna," he repeated, his voice breaking. "It's you."

I shook my head and looked at Dad in a panic. "It's okay," he affirmed. "Give him what he's needing."

I took a breath and looked back at the boy, into his eyes so desperate and scared and hungry. I placed my gloved hand into his, the bright blue of the latex tingling

172

with the cold of his skin. "Hi," I said. "It's me, María."

"María," he murmured, the trace of a smile flickering across his chapped lips, and he squeezed my hand. "Tell Mama," he said. "That I'm alright." He took a breath as Dad pulled a chunk of shoulder blade from the bullet hole, then sighed. "I'll be home soon."

DAYS PASSED INSIDE the shed. Someone opened the door and threw in rice gruel every few hours. Dad and I scarfed it like starving wolves and guzzled water from the jugs desperate as the dry forest floor itself. Angry, muffled conversations outside the door suggested we were being guarded. Dad made delicate efforts to rummage through the other boxes in the shed and found a pile of bedding to warm the boy. All matters of housewares overflowed from the boxes: dishware, cutlery, light bulbs, packing tape, sewing kits, rubber bands, coiled hoses, and clothes hangers. Any would have served a million uses back at Pluto Cove, but we dared not leave a single item out of place.

We alternated sleeping in the corner while the other kept watch over the boy. Sometimes he roused and whispered, *María*, before again descending into the vapors of his mind. Dad debrided the wound and packed it. We dribbled children's amoxicillin – bubble gum flavor – from the Nanwalek Clinic into his mouth every six hours. The risk of infection dictated every move: changing his dressing, checking for red streaks on his skin, for capillary refill in his fingers and fever across his forehead.

On the third night, the boy became lucid. Just for a few moments. I was on duty, funneling drips of water into his mouth when his eyes opened in a halting flutter.

173

"Who are you?" He whispered.

I looked at Dad sleeping on the floor in his filthy clothes. I didn't want to wake him. But the boy was more awake now and would see that I was not María.

"My name is Enna," I said.

"What happened?" He asked.

"You were out hunting and got shot," I said. "Do you remember?"

He took a moment to consider. "I don't think so," he replied. His voice was barely audible. I crouched to the level of his face at the table. "Is this a dream?"

Now I took a moment to consider. "I don't think so," I said. "I kinda wish it was."

He nodded slightly, then grimaced with the pain of movement. "Are you a good person?"

In normal times it was such a monstrous question, an impossible question, a question mulled by philosophers and savants over millennia. But these were not normal times, and I knew what he meant. There was a line now between good and bad that required no definition.

"Yes," I said. "I'm a good one. My dad's here and he's a doctor. He's taking care of you."

"Okay," the boy said weakly.

I had so many questions. A thousand. By the look on his face, he might fall back asleep any moment, so whatever I asked had to be good. It had to be big. But there was only one above the rest. "Who is María?"

He grimaced more deeply, ripe with pain. "My baby sister," he said.

"Oh," I said, realizing this caused him a certain agony for which I had no remedy. His sister could be anywhere, felled by any fate. So I said something small and meaningless just to keep talking. "I have a little sister, too."

"They told my parents they'd pay in food and water," he went on, his sentences gaining strength and complexity. "If I worked. They'd help my family if I worked. But they just took me." He cracked. Had there been any water to spare in that busted body he would have cried freely and hard. "But they took me. And now they don't give me food or water unless I work. They tell me I won't see my family again unless I work. But maybe María isn't even alive…" he trailed off into a place of terrible mourning.

I knew the answer. We all knew it. But I needed to hear it. "Who is *they*?" I asked. "Who took you?"

His eyes blazed. "The Birds."

"Where'd they take you from?"

"Kenai," he said. A bigger sized town on the peninsula, one that we drove through on our escape from the road system.

"They only give us water," he gasped, closing his eyes. "If we work."

"Who are they?" I asked, desperate. "Who are the Birds?"

"They're…" he started, his voice losing its urgency and strength. His eyelids quivered. "The Kittiwake Clan, who lost the Seldovia War…" he said, faltering.

The window was closing. He was going to slip away again. "What's your name?" I pleaded. He did not reply. I asked again. "What's your name?"

"María," he murmured, slipping back. "My

María."

"How old are you?" I urged.

He did not reply.

He was an impossibly skinny person when we arrived and wasted steadily by the hour. By the time Dad stitched the wound, satisfied the risk of infection had abated, the boy's skin looked translucent. His ribs were piano keys, and his cheeks arched as Roman aqueducts. Dad put his right arm into a sling that dangled from his side like the broken wing of a sparrow.

"We've done everything we can," Dad said, as he prepared to knock on the inside of the door.

"Is he going to live?" I asked, taking one last look at the boy, his eyes still closed but his breathing soft and steady.

Dad paused. Looked down at the floor. "The body is an extraordinary healer," he said. Then he knocked.

Keith Bird ripped open the door and forced his way inside. The blast of fresh air hit me like being plunged into clear, cold water. I had not realized how warm, how confining, how much the shed reeked of sickness and death. "About fucking time," he said. "Are you done?" he closed the door on its rope hinges with a thud.

"Yes," Dad said with certainty. "It is up to you now to feed him and get him enough water."

"Hmph," Keith Bird gruffed, tossing the suggestion aside like rancid meat. Still, he would not bring himself to look at the boy. He angled his bad side – the eye burned shut – toward the boy and spun the remaining pupil toward us. "Put these back on." He handed us the same black t-shirts we wore on the way in.

I looked to Dad and he nodded softly. I gulped hard for the smells that awaited, but having the agency to put in on myself, to have some warning, helped.

"He's not awake," Keith Bird said as I donned the headcover.

"He will be sleeping for several more days," Dad said, his voice muffled under the cover. "Food and drink will help. But he'll need lots of rest, especially on his shoulder and arm."

"Like hell," Keith Bird growled. "We need him back out getting goats."

I could not see the boy, but suddenly I heard him again. Perhaps it was the sound of Keith's voice or the blast of light and fresh air as the door opened. He screamed. Not the faint, soft whimpers of the last three days, but full, ripping, electrifying screams that shot up and down my spine and crawled over my skull like centipedes.

"What the fuck is he doing?" Keith Bird demanded.

"It's fine," Dad said, betraying his hesitation – of wondering if it would be more humane to let the boy die. "It means his lungs are working again."

We marched down the beach to the sounds of those screams. Summer wind brushed the skin on my hands, flushed and reactive after the barricade. There was a steady drumbeat in my ears, the fear that there was no returning to Pluto Cove, that they had no motivation to take us back, that they would dump us out in open water or take us to a hidden prison in the mountains. But to my surprise, the drumbeat was soft. It did not thrum in my ears. It did not hammer at my heart. It was there, but it was bearable. It was familiar. It connected me to a piece of myself unknown. The piece of myself anchored in something deep and strong, anchored in a million stories of people in fear before me, the piece of myself that knew, at its core: it's going to be okay. Even in death.

But we did not walk the plank. We did not waste in a mountain prison. They dumped us at Pluto Cove and pulled off toward their fortress before Dad and I could unwind the t-shirts from our heads. We took off running toward the cabin, still there, still intact, the same in all its smallness and isolation and worry, and I had never been so heartbreakingly happy to be anywhere on earth.

Mom and Callie tore from the cabin like animals set free from a cage. Benji sprinted down the gravel, his feet barely touching the ground. We collided into each other in piles of limbs and hair, gasps and sobs. Mom kissed me all over my face until my skin turned hot, and Callie grabbed so hard at my legs that I lost my balance. When I toppled over, we all toppled over. Benji licked at me and pounced at my chest. Something flooded through me like the breaking of a long-dammed river, something more nourishing than food, more refreshing than water, more comforting than the sound of rain on the roof. I let it wash over my bones, and let myself feel, for just a moment, that this was all there was. A place to call home.

MOM SHOT A canvasback duck and fed it to us, roasted and sweetened with canned peaches. It was a round, plump bird whose fat emulsified into the sugars, and I let the sticky grease coat my teeth before swallowing. We sat on the beach and watched light bounce on the water, as greedy for air and daylight as we were for food.

We did not speak of the fortress or the boy. I wanted to tell Mom everything – and knew Dad did too – but the words were not yet ripe. Images and sensations tumbled around like driftwood in the tide, not having consolidated into something real. Mom seemed afraid to ask, but she did venture one question.

"How old do you think he was?" she asked softly as I ate well past the point of stuffed.

"Fifteen or sixteen," Dad replied solemnly but still chewing. "Enna's age."

It startled me to hear my age spoken. Two birthdays had come and gone at Pluto Cove without fanfare. Everything stood still, but somehow, I got older.

Dad swallowed his bite, then reached into his pocket. "Brought this back for you, Lisa," he said. He pulled out a small notepad with *Nanwalek Clinic* stationary. "Some paper."

"Alex!" She exclaimed, in delight and dismay. A previous version of myself would have been shocked. *Dad doesn't steal,* that voice would say. But nothing disappointed me anymore.

He reached into his front pocket and dug around for a thin ballpoint pen with the Nanwalek Clinic phone number. "This too."

Mom shook her head, her neck stiff from the pistol whip, her hairline black and purple, crusted with blood. But she smiled.

He pulled off the cap and scribbled onto the paper. I craned my head but couldn't see over the ruff of Benji's fur. He had not permitted me more than an arm's length away. "I better write this down before I forget,"

Dad said.

"Write what?" Callie asked, angling for a peek.

Over Benji's shoulder I saw Dad was not writing at all. He drew a picture, a map. "Here's what I think I saw," he said, casting long lines down the page as he sketched the outlet of the Qaneqiraluq River.

"But Dad?" I asked, my mouth thick with duck fat. "How? They had us blindfolded." Mom visibly shuddered at the word.

"On the way out," Dad said, "one of the guys escorting me let my hood slip. Or maybe he even pulled it down. Just a corner of my right eye. But I could see a bit. It was like he wanted me to see." He drew boxes representing the cabins and outbuildings that I had completely missed. "And there were a few cracks in our shed where I could see out. Not much, but a little. I took glances whenever I could."

I felt so foolish. I had been there too, in the same place, and gathered no intelligence.

"This is where we were," Dad said. "The storage shed. But it was more than a shed, it was *big*. Had a lot of stuff in it, some essential and some totally random stuff. Like a pile of bike handlebars. We were about a hundred feet from the river. Up the river were a few big cabins, where I saw Keith and Johnny come and go." He sketched in a palatial looking home. "To the west were several small structures that looked like bunkhouses – for their workers, I think." He shot a Mom a sideways glance at the word *workers*. "Boys were out clearing the slope on the east side of the river. There must be a bridge somewhere, but I didn't see it. Over here was a timber pile, these huge, downed trees. And here," Dad said, circling a

180

nondescript square in the middle of the page. "This one had a whole mess of wires coming out of it that went to all the bigger cabins. They must be generating power in this one."

"But how?" Mom said. "It's not near the river so it's not current powered. Was it wind? If they had a generator, the fuel would've gone bad by now."

"When we were walking by it on the way out," Dad mused. "There was a humming sound coming out of it. A spinning sound. I couldn't quite place it."

I knew the sound. I heard it while trying to sleep in the corner. At first it sounded like insect wings, and I willed it to lull me to sleep – until I realized it was nothing at all like insect wings. It was mechanical but irregular. It went fast for a while and then slowed down. It skipped moments all together. It was a vaguely familiar sound, but I could not identify it until Dad mentioned it back at Pluto Cove.

"It was bikes," I said. "That sound. It was stationary bikes."

Mom and Dad titled their heads in unison. "Enna, I think you're right," Dad said.

"Wow," Mom said in awe. "They are generating power with humans pedaling bikes."

"I think so," I said. "Mom, it's just like your turbines. But instead of being spun by a current or by the wind, it's by feet."

She wanted to feel pride in me, but was overwhelmed by the information coming in. Barring any other meaningful comment, she said, "That is super inefficient."

"Obviously it's solstice now, so their electricity

needs are probably lower," Dad said. "But they had some huge spotlights around the place. Like those light plants road maintenance workers use in the dark. In the winter, their electric demands must be through the roof."

"Yeah…" Mom whispered, elsewhere in her mind.

"They also have little scoping stations up in trees," he said. "Little platforms or treehouses. Lookouts."

"Daddy," Callie asked. "Were there any girls over there?"

Dad looked at Mom, who tried to meet his gaze without it being an alarming gesture. "I think so," he said. "I heard some voices that sounded like girl voices. But I never saw any outside walking around."

"Oh," Callie said, disappointed for the wrong reasons. I had lost a formidable chunk of standard education but knew the implications of this gender ratio. Without females, the Bird Fortress was a temporary camp, a moment captured in time – not an emerging city rising from the river plain to become a perpetuating civilization. From what we knew of the Birds and what they built, they would settle for nothing less.

"Pluto Cove is a narrow beach," Dad said, picking up the thread running through my mind. "Just a little thumbnail. Where they are is massive. It's where the Qaneqiraluq River comes out and has cleared everything for more than a mile. It's flat and open. It's absolutely huge."

"But it's a river plain," Mom said, rubbing so vigorously at her triceps the skin went red and thin. "Which means it floods."

"Sure," Dad said. "If the rain ever came back."

That night I crawled into bed flushed with gratitude. The old sheets, the thinning blanket, the view of serrated mountains from the porthole. I loved it all. My bones sunk into the lumpy mattress, and I pulled Benji in so close that his heartbeat fluttered inside my stomach. But for all the relaxation and relief, sleep did not come. I lay awake, thinking about the green-eyed boy. About his parents giving him willingly to the Birds in exchange for food. About María Luna. I thought about our trek over the mountains to the mainland, about running away from this place. About how leaving the cove meant leaving behind captives at the Bird Fortress: the boys and young men and, somewhere, the girls.

I heard rustling under the loft. Mom and Dad couldn't sleep either. I rolled over and peered over the edge, expecting to see them at the kitchen table talking over a plan or a fear or some terrible unknown. But they weren't at the table. They weren't speaking at all. They stood in the middle of the living room floor, holding each other close, swaying back and forth. I strained my ears and heard it: Dad softly humming a song into her ear. They were dancing.

CHAPTER FIVE - *Three Months Later*

Where there is drought, there is fire. And in the Polar Storms, with the globe tyrannized by prolonged, sustained drought, we were all at the mercy of fire.

I could draw you a map of the world from memory, but it would not do justice to the size of these fires that swallowed our small gem of a planet. Millions of acres burned in Siberia, so much that the smoke dispersed across the entire northern hemisphere and not a soul from Nebraska to Ukraine could draw a breath without inhaling shards of tundra shrubs from that faraway place.

The Amazon burned from Bolivia to Suriname and coated both Pacific and Atlantic oceans in undulating films of ash. A fire in the Congo Basin drove herds of elephants into villages and settlements, fleeing the fires by stampede. Drone footage of the Sumatra Rainforest showed a blurry inferno dominated by the sound of snaps, fizzles, and explosions as the moisture trapped in plants steamed up and burst like popcorn.

A fire is only as good as its fuel, people said. *The fuel can't last forever.*

But there was so, so much fuel.

Armies were dispatched to fortify the great urban centers of the world using a blood-red powder by the ominous name of BOM – a solid-state form of butyllithium oxalyl-hexabromide methacrolein – a chemical fire retardant that did not require water to activate. It coated the shrines of Kyoto to the cobblestone streets of Amsterdam to the fabric tents of the Onitsha market. BOM was a teratogen that caused perilously low birthweights and an increase in cleft palate deformities. But this was deemed an acceptable trade-off for the preservation of population centers. Pregnant women of means sought refuge in BOM shelters, which provided quiet relief from exposure to the red dust as well as a calming space in tumultuous times.

Humans caused some of the fires: cookstoves, bonfires, firecrackers, garbage heaps, and discarded cigarette butts. Bombs and gunfire. Trains sparking as they came to a stop, or airplanes sparking as they landed. Nature caused some of the fires, too: lightning, black kite birds, and, as the drought intensified, spontaneous combustion of profoundly dry materials like wood chips, sawdust, or leaves.

In Sub-Saharan Africa, the World Health Organization proudly declared an eradication of malaria. Mosquito habitat dried up and burned. It may have been a victory had there not been so many defeats.

In Alaska, virgin forests blazed like hell itself. In the summer before our escape, forest fires raged to the north, east, and south of Anchorage, turning the air thick, sticky, and yellow. Our eyes burned against the smoke. Our lungs heaved. No one dared to go outside or even open their windows. Summer camps were canceled. Businesses shuttered their doors. Lines for HEPA-filters queued from the comfort of people's vehicles and extended for miles down the street when a barge shipment came in. The world was yellow, hazy, blurred at the edges like a sepia photo. The city was so quiet on the smoky days, not even songbirds could sing.

Remember how I told you there were satellite

photos showing our earth in crystal relief with the only clouds gathered at the poles? How, for the first time, astronauts could see every feature on earth simultaneously, without waiting for a storm to pass? This wasn't the case in the fire days – the days leading up to that November election, the days leading up to our escape. Satellite imagery then showed a planetary Christmas tree of flames. As light waned up and down the Americas, the photos lit up from the boreal fires of Canada to the jungle fires of Costa Rica to the plains fires of Argentina. The only places not on fire were the oceans.

Geologists said it heralded a new epoch of the earth's history: the Pyrocene. Codified forever in the earth's history by layers of ash, like a bookmark, in the planet's crust.

It was a sepia-toned day, a yellow day as autumn approached, that Callie disappeared.

There was a fire somewhere nearby – smoke lodged in our throats like unchewed food, but it was not visible from our small view of the world. Few things were. Mom and Dad started cutting a wide clearing of trees around the cabin so that any approaching fire would run out of fuel before reaching our home. The fire could have been hundreds of miles from us, but there was no way to be sure. All we had were smoke signals. Mom hauled branches and trunks until her hands bled and knees buckled. If she slept, it was between the hours of my own sleep. If she ate, it was from a secret food source. I suspected she did neither. All she did was work. Not the mindful, creative work of our early months at Pluto Cove that tied together our resources and trash into renewable assets. It was manic work, masochistic work. All she talked about was fire. All she consumed was smoke.

Dad tried to assuage her. "We will be safe if there is a fire," he said late one night, coercing her to bed. "We will head toward the ocean. We will be okay there."

"But the cabin won't," she asserted, holding the axe against the bony protuberance of her hip.

"We can rebuild the cabin," he said. "We can evacuate all of our tools and belongings down to the water. We can rebuild."

"You make it sound so easy," she dripped. "Like the water isn't two degrees above freezing."

He knew he was wrong. The evacuation he described was a week of labor – not a rapid response to an approaching fire. But he saw, as I did, that Mom was sick. She was working herself to death. Her mind spun and reeled, ever downward, and she brutalized her body so systematically it frightened me to see her willingly, wittingly, disappearing.

Finally, Dad said, with more sadness than any one person could convey to their loved one, "There are a lot of ways to die out here. We don't have to do it to ourselves."

Mom gave a long, pained look and set down her axe to come inside. To rest her body. To calm Dad's mind.

Except that she would not rest that night. We came in for supper to a bouquet of fresh cut flowers Callie had gathered and assembled into a glass jar. "What is this?" Mom demanded.

Callie, taken aback by the rocks in Mom's tone, nevertheless stepped forward with pride. "I made them for you, Mama. Something beautiful to have in the cabin."

"Callie," Mom said, slowly turning to face her.

"Where did you get these flowers?"

Callie paled, confused, not understanding why Mom was angry over something as beautiful and benign as a bouquet of flowers from a six-year-old. But I saw it right away. The bright orange flowers like tangerine starbursts. "Umm…" Callie said.

"Did these come from the greenhouse?" Mom demanded, her voice rising to a near shout. "Were these from the greenhouse?"

"Y-y-yes," Callie blubbered, beginning to cry.

"Callie!" Mom yelled in rage. "Callie! Those are squash blossoms! Those were going to turn into food! A lot of food! How many zucchini and pumpkin did you just kill? Huh? How many?!"

Callie fell to the floor, sobbing. Dad and I stood immobile, transfixed. Mom became depressed. Mom became quiet. But Mom never became explosive. She never erupted at her youngest daughter, cowering on the floor. But she could not stop. It erupted from her like magma in a fissure – all her frustrations and anger coming out on the one person who could least understand it, let alone mitigate it.

"Get her out of here!" Mom screamed at Dad, pointing toward the door. "Get her OUT!"

Dad did not wait. He scooped Callie up into his arms. I ran to hold the door open and hurried out after them. I closed it tightly, but that did not stop the sound of Mom's screams from following us as we ran toward the beach.

"I am not ill!" She screamed at no one. "I am not a freak!"

"It's okay, Cal," Dad said, holding her tight, stroking her braid down her back. "It's okay. You're not

189

in trouble. You're okay. It's okay."

Callie squirmed out of his grasp, pushing him away, and lunged toward me. I took her into my arms and felt her sobs into my shirt. And I started to cry, too. Onto the top of her head, into her hair. It had been nearly two years since I had cried. But now it seized me. Like a burglar who has been lurking in the closet all along, it pounced and did not let go. Her cries rattled the tears out of me like coins from a piggy bank. Smoke burned my throat with each gasp. Benji whimpered at my feet as I lowered the two of us to the ground where I did not have to hold us upright.

We fell asleep wrapped up in each other on the beach. When I awoke in the middle of the night, a colorful, smoky dusk shone weakly over the mountains as the sun descended and the earth slowly turned us away from its light. We huddled in a pile of blankets and Dad lay next to us, staring up at the stars poking their way through the twilight sky, his eyes wide open and full of sorrow.

"Dad," I whispered.

He jerked his head, too accustomed to a world where being startled meant being terrified. "Enna," he whispered back, looking at Callie where she nestled into me. "Go back to sleep."

"I don't know if I can," I said.

"I get that," he acknowledged, turning his gaze back toward the sky.

"Dad?" I asked softly.

"¿Sì, mija?" he replied.

"Can I use you as a pillow?"

He smiled. "Sì, mija." He scooted closer toward

me and angled his body so that I could rest my head upon his belly. It was barely softer than the beach rocks, but at least it was alive, warm, breathing. "Enna," he said.

"Yeah, Dad?"

"Can I tell you something?"

This was unusual. Dad was not a gossip. Not a revealer of secrets. What secrets could we hold from each other in this place? It must have to do with Mom. Dad felt something deeper than loneliness to need to confide in me. "Yes."

He paused, wondering if it may be too late to walk back his words.

"I think Mom might be pregnant."

"What?!" I exclaimed, then reflexively put my hands over Callie's ears to insulate her from the intrusion. "What?" I repeated, more softly, but still as full of bewilderment and shock, unable and unwilling to process how this happened.

"Yeah," he whispered sadly, helplessly. "She hasn't said it explicitly, but I think she suspects. And I think she's been trying to self-abort by overworking herself."

"Oh my god," I said, watching as a million new stars burst through the dwindling light, overwhelming me, pushing down on me, oppressive in their brightness and their allure of another world. "What are we gonna do?" I pleaded.

"I don't know, Enna," he said.

There were so many exclamations, so many questions, so many accusations whirling in my head. So many that they cancelled each other out into a dull, persistent white noise. At the bottom of it was just one small, empty statement. "I'm sorry, Dad."

"You have nothing to be sorry for," he said firmly. "I don't ever want to hear that from you about any of this."

"Okay," I said "But I am." And I was. There were photos of Mom and Dad in our old house, photos of them young, radiant, and oozing a happiness almost tangible in the glossy ink. These were people in control of their futures, and those futures were good. Stable. Plentiful.

Lying there on the beach with Dad, Callie and Benji, I realized my young age was an asset. For all I had left behind in Anchorage, it was a fraction of what Mom and Dad had abandoned. For as many dreams and goals and ambitions as I had, most of them ended with soccer scores, test results, and school dances. Mom and Dad had more than dreams or ambitions – they had an expectation, a confidence – that they would lead secure, contented lives, and raise me and Callie in the same way. For me, Pluto Cove was a change. For them, it was a failure. I did not fault them. Or blame them. Or resent them. I just felt so, so sorry for them.

The next day we tiptoed around Mom – Callie did not dare enter the cabin. Instead, she made flower patterns from rocks in the gravel by the outhouse. Dad suggested she and I go out blueberry picking with the sandcastle bucket, something for us to do away from the cabin, something to help Callie feel redemptive and useful, while he sat with Mom and struggled to convince her of his unconditional love.

The air hung smoky, hazy that morning. Visibility was low. But the berries, in patches where we had diligently delivered water to their roots, were abundant.

"I wonder if Mom's okay," Callie asked as we sat together, picking the bush clean from different sides.

"She is," I said, thinking that there could be a baby squirming in her starving belly and that she was very far from okay. "Just give it time."

"Sometimes I think she's just so brilliant that her brain doesn't know what to do with it all," she said.

I rolled my eyes. This was a generous assessment. "Sure," I said. "Maybe."

"If we were in *Little Women*, I'd be Beth," she mused to herself as the drop of each berry plunked dully into her bucket.

"Like the movie?" I asked.

"No," she said. "The book. I think it's my favorite."

"Maybe I can read it to you someday," I offered.

"That'd be nice. But I already finished."

"Okay," I shrugged. Little kids and their fibs.

"And you are Jo."

"Is that right?"

"Yes."

"Well, at least she had Laurie to hang out with when she was stuck at home. She was never lonely." I paused, running my fingers over the leaves. "And her mom wasn't crazy."

"That's why you're Jo," Callie sighed. "Like what Laurie said, *Don't spoil so many good gifts because you can't have the one you want*."

The words were nonsense from the mouth of a child. She might as well have made animal noises. But she'd had a hard night, so I smiled out of the corner of my mouth and said, "Okay, Cal."

We filled the bucket. We readied to head down the hill when Callie saw one more bush teeming with glittering blueberries, like topaz jewels, and stopped to top off, hoping that a good haul – not only filling the bucket, but overflowing it – would earn Mom's forgiveness. And when I looked back, she was gone.

I CALLED HER NAME, louder and louder. I went from annoyed, to thinking she was playing a joke, to pure panic. I could see the bush, the one with all the berries, the one where she had just been standing. Her bare feet were too tiny and light to leave prints in the dirt. Everywhere I looked I saw branches moving around the shape of her body, heat traces of where she had just stood and where the air was still warm. With every cell in my lungs I pulled in a breath and screamed, bloody and ugly, "CALLIE!" But not even the forest replied.

I took off running to the cabin, my feet skimming the ground as gravity and hysteria propelled me down the hill. I ripped open the front door where Dad knelt in front of Mom. She sat on the couch with her head in her hands. Benji curled up at her feet, sleeping off the unrest of the night before. "Callie's gone," I gasped, struggling to form the words as tremors overtook my lips, tongue, face, hands, body. "Callie's gone."

"What do you mean?" Dad asked, jumping to standing and making for the door.

Before I could answer, Mom cried out. "It's my fault! I scared her!"

"We were berry picking," I said, crying. "We were berry picking, and when I looked over, she was gone!"

"What do you mean?" Dad repeated.

"It's my fault!" Mom repeated.

"Come on," I said, pulling Dad's arm toward the door. "We gotta find her. We gotta find her."

The forest grew a million times as I led them toward the berry patch. The trees had never been so dense or so tall. The green and gray and brown of the plants and earth had never been so impenetrable, so swirling and indecipherable. It bore down on me like a gathering wave. We called Callie's name. We yelled her name. We screamed her name. We split up and combed the slopes of the mountain. We formed a daisy chain and linked arms so that no square inch of ground went unexamined. We dropped to the ground and down pressed our ears to hear something, anything. We gazed out sideways across the forest floor to see what the mice see. We followed Benji as he paced and barked, but he took us only in circles back to the berry patch.

"We had a bucket," I said. "The sandcastle one. It was full of berries. It has to be around here somewhere."

No one said anything except for the calling of her name.

I took Callie to the berry patch in midmorning. Now, I walked Lamplighter Mountain all night and into the next day. I walked until my vision blurred like water poured on wet paint. I walked until my body could remember no other motion. I called out her name until it felt foreign and absurd in my mouth, an assemblage of sounds devoid of meaning or attachment to any person or thing. I called out her name until my voice receded into the deepest tunnels of my throat, where it came out hoarse and alien sounding.

When do you stop searching a forest that has no

end? When do you give up and try to sleep? When do you say that the universe opened into a bottomless pit, edged with teeth and halitosis, and swallowed a child? When do you surrender the brain and body of a little girl to the unknowable forces of the world that only ever act in cruelty?

For Mom, the answer was never.

I found three more of Great-grandpa's old mining trails, hacked out by a machete, the stumps of trees smoothed over where new growth took hold. Maybe Callie had started the walk, the escape from this place – the journey we were weeks away from embarking upon. Two of his old trails merged and dead-ended at a shale cliff. Another trail led across a ridge to an old shaft blasted into the mountainside. I pulled aside the devil's club and pushkie grown over the entrance, caring not a moment for the pricks and stabs of their leaves and stems. The shaft was cool and wet, breaking open into a cavern. I called out her name. It echoed back into my ears. I briefly thought someone had answered me. I called out her name again just for the echo, just for the company.

I pushed deeper into the mine shaft until all light vanished save for slivers flashing through the smoke and plants behind me. I raised my hands in front of my eyes, but there was nothing to see but darkness. I looked down to my feet, but there was only black. I had no body, no form, no presence. I diffused into the darkness, disappearing and mixing like salt mixed into water. I would dissolve into nothing. And it would feel so good.

Which is when I heard Dad calling my name. His voice. Far away. Familiar, caring, strong in the face of everything. I could not disappear into the darkness. For his sake.

I felt my way out of the tunnel, following the thin beams of light, brushing the edges of rock so I did not stumble into oblivion. Then I felt something that was not rock. It was hard, but smooth. Round. Cylinders stacked atop one another. I worked my hands over the edges and contours to draw a picture in my mind. It was a stack of something bundled together, bound by ropes. It was nothing I had ever felt before. There was no reference for it in my tactile memory. But I knew what it was. Only one thing had such a shape. A thing of Sunday morning cartoons and the cut-and-paste word art next to the hardest questions on Miss Ritter's math tests. It was dynamite.

I took a breath with my hand on the sticks. Dad called my name again, a rope descending into a well where I had fallen. I left the cave, crossed the ridge, and found him. I said nothing of the dynamite. We continued our search.

SOMEHOW I ENDED up at the cabin with Benji at my side, collapsed in front of the fireplace although no fire burned. That was the place where Callie spent her days and nights at Pluto Cove, there in front of the fire, tending to it with all the meticulousness and care her small hands could muster. The Little Match Girl. If there was any place on earth where she might spontaneously materialize from thin air, the fireplace seemed likely.

I woke up to Dad placing a plate of fried cod in front of me, hoping the smell would lure me to consciousness. It did. "You need to eat," he offered, sliding the plate under my face. "You gotta eat."

I pushed myself up onto my elbow and squinted into the cabin, trying to ascertain the time. It could be anything. Midday. Middle of the night. Evening. "Where's Mom?" I asked groggily, half hoping the entire ordeal had been a delirium borne by fever or pathogen.

"Still out looking," he said, turning toward the sink so his back was to me.

I scooped up a fingerful of the fall-apart fish and brought it to my lips. My mouth would not open. The smell was overwhelming, repugnant. Hunger oozed out of my skin and stank in my mouth, but the thought of food was worse. I dangled it in front of Benji, who swallowed it whole.

"When is she coming back?" I asked.

"I don't know," he said, still not looking at me. "She went out on the boat to see if there was any sign of her from the water."

That leaky, sea-shaky boat. Mom out in it. "Is she ever going to come back?" I asked.

Dad was quiet.

I laid back down on the floor, curling around Benji. I looked at the cabin from the view of the wooden planks, examining every splintered board, every grooved track worn by footsteps, and every dust mite and hair clump gathered in a corner. I could see under the couch where Callie stored her stack of books and dolls. *The Giver*. *The Adventures of Huckleberry Finn*. *Holes*. An American Girl doll with a backstory from the Revolutionary War. A Barbie who came packaged as a doctor but who long ago lost her doctor-identifying pieces: lab coat, stethoscope, and clipboard. A crochet doll with brown braided hair that Mom crafted on the advice of her therapist as a way of physically engaging with the world. It was a terribly ugly doll, its features disturbingly out of proportion. Callie loved on that doll until it was worn down and floppy, somehow even uglier than before.

I tucked my chin into my chest, driving it into my ribs, hoping that if I pressed in hard enough my body cavity would simply yield and swallow me into it, a snake eating its tail. But no matter how small I curled, nothing took me off that floor, out of the cabin, away from Callie's relics, her smells and her errant hairs stuck to the brush. Benji pressed himself into me, sensing my distress. But even he, my partner in all things, served as a reminder that he was a furry, slobbering, nonverbal animal who was not my sister or the same species as my sister and could never replace her.

It felt as though my insides had been carved out by a spoon. Whereas before I had pulsed with a mosaic of blood and plasma and lymph – whereas before the thrum of my heart and slow churning of my belly made music and rhythm inside of me – now, there was nothing. An ocean whose reefs had turned to skeleton stone and all life had gone extinct.

I stayed on the floor longer than I can say. Benji anchored himself to my side and nuzzled my neck with his sticky nose that I had no energy to wipe away. Sometime later I fell asleep. Sometime after that I woke to the sound of Mom, far away, calling Callie's name. Her voice was deep and desperate, the song of a baleen whale in a hundred fathoms of water, calling out for her calf, slow, mournful, and haunted.

Every day Mom searched for Callie, covering the same terrain again and again. I wondered if she would find Great-grandpa's old mining shafts, if she would find the dynamite. If she did, she never said anything. Then again, neither did I.

Even as she spent her days up in the mountains and out in the boat, even as the air grew biting and cold, and the wind blew in from the south with fury and ire, even as our window for leaving Pluto Cove over land shrunk and closed in the menacing fist of winter, I watched her belly grow a little rounder, a little tauter. At night, Dad fed her fish and vegetables – sometimes by hand – coaxing her to open her mouth like a child. She did not want to eat. She did not want this new baby to survive. She wanted only Callie. Her suffering was endless. No physical creature should experience pain of that magnitude. Any merciful god would have installed a kill switch, an automatic shut-off, an overfill alarm. Some mechanism to detect and plug the threshold of suffering. But not only did she experience the pain but was forced to endure it – day after day after day.

Dad dug out a pair of ear plugs from the toolbox and gave them to me. I asked why. He said for sleeping. Lying in bed, listening to Mom sob below me, I understood. I shoved them into my ear drums as deep as they could go.

He wanted to collapse, that was clear. He buckled under the weight of his grief. His posture stooped – this tall, proud man – like a shelf sagging under too many books. His brown skin paled. The sclera of his eyes yellowed. I knew the dynamic between him and Mom, the unwritten code, the habits they followed and had no means of defying: only one person could break down at a time. When Grandma Julienna died, Mom did everything for him as he grieved. When Mom had her episodes, he rose up. When Dad lost a child in his care or was passed up for a promotion with words like *not a good fit*, Mom took the reins. It was an exchange, a balance. It had always worked for them. But they had never truly grieved at the same time.

He waited for any sign of strength from her, any source of light, any indication that it was safe for him to confess his sorrow. Some whisper of stability that, were he to express vulnerability, she would not tumble deeper into the crater Callie's asteroid had blasted. But that sign never came. Like the book of Greek mythology I read waiting for sleep to come, he was Orpheus, scouring the layers of the underworld to save his Euridice, to pull her back to life. But she did not want to follow him to the surface, and he stayed there alone, calling down into Persephone's clutch of damned souls.

He went out on the searches. Not for hope of finding Callie – by now the sky was pasty and frozen, the earth hard and dead – but to keep watch over Mom. To make sure she did not throw herself over a cliff or into icy water. To stop her from crawling into the den of a hibernating bear, or simply lying down in a place we could not find her. These were the fates she desired. Dad and I were not enough to make her want to live, just as we hadn't been when I was six.

They scarcely noticed me. Dad murmured appreciation for my meals of overcooked rice and gamey ptarmigan breast. Occasionally Mom reached out from where she sat and grabbed me like an awakened mummy

– squeezing me eerily hard without a word, then letting me go as though nothing ever happened. But she would not look at me.

MY OWN SEARCHES for Callie took Benji and me to the furthest reaches of Lamplighter Mountain. Cliff faces undulated in shapes and patterns like the carvings of ancient giants. Meadows slashed by game trails crisscrossed the dried grass like scoring on fresh bread. My legs grew long and skilled at navigating the forest floor, dodging the eye-level branches, taking wide strides over burrows, and jumping from hummock to hummock. I carried little but a pack for water, a fixed-blade machete, and a 30-30 Winchester that slapped my back as I ran. My quadriceps and hamstrings grew dense and reactive. From the too-short hems in my pants, veins popped from my calves. It was a level of fitness I had only seen in posters of sports heroes – but at the expense of endless climbing up slopes, and bounding back down them, for a sister whom I could not find.

Over a knob of Lamplighter Mountain, I wandered into a scarred gash of burned trees, a ghost forest – a fire far closer to us than we had known – blocked from Pluto Cove by a steep ravine. Blackened, charred trees loomed over me like tombstones. An unsettling quiet bore into my bones as Benji stuck close to my heels. There was no Callie here, I knew, but something lured into the ruins. The stillness, the proximity to something so destructive, it whispered my name. *Enna*. Benji whinnied, urging me out of the scorched forest. But there at the base of the trees, I saw morels. Mushrooms. Clustered like candles at a shrine, their caps the same etched black as the tree bark around them.

I stuffed my pack, stuffed my pockets, even lined the edges of my socks, yanking them from the ground. If I returned the next week or even the next day, the ephemeral mushrooms could be gone. It had to be now. Greed surged through me. *Enna.* But then the forest trembled, rumbled. An earthquake? Harder, and harder. Branches crashed to the forest floor – the tops of trees tore from their trunks and landed with explosions of soot around me. Benji squealed, and I put my body over him, huddling down, covering my head with my hands. It was no earthquake – it was a windstorm ripping through this decimated ecosystem, bringing down burnt limbs and branches like landmines detonating in a forbidden land.

"It's okay, Benji," I whispered, shaking. "It'll be over soon."

At a break in the wind, we sprinted from the phantom forest, my arms shielding my head, morels flying out of my pack, my pockets, and my socks. Without Benji's fear, I would have stayed in that forest, felt the ripping apart of the air as trees crashed down, watched their decapitated pieces land inches from my head. Like George trundling up the porch steps, it was a fear that felt alive. Grounded. Rooted in something real. All my life was consumed by threats unseen – but this was real and present danger. It bewitched me. *Enna.*

Later that week I conducted another search, going up, up, nothing but up. Past the timberline, to the place where no trees grew, higher up Lamplighter Mountain since before the Polar Storms when I hiked to the jökulhlaup with Dad. Alpine tundra rose from the tree line like exponential growth curves, billowing with sedges and lichens in the wind of a thousand fall colors. Here, massive boulders protruded like knuckles from the ground, long ago dropped out of ice by receding glaciers. Benji ran at full bore, unused to a wide stretch of land uninterrupted by trees and topography. He was getting older, slower, but I had kept him healthy – often with food from my own plate – and up in the tundra his energy boomed, his spirits high.

From there I saw the entirety of Kachemak Bay, miles of peninsula ragged and ridged, the scars of avalanches, the white lapping of waves along endless coast. Up over a secondary summit of Lamplighter Mountain, I saw the white edges of the ice field – that place where Dad I had hiked so many lifetimes ago to the jökulhlaup. It was another half day's hike to that place, and there was no point.

Callie would never be in a place like this. There was no version of events in which she ended up so high above the trees. Was I really looking for her anymore? Or simply carving out a path to somewhere else? Still looking for the exit? If I was, I could not find it. From my bed in the cove I easily pictured the trail to the mainland: hugging the mountainsides without ever summiting, passing through spruce forest not too bogged down by brush and poisonous plants; a way around every drop-off and escarpment. But here, out in it, up high with a view, there was clearly only one way back to the mainland: by water.

There in the tundra I saw my first mountain goats. They grazed in a herd around some tussocks not 400 feet away, ostentatious by their angel white fur against the fading colors of the mountain. I called Benji in and kept him close as we approached the herd, quiet and slow. Pulling the 30-30 from over my shoulder, I found a perch behind a boulder. I watched the group, waiting for one to present itself. In less than a minute, a large horned male turned his flank my direction, the perfect shot. He was massive, nearly the size of a dairy cow, white as ivory with enough fur to wrap my entire body twice in warmth. It should have occurred to me sooner: of any animal capable of weathering drought, the alpine goat herds were well situated with their glacier water sources. I held my breath, steadied the barrel, and took my shot.

He went down fast, and the herd scattered around the bend of the mountain. I shouted out in glee, whooping and cheering. Goat – a delicacy. I approached the kill and admired the lushness of his white fur, the power under his shoulder humps, the shining onyx rings of his horns. It was a tremendous amount of meat, a windfall. It would take hours to process … when I realized that I could never process him all before darkness fell. That I could never carry an animal of his size down the mountain by myself. That I lacked the tools to gut and quarter him.

I pulled out my machete and began the rough, terrible work of hacking his limbs from his body. What should have been careful, deliberate work with a carving knife through joints and around edges of bone was now the great, haphazard swings of a lumberjack against a tree. I was furious at myself and would carry whatever of him I could carry, use of him and eat of him whatever I could use and eat. Blood spattered hot on my face, my punishment for being so stupid, for killing so recklessly. I took off my jacket laid it down on the ground as a tarp. It would ruin my clothes – clothes I needed. But it had to be.

I pulled off his legs wrapped them in nylon line. I ripped the shoulder straps off my backpack and tied them to the nylon. The bloody, sopping remains were my backpack now. Benji licked up the drips. I turned to the remainder of the goat – so much meat, so much hide, a single black eye staring up at me reflecting the blue sky above – and told him *I'm sorry.*

An hour down the mountain, I was saturated in blood down into my socks. By halfway down the mountain, the backpack straps came apart. In the rapidly approaching darkness, there was no time to fix them. Instead, I dragged the parcel through the brush, heaving it up and over rocks so that it did not split apart.

I arrived at the cabin looking like the victim of a botched murder. Bare twilight sighed across the inlet. Maybe I imagined it, but I smelled the meat beginning to rot. I didn't even go into the cabin to change my bloody clothes. I unpacked the pieces of the goat and got to work at the plyboard table outside the greenhouse: skinning, cleaning, and boning. I worked until the middle of the night by a bright moon shimmering above the cove. I hated myself for what I had done. I cursed and swore at the pieces of ligaments and tendons that once held the pieces of this great animal together. At one point Dad called out from the porch, "Enna, is that you?"

"Sì, papì," I said.

"Okay," he said and closed the door again.

The air temperature dropped. My breath came in puffs haloed by the moon. Steam hissed from the goat as I cut into the deeper parts of his flesh. In my descending exhaustion and hunger, I muttered *Why do I even try why do I even care why do I even try.* And in this chant, this meditation, came Callie's voice small but clear. *Because you're lucky.* And though I filled with anger and resentment at the sound of her voice, she was right. My little sister. The one who saw the gratitude in all things hard and ugly.

I retreated into fantasy. Another place all together. Another time, another body. I was a princess marooned on an island in frightful Nordic seas. There would come a rescuer, turning up by boat or stumbling out of the forest to land at my feet. He would whisk me away from this place, to the burning world of color and fruit and music, and there would be no more loneliness or heartache left inside me.

It was pedantic. It was the 13-year-old version of myself left behind in Anchorage. It was the movies and storybooks she had known.

At the cabin I read Mom's old copy of *The Constant Princess* – the tortured and powerless life of Catherine of Aragon – and learned that princesses were not what I believed them to be. Their lives were brutal and mean. I was no longer a child. But a piece of my mind was stuck there. Pluto Cove was my tower in the castle. Benji was my songbird. The waves rushing up the shore were the sound of an approaching carriage over rocks. At any moment my clock would strike midnight, and everything would change.

When I finally went inside, barely moving under my fatigue and stiff, bloody clothes, Mom and Dad were both asleep. They did not stir as I made myself dinner without turning on the lights.

IT WAS MY ROLE, my place. Memories of soccer, of Sylvie, of my bed at home, of TV reruns on the weekend, faded to the point of becoming not history but fiction. Hopes of getting a driver's license, applying to college, or going on a date were abstract concepts that had no foothold in my mind. Even the drought had lost its sting, its acuity, its feeling of being so totally personal. Hope was no longer a feeling I had the vocabulary to describe.

There was no one to bury, no autopsy report to read. No memorial, no funeral. There is no ceremony for a sister who has disappeared. There is no closure. Unendurable anguish nested in the uncertainty. Unlike the books I read, there was no last page revealing the truth or solving the mystery. She was just gone. How much energy did I spend listening for her footsteps coming through the woods? Believing movements or a shadow in the trees was her standing up from a crouch? That a branch in the wind was her waving? Watching the door so that she might open it, shake off her coat, and settle in next to the fire as though no time had passed? Any hope at all was senseless, wasteful. So instead, I worked.

Irrelevance would have been worse. In that scenario, I would have decayed like dead leaves on the forest floor, slow and slimy. I would have suffocated under the weight of her disappearance: did I hear anything? See anything? Where could she have gone so fast? *Think think THINK.* I could invent stories. I could fill in blank spaces in my memory and contrive any number of events that were not true. The reality was that I didn't know. I just didn't know. One moment she was there, and the next she was gone. So was her bucket. Dad finally stopped asking so much, *Think think THINK*! He saw how it hurt me, to be the one person who should have answers but did not.

Instead of answers, I worked the greenhouse down to the last breaths of growable air and mounded the potatoes until our last frost-free night. It gave me focus, purpose. At night when it was too dark to fish or haul ice, I sat by the fire and sewed clothes for the baby. I pulled threads and cut fabric from Callie's clothes pile and repurposed them into awkward garments that I theorized would fit an infant. I didn't know how big a baby should be – or how big a baby growing in Mom's stricken belly could possibly grow. But it grounded me. It calmed me. I used the remains of George's furs and fashioned a coat with tufts of fur for ears over the hood. In it, the baby could look like a little monster, a little bear cub, and feel powerful and strong when the rest of us were not.

One evening I cut up rags and sewed them into the approximate shape of diapers. The light in the cabin was low. Dad made a comment about the battery bank running down, but not even this reanimated Mom. The pieces of her so passionate and obsessed with electricity were gone. I sat directly under the bulb in the kitchen to soak in its light, but still it was dim and orange. It was early in the winter. Without any new sun to recharge our rapidly draining batteries, by the deep center of the season, we would be totally in the dark.

The thought did not phase me. Few things did. Not that I could shrug them off with optimism or ambivalence. Not that I was sturdy or bold. But because I now perpetually inhabited the darkest place in my mind, and I had made myself at home there. A weight was tied to my ankles, and I sat at the bottom of the ocean floor. Instead of running out of air and drowning, I simply looked around. Waiting.

"You're going to ruin your eyes," Dad said to me. "Sewing in light like this."

"Well, I don't have another option," I said.

"You don't have to make things for the baby," he said, aggressively washing a dish in the kitchen sink.

"I want to," I said.

"It's a waste of time," he said.

"I don't think so," I said.

He spun around from the sink and grabbed the sewing from my hands. "This is ridiculous, Enna." He threw the fabric to the ground. In the silence between his breaths I heard the needle hit the floor. "Do you know what the odds are that a baby born in a dirty cabin in the middle of nowhere will survive? Even past its first day?"

I folded my hands in my lap. I was still. My spine was straight. *Bottom of the ocean*, I thought. *Just wait it out.* In my imagination, I ran my fingers through the fine sands of the seafloor and watched a yeti crab scuttle by. I could shut myself out of this scene. Be somewhere else.

My silence was palpable and violent. Inside of it, Dad broke. "Oh god," he gasped, his vision coming back into focus. "I'm so sorry, Enna. I'm so sorry." He bent down and picked up the fabric, the needle glinting from its thread like a spider dangling on a web. Without making eye contact, he set it back on my lap. "I'm so sorry," he muttered. He turned and walked out of the kitchen and into the living room where Mom slept on the couch. For as much as she did not want this baby to survive, I knew that, should it die, her suffering would escalate. And there was no room inside her for escalation.

What Dad said was true. He had some medical equipment, but we were not a hospital. Mom made every attempt to have an unhealthy pregnancy. The baby might die. From my reading – the stacks of books with *A Farewell to Arms*, *Wuthering Heights*, and *One Hundred Years of Solitude* – I knew Mom dying during childbirth was just as likely. Maybe even more.

I boxed the thought up in my mind and put it into the stack of thoughts where Callie was stored. Where I boxed up the haunted voice always singing *It's your fault she's gone, it's your fault she's gone*. I went back to sewing the little cloth diaper, letting my mind drift back down to the place it now dwelled at the bottom of the ocean.

CHAPTER SIX - *Two Months Later*

They came back.

We had not seen them since summer solstice, and now it was only days from winter solstice. The dark crushed us like cans in a vice. The cold choked us like a bad smell. And with it, Mom lost her energy for the daily searches. She and Dad went out in the late morning when the sun hit its peak – even then, she took a headlamp. By early afternoon, she came back to the cabin, back to bed.

The need to work was dire, but darkness and frigid wind zapped my sense of industry. I split firewood for hours on end, even though I had stacked enough to last another three winters. It was the only plentiful resource. I climbed out to the furthest edge of the gravel spit and cast a fishing line, pulling in loose trash which I kept. I walked the traplines once a day, sometimes twice, but had better returns carrying the Winchester and shooting rabbits and squirrels, ptarmigan and grouse hiding in the brush. My aim was good. Really good. And Benji became a worthy retriever, fetching fallen creatures from the brambles and dropping them at my feet in anticipation of praise. The memory of the goat burned into the barrel of my rifle; I never killed more than I could carry.

The morning the Birds came I awoke to the most extraordinary sight. Snow. So much snow.

A few years before, such a morning would have been nothing. Routine, rote, beautiful but otherwise expected and unremarkable. But it had been so long. Ice storms and hail flurries and whispers of rain kept the toughest of the evergreens clinging to their roots – and occasionally we had dustings of snow, a skim, that blew around in winter wind like loose Styrofoam. But this. This was the real, heavy, shining white snow of Christmas cards and the winter Olympics and glass globes with rosy ice skaters. It rimmed the edge of the window, and I leapt from bed to press my face against the glass. It went on and on, piled against rocks and hanging in fat bellies from the spruce boughs. The sky was dark but the ground was alight. The white blanket absorbed the light of the stars and threw it back into the atmosphere, glittering and glossy.

I hurried down the ladder, threw on my boots next to the door, and launched myself into the dark morning air, the survivor of a marooned ship throwing herself onto land for the first time. Mom and Dad did not stir from their tortured sleep, but Benji came out and jumped in snow drifts nose-first like a dolphin in calm water – not for survival, simply for joy.

I neglected a coat in my haste, but it was irrelevant. My skin was toughened to the cold, and this was a different sort of cold. A snowless cold is hollow and barbed. But cold in the snow is thick and gooey as honey. It wrapped around me like a scarf and softened my skin with its wet, velvety grip. I leapt from the stairs of the cabin into fresh, pillowy snow up to my knees. I took a jump with both feet and landed again in its embrace. And again. Snow brimmed the tops of my boots and melted into my bare feet. No matter. There would be a fire in the stove later, and darned socks to warm my toes. There would be time to register the tingling and numbness in my fingertips, but for those moments, there was no need.

There was snow, so much snow. And snow was rain.

The snow hushed the forest, absorbing into its empty spaces all the sounds of the ocean waves, rustling branches of trees, and heartbeats of wildlife. Each flake, the size of rose petals, dampened the small noises of the cove. I pulled that quiet into myself, letting its peace and stillness cover me like a soft blanket in whose comfort I could hear the simple sound of myself breathing, digesting, living.

Which is why I did not hear them when they pulled to shore.

Johnny Bird was ten feet away when he barked out my name from the morning darkness. "Enna."

I spun around, my boots slick at the base of the snowpack. He shouldn't know my name. I was the child, anonymous. The darker one. Mija. Not Enna.

"What do you want?" I said, my voice strong but lonely in the muffled air of falling snow.

"We got a sick kid. Get your dad." Perhaps this seemed too cordial to him on first blush, so he followed up more menacingly. "Now."

I ran up to the cabin, slow and sludgy through the drifts, the static, ineffective running of a nightmare. Benji jumped behind my tracks and nuzzled through the door first. I blinked my eyes going from the purple shine of the snow outside to the flat, deadened dark of the cabin.

"Dad," I whispered loudly in the direction of the bed. "Dad, the Birds are here. We've gotta go now."

Through the dark, I heard him rip the blankets from his body and jump to his feet. "Where?"

"They're right outside the door," I said. "Johnny Bird. He said someone is sick and we have to go now."

He fumbled his way down the length of the bed and hit the light switch. The light flickered, orange and brown, then died. He flipped the switch up and down, the light sputtering like a car low on gas until we heard Mom's weak and groggy voice, "What's going on?"

The light flicked on and stayed on. I went for the loft to add layers. The boat ride to the Bird Compound would be cold. And the storage cabin where they kept the ill and injured would be even colder.

"The Birds are here," Dad said. "Get dressed, Lisa."

"Are you crazy?" She said. "I'm not leaving here."

"You have to," he said. "We're all going."

"No," she said. "I'm not."

"Lisa."

"Alex. I said no."

I pulled on a second sweater and savored the brief moment my head suspended in the collar, the world dark, muted, and private.

"You cannot be here alone," Dad said.

"What if she comes back?" Mom said, loud and pleading. "What if she comes back and there's no one here at the cabin?" Her voice broke. "I won't leave this place unless she is with me."

I knew the implied end to her sentence: I won't leave this place unless she is with me. *Ever*.

"Lisa, you have to come. I can't leave you here alone."

"You have to. I'm not leaving without her." *Ever*.

This was the truth of it, the heart of it. Mom would never leave Pluto Cove without Callie. Dad would never leave Pluto Cove without Mom. And so someday it would be me, alone, setting out into the forest deep and dark, in search of the world. In my head, I walked the mountains with Benji, hunting food until we came upon the others whom I believed were out there. The ones with music, with children, with fruit trees. I would rest with them, gather my strength. Then come for my family by boat, back to Pluto Cove, and save them from this place that digested us whole and squirming like a mouse into an owl.

"Lisa," Dad begged.

"No," she said. I inched down the ladder and she pulled the covers back over herself, digging into the trench of the bed from which she would not move.

Dad looked at me as though I may have an answer. I refused to meet his gaze, and instead opened the cellar door to retrieve the medical kit.

"Hurry up!" came Johnny's voice from outside. "Another minute and I'll break down that door and get you myself!"

When I came back up, Dad had ripped a piece of paper from the Nanwalek Clinic notepad and wrote on it next to Mom. He shoved it and the pen into her face under the covers. "Lisa," he said. "Sign this."

She peaked out like a fox from her burrow and read the paper. She looked at Dad. "Are you serious?"

"Very."

"I'm not a freak," she said. "I'm not ill."

"Then sign it."

I wasn't sure what was happening. Mom was in a deep but brief contemplation. She grabbed the pen and scribbled on the page. Dad bent down and gave her a kiss. "I love you," he said. "We'll be right back."

"Okay," she said.

Dad made for the door and I followed. I didn't want to speak first, to remind her of my existence, of my persistence in this world when she wanted only Callie. But she was not going to say it, and I needed to hear it, her voice, her words. "Bye, Mom," I said. "I love you."

"Oh," she sighed, propping herself up in bed. "I love you so much, baby. Be safe out there."

"Okay," I said, longing for her to jump out and run to me, throw her arms around me, shower me in her kisses and tenderness, pull the tangled ends of my hair through with her fingers. But that Mom was gone.

Dad tacked the piece of paper next to the door and stepped into the snow-laced world where the sun rose just a sliver in the east like a blackeye in the clouds. I glanced at the note as I pulled the door shut. *I, Lisa Sjöden Martinez, know that I am loved by those around me and promise to my husband that I will not harm myself in any way. Signed __LSM____.*

THE BLINDFOLD WAS a burlap sack that smelled of potatoes. I didn't mind it. Though loosely woven, it protected my face from the snow blowing off the water. Through the fibers, I saw the sky lighten from black to gray. Dad did not call out for me. And I did not call out for him. Having done it once made it feel routine. Or maybe in a world where Callie had simply vanished into the air, there was nothing that disturbed us.

What layers I donned were insufficient against the winter wind whipping over the wooden hull of the boat. The sack grew wet and heavy as snow fell and melted under my diminishing body heat. They bound my hands behind me – a new development – and I flexed my fingers back and forth, flicking them out, sending blood to the tips. But eventually they went completely numb. When I wiggled my fingers, I received no signal that anything had moved. So I stopped.

The boat slowed as many invisible hands lashed it to the dock. Someone grabbed me by the armpit, his own hands freezing in the lingering warmth of my core, and yanked me hard off the port side. My feet fell into uneven hills of snow. With my hands tied behind me, I fell to my knees, stuck. In that moment I saw myself from the outside, from above. A captive, her head in a brown sack, faceless, headless, hands tied, outnumbered and surrounded, half buried in a snowdrift. It was a movie scene I had to close my eyes for, a snapshot from a nightmare that left me plastered in sweaty sheets. But that was from the outside. In my own head, on my own knees, if I kept myself there as a denizen of the ocean floor, my eyes closed inside the soggy bag and my legs in a cradle of heavy snow, I was the octopus in my grotto, silky and invertebrate. I was alright.

Someone pulled me up by my wrist, but his force was dull and anesthetized by the cold. I stumbled over the snow where footprints had carved out deep pits. I kept my head down. There would be no reconnaissance, no spying attempts. Just survive it.

I went up the steps to the cabin, familiar now, and felt a blast of warm air and bright light as the door opened. Johnny Bird pulled the sack off my head and untied my hands. Dad stood next to me, sopping wet and shaking. The room was changed. Plaster mud covered the gaps and holes in the walls. Shelves sat bare. The single

219

overhead bulb shone hard and blazing. And the warmth. Warmth like bread just pulled from the oven. Warmth like the insides of a fresh cut animal. But how? There was no hearth, no fire.

I saw it: in the corner of the room, a space heater. Gray and square, a Honeywell. A brand name from an old world. Mom's voice – Mom's healthy voice – commented with curiosity in my ears: that heater takes *power*. Tremendous power. In a world of dried wood, where fires raged hot and endless, surely there were more efficient ways to warm the shed. But there it was, steady and humming. I yearned to lunge for it, to press my hands into the slats until they burned like grill grates and sensation returned. But there on the table, covered in blankets, was the patient. And she was dying.

It took me aback – a girl. A she. Her head was shaved close to her scalp, but there was no denying her gender. Her skin was somehow both dark and pale, an ashen black that spoke of vibrant color with not enough air. Her lips parted, dusky and blue. She was curled up on her side, facing us, whimpering, but did not acknowledge our presence. Below her thin neck she was covered in a red quilt stitched of cardinals and rose peonies, a hobby craft from other times. Her face was young, and her features fine and delicate. A teenager. Like me.

"Get to work," Johnny Bird barked. "And none of this shit like last time where you try to gross out Keith so he'll leave. Ain't gonna work." He pulled up a chair next to the door and sat, blocking the door handle. "I ain't grossed out by nothing." His good eye glimmered, and he stuck out his tongue for a slow, vulgar lick across the scarred side of his mouth.

"What happened?" Dad asked, blowing into his hands.

"She got sick a couple days ago. Said her stomach was bugging her. She's a real whiner, though. Then last night she starts screaming an' passes out."

Dad moved toward her, his hands trembling. Not for cold. Dad struggled with sick kids. Girls, in particular. In the emergency room he tried to transfer any patient who reminded him of Callie or me. He extended a hand to her forehead. "Good lord," he said. "She's on fire." The words were too much, the promise of warmth was too great. I walked to the girl and placed my hands on her forehead using the terrible pretense of assessing her condition when I only wanted to warm my fingers. She was, indeed, burning. The heat of her skin rivaled any space heater. With immense, repulsive shame, I kept my hands on her head, letting the warmth flow into me with the pain of knives and needles as sensation returned. She moaned under my touch and rolled toward me. I looked to Dad. He nodded. "You can help draw the fever out," he said, understanding. "It's okay."

He took a tentative peak under the blanket and she was naked, bare. "Hey, sweetie," he called out. "What's your name?"

Johnny stuck a wad of chew into the pocket of his cheek. "Don't speak to her."

"I have to–" Dad pressed.

"Shut up and get to work. She has been instructed not to say a damn word to you. Any questions you have go through me. One'a the other girls thought it might be her appendix."

Dad looked down at the girl, his face a hundred

years old, wrinkled and dehydrated as an old apple. If both people he treated here were children – and both were close to death when he arrived – how many more had laid on this table in pain, sickness, and injury? How many had died before the Birds dispatched to Pluto Cove?

"Mija, get more blankets. We need to cover her."

I left the warmth at her forehead and went to a shelf with neatly stacked linens. Dad shielded the girl's body from Johnny as I placed blankets over her breasts and pelvis, arms and legs. As though Johnny hadn't already seen it all. Dad pressed gently upon her abdomen and her eyes flew open, full of fire, baring straight into heaven as she writhed. A stream of vomit tumbled from the corner of her mouth. Dad reached in with an ungloved hand and swiped her cheek so that she would not choke.

"What else did this other girl say?" Dad asked, keeping his back to Johnny. "If you won't let me speak to her then you have to give me the information. If it's appendicitis, I need to know."

Johnny gave an exasperated sigh. "You fucking academics. Can't you just take it out? She said her tummy hurt," he said with a sickly whining voice. "First all over, then down low. Said it ain't cramps. She threw up a bunch, couldn't walk. Here we are."

Dad looked at me. "That does sound like appendicitis," he said.

"So what do we do?"

He shook his head. "I can't get an image or run any tests. I guess … I guess I just have to cut into her and take it out. And we hope that's really the problem." The girl moaned, screwing her eyelids close, arching her back upon the table.

"Oh," I said. As though it were normal to cut her open on a guess.

"Stay with her," he said. "I'm gonna get the supplies together."

He combed through the box of medical equipment from Nanwalek Clinic, already open at the foot of the table. The box was significantly emptier than the last time. Bandages and tapes had been pillaged nearly to extinction. But the tools, the reusable things, and the IV bags were still there.

From his backpack, Dad pulled out two small mason jars of clear liquid and set them on the table out of Jonny Bird's sight. I faced Johnny, who already looked bored. Dad moved to obscure Johnny's view as he mixed the two liquids together and quickly sealed the cap.

"What is that?" I asked.

Dad shook his head. He would not tell me when Johnny could hear. "I'm going to take care of you," he said to the girl in a loud and clear voice. "You don't need to be afraid."

"I said don't fuckin' talk!" Johnny Bird barked from his chair.

The odor of the mix was pungent, astringent. One I immediately identified as bleach. The other I knew but could not name. I expected him to apply it over her belly as disinfectant, but instead he grabbed a corner of the blanket covering the girl's chest and whispered to me, "Hold your breath," before he poured it onto the fabric and pinned the blanket to the girl's nose. Her body relaxed. Her arms dropped and fell limp at her sides. Her eyelids went loose and heavy, her breathing slowed. Then he moved to her belly where he pressed softly, feeling the contours of her abdomen, watching her face for reaction. "There's a mass here," Dad said. "That's where I'll cut."

His voice faltered as he scrubbed iodine over her belly. "Have you done this before, Dad?" It occurred to me appendicitis patients in the emergency room were likely shipped out to a surgical floor.

He glanced up at me as he donned his surgical mask. "No," he said. "I watched a few in school and residency." He paused. "That'll have to be enough." He took a breath. "Are you ready, mija? You're my nurse."

"I'm ready," I said.

"First, we sterilize."

Though my fingers and toes still tingled and burned in the warmth of the cabin – and though my stomach howled having skipped breakfast – my brain felt alert, alive, awake. My vision was sharp, focused. My hands moved swiftly around the instruments, scrubbing them down with alcohol and enjoying the clink each tool made as I set it into the tray. I understood then that, had I the opportunities of life on the mainland – a life free from the Polar Storms, a life as something other than a refugee – I would have done what Dad did. Followed in his footsteps. Watched the world from over the white horizon of a cloth mask with my hair tucked into a bouffant.

No such thing came to pass, as you well know. But I pictured the photos from my old history textbooks. Nurses at the bedside with opium and bandages of torn linen. Doctors rotating tourniquets made of sticks and ropes. Wading into the middle of turmoil to relieve pain, offer comfort, and untangle the web of blood and nerves

224

that make the human body.

The skin on her belly opened easily under Dad's knife and glistened shining and dark like the ventral scales of a fish.

"Two layers of fascia," Dad said. "Fatty and fibrous." He spoke partially to educate me, but mostly to remind and reassure himself. "The muscle will be underneath. Enna, keep that soaked blanket near her face. When she starts to stir, reapply it."
"Okay."

"Here," Dad said, holding out the retractors. "Pull the incision open. This is the external oblique muscle. See how it runs up and down? I need to cut along the direction of the fibers. But the muscle underneath it, the internal oblique, runs perpendicular to it, so I have to be very careful not to cut too deep."

"What happens if you do?" I asked.

"She could herniate," he said. "Give her more of the fluid from the jar to breathe. This is going to hurt her."

I looked past Dad's shoulder at Johnny Bird slumped in his chair by the door. He snored, a raindrop of drool shining off the maimed side of his chin in the incandescent light.

"What is this stuff, Dad?" I whispered, reaching for the jar, keeping one eye on Johnny.

"Is he asleep?" Dad asked in a barely audible voice.

"Yes," I said.

"It's chloroform," he answered with his teeth clenched as though someone might read his lips and learn his secrets. "Or something like chloroform. They can't know that we have any kind of sedative, you understand?"

I nodded and bit my tongue.

Leaning in with the retractors, I saw the lines of muscle running tightly together like a school of snapper fish. Dad cut slowly, carefully, separating the fibers, unwinding a rope one thread at a time. "There," he said. He took the retractors from me and moved them deeper into the girl's abdomen. "Here's the next layer." And there was the interior oblique, indeed running at a right angle to the muscle above it.

"Good job, Dad," I said.

He softened. "Thanks," he said. "Now is the peritoneum. It's the sack that holds all the organs in the abdomen. See it here?" There was no missing it. It was rubbery and translucent like the glea of a compass jellyfish. "Her organs are going to shift when I cut here," Dad said. "Are you ready?"

"I'm ready," I said, and meant it. I was Florence. I was Clara.

He sliced into it with the gentleness a mother uses to stroke the cheek of her baby. The sack gave way by the nanometer as he strained against sudden shifting or accidental puncture. When the peritoneum finally gave way, it gave way quickly. Into the incision erupted an intestine, pink and corrugated. Fleshy and flexible but sturdy. Like the water pipeline to cross Alaska. I wondered if anyone ever built it. I suspected not.

Dad pushed it back into her abdominal cavity. Then something red and angry rose to the surface like a navigational buoy. It was the length of my pinky finger but nearly the width of my wrist.

"Yeah," Dad said. "That's it."

"The appendix?" I asked.

"Yes," he said. "It's in awful shape. See the stain down here?" He pointed his gloved ring finger to the base of the organ where it anchored to the intestine. "That means it was about to rupture at any second. This should look like an earthworm. Not a firehose."

His eyes shone in visible relief over the mask. He had identified the problem. He had not cut her open for naught. I replaced the dressings around the incision. I reached up with a bloody glove and pulled the lightbulb down from its slack wire, bringing the light a little closer to our work. It shone brightly as ever.

Dad cut the appendix from the ileum and set it on a tray. Yellow fluid oozed down the sides like ice cream melting from a cone.

He initiated the painstaking task of sewing up each layer of tissue. I suspected he could have simply stitched the top layer and let everything underneath it heal over time. But Dad did not play. If he saved a life, he saved it properly. Only, neither of us were sure of the life being saved. I thought of my book back at the cabin, *Beloved,* and Sethe, running a knife over her daughter's throat to free her from slavery. Death as an act of love. Dad healed this girl from a place of love, I had no doubt. But love in this world was a complicated and unmerciful thing.

As he stitched the girl together, I kept the chloroform near as she stirred, ever more agitated in her stupor. Johnny Bird awoke and righted himself as though he had been attentive the entire time. Several hours had passed and I desperately needed to relieve myself, but couldn't face the bucket behind the curtain in the corner.

So I ignored it.

"Ain't you done yet?" Johnny Bird demanded.

"Getting close," Dad said without flinching. "But she'll need quite a bit of care after I'm done with the suturing."

"You're outta here after that last stitch," Johnny Bird said, standing up and shaking out his feet.

"Last time we were here for several days to monitor recovery," Dad said.

"Well this ain't last time, is it?" he snarled.

Dad was quiet. He continued suturing while I supplied him with thread. The movements were a craft into which he could let his thoughts disappear, take on new forms, and reappear changed – as one does with knitting or playing piano. After a while, his thoughts manifested, and he spoke again.

"Seems like a lot has changed around here since last time," he said.

"That's none of your business," Johnny Bird said.

"The cabin is looking in better shape. Good woodworking. And this light and the space heater? Must be using a lot of electricity. Where are you getting it? Solar? Tidal? Wind?"

"I said stop with the fucking questions," Johnny Bird said, more upset. "Or you'll be sorry you did."

"Just trying to make polite conversation," Dad said.

"Well quit it. You're lucky we ain't shot you and your daughter already."

"Seems like we serve a necessary purpose."

Johnny stamped his foot like a toddler. "Yeah, well then you're lucky we ain't taken you from that shithole cabin and are keeping you here full time. Could have you whenever we wanted."

"Yes," Dad said. "That's odd you haven't done that."

"Quit the talking!" Johnny Bird shouted. He stepped to the table and peered over Dad's arm to see the girl. She had less than inch now of exposed wound. "That looks good enough to me," Johnny said. "Time to go."

"But I still have–" Dad started.

"I said now!" Johnny yelled, grabbing the suturing needle from Dad's fingers and stabbing himself with it in the process. "I've gotten over cuts way bigger than that, she'll be fine."

"But she needs–"

Johnny pulled a handgun from the waistband of his pants and aimed it squarely at Dad's head. The gun transformed Johnny. He didn't yell. He didn't emote at all. "I said now."

Dad slowly raised his arms into the air. A rock formed in my stomach, pulling me down. "Okay," Dad said. "Okay. We'll go. I just need to get my backpack."

Johnny Bird pushed the hammer back, cycling a bullet into the chamber. "Leave the backpack."

"But–"

"I said leave it." The barrel hid Johnny's face, a roundness and symmetry he otherwise lacked. Both men stood stock still, breathing heavy but with no rising in their chests. Again, I put myself at the bottom of the sea, this time a squid, old as the dinosaurs, propelling myself backward through a cloud of ink. It calmed me. But if I considered the scene outside of myself – as a spectator – I filled with sickness as a sore fills with pus. I did not move, I scarcely breathed. There was a total stillness over my body, which made it all the more shocking when she grabbed my hand.

Her grip was weak, her fingers cold. But the touch shocked me from the thin veil of reverie I occupied as the ancient squid. She stared up at me, wordless, terrified, in great physical agony that billowed from her eyes like steaming water from a kettle. It was not just her eyes I saw in that moment, but Sylvie's eyes. Grace's. Margot's. Sofia's. The eyes of every female friend I'd ever had. The trust and safety that exists between girls growing up in a world stacked against them. A language only we speak. How long had it been since I saw a girl my age, a peer, a child growing up at the furthest reaches of inhabitable land, at the end of all time, whose own body was proof that life continued and altered and grew even when all else stopped?

"Help me," she mouthed without sound.

I broke my gaze with her to look at Johnny Bird. He was intent on Dad, keeping his gun cocked with both hands. I looked back to her and mouthed back, "I'll try."

Before anything else could transpire – before I could learn her name or tell her it would all be okay – the door opened. The Birds appeared, and the wet sack was over my head before I could feel winter come in through the door.

Hands of different sizes and temperatures touched me, passed me around. I knew the Birds' hands because theirs were large and covered in thick, heavy gloves. They touched me between my legs and over my chest. They laughed. I steadied my mind. *Bottom of the ocean.* Even deeper than the squid, now I was a frilled shark, five thousand feet below the horizon of the sun's reach. But there were other hands. Smaller, colder. One, I swear, was gentle. When I stumbled on snow, the hand reached lightly for my elbow and propped me up. There was shouting, barking, angry voices from unseen faces. But in the calamity of boarding the boat I heard another voice, soft, barely perceptible, straight into the burlap covering my ears. A voice I recognized only because there were so few voices I heard in the last two and a half years. "It's me," he whispered.

The boy with green eyes.

"Hi," I whispered.

And with that they shoved me onto the boat, and I was swept through the choppy wintertide back to Pluto Cove.

IT WAS FEBRUARY now. There was a book of poetry on the shelf with a line reading *April is the cruelest month*. I did not read past this line because it was so inane. February is the cruelest month. It reaches into your throat and chokes you from the inside. It is a smooth wall of darkness and cold on all four sides with no rungs or handholds from which to climb out.

Our power was dire. No sun shone upon the solar panels and no water flowed through the turbine in the creek. I did not understand what was different about this winter compared to the last, or the one before that – except that we as a family were bleak. We have drained the battery-bank by our own melancholy sucking it dry.

I went to Mom one terribly cold and dark morning, missing the warmth of the space heater in the Bird's cabin, remembering the fire on the girl's forehead that resurrected my fingers. The stove in our cabin was adequate, but on some days – like this day – the cold seeped in like haunted spirits and gripped us around the ankles and neck. It was magnified by darkness that strained my vision and left my brain aching for daylight.

I traced every wire from the solar panels to the battery-bank and every wire from the battery-bank to the light fixtures. I found nothing amiss. I climbed up on the roof and cleaned each photovoltaic cell with warm, soapy water that sculpted bizarre and otherworldly icicles as it dripped over the gutters. I hammered ice out of the surface of the creek to make the rotor spin, then traced the wires from the turbine to the cabin, still finding nothing. What I was looking for, I wasn't sure. I hoped for something obvious – a connection loss or breakage. But I found no such thing.

"Mom," I whispered, approaching the S-curve of her body in the ratty bed. Her arms curled around her belly which stuck out from her spine like the burl on a tree, its mound pulling so tightly at her skin I saw each vertebrate through the cling of her sweater. I knew she was awake. She snored now when she was asleep – the baby and her insides pressing hard on her lungs. "Mom," I repeated. "I need your help. There's no light. It's too cold for me to work outside, and I have two geese to skin." I had tried processing them on the deck, but they were frozen. "Plus, it's going to be dark again in an hour or so. Is there any way you can help me get some lights on in here or the greenhouse so I can work?" She did not respond. "Please?" I begged. "I can't do this alone."

The blanket crested and fell where she took a breath. Using an exhale as momentum, she hauled her legs over and rolled to face me. I saw her every day but never got used to seeing her like this. Her eyes were rimmed with concentric circles like two stones dropped into water. Her lips were pale and cracked as fish bones. Her cheeks had cavetized like the hollows of trees where owls sleep. She looked up at me from the bed.

"We lost our power," she said.

"I know," I said. "How do we get it back?"

"If I knew that," Mom said weakly, closing her eyes. "I wouldn't be here."

I sighed. "Why'd you put the turbine in the creek?" I asked. "Why not try to get the wind instead of the creek?"

She paused for a moment, digging hard into the chambers of her memory. "Maintenance," she said. "Easier to get to and modulate. And sometimes the wind is so strong here. I thought it might rip the blades right off."

This was the most she had spoken since Dad and I returned from the Birds. It lit a small fire in my chest, a flicker of warmth.

"Okay," I said. "I might try to convert it to wind power. See if we can get some more electricity into the batteries."

"Okay," she said.

"Do you have any advice for me?" I asked.

I expected another long pause as she gathered the strength to form words. But she spoke right away, opening her eyes to look at me. "You can do it," she said. "You are extraordinary."

Entire seasons had passed permitting myself only basic body functions and drives. There was little tenderness left in me. But what remained reflexively awakened at her words, surging like a canyon wind through my core.

"I learned everything from you," I said quietly, reaching down and brushing her cheek. I had never touched her this way, though I had received it many times. I knew how it felt. How the simple act of touch could bring a body back to the ground, to earth, to the soil, to roots, to the places from which we came. "I hope you come back soon," I said, then went outside.

Her words were meaningful, but what I really wanted – needed – was *her*. The way she thought, problem-solved, improvised. I could not rival her knowledge and ingenuity. She designed our elaborate hydropower system using repurposed pieces of Daisy and Dennis' generator. Now I needed to repurpose those same pieces into a wind turbine – something that, even if it worked and generated power, may not solve our problem.

I had to think like Mom. Break down the constituent parts of a wind turbine. A tower. I could use a standing tree, still living, and limb it down into a pole. The brake, gearbox, and rotor hub I already had. The nacelle was mostly ready, but it would need a different cover. I would also need blades, larger than what was in the stream. And an anemometer. And a yaw for the whole mechanism to spin toward the wind. It seemed insurmountable. There were other things I could do with this time: hunt, trap, and fish. But we needed electricity. Without light in the cabin we would wither like roses. Seedlings in the greenhouse would be late a month or more. Our cold storage would fluctuate, meats would spoil. Our stovetop would go dead, and I'd be left hauling ice chunks into the sink instead of flipping on a pump.

I started with the blades – the biggest and most daunting component. The blades needed to be light but not too light, capable of catching the wind without ripping away. I circled the cabin, combing through our storage piles and covered spaces. Here were all the items Mom packed out from Anchorage or pulled from Daisy and Dennis' cabin, all the items we squirreled away, and the trash pile that only ever grew with each pull of the fishing nets.

The trash pile. Mounds of plastic that made a sea journey from all across the Pacific to Pluto Cove. Soda bottles, straws, caps, food wrappers, and grocery bags. Shower curtains, disposable cutlery, shampoo bottles, and chapstick containers. A pile taller than me, anchored down with willow netting and rocks. It was perfect. It would be disgusting and toxic to make, but it was perfect. I hauled armfuls of plastic trash to our fire pit in front of the cabin and ignited an uneasy flame with a nine-volt battery in the vacuum-like cold. I built up the fire, donned heavy work gloves, and melted plastic into deformed, Picasso-esque shapes, fusing them together into long sheets. The smell was noxious, but the plastic blended together well in the fire and congealed quickly in the cold. I could build three and cut them into similar shapes. I could warp the sheets into scoops over fire to better gather wind. I sucked all the daylight into my quest, pounding out the still-warm plastic with a sledgehammer like a metalsmith.

So engrossed was I that I did not hear Dad when he came outside. He was standing next to the fire when I looked up.

"What's going on?" I asked, unable to read the look on his face.

"Your mom," he said. "Her water broke."

WHAT PASSED THAT NIGHT is a patchwork of sensations and images stapled into all the sensory parts of my mind: the sound of Mom screaming, the sight of her contorting, the feeling of her fingers ripping into my hair, and the smell of the baby's head against Mom's shoulder.

My mother, the engineer. My mother, the depressed. My mother, the backcountry survivalist. My mother, Nephthys, the Egyptian goddess of perpetual mourning. It all evaporated. She became no person resembling my mother, no person resembling a human. That night I witnessed my mother transform into a great howling bear. There was no language in her brain, no high order functions. Dad and I were her zookeepers as she paced and whimpered and roared and clawed.

"This isn't like our other procedures," Dad said as we hustled around the cabin, readying supplies. "We are not in charge here. She is. There's not a lot we can do except try to make her comfortable."

"Is she far along enough?" I whispered to him by the cabinet holding our towels.

He nodded, his lips thin. "I think so," he said. "Pretty close to nine months."

It started slowly, each contraction coming on like the gradual, predictable movements of the tide. But then they came harder, faster, each one a tsunami that swallowed her whole and spit her back out, battered and weak. I offered her water while Dad rubbed her back. He dabbed her with wet cloths and massaged her hips. I gathered clean towels and warmed a kettle of water on the stove. In moments of reprieve, Dad used a gloved hand to check her, but he was unsettled, insecure in his assessments. "I think that's a head there?" he said, straining. "I think so? Not a bottom? I think the position is okay. I think you're maybe four or five centimeters?"

"But it's not a foot?" I asked.

"Definitely not a foot," Dad said, withdrawing his hand. "Yeah," he said on further consideration. "Probably not a foot."

I put my hands on Mom's belly; she looked at me, feeble and anemic. There was a hardness to her abdomen unique to rocks and metals. But it was not inanimate. It wiggled and shimmied under my hands, alive. I let out a little gasp. Something tiny and knobbed rolled across the palm of my hand. "Dad I think I feel a foot up here," I said. "I don't think the baby is breech."

Mom rolled away from my hand and groaned from a place in her throat older than biology itself – the sound of stars being born at the edges of the expanding universe.

"I can't do this!" She shrieked.

"You can," Dad urged. "You can. You already have, twice. You can."

"I can't!" She yelled again. Those were the last words she uttered as she made her full passage into animal.

It was an illusion, I believed – a trick of the mind as events intensified – but I swear the lights grew brighter during her contractions. I saw the skin on her belly pull and retract, exposing the lines of her ribs like fish gills, and the lights grew so bright I could hear them buzzing, burning. The cabin was hot and sweaty. The lights shone as though day, and that cabin could have lifted up off its foundation and blown in a tornado a thousand miles south without shocking me. When I looked out the window, it was dark as death, not a star hanging in the sky. Only our cabin was ablaze on that mountainside with the lightning Mom cast from her body, throwing great javelins of light and commotion like Zeus himself. Too dark for me to see that someone was outside, looking in.

When it came time to push, so many hours later, well into the next day's morning which was still night, she screamed harder and grabbed onto my shoulders like they were the gutters on a roof from which she slipped. I kneeled with her on the floor of the cabin, face-to-face, with Dad behind her, ready to catch. Sweat poured off her like the Polar Storms themselves, and her eyes were somewhere else – not here – somewhere in outer space where the stars and planets hung like windchimes and sang her outside of her body.

"You can do it, Mom," I said, though I had no hope she heard me. "Push! Push!"

"Push, Lisa!" Dad called from the other side. "You're doing great. Push!"

Mom howled like a pack of wolves warning off predators. It went straight into my ear and rang my head like a belfry.

On and on it went, her clutching at me, screaming into me, my knees going numb from the floor where I dared not to move.

"The head!" Dad exclaimed, snapping me from the rhythm. "I can see the head!" Despite the simultaneous adrenaline and depletion of the last 12 hours – and the last two years – his voice bore a genuine excitement. "Almost there, Lisa! Almost there!"

She sucked in a breath as though she were surfacing from drowning and threw her arms around my neck with her fingers in my hair, pulling so hard my scalp twisted and shifted. The light bulb overhead hummed like cicadas and danced on its wire. She let out one last feral call that echoed into the walls of the cabin, the walls of the cove, the great Gulf of Alaska itself, and that was the moment she broke in half. Fluids gushed out of her and covered the wood floor around my knees. The roof of the cabin ripped off the frame and the sky above shattered. All the grief and mourning were sucked into the vacuum it created – where everything old and stale became new. The baby let out a cry, long and piercing and pure.

Mom sobbed, not in agony, but joy. "Oh my god," she cried. "Oh my god," bringing language back into her brain, movement back to her tongue.

"You did it, Lisa," Dad said as he wrapped the little bean in a blanket, wiping the wax from its skin. "You did it." His eyes shined with tears as he maneuvered to contain the wiggling, howling bundle. The first new thing to arrive in Pluto Cove in so very long a time.

Mom released her grip on me and turned to Dad, moving her leg over the rubbery blue cord that descended from the blankets. She reached out her hands and took hold of the bundle, pulling it into her chest before even looking at its face. I sat beside her, supporting her back, unsure of what I saw except that Mom appeared to be –

unbelievably, almost inconceivably erased of all memories that preceded this moment – happy.

"My baby," she cried, rocking it back and forth. "My baby, my baby, my baby."

Dad knelt at her feet, one hand on the back of the little baby who I still had not seen. He kept a towel ready for the afterbirth but seemed utterly consumed by the moment.

"Let's see, Lisa," he whispered as the baby's cries subsided into gentle whimpers. "Let's look."

She slowly, ceremoniously, lifted the blankets back from around its face like the fabric of a knight's chainmail hood. "Oh," I gasped, my knees wobbling under Mom's weight. It was beautiful, this creature. Eyes bright and dark and wide, looking at us, squinting under the lightbulb above. A nose so tiny it seemed impossible air could pass through it. Cheeks plump as pumpkins and a mouth with full rosy lips that puckered as though unconvinced of this new world. Dad wiped away the wax and blood giving way to a mess of long dark hair, held straight up as though ignited by a plasma globe.

"It's a boy," Mom said, sobbing. "It's a boy."

"A boy!" Dad exclaimed. "A boy!"

Back in school we took a field trip to the Alaska Native Heritage Museum. There I saw a Chilkat blanket preserved under glass, perfectly lit in the dark hall, intricately woven in black and red thread to tell the story of the Clam Woman. Of all the precious, ancient artifacts in this museum, I lingered at the Clam Woman blanket the longest. Frozen to her story and the way I felt I knew her. I read from a small plaque under the exhibit that the Clam Woman was from a village in famine. One day she

240

walked to the mudflats to harvest shellfish in the low tide to feed her family. She reached down for a clam, and it closed on her hand, pulling her down. She fought and fought, but no matter what she did, the clam held her there. And the tide began to rise. Held prisoner by the clam, she was swallowed by the rising tide and never seen again.

Even then, before the Polar Storms, before Pluto Cove, the story brought me to Mom. The Clam Woman. It stuck to me like thistles on my clothes. For as long as I could remember, Mom had been trapped between the rocks and the rising tide, trying to pull free.

That night, a piece of her pulled free.

She held her son, quiet and full of light. At some point, she wiggled a hand free and pulled me in, too. I huddled there with them, the three of them. Now the four of us. What should have been five. Mom and Dad's embrace brought me close to my little brother's face where he looked up at me in curiosity and tiredness, and I looked at him the same. A new person, a baby of the Polar Storms, a child of Pluto Cove.

You.

PART THREE

THE JÖKULHLAUP

CHAPTER SEVEN – *One Week Later*

Each moment passed like the stretching of a rubber band beyond its elastic. Would the baby keep breathing? Would Mom stop bleeding? Was this warmth on her forehead a sign of life or fever? I tracked the days by the sun across the greenhouse window, its light slumped and sagging as the walk of an old woman across the sky. I sucked the light into my eyes like water through a straw while I washed rags and towels from the birth in a bucket of warm water. Then I dumped the bloodied water straight into the soil. Body waste caused me no distress. In a lonely, hollow world there is no shame or taboo around amniotic fluid or meconium. They would enrich the soil for our garden. That was all that mattered. From my wash station behind the window I counted the minutes of daylight. It came back each day, a few minutes at a time.

Back in the before-days, just as the Polar Storms came on, there were changes in the angle and rising patterns of the sun. Many people subscribed to a brief hysteria that the tilt of the earth was changing. That our axis, which had held so steady throughout our evolution from fish, got off course. This made sense to me as a child. If all the storms and rain went north, it must be that all the planet's water flowed to one side like a tilted cup.

It started in the north, the far north. Places so far north that even Alaskans like me could not conceive of their latitudes. Inuit elders reported that the sun rose in the wrong place. People who had tracked the movement of the sun for all the decades of their lives – people for whom the sun vanished entirely for portions of the year and then one day emerged to great celebration and ceremony – they witnessed an oddity. It rose at the wrong time, in the wrong place.

A podcast crew dispatched to a village in Northern Canada where an elderly man pointed to a window in his prefab home. Through an interpreter he testified that, on January 23rd, the first sun of the year always rose precisely through the bottom center of the window. Every year. He was not wrong. If anyone on earth knew where the sun emerged on a specific day in January it was someone who lived in seasonal darkness. But now when the sun appeared, it came in through the upper left corner of his window – on January 17th.

Others noticed, too. From the Inupiat of Utqiagvik, Alaska to the Inuktun of Qaanaaq, Greenland, the northern inhabitants of the world reported that the sun rose in the wrong place at the wrong time. I listened on the radio, just 10-years-old, as scientists dismissed their testimony as the ramblings of an isolated people. Subsequently, news commentators were fired en masse over their comments. Like the famous morning duo *First Blush with Kevin and Kelly on KTVR* that I watched over my cereal one morning:

Kelly: Well, now these people also believe that the sun is held up by a raven. Isn't that true, Kevin?
Kevin (laughing): That's what I hear, Kelly.
Kelly (picking up her papers to close out the segment): Well, I don't know about you, but if a bird is holding up the sun, I couldn't blame it if it shifted around every once in a while.
Kevin: I mean, what if it has to go to the bathroom?

Kelly (laughing): Can't really blame it, can you? Even a bird who created the universe has to go to the little boy's room every once in a while.

Both (stacking papers, signing off): And that's our show. You heard it here on First Blush. Have a great day, everyone.

Then the Antarctic researchers – American, Russian, British (people of white skin) – reported the same findings at the South Pole. The sun was not where it should be. Instead of oral accounts, they provided timestamped photos and pages of inscrutable data. Then the world paid attention.

The theories people spun! Flat Earthers gained members not seen since the days of Eratosthenes. A powerful online presence exploded with the belief that the USA was secretly detonating bombs that tilted the earth on its axis. There were those who posited the earth was beginning its inevitable suction into the gravity of the sun, and they threw massive raves harkening the end times. Some believed it was not the earth changing but the sun itself signaling the return of the Prophet. But no one agreed on exactly what prophet it was.

These were the very early days of the Polar Storms, when it was just an aberration. If anything, the Solar Wobble (as it came to be known), generated more spectacle and inquiry. It was more dramatic than a shift of rain patterns. Rain comes and goes. Our sun stays in one place.

Ultimately, the two phenomena were tied together. The Solar Wobble had nothing to do with the position of the earth but was actually a trick of the atmosphere. A mirage showed the sun rising in the wrong place – a bend of the light around the top of the world so that the sun appeared full and bright where the sky was truly dark.

It was an inversion of the atmosphere, a flipping of the usual gradients that governed the meteorology we had built civilizations upon. Low pressure systems chased high pressure systems and vice versa. But now all low-pressure systems moved toward the poles – north and south – and high pressure bulged at the equator, pushing the clouds away like a belt cinched too tight.

A divorcee from Chile solved the mystery. This man, in his cuckolded anguish, embarked upon a transcontinental bike trip from Tierra del Fuego to the Chukchi Sea. He maintained meticulous records of environmental features and site conditions to calm his ailing mind. He observed the pattern of bulging pressure systems from a keychain aneroid barometer that hung to his jacket zipper. From there, photolithography from a dozen weather stations in each hemisphere confirmed his findings.

But maybe that man is just a legend. Who is to say how these stories get told?

The sun looked the same to me as I stood in the greenhouse, bundled up beyond any human shape against the cold, washing the rags and towels. We were far north, but not that far north. Light did not bend at this latitude. Our lives would not have changed if it did.

There was a baby now. We were marooned. Callie was gone no matter how often I searched for her face in every tree or the print of her bare feet in the snow. So I cleaned the towels without thinking about their contents the way a landfill scavenger forgets the smell and thinks only of getting to the next day.

During moments of reprieve, I went back to my windmill, starting in on the wiring so as to not burn plastic near the baby. I pulled out Mom's roll of copper wire – its spool nearly as big as me – and cut little pieces as I dissected the generator in the turbine. It was mindwork, busywork. The reality was that we did not need the supplemental power now. The sun did not move from its stubborn February peak. It did not generate any more power in our panels. But for whatever reason, there was enough electricity now. Whenever I needed a light, or to warm food on the stove, or pump water from the cistern, there it was – the power, on and strong. We did not need the wind or the sun. Our electricity was back.

THEY NAMED HIM MILES.

Mom liked the name because it conveyed how far away from the world he would be raised. His name reflected our isolation, our remoteness. Dad liked the name because in Spanish it meant *thousands* and suggested abundance and prosperity.

My exhaustion that night after the birth exceeded any tiredness my body had known. Even though he fussed for hours on end, I slept with the heaviness of a settling glacier. If I thought the age gap between me and Callie was big, the gap from me to Miles spanned entire mountain valleys. I was old enough to be his mother, and I didn't know how that would fit into my role within the family. I did not want to be in the cabin with this thing so fragile and pure. I did not want to stare into his face the way Mom did, as though he were a deep pool of water under which the mysteries of the world were etched in sand. He was a beautiful baby; I saw that plainly. When Dad handed him to me, I relaxed in the scent of his hair, ran my thumb along the river stone smoothness of his skin, and smiled in the way his tiny bottom fit perfectly into one cupped palm. But attachment to him was not mine to have. What I had let happen to Callie I would never let happen to Miles. I would never give the universe the chance.

MOM AND DAD alternated sleeping, with Mom awake when the baby needed to eat. From the loft I watched each of them, in turn, pace the floor of the cabin in a circle, bobbing the baby up and down on their shoulders, shushing quietly, pausing at the frosted windows so that he might gaze out upon the icy world.

Mom had struggled for so long, but now the quality of it changed. Her body was broken, piling physical pain atop her emotional pain. Sometimes she was loud – louder than she had been in months – with a cackling, almost manic voice. Shrieking. Then she openly sobbed like a bad actress in a silent film. Sometimes she was productive in a way unmatched since before the Birds arrived at Pluto Cove: fixing, mending, scurrying from corner to corner of the cabin. But sometimes she did not even move when Miles needed milk; Dad simply laid Miles on her chest until he had his fill and nodded off to sleep. Sometimes she shook like a branch in the wind, her nervous system detached from her brain like a junkie on detox. "It's hormones," Dad said to me. "They crash hard after having a baby."

Three days passed. Then a week. Miles put on

weight, and Mom was surprisingly compliant about eating what Dad handed to her. Seeing her belly grow had not spurred her appetite – but seeing the food physically extracted from her by a creature so tiny, lovable, and warm awakened her hunger. Then, he was a month old and Dad seemed to finally accept what was happening: Miles and Mom would survive.

The hair around Dad's ears and in his beard flecked deep with white; sometimes I looked at him and mistook him for a lost old man who had fallen asleep in the forest. He was Rip Van Winkle. But in holding Miles, assessing him, listening to the movements of his heart and stomach under a stethoscope, some of the lines on his face smoothed. Some elasticity returned to his skin.

I wondered if I looked older than my age. In the tiny round mirror of the ceramic owl I saw a different face from the one who had piled into the minivan that November day two-and-a-half years before. Under my own fingers, my skin turned from soft and plump to tough and lean. My raven black hair fell to my waist in a single braid. I could have cut it; we still had functioning scissors. But my hair was a clock, an inscription of our time at Pluto Cove. At the end of my braid was hair from my former life, hair I grew during soccer practices and sleepovers and from the depths of my deep, cozy bed with the lilac comforter. I often pulled at the end of my braid and swiped it across my cheek, an annoying tic to my parents. But it calmed me. In that hair I could feel what was lost. Callie lived in that hair.

I was tall – looking easily over Mom's head – but filled out in the chest and hips. Dad made no comment about my appearance, but it relieved him to see me develop normally, even healthily, under our circumstances. No matter what other disruptions life launched our way, the steady march of the body could not be stopped. Mom had shown that, too, as she grew Miles. And now Miles also, miraculously, grew.

But we entered that May at our lowest food stores ever. Hierarchy ruled. Miles needed to eat first. For him to eat, Mom needed to eat. For Mom to eat, we needed to hunt, garden, and forage. We spent that winter in a haze of the baby and under mounds of snow. We fell behind. The pile of potatoes and carrots in cold storage whittled down to bare ground. The dried strips of red and gray fish were just the empty racks where they once hung. The jars of preserves and jams from our berries were wiped clean by our tongues. The meats I harvested during searches for Callie were now bones – already boiled off – in the compost pile.

I slaughtered a handful of the older chickens, the ones who laid fewer eggs, and braised their meat for four hours. Still, it had the taste and texture of old football leather.

The snow, for as fresh and welcome it had been, kept me from heading up the mountain to hunt. While winter travel was normally easy, the snow persisted in a mucky, mashed-potato consistency for which I did not have the boots to cross. Twice I attempted ptarmigan hunts and both times Dad treated my feet for frostbite. There were some rosehips still dangling from bushes that I swallowed whole like vitamins, ignoring their pulpy, bitter seeds. The spruce tips emerged sometime in March, and I pulled them from trees until my hands were sticky and tarred with sap. We ate them cooked in flour and water, a sickly soup the color and texture of mucus.

It was erratic, and it was never restful, but I slept a lot in those days. Sleep for lack of energy, sleep to push out the sound of Miles crying, and sleep to forget the hunger. But the sleep was not sweet. It was only a pause in the movie whose ending I did not care to see. Sleep passed the time and was a dull and stupid relief from stress. Each time I woke up, I had to reconstruct my own hunger, to remember where I last left off. The first thing I saw was Callie's empty bed next to mine. As much as I needed to be out working, I just willed myself back to sleep again.

Finally, it seemed as though the weather might turn, that a warm spell would descend upon us and thaw out the earth so that we might make and find food again. But then, that last week in April, a raging, furious storm blew in from the Gulf. The windows in the cabin rattled as wind drove icy snow into the glass like pebbles. Snow drifted up and over the logs of the cabin as though we might get buried inside. It piled so high and deep on the roof that the frame sagged on the south side. Miles slept peacefully through it all, oblivious to any change in his environment, on a small nest of rabbit furs near the fireplace. Benji dozed at his side, his new protector. Dad and I hauled plyboard from the cellar – the same boards Great-grandpa used to close up the cabin when he left for the season – and tacked them to the windows with recycled nails. Mom sat by the door, her knees tucked up to her chin, thin arms encircling her legs. No words were needed. She thought of Callie. We all did, all the time. Snow would bury her, wherever she was. No little girl could survive such a storm. But then again, no little girl could have survived any part of the winter. Logic was irrelevant to us. Callie was missing. It was a purgatorial death.

In the thick of that storm, I resented that land, hated that place. In everything I learned growing up – from the Hoover Dam to the Erie Canal to the Roman viaducts – humans control their environments, not the other way around. We find water in deserts, we barricade our cities against unflappable tides, and we leave our footprints on every square inch of this world and declare it ours to own. But no matter how many gains we made at Pluto Cove, nature snatched it away, presenting her poker hand, hiding the ace all along. If there was a place on earth not meant to sustain human life, Pluto Cove was it.

But the Alutiiq lived on that same land for many thousands of years. An old map tacked above our bookshelf drew a great sweeping line across the coastal lands of the Pacific Eskimos. They thrived here. They adapted. They moved with the rains and with the food, but we had anchored ourselves to one crumbling cabin and hoped the food would come to us. Ten vicious seasons had shown that we were adequate at survival, but we were not thriving. We were not building an empire. We knew what berries were good to eat, but I could pass a hundred plants in the forest and not name them – let alone know their uses. I could fish using a carbon fiber pole purchased from a big box sporting goods store, but I could not build a weir made of fyke net. I watched whales breach in the open water, large enough to spin their own gravitational force, but could not fathom setting out on an open craft and spearing one before rowing it back to shore.

Mom had taught me the methods for field dressing small animals using a steel switchblade, but I always left meat on bones, body parts I could not repurpose, knicks in the skin. When my knife dulled, I was stymied. When the snow came, we were stuck. Without a boat, we were grounded. We had knowledge, but it was a wisp of smoke to what the Alutiiq had passed down over a hundred generations. We were a joke. Imposters. We started with a surplus. Now subsistence was all we had – and it would never be enough.

But, sometimes, nature has miracles too. Quadriplegics who walk again. Bullets stopped by a pocket Bible. Mudslides that spare a school and the children inside of it. Our miracle was coming.

The storm ended on the third day. It blew away, north, where all storms went. And at its heels came a swell of warm weather, fresh and heavy. The snow melted away flake by flake, and all that water penetrated the hard crust of earth. Our creek swelled and the deciduous trees exploded with green leaves. We had no airs that rain would come – this was surely an anomaly in the drought – but it was enough to jumpstart spring. It would be weeks or months before the seedlings in the greenhouse recovered. But just the promise of food was enough to stave off hunger for a few days.

Once the last of the snow shrunk to just a few stubborn patches at the bottoms of trees, I went to the shore to collect seaweed. I would boil it, ribbon it, and serve it spaghetti-like in bowls. The human-sized spool of copper wire lay in the cove, half submerged in seawater. My shoulders collapsed, realizing the storm had blown down the beach. I'd have to wade in up to my hips in icy water and push my weight against slippery gravel to roll it back to dry ground. I dreaded the chore.

Birds circled the mouth of the creek as I approached, hysterical in their swoops, dives, and calls. The water glimmered red, alive, shimmering like rubies in a jewelry case. I peered in closer. It couldn't be. I was hungry and delusional. Starvation makes the brain eat itself. It was the mirage of water at the desert horizon. It was the dream of cake in a crash dieter's sleep. It was the cartoon mouse dangling himself over the cartoon cat. I blinked until I was sure it was real.

It was salmon.

King salmon clustered at the mouth of our creek, pressing themselves into the shore, flopping over each other, pushing to be at the front like rock fans at a rock concert. Hundreds of them, thousands of them, silver finned and red tailed, as far out into the cove as I could see.

I was stupefied. Salmon did not spawn in this creek. It was not anadromous. I had never seen salmon here before. Mom had never mentioned it. Salmon return to freshwater in the fall, and now it was spring. There was no explanation for it, no sense. It was a miracle.

I waded into the water, unperturbed now by sopping wet feet, and picked up a salmon by the belly with my bare hands. It flexed its powerful tail, fighting me, but my grip was strong and sure. Even holding it in my fingers, feeling it resist me, I scarcely believed it was real. But it was. I turned on my heels and ran up to the cabin, holding it up in the air like a trophy, crying, "Mom! Dad!"

WE FEASTED. We feasted until we were sick, and then we feasted again. My stomach groaned and stretched until the sight of that pink flesh turned me inside out. I gutted fish until my hands blistered. I rendered fat into glass jars and, once congealed, licked it from my fingers like whipped cream. Even Benji ate himself into a coma. Our little corner of the earth had never delivered a gift so great.

Over several days, we developed a theory. Rather, Mom developed a theory. In the storm, wind blew the spool of copper wire from the cabin down to the mouth of the creek. Though poorly understood, biologists had some concept that salmon navigate the ocean using magnetic fields; Mom, massaging her belly full of fish, postulated that the copper disrupted their delicate magnetic sensors and drew them toward our cove. With that, and a combination of aberrant weather and ocean patterns, it was possible they were so thrown off course that the homing devices in their wee brains shut down.

The theory required testing, but we did not rush to do it. Moving the spool of copper risked them leaving. Though I canned, jarred, and dried hundreds of pounds of fish, no storage compared to having it fresh and alive. After the cellar overflowed with their meat, Dad and I went down to the creek and hauled the copper out of the water together, rolling it up the beach gravel like a circus ring.

Sure enough, when we awoke the next morning, the sky was silent. No birds squawked or fought overhead. No silver fins glittered in our waters. Only a few carcasses picked over by the eagles remained as testament to their visit.

We rolled the spool back to the mouth of the creek and waited. One day, two. No salmon, not even in my nets at the head of the cove. I panicked – we had ruined it. Their presence was a moment in time whose conditions we disrupted for scientific hubris and now could never replicate. But two mornings after that, gulls stirred me from sleep with their caws, fighting and feasting. The salmon returned.

The fish woke me up. It cleared my brain of cobwebs and scrubbed the film built up around my eyes. It was May now; sunlight careened out from every corner of the horizon. With energy to burn, I dared to dream again outside of the cove, to the world beyond, to the people, music, and fruits awaiting me. A full belly even rewrote history; I told myself the impossible passage over land that I traced from the top of Lamplighter Mountain had been wrong. The product of a weak and starving mind. I hadn't looked hard enough. There was a way. Mom, Dad, and Miles would stay here. I would walk out on foot and return by boat. I would leave, but it would not be the end. Not like Callie. That fall, in five months, I would set out.

I went about my spring chores with renewed stamina and motivation. I sowed each seed, believing it my last. I mucked the outhouse, believing I never would again. I washed cloth diapers, believing they were finite.

But for Mom, the clarity of food and open skies had a different outcome. It renewed her agitation for Callie. She had the energy to actively mourn again, to pace, and to gaze up at the mountainsides with binoculars looking for a path she may have missed. Her hunger had one perverse blessing: she was too famished to punish her body searching the mountain, her sleep was too starved to generate dreams or nightmares – but now she passed the nights in fits of sweat and screams.

One morning, Dad and I awoke at about the same time. He rose from bed and I came down the ladder to see Mom leaning over the kitchen table. Her shirt hung loosely at her chest as she expressed breastmilk into a glass jar. Miles slept quietly with his hands stretched over his head, the tips of his chubby fingers barely reaching the top of his scalp. Dark hair spilled onto his rabbit fur blanket like ink leaking from a pen.

"What are you doing, Lisa?" Dad asked, groggily.

"I'm gonna go out on the boat," Mom said without looking up from her task. "I'm pumping milk so you can feed Miles."

"You can't leave," Dad spurted, suddenly awake. "You can't leave Miles."

"I had a dream, Alex," Mom said with disturbing calm to her voice. "I dreamed about her. She's alive. I can feel it. She's out there. I have to look for her. The boat is the best place to start. It'll only be a few hours."

"Lisa–" Dad said, fumbling over his words. "Lisa, listen to yourself. The boat is trashed. Callie's been gone for–" he could not finish his own sentence. *Seven and a half months,* I wanted to say.

"I am listening to myself," she said, steady. "I am really listening to myself. And something is telling me she is alive. So I am going to listen to that, and I am going to find her."

"Mom," I said, inserting myself. Something I rarely did. It surprised them to hear me. For all the rich and complicated and interesting dialogue in my head, those days I rarely spoke out loud. "Mom, you know that can't be true. Think of the winter we just had."

She shook her head, turning back to the jar that she painstakingly filled with milk. "I just know she's alive," she said. "It'll just be a few hours. Then I'll be back."

"But then what?" I asked. My voice rose in volume and pitch. "Then what? You go out again tomorrow? And the next day? You abandon us because of a dream you had? You make me take care of Miles because we aren't good enough for you?"

She stopped cold. Even Dad straightened. I had not meant to be so direct. But while I understood I could not replace Callie, I expected Miles to succeed where I failed. He could take away Mom's hurt. She could fail me, but she could not fail her baby, the baby she had ripped open the universe to bring into the world, the baby made from some little spark of love at the fringe of reachable land, the baby with hair like a punk guitarist and cheeks like scoops of ice cream warm with hot fudge. She could not fail him.

And yet.

"Enna," she said. The sound of my own name was foreign to me. It had been a long time since it was spoken. "If it was you missing, I'd do the same."

"I don't know if you would," I whispered.

She stood up and pulled her shirt down. "If that's how you feel," she said, screwing the lid onto the jar. "Then there's really nothing I can do to convince you." She handed Dad the milk. "I'll be back in a few hours."

Dad looked at me with confusion and fury, as though I were the one driving her out the door. "Lisa!" he called out.

"What?" she asked curtly, pulling a jacket over her bony shoulders.

He faltered. There was no changing her mind. "Just…" he started. "Just…" he looked at the paper tacked next to the door and pointed it out. "Remember your contract," he said.

"I will," she said, without looking at him.

"Promise," he said.

"I already signed it," she said. "What more do you want? I am not a freak. I am not ill." And she left.

There is only one outcome to a story like this. A grieving mother in the muddy lakebottom of postpartum. A teenage daughter who angers her with conceit and self-righteousness. A woman with excessive confidence in her outdoor skills. Unresolved trauma from an unspeakable accident and a brilliant career abandoned. A vivid dream with the voice, eyes, and skin of her little girl, pulling her toward the water like a mermaid singing relief to the drowning sailor.

We did not see her again. Mom was gone.

HOURS PASSED. Darkness fell. Dad stood at the edge of the cove and gazed into the infinite expanse of ocean. He walked from corner to corner of the beach, out to the furthest reach of the gravel bar. But there was no sign of the boat, no sign of her. I stood by the cabin cradling Miles, trying to feed him milk through a plastic syringe meant for children's Tylenol. He twisted his head away from the plastic, resisting the milk, denying his own hunger.

"Come on, baby," I whispered. "Come on, Miles,

just take a little bit. It'll make you feel better. I promise."

But he refused. He wanted Mom's soft skin, the freshness of her milk, her scent. Not his older sister struggling to support his flopping neck, pushing cold milk at him through a plastic syringe. He twisted his head and tightened his body, curling against my pleas.

It went on for hours. His screaming penetrated my brain and rattled around inside of my skull like keys on a chain. My skin tingled under the anxiety and my lips buzzed with the relentlessness of his screaming. Surely he must fall asleep soon – no mammal so little could scream so long. But he kept going, going, going. We stayed on the porch, away from the lights in the cabin so bright, so punitive, so much like an interrogation lamp for questions to which I had no answers. I begged him. I negotiated with him. When all else failed, to my utter and forever shame, I yelled at him. "Please! Please! Please! Stop crying!" But he only cried harder.

Twilight smeared its glow around the cove, a candle's flickering of orange light. She had been gone all day. Still, Dad maintained his watch post at the shore. I was hungry, thirsty, and angry. I set Miles down on the porch over his blankets and instructed Benji to stay with him. Benji obliged. He was a better, more patient creature than I.

I walked to the beach. I called out, "She's not coming back, Dad. You need to come inside."

He whirled around to face me, kicking up a rooster tail of gravel. "She is coming back."

"Whether she is or she isn't," I said matter-of-factly. "You standing there isn't going to make it happen any faster. I need your help with Miles."

His eyes widened. "Where is Miles?!"

"He's on the porch," I said.

"Enna!" Dad shouted, taking off at a run up the beach. "You can't leave a baby alone!"

I threw up my arms, exasperated and bitter. "Then where have you been all day?!"

I trudged up the beach, following him slowly. I had no urgency to see the screaming baby. Which is when I heard it. The plunging of oars into water, the scooping of waves as a boat moves through the sea. It was not the sound of Mom's outboard motor. It was not the sound of her single emergency oar. It was a big boat. I heard it before I saw its shadow.

They were back.

Maybe they found Mom and brought her home, I wondered. *They rescued her and are returning her.*

So childish for a teenager, don't you think?

DANNY BIRD STOOD at the bow, clutching his face with towels. His posture was of a man in tremendous pain. Was he our patient? Why did they bring him to us – and not us to him?

"What do you want?!" I called out as the boat approached and landed in the gravel. My voice that day had ruined my mother, my little brother, my life, so I felt nothing about yelling, hostile, as they approached.

"You!" Johnny Bird called out, jumping from the boat and into the water, picking up a roll of rope to tie me. The dwindling light cast a pale shadow over the mangled side of his face. With a dirty blue windbreaker that rippled in the sea wind, he was *The Phantom of the Opera* from the moldy paperback holding up one leg of

263

our kitchen table. "Get over here! Now!"

I hesitated. I did not want to be still, but I did not want to run away. Adrenaline coursed through my body like wildfire. I wanted to stand there, and I wanted to fight them. I wanted to protect Miles. I wanted to protect Pluto Cove. I wanted today to have never happened, for Mom to have never left, for me to never have yelled at a three-month-old, and for Dad to have stopped Mom at the door with more than just his stupid contract. For too long I had been the Lamplighter, doing the same thousand tasks a day with no pushing back. Now I was going to push. I was going to fight.

I counted the men in the boat. Twelve rowers, six on each side. And the three Bird brothers. As I scanned their faces, I saw the green-eyed boy sitting with an oar near the back. He seemed to read my mind, detecting the clenching of my fists and the hardening of my jaw. He gave me a quick shake of his head *no*. The water surface glimmered over his eyes, and I saw that he really meant it. No.

I took a breath. I took a step back and turned on my heels, running at full speed toward the cabin. They could chase me. But I knew this land and I knew my legs. I was fast.

I burst through the door where Dad soothed Miles on the couch, forcing milk into his screaming throat as it bubbled up around his mouth. "They're coming!" I yelled. "They're coming!"

Dad stood up. He crossed the room in two steps and handed me the baby. "Go," he said. "Run."

"What?" I asked, holding Miles uncertainly, my heart like thunder crashing on a prairie. "I'm your nurse,"

I gasped. "You need me."

"Go!" Dad shouted. "They cannot know about the baby!"

"But Dad. Dad…"

"Mija," he said, grabbing my face with both hands. "You know this mountain better than anyone. Go hide. Hide well. Hide Miles. I will be okay. I promise."

I gulped. I looked at Dad. I looked at Miles. And I turned and ran out the door. Benji raced beside me. Up the mountain, Miles in my arms, quiet and stunned under the motion, tearing up the corridor of trees I knew like the contours of my own bed, running as I heard the sounds of Danny Bird screaming in great fits of pain, crashing over bushes and brambles, trampling the earth and scouring my skin over thorns and barbs, up and up the mountain, my long legs reaching over roots and plowing through devil's club, conditioned for this, ready for this, pushing through the brambles with one hand and clutching Miles in the other, up and up and up as their voices called out behind me *Girl! Enna girl, come out! Benji boy, c'mere, puppy!* until their voices disappeared into the air, up and up and up across the ridge to Great-grandpa's mine shaft, safe and dark.

From inside, I heard only my own breath, heavy and terrified. Benji stopped at the entrance, afraid. Out over the cove a crescent moon rose from the mountains like the corner of an all-seeing eye. I pulled Miles tight into my chest and sobbed softly over his small body. "It's okay, little baby," I said. "It's okay, little baby," over and over. "It's okay, little baby."

Benji took an uneasy step into the cave and put his chin on my knee. "Good boy, Benji," I said. "That's a good boy."

Miles went soft as he fell asleep on my shoulder, relaxing into me like melting butter on bread. "It's okay, little baby," I whispered in a trance. We sat there in the cave until the moon vanished and the sun rose. I was cold and hungry and stiff. I did not dare think of Dad. I did not dare think of Mom. "It's okay, little baby." I did not shiver. My belly did not growl. Miles, Benji, and I kept each other warm. "It's okay, little baby." For the first time in a long time, no matter my terror, I did not feel alone.

I STRAINED MY EYES against the laser of the rising sun, looking for a boat in the ocean, the tracks of oars across water, any footprint of the Birds leaving the cove. Spots danced in my retina, but I held my gaze through that morning and all through the day. I scooped handfuls of snow from a determined drift at the mouth of the cave and licked it from my fingers, easing the stickiness of my tongue. Miles uncoiled, weak and lethargic. I warmed snow in my mouth and dripped it down to him like a baby bird. He did not resist. He needed to get back to the cabin, to warmth and to milk.

We waited and waited. Miles slept, whimpering and hoarse, dehydrated. I held him as close to my body as our repelling electrons allowed, to let him know that no matter what other distresses he suffered, the lack of a loving person was not among them. Benji chewed on sticks and roots but never ventured more than a few feet away. I shoveled more and more snow down my mouth to stave off hunger and feel awake, but it only deepened my thirst.

The sun arced across the sky, a vertex parabola,

throwing shadows across the mountain pointing us home. As darkness fell, in the dusky dark of that spring sky, I traced the spiny shadow of Lamplighter Mountain, the Bird compound just over the other side. Clouds hung low in the sky and kicked back light from the compound like a distant city. *Even with all of them at Pluto Cove*, I thought, *they have the power to leave the lights on*. I kept my eyes trained on the orange glow, eerie and otherworldly in a place where I had not seen the lights of a far-off civilization since the last barges came through the Gulf, bright as satellites in orbit. *So bright*, I thought. *Looks warm.*

The western mountains gobbled what was left of the sun's journey. Miles' breath came in tiny slurps; his skin was pale. We could wait no longer; darkness was imminent. This was our moment. I nestled Miles securely in both arms and started down. "Come on, boy," I whispered. Benji did not falter and fell into perfect step in front of us, clearing our path.

It was so much further than I remembered. I picked our way down carefully, slowly, protecting Miles from the whips and lashes of the brush. What had I done the previous night? There were no accessible, coherent memories in my mind – only flashes, pieces, sensation, and speed.

When we came into view of the cabin, I paused. Listening. Snow melted from the roof and ice snapped in the thawing creek. I whispered pointlessly, "Dad?" And, even though she was gone, "Mom?"

There was no visible movement in the cabin, no smoke from the chimney. I pulled Miles in close and walked, silent, invisible. The windows were too high for me to peer into. I took the rickety porch steps one at a time, knowing all the places where the wood had gone soft and would not make a sound.

The cabin was dark. The lights were off. But there was no mistaking the figure of my father on the floor, unmoving.

I took a fast and desperate breath but controlled the urge to rip open the door and rush to his side. Assess first. Make sure it is safe. I scanned the rest of the cabin from outside the window and looked out to the cove. Empty.

Now I rushed in.

"Dad!" I screamed. "Dad!"

I set Miles down on the floor where Benji wrapped around him, a life ring, and I went to Dad's side. I shook him lightly. "Dad!"

He moaned. "Lisa," he choked, not moving his head. "Lisa...?"

"It's me, Dad," I wept. "It's Enna. I'm here. I have Miles. Are you okay?"

He did not respond. He rasped; his breathing only audible if I kept my ear just inches from his face. Even in darkness there was no mistaking blood seeping from his mouth, the bruises blooming like a toxic alga across his head.

"Dad," I said. "I need you to talk to me. You gotta talk to me, okay? You gotta tell me what happened. You gotta tell me what you need. I'm going to take care of you. Okay? I'm going to take care of you. I'm your nurse, remember?"

"Lisa…" he drifted.

I stood up and ran to the wall to turn on the light.

It was faint, candle-like. It illuminated the tatters of the cabin. Our possessions in ruins. The table broken and tilted like a kneeling horse. The stuffing of the couch disemboweled. Synthetic cotton stuck to the blood stains like fly paper. The blankets gone from the bed and the pots and pans gone from the kitchen. A single bullet hole burned into the floor about eight inches from Dad's left ear. There had been a pillaging, and there had been a battle.

I looked to Dad on the floor, curled into fetal position, then scrambled up the ladder to my loft. It was intact. For all their manpower, they had been hasty. I grabbed my blanket from the bed and pulled it down, draping it over Dad. I grabbed a cup from the floor and filled it with water from our tap, the electric pump running slow and in fits. "Here, Dad," I said. "Here, Dad. Have some water. Take a sip of water."

He struggled to pull his head back but did as I instructed. I poured the water into his lips, cracked open, purple and swollen as carrots. I could barely look at them. I could barely look at any part of him. They had beaten him. They had beaten him and left him to die. "Good job, Dad" I said. "That's good." Because there was nothing to say.

He had taught me a lot. First aid. Treatment for shock. Infection prevention. But more than anything, how to think clearly and methodically under pressure. I did not hurry. I did not rush. I fed him the water. I brought the fire to life and warmed the cabin. I irrigated his wounds and packed the big ones that I could not stitch, covering them in gauze and butterfly tape. I drew a circle in pen on his belly where a deep and ugly bruise signaled

269

internal bleeding and monitored it every hour for growth. While rocking Miles in one hand, I kept the other open to the pages of *The Second Edition Field Guide to Wilderness Medicine.* I could not start IV fluids or suture Dad's wounds, but I went to the cellar and ground the very last beet into a paste and rubbed the mash under his tongue for some sugar. I took his temperature and wrote the results down on my forearm. I watched his pupils under swollen eyelids and begged them to stay equal.

Mom's jar of milk had rolled under the couch and I tried the syringe again with Miles. In his stupor, he did not fight. The milk went down easily. He suckled in his sleep. Milliliter by milliliter I fed him the jar until only a fatty film remained. I laid him next to Dad to nurture each other in their warmth and smell. And then finally, I curled up next to Benji on the floor and closed my eyes.

I awoke to the sound of my name. "Enna."

I startled, swearing I had just laid down, but unsure of how much time had passed. A purple-orange light outside could mean dawn or dusk.

"Dad," I said. "You're awake."

His eyes swelled and oozed like beehives. He looked at me through a slit as he blinked away some combination of tears and pus. "Enna," he repeated. "That's you?"

"It's me, Dad," I said. "And Miles is here, too."

Dad drew in a thick and tortured breath suggesting he wanted or needed to cry – but out of physical pain could not. "Mija," he said. "Mija."

"What happened, Dad?" I asked. "What did they do?"

"Where is Lisa?" he asked, his eyes closed. "Did

she come home?"

I paused a moment. Bad news might crush him, and he could not afford despair. Before I answered, his eyes closed again, his wheezing breath in ragged intervals.

The story would not emerge for many days, as I changed his bandages and makeshift bedpan, and fed him watery pastes. I suctioned out pus from his draining wounds using a nasal aspirator that I disinfected in boiling water. It was humiliating for both of us, but I thought of Sophia whose grandpa had dementia and needed help changing his diapers. The class had all laughed and told her that was disgusting, but she answered with a simple response: you do anything for the people you love.

There was little I could do but make him comfortable – but he had taught me the body is a powerful healer and, sometimes, that is enough. There was no more milk for Miles, so I mixed flour and water, rice and water, boiled root vegetables and water, anything at all, and fed it to him through the syringe. A box of powdered milk sat in the back corner of the cellar, and I rationed it out like chocolate bars in a war. There was no replacement for breast milk. But from *Beowulf* and *The Canterbury Tales* I knew babies were sometimes sustained with paps and gruels, so I crossed my fingers and prayed. He accepted food through the syringe. Sometimes he even sucked on a spoon. One day, he discovered his fist and I implanted in his chubby hand a nub of dried salmon that he sucked at happily, drooling pink juices down his bare chest.

I worked my hands bare to my knuckles. I cared

for them both in every conscious hour. Each passing day was another day not spent in the garden, not working the soil, another day our basic survival requirements went ignored. I was setting us up for long-term failure. I knew that. But short-term failure was so much scarier – and more imminent. So I did what I could.

And Dad, over time, recovered some strength. He sat up. He drank water from a thermos, and the wounds over his face went from black to purple to brown. His breathing came stronger, surer. The biggest gash of all – the one over his shoulder – briefly turned an angry red but, after hourly washings with warm water and soapweed, returned to calm and the edges of the wound found themselves. One day, four weeks later, I came into the cabin from refilling the cistern and saw him sitting up, holding Miles and cooing.

And I knew he would survive.

Danny Bird had been wounded, Dad explained. His injuries were consistent with an assault using a metal pipe. One swipe to his head, another to his face, and a lesser hit to his ribs. Whoever had done it delivered some effective blows, but only a few before he or she was stopped. Most of his front teeth were gone. His nose was broken and maybe a cheekbone too. There were at least three palpably cracked ribs on his right side.

Dad tried to administer care, but there was nothing he could stitch together, no bones he could cast or splint, and no way to image his brain.

This did not satisfy the Birds. They wanted procedures. They wanted instant healing. They wanted assurances. Dad cleaned out Danny Bird's mouth, scooped up the loose teeth, and conducted some symbolic suturing of his upper lip though it would not help. He even rubbed some camphor over the broken ribs calling it an intradermal balm, hoping the attempt at concrete action would pacify them.

But Keith grabbed the little tub and took a sniff. That's when they decided Dad's life was not worth preserving. What good was having a doctor around if he was a trickster? If he was useless? He had worked for days field operating on a servant and a slave, but only took one look at the master himself, shrugging his shoulders.

So they beat him. First with fists, then with electrical wire. They could have taken their time – no reason to rush – but they were hurried, sloppy. One brother beat Dad while the other pillaged the cabin. Danny Bird watched it all through puffy eyes, barking demands and orders.

"Where's Enna?" Danny Bird screamed as Johnny Bird delivered kicks to Dad's torso.

"I don't know," Dad sputtered, barely able to form and execute words.

"She's around here somewhere!" he hissed.

"I don't know," Dad managed to say.

"We saw her run to the cabin," Johnny Bird added before spitting on Dad's head. "She's around here somewhere. And both of you'll suffer when we find her."

This triggered a surge of strength in Dad, his last. He rolled to his back, gripping his torso.

"If I had to guess," he said in a voice barely recognizable as human. "She's out in a tree with her .44 and is going to pick you off like wild pigs. There's no better shot in this wilderness than her."

This unnerved them, the prospect of a sniper hidden in the darkness. "Shoot him," Danny Bird directed.

Johnny Bird drew his gun. Even hearing the story from the lips of a survivor, I grew cold and hollow on the inside.

But then. "Hey!" Keith Bird shouted from outside the cabin. "They're tryna row away! The boat! The boat!"

With the three Bird brothers at the cabin, the boys of the boat staged a hijacking. Keith, Johnny, and Danny tore out of the cabin. Johnny raised his pistol and took one point-blank shot toward Dad as he ran out of the cabin – not stopping to see he had missed.

"Who do you think beat up Danny Bird?" I asked Dad.

He attempted to shrug, but his shoulders resisted. "I don't know," he answered. "Someone who probably suffered a lot after trying."

I nodded, musing. Why now? After all this time, what had happened on that particular day to make a slave start an unwinnable fight?

I walked down to the water to examine the scene of the coup. What kind of struggle had transpired there as the boys tried to leave with the boat? I half expected to find a corpse. But it had been days since the altercation, and the tide washed away all evidence. There was nothing to see.

But something caught my eye as I headed back toward the cabin. Off in the forest, tucked neatly into the moss at the base of a hemlock tree was something smooth and orange. I veered toward it, holding my breath. The thing I had searched for so strenuously – the piece of Callie's disappearance that I obsessed over most.

It had been placed there in the moss intentionally – concealed without being invisible. Subtle while still conspicuous. To catch the eye of someone who knew the land well. Which is exactly what it did.

Callie's berry bucket.

TRUTHS FORMED IN my head, but they were fuzzy, amorphous, disconnected. There was a story I had no words to explain. But there was a connection between all that had happened, a thread stitching it together. I just did not know what it was.

"What happened in Mom's accident?" I asked Dad one afternoon while I cooked salmon on the stove, handing fatty belly to Miles that he gummed with his one tooth.

Dad sat at the table, struggling to work some willow lashes into a plait, trying to keep his fingers dexterous and his mind awake. He did not look up at me. "Why are you asking?"

I shrugged. "Seems like whatever happened to her was too tragic to talk about. But we're past that now, I think."

I spoke casually, even coolly. Mom's disappearance coincided with Dad's attack and there had been no wide-open times or suffocating quiet spells to acknowledge she was gone. When I did consider it – when the thoughts pounced like a predator stalking me from the trees – it was with rage. This was her fault. This was her pit she carved. Anger flexed and bulged in me like a twitching muscle, a reflex born from her suicide attempt ten years earlier. How can a six-year-old know that the thing jamming up the bathroom door is a human body? What is it about the weight and resistance of a motionless human that is so obvious, even to a child? The sensation of forcing that door open had engrained itself upon me, and every motion – from lifting Miles to adjusting pillows around Dad – had that same friction and triggered those same thoughts. *If I had been better, she wouldn't have taken those pills. If I had hugged her harder before going to school, she would have called for help before swallowing.* No matter how many times Dad tried to convince me otherwise, my brain clung to that first-grade logic. Except now, it echoed off the chambers of my skull like a shot ringing out in the mountains: *If I hadn't challenged her that morning, she might have stayed. If I hadn't lost Callie, she would still be here.*

Anger was the only emotion that allowed me to recognize she was gone but continue the tasks essential to Dad and Miles. I let the anger keep me awake and used that extra time to wash diapers. I gave it space to agitate my blood and used that energy to haul double buckets of water. But somewhere inside – in a place I could not access or name – I was shattered. I was the egg, hideous and absurd, that all the king's men could not repair. I needed an embrace that I could not get. Hair tussles, strokes of the cheek, whispers of goodnight for which I languished. They covered my body like scabs refusing to heal. I was not a little kid who needed her mom to dress and feed her. I was not an adult who needed her mom to be the grandmother and celebrate a wedding or visit for Christmas. I was a 16-year-old who needed her mom for no other reason than she was my mom. Even at her worst, even at her darkest, she was my mom. My guts and spine and skin swelled with a love and longing for which I had no outlet. I wanted to tell my mom I loved her. But she was gone. Not just a bedridden shell of depression who was as good as gone – but actually gone. And that love had nowhere to go.

"She was on an offshore drilling platform," Dad said slowly. "Out in Cook Inlet. She was there with a crew of twelve guys, doing circuitry. The crew was taking out drill pipe from the well, but the company hadn't wanted to spend the money on high-density muds. They bought the cheaper stuff. The crew didn't know that. They didn't know they weren't using enough mud to offset the pressure in the well." He remembered with a level of detail suggesting he was lost in the memory, and I did not dare interrupt. "Gas started leaking out. Mom was in the control room. The gas ignited. There was an explosion that killed five men instantly." He took a deep, shaking breath. Smoke came from the salmon fillet, and I flipped it on the pan. "Then it caught on fire. The whole rig. The fire burned through the blowout preventer hoses, so gas kept coming up and kept burning. The exits in the control room were blocked by the fire. There was a guy in there, a young guy, a welder, named Ben. Not even twenty years old. He grabbed an emergency blanket from the first aid kit and covered himself and Mom with it. They made a run for it, out through the fire." The spatula shook in my hand. Dad's words slowed. Any memory of Mom was torture for him, let alone this memory. But he seemed to understand what I had said: there was no limit to our pain and fear. So why keep secrets?

"They got out, her and Ben. Four more guys were

dead at that point from the fire. So it was her, and Ben, and one other guy named Roger. Mom found the lifejackets. They jumped from the rig platform, eighty feet. Roger died on impact. Mom and Ben were in the water, that water in Cook Inlet. Barely above freezing, muddy, turbid, silty. They had five or ten minutes to survive in that water, maximum. A piece of blown-off platform was floating in the water and they crawled on top of it. Part of it was steel decking, and part was rubber insulation."

Dad's voice broke. I turned off the stove and scooped Miles into my arms from the floor. I pulled up a chair next to Dad and sat down. "And then an entire quadrant of the rig blew off, into the water. Including the control room with the open circuits Mom had been working on."

I nodded. I understood now how this ended. "And it landed in the water," I said, offering to help him finish the story. "Electrified."

"Yes," he whispered.

"And Ben was on the steel piece of the debris, and Mom was on the rubber piece."

"Yes."

We were quiet. I could not fathom the amount of voltage coursing through the flotsam that held up two human souls.

"Mom was electrocuted, too," he said. "Just the smallest part of her hand was on steel. But it was enough that her hand was nearly amputated."

A light flashed through my vision like the silver of a fish jumping from the water. "Is that why she always rubs her wrists, Dad?"

278

But he was too lost in the story. I knew the answer. "She floated there with Ben, who was dead, for three hours before a helicopter spotted her out in the tide and picked her up. The other guys on the crew had to be identified by dental records."

"She was the only survivor," I said.

"She was the only survivor," Dad repeated. "But barely. She barely survived. No one had much hope. But she survived."

I nodded. Mom was a fighter. Despite everything. Her trauma, her demons, her grief. She fought. Maybe she was doing that now. But I did not dare speak that to Dad. There was nothing more awful shared between us than hope.

The salmon sat there cold. Neither of us ate. We stayed at the table, watching the light fade out the window. Eventually Dad spoke. "Back then," he rasped. "Back then, I thought she was gone. Spent so long in a coma. I thought it was just going to be me and you. The two of us." He had told me this once before, high above the cove, before the Polar Storms. "Looks like it's come up that way in the end, hasn't it?" Dad cried into his open hands.

I felt in that moment a surge of something unfamiliar. Something warm and smooth as hot cocoa running into my belly after coming inside from building a snowman. It softened my muscles, relaxed my nerves. It was a tangible, physical thing. But it could not be seen, could not be touched. It was forgiveness. Forgiveness for my dad. For all he failed in the things he could not control – the drought, the Polar Storms, the Birds – and for all he could control but had forsaken. Me. Talking to me, checking in with me, spending time with me. All the nights I spent reading books beyond my academic league simply to fill my head with voices and beating hearts because the ones inside the cabin had forgotten me. I forgave him. "We're a team," I said, putting a hand on his back. "Then and now."

I CONTEMPLATED MOM'S story for many days. I wanted to digest it, to process it, but really it digested me. I had been swallowed by the story and was passing through its system, churning and grinding, being crunched into tiny pieces for extraction. I wished she had told me. But I understood why she hadn't. I slept with Benji's face next to my face and thought of his namesake, the man with the blanket who pulled Mom from the fire.

It was laundry day, and I filled a tin bucket with water to warm over the stove. Dad was up and moving – gingerly – and announced he was taking Miles to the beach for some Vitamin D.

"Okay," I said at the sink where the bucket filled at a steady clip.

After they left, the water slowed to a trickle and stopped. The cistern was full, I had just filled it. It sounded like the pump. I dropped the bucket in frustration. Our power problems were – too much or too little, and I couldn't modulate the flow from the batteries. It made me miss Mom in a way that gnashed at my skin and wore me down to the thin, spidery veins pulsing under it. Even when she was detached and lost within herself, she was another chamber of my heart, another hemisphere of my brain. Without her, I was half a strand of DNA, built of limbs without joints, a mouth without teeth, a nerve without a synapse.

Dad came back through the door with Miles. "I'm going to bring a blanket to set him down on," he said, grabbing a towel because most of our blankets were gone. The pump kicked back on, and the bucket again filled steadily.

"Thank god," I muttered to the sink.

Dad left again with the towel, and the pump slowed again, eventually stopping.

Why it was that moment and not the thousands of moments that preceded it, similar in scope and situation, I do not know. But it clicked. The skies parted and the realization struck me like a tree collapsing in a windstorm.

It was electricity. It was all electricity.

"Dad!" I shouted, running from the kitchen and out the door. "Dad, come back here a sec!"

Dad looked worried and puzzled – summons only came for terrible reasons. He moved slowly and with great pain, but moved nonetheless. I ran back into the kitchen, waiting for what would happen when they returned to the cabin: the pump turned on, strong, once again.

I grabbed Miles from Dad's arms. "Let me see the baby," I said. I switched on an overhead light even though the cabin was bright with sun. The light came on. Then I did something unthinkable: I pinched Mile's foot. Hard.

"Enna!" Dad scolded.

"Shush!" I replied forcefully. He did not argue.

Miles cried and the light brightened.

I ran to the stove and turned on a coil burner. It

came on with a buzz and gradually turned red. Then I grabbed Miles' other foot and pinched it even harder. He screamed and wailed, and I watched the coil go from a deep crimson to a blinding cardinal, smoking off its own nichrome.

I turned off the stove and turned to Dad. "What's the meaning of –" he started.

"The Birds have them," I said. "Mom and Callie. The Birds have them."

THE STORY WAS an unbelievable one. An outlandish one, the fiction spun of a distressed and disjointed mind. But I knew it was true. Miles was my proof.

"Mom has powers," I said, as Dad worked his way down into a wooden chair, looking at me with a sadness and disappointment that did not deter me. "After her accident. It gave her powers with electricity. She can't generate it, but she can amplify it. She can take an existing circuit and make it stronger. Her nerve synapses, her action potentials. Just like you taught me. We all have a current and a charge. Her shock on the drill platform lets her amplify those through the action potentials in her nerves. And when she had Callie, she passed on those powers. And now Miles, too."

"Enna," Dad said sadly. "Enna, this is absolute nonsense."

"It's not," I insisted. "It's not. Think of all our problems with electricity and making power. They didn't really start until Callie disappeared, right? Why do you think Mom put the battery bank under her bed in the loft? And then it all miraculously recovered once Miles was born, even though it was February and we were getting basically no sun in the solar panels. Did you see what Miles did just then? How the pump and the light and the stove all worked better when he got closer? It's magic, Dad. They have magic."

Dad said nothing. The word magic was anathema to him. It turned his hearing off to anything that followed. "What on earth would this have to do with the Birds?" He said. "Enna, you're wanting to make a reason for why your mom and sister are gone. Sometimes things –"

But I didn't let him finish. "They figured it out," I said. "They figured it out before we did. Do you remember on the beach the first time we met them, when Danny Bird threw a headlamp to Callie and she turned it on even though he insisted the batteries were dead? I think they started spying on us and I think they could see that she was drawing electricity. Do you remember when Mom was in labor? Do you remember how bright it was in here? I thought that was just in my head, like just the intensity of what was going on. But I think it *was* actually brighter. I think she was making the light bulbs burn brighter." I was on a roll now. "And did it ever seem weird to you that Mom was able to make the boat run so, so, so long after it ran out of fuel? She said she converted it to electric, but we never really asked her what that meant. How was she charging it?"

Dad took a deep breath. He was so close to these things that he never thought about them, never considered them. Mom handled the electricity, the power. He handled the health, the injuries. That was the separation of duties, and they did not cross. But something in him cracked open, just a little.

"Think about it. Think about their compound when we went over for the green-eyed boy with the gunshot wound. It was all dim and dark. Then when we went over for the girl with appendicitis. And it was bright! So bright in there! And that space heater in the corner. That's a huge amount of power, and you know it. That was after they took Callie, after they were using her for extracting electricity."

"This is crazy," Dad muttered, his words discouraging but his tone unconvincing – as though they were the words he needed to say, but not words he necessarily believed.

"What about how when they got here the other night, they asked for your daughter? For me? But just one daughter, singular. They even asked for me by name. How could they know there weren't two of us? I always assumed they'd come for me since I'm a teenager and clearly that's what they want …" my voice trailed as I considered the undertones of pure evil – of rape, assault, pregnancy. "But they didn't. Callie was more valuable even as a six-year-old."

His face went pale and the ugly colors of his injuries faded. Miles reached up and put a tiny finger into my mouth, hooking the back of my teeth as I spoke. I had not spoken so many consecutive words since Callie disappeared. The sound rubbed at my throat like sandpaper.

"Listen, Dad," I insisted. "When I escaped with Miles that night, that night the Birds came, that was the day Mom disappeared, right? We were up on the mountain and I could see over the edge of the spine by where their compound is. And it was so *bright*, right? Like

284

a whole city in the darkness. Like, how could it be so bright? And I swear, I know it sounds crazy, but I swear it got brighter as the night went on. Which would have been Mom's first night there."

Dad said nothing. He stared into space. I adjusted Miles on my hip who had forgiven my pinching his feet.

"And Dad," I said, lowering my voice hoping he would really hear, really listen. "Dad, do you think it's a coincidence that the day Mom goes missing is the day Danny Bird gets beaten by someone? Who would do that to him? Who would dare fight him?"

Then Dad broke. His hands flew to his face, over his fresh scars and open cuts, as tears welled in his eyes like water into the hull of a bullet hole in a boat. "Mom," he said. "Mom would."

WE WERE SCIENTISTS. We conducted experiments. I left Dad in the cabin to work appliances while I held Miles at different distances. We recorded lumen outputs in the lights when Miles was asleep versus awake. We compared relative heat in the stove coils when he was in the cabin versus on the porch. We measured the volume of water out the pump when he was mellow versus when he cried. Something other than the known laws of physics were at play in our little cabin – and over Lamplighter mountain, across the Qaneqiraluq River, at the Bird compound.

That night, Miles snored contentedly from his bear skin nest on the cabin floor. Dad was exhausted from the long day of experiments. We sat on the couch, comically deep in the collapsed cushions, watching the baby sleep as though he were a bonfire burning in a mountain range. Neither of us spoke for a long time, and my eyes fluttered as my neck sunk into the flattened foam of the couch.

"You know," Dad suddenly said, startling me from my oncoming sleep. "Back in the days, in the Polar Storm days, I really thought I had things figured out."

"Oh," I said, groggy.

"Yeah," he continued. "I remembered each day thinking *This is it. This is as weird as it gets, this is as bad as it gets. I am ready for whatever comes tomorrow.* And then the next day it'd get weirder, and it'd get worse."

"Huh," I said.

"You're just a kid," he said, as though confessing to a crime for which he had not been accused. "So you might not get it, and that's a good thing. But it was so disconcerting to me as an adult. Especially as an emergency physician. I had been trained to always think that the worst thing is coming yet, to never get complacent. But those storms … the ways people started acting … I started to feel, just, so naive. Every night I went to bed feeling a hundred years older than I had in the morning. But still I would think, *This was the last day, tomorrow will be normal again.* And then, in the morning, I'd have to go age another hundred years before I realized I was wrong. Again."

"Yeah," I said, drifting.

"I guess what I'm trying to say," he started, then leaned forward and put his face into his palms. "Nothing should surprise me anymore. Not even this." He gestured at Miles, snoring in the furs. "There are so many mysteries to this world, still."

"There are," I echoed.

"And tomorrow," he said. "I'm not going to be passive anymore. I'm not going to wait for things anymore. Your mom didn't. You didn't. I'm going to meet the world where it's at and stop waiting for it to behave how I want it to."

Somehow, I ended up asleep in my bed that night. I awoke in the middle of the night to a dark and quiet cabin, and scooted over to Callie's bed, dragging over the blankets, breathing in what was left of her faint and precious smell. I gazed out the small porthole of our loft and saw the North Star, Polaris, glowing down at me in the small hours of darkness, the bright star at the tail of the little bear. I thought of Ovid's *Metamorphoses*, the hardbound book with the cover of a half-woman, half-ram. I remembered the verse as Jupiter cast Callisto into the sky at the moment before her death, forever enshrining her in the stars as a bear. Ursa Major, Callisto the bearwoman. There lay Callie, my Callista, in the stars, a bear pacing across the sky. I missed her so much I felt it in my teeth, and bit back tears before rolling away from the window and spiraling into sleep once again.

Hours later Dad startled me awake by ripping cover pages from books. Blank paper – a precious resource – for a final plan. A rescue mission.

Something in me nagged that I was wrong. Maybe Mom and Callie were not hostages with the Birds. But I assured myself: even if I was wrong, our plan was right. Freeing their slaves, the green-eyed boy and bald girl. We would get one shot at destroying the Birds. Far from my childish righteous virtue – my alarm as Mom stole the skiff, my horror as Dad pillaged Daisy and Dennis' cabin, my inability to see that some wrongdoings were both necessary and humane – I was now consumed by adrenaline and monomania. I was cynical, confident, and irascible. Destroy the Birds.

It had to be fast – it had to be out of nowhere. It had to be cataclysmic. We pulled out Dad's old maps of their compound and considered the resources at our disposal. We had guns, but they had more. June was never dark, so we had no natural cover by which to infiltrate. And of course, we had a baby, who was never totally quiet, not subject to instruction or keeping a low profile.

Even back during the first visit, when Dad caught a few glimpses of their layout, the compound was huge. They could be anywhere in those cabins, out in the forest. Surely it was even bigger now, more elaborate, better guarded.

"What about setting a fire?" I suggested late in the afternoon, tired of talking over plans and simply wanting to act.

Dad shook his head. "They could escape a fire. They could ride it out in their boat. And in this drought, we'd risk burning the entire mountain all the way to Pluto Cove and beyond."

I sighed. "Yeah, but at least it'd wipe their compound off the map."

Dad slowly straightened, going rigid, his pupils dilating. "What?" I asked, breathless. "What is it?"

He looked at me with the wide-eyed, disbelieving, hopeful eyes of a man who has just sailed his boat onto an undiscovered continent or stumbled on the cure to disease. "The jökulhlaup," he whispered. "The flood."

I blinked hard. "The ice dam at the top of the

mountain…" The hike with Dad to the top of Lamplighter, to the cathedral of ice holding back the subglacial lake. "If we could break it, it would destroy everything downriver. It'd destroy them instantly."

"But maybe give us time to get some people out, first," Dad said, thinking only of his wife and daughter.

"Yeah," I said, unconvinced, but not wanting to abandon our momentum materializing from nothing. "One of us breaks the jökulhlaup, and the other gets people to safety somewhere."

"But how do we break it?" Dad asked. "How could we possibly destroy that much ice?"

I looked at him square in the eye and smiled for the first time in so long it was like carving marble. "I actually know where there are a lot of explosives stored on Lamplighter Mountain."

CHAPTER EIGHT - *Three Days Later*

We had a plan. It came to us in bits and pieces, fits and starts, but eventually it melted into a cohesive shape that we could pound into sharp, pointed edges. It was a carefully choreographed dance, a flow chart, a treasure map. Once the jökulhlaup blew, we would have only minutes. At most. There was no room for error.

We fought. A lot. We had Doubts that mom and Callie were at the Bird compound at all – but decided that it was worth wiping the compound clean either way. We were playing god and had deemed the Birds not fit for existence. It was the end product of tortured minds and bodies, of humans living in perpetual terror whose sense of reason and conscience had wasted away. The world, in all its open spaces and profound complexities, had come down to just one choice: us or them.

We fought over whether anyone at the Bird compound could be trusted to help, and how to recruit them. We debated the existence of the large timber pile Dad saw near the mouth of the river. One of us, Dad or I, would have to shelter with Miles. Dad insisted he go, as the aging man who lived a big life. I insisted I go, for if something went wrong, Miles would need his dad far more than he needed his sister. Dad could keep him alive.

Even as we set out of the cabin, boarding up the windows and doors and taking one last look at its rundown walls and collapsing roof – never before had it looked so small, so decrepit, so impossible to have held us and our lives and our grief for so long – we did not know who would stay behind with Miles on the mountain.

We started up the mountain on the fourth day. Dad was weak and bruised. He carried the shotgun and a backpack holding incidentals like nine-volt batteries and steel wool, the first aid kit, dried salmon, root purees, a jar of motor oil, and a switchblade. In the pocket of his jacket, he stuffed the small blasting cap I had crafted from parts of the turbine and cook stove. Even that small load was a great weight on his injuries, and he suffered up each step, struggling to pull air through his broken ribs.

Benji trotted at our feet with several hundred feet of spooled copper wire strapped to his back. My boy was getting old, but – elated – to shoulder some of our burden.

As for me, I carried sixty pounds of TNT on my back. In one hand, a machete. And on my chest, anchored by one of Mom's old sweaters tied at the sleeves, Miles.

Our progress was impossibly slow. I was fit and mountain-worthy but had never carried a weight so great. I broke trail for Dad; Benji ran ahead as our scout. For every two minutes of hiking we took one minute of rest. Our steps were like those through thick and sticky mud, not the dry and crackling forest floor stretching up around us. We followed the creek for water and game. But the sound of our labored breaths and heavy footsteps on dry twigs frightened creatures before I took aim.

One afternoon we spent two hours completely motionless, waiting, before a grouse poked its head up through the brambles. I punctured its neck with one clean shot. Just feet from its body, I found a nest of eggs. We sucked the marrow from its bones and ground up the eggshells to drink in our water. Dad packed a small bag of powdered milk and rubbed it into Miles' gums. Miles mostly slept on the steady rocking of my chest as I walked; but when he awoke, we knew he ailed. We all did.

I patted his rump as we walked and sang ambiguous melodies into his ear – the tunes of songs I had long since forgotten. I thought of Sacagawea, traversing the Rockies with a baby strapped to her back, leading the way into dangers and obstacles unknown. I thought of Signe Bergman, marching to Stockholm for women's suffrage with a baby on her hip and a picket sign in her hand. I thought of Mom, ripping open the sky as she brought Miles into the world a hundred miles and a hundred years from any modern medicine. This is what women did, I told myself. This is what women do.

With no threat of rain, we camped without tents or tarps. The first two nights we spent in the root caverns of spruce trees. The second two nights we rested above tree line with the summit of Lamplighter in full view. Though the icefield was there, visible, the distance to it seemed insurmountable. But at least now we were out of the trees and brush. Passage would be clear now, but steep.

The sun did not set. On the mountainside with nothing for cover, there was no sleep to be had. Dad lay against the pack with Miles in his arms, both of us willing ourselves to forget the pyramid of unexploded bombs under the nylon and zippers. Miles was wrapped in George's fur, the ones I had sewed before his birth, with bear ears poking out over his hood. I lay against Benji's side and felt his steady breathing.

"Remember the last time we were here, Enna?" Dad asked quietly, watching the sun that refused to set.

"Yeah," I said, lingering briefly in the memory of digging our snow cave on our way to the jökulhlaup. Everything then was simple, easy, comfortable. We went outside for fun and recreation and exploration. Pluto Cove was a vacation. No one hunted us. No drought. No hunger. When I needed to be warm, I went somewhere warm. When I wanted a snack, I opened a cabinet. When I was dirty or sweaty, I stepped into a shower and then into clean sheets. When I was lonely, I picked up a phone or walked down the street. The memories felt distant and hazy – as though remembering a story told by someone else.

Dad was in the same space. "Sometimes I wish I had known then what we had," he said. "I thought so much about my mom, your Grandma Julienna, and what she ran from at the border and what she struggled to create. I just assumed we only moved forward from there, not backward. That anything to come would only be better because we work hard and are good people. But that's not how the world works, is it?"

His question startled me. Matters of fairness and function were for me to question, the kid. But he knew no more than I did. The great secret of adulthood. "No," I said. "It's not."

"If I could do it all over…" he started, trailing off like the great streaks of orange painting the sky.

"No," I said, cutting him off. "It's not worth it to do that, Dad."

He sighed. "You're right."

Neither of us said anything. Then I felt her, Callie, near to me. The heat from her body warmed mine. Her light hair drifted over my shoulders as though she leaned against me. "Callie would say that we were the luckiest people alive," I said. "No matter how bad things got or have gotten. We were together, our family. We had a place to go. People who love us. Parents smart enough to hack it."

Dad chuckled a little. Just a little. "I don't know about hacking it," he said.

"Clearly you did," I said. "Because here we are."

He took a deep breath. "You, too, you know."

"Me what?"

"You also hacked it," he said, committed to using my language. "You are the smartest, toughest, most incredible girl – young woman – I could have ever imagined."

"Dad –" I said, senselessly embarrassed up there at the top of the earth, holding the sky in my hands.

"Mom and I got us started," he conceded. "But you kept us going. With everything. I can't even tell you my shame in those times after we lost Callie, how I gave up. Mom and I both did. I saw what was happening, I saw you going out day after day and working yourself ragged. I saw the meals you put on the table and the fire you kept going in the stove. And I wanted to say something for so long. I wanted to thank you, to acknowledge you. But," he paused, catching his breath. "But I was so ashamed. I couldn't even look you in the eye because I thought you would see how weak and cowardly I am. I shut you out so that you would keep thinking I was strong. Enna, my Enna. Mija. I'm so sorry. I'm so sorry. Until the end of the time. I'm so sorry."

And to my dismay, without any permission from my body or brain, I cried. "It's okay, Dad," I whispered.

"I forgive you. It's okay, really."

"It's not," he said, reaching out and grabbing me by the hand. "It's really not okay. A parent is there for their child, no matter what. I abandoned you. Mom did too. We were in the same five hundred square feet, and we just completely left you behind. But it didn't stop you from saving us, saving our lives. And reading. Every night, you read your books, still wanting to learn, still filling your brain. And you helped me after I got hurt … and you helped bring Miles into the world… mija, you are the light of my life." His words tumbled out, staccato and hurried as though if he did not say them all at once, he may never say them at all. "La luz de mi vida. Do you know that? No matter what else happens on this mountain, watching you grow up here at Pluto Cove was the best thing that ever happened to me."

I could say nothing to this. But I felt it. I knew he meant it. I knew all along that my mom and dad loved me, appreciated me, respected me. If I didn't, I wouldn't have worked so hard. Though they had fumbled and erred and missed many chances, I knew. From those months when Mom was in a coma after her accident and he curled up next to me in my toddler bed each night, to the day Callie was born and Dad promised me I was always his niña and first love. From the trust he put in me to be his nurse and care for the sick and dying, to Mom cutting up the apples in my lunchbox into flowers and stars. From cuddles with her on the couch under a dozen fleece blankets watching *Elf* every Christmas Eve, to the days when she was so sad and sick she could not leave her bed but cracked the door to signal that I could come in and lay on her bed, and she would place one hand on

my back, pulling out the tangled ends of my hair. I knew
in my marrow that I was deeply and unconditionally
loved. It grounded me. It flowed through me like blood.
But hearing it there, out loud, in this place we had shared
when I was little, simply for the thrill of seeing this
beautiful and wild world into which we were born, was
more than I could bear. I rolled over into him and let him
wrap one arm around me, the other holding Miles. He
winced as I touched his ribs but tried to hide it. "Te amo,
papí."

"Te amo, mija."

And I decided I would go down the mountain to
face the Birds. Miles needed his dad.

THE TOE OF THE jökulhlaup spread before us like a
great Roman wall, massive and crumbling. It was smaller
– so much smaller – than the day we saw it six years
earlier. The subglacial lake behind it stretched over many
square miles. The ice atop it glittered in alpine winds blue
and white. The ice was vast, epic. The water below it
could have nourished a city for a century. Creeks and
gullies flowed from the edges of the ice like spider legs,
braiding and weaving as they parted and joined down the
mountain. But there was one true river coming from the
dam: the Qaneqiraluq River. And at its bottom, we
believed, were Mom and Callie.

We set up on the eastern side, the Pluto Cove side.
I needed to cross to the west side to be on the Bird side. I
would walk across the jökulhlaup, plant the explosives in
the middle of the ice, and then keep walking to the other
side. I would wave to Dad from the other side. And then I
would descend.

The ice was cracked and rimmed with crevasses. It was strong enough to hold back all that water – surely it was strong enough to hold me. But I could not fall. The June sun had melted down most of the snow, and the canyons of ice were clear and translucent. But each step was a risk, a held breath for stable footing, a sigh of relief before the next one.

We ran through the plan one last time. And then we looked at each other. "Enna, are you sure?" Dad said. "It should be me."

We had talked it over for hours in the last stretch of the hike. At one point he leaned over and vomited at the idea. But I convinced him. "Dad, you're still so weak," I said. "We need someone down there who can be quick. It has to be me."

"This is going to work," Dad said.

"This is going to work," I repeated.

I looked away, unable to meet his eyes. "I don't know how to say goodbye to you," Dad said, choking. "I never thought there would be a day in my life like this one."

"I'm going to see you at the cabin," I said. "You and Miles. You'll be there. I'll be there soon with Mom and Callie. That's all this is."

"Okay," he said.

I hugged him and Miles. Tight. I felt his embrace radiate into every cell, anchoring itself into my spine, and felt it impart strength.

"Your abuela crossed the desert to get to a better world," he said. "Now you'll cross the ice."

I blinked back the burning in my eyes. "Sì, papì."

The pack listed me side to side like a branch in the

wind. My legs fought beneath its weight, knees braced. Benji leapt at my heels, eager to follow. "No, Benji," I said. "You have to stay with Dad."

He understood the command – but ignored it. He bit the fabric around my ankles and whinnied. "Stay," I said. "Stay." But he would not stay. Each step I took, he followed.

I fell to my knees before him. "Benji," I pleaded. "You have to stay here. Stay with Dad and Miles. You can't come with me." He barked softly and licked my cheek.

"Take him with you," Dad said from behind me.

I turned to look at him. He gave a nod.

"This isn't part of the plan," I said.

"That's okay," Dad said. "You need your Benji. He won't let us down."

I grabbed Benji behind the ears, pulling him close to smell his fur. "Okay, boy," I said.

"Let's go then." He gave a little jump with his forepaws onto my collarbones before I stood up, wobbling less now under the weight of the pack, buoyed by his joy. His loyalty.

I turned with the massive pack and walked toward the glacier. "Dad," I called back.

"Yes, mija?" He answered, gripping Miles to his chest.

"Did we come to Pluto Cove because of me?" I asked. "Because of my skin? My name? Because of who I am? Am I the reason for all of this?"

He did not say anything for a long time. His face betrayed nothing but the agony that, for years, had entrenched it, eroding his skin like water down granite.

"If I said yes," he answered, "would it change anything?"

I thought about it for a moment. "No," I said.

"We would do anything for you," he said.

"I know," I said. And I took the first step onto the ice, Benji at my side.

THE ICE WAS ANCIENT. Ailing. I swear it creaked and shuddered under my careful footsteps. Benji and I walked in tandem, one step at a time, unraveling the copper wire behind me like Gretel leaving breadcrumbs in the forest. The passage was clear at first, just open ice, pitted and smooth. But that gave way to breaks and cracks that fell a hundred feet into nothingness, into a cold and darkened hell. It was here, at a point of existing weakness, that I knelt and pulled off the backpack. I roped the sticks of dynamite together high and wide, so that the explosion of one would amplify the explosion of another. I plugged in the copper wire to the blasting cap and traced it to the detonator at Dad's feet, and unspooled the wire.

Bating my breath that the wire would hold, I lowered the TNT over the edge of the deepest accessible crevasse, wide and yawning like a monster embedded in the arctic earth, so that a failure in one spot would give way to collapse in another and another and another. I let the wire descend, inch by inch, into the crevasse, until it disappeared into the ice and the wire lost all slack. The bomb was maybe a hundred feet deep into the glacier. The wire would need to hold it for as long as it took me to signal to Dad. I turned around and looked at Dad and Miles from across the ice. I gave a wave. He waved back.

Then Benji and I continued onto rougher and

rougher ice. It was rotten and soft on top like old cheese. I didn't trust my feet to hold me upright and fell to all fours, spreading my weight. Benji stayed low next to me, and we crawled across the remnants of the glacier, using my elbows to protect my hands and fingers from frostbite. Then even my elbows and knees became too much pressure upon the decomposing ice, so I moved to my belly, scooting across the full weight of my body like a caterpillar. We were back at the solstice, back at the peak of summer once more, but there was no warmth on a million tons of ice. It was a perpetual winter, though the sun reflected high and bright off the surface.

Finally, finally, Benji and I reached rock. Solid ground. I stood up and held my body, enclosing myself around my own shivers, breathing warm air back into my blue-tinged skin. I looked across the ice. Dad was a shimmer in the distance, but he was there. I did not know how to walk away, how to keep moving until I could no longer see him. But people vanish in this world. Now it was my turn.

We started our descent down the other side of Lamplighter Mountain, a mountain I knew so well. But here was its shadow side – the side I could never see, obscured, like the backside of the moon. I crossed the alpine tundra past a herd of mountain goats and took a moment to observe them. One female with ragged, coarse hair looked straight at me out of her left eye, black and gleaming. I gave her a salute, then continued on.

The bushwhacking was fierce through the tree line. My arms rapidly fatigued as I preceded each step with violent whips of the machete through the brush. Sweat matted my hair and I stopped often to drink greedily from the river. This was not the soft trickle of water from our creek. This was a deep, swift body of water that propelled tree stumps and tumbled rocks down the length of the mountain. There would be no crossing it. I thought of Dad and Miles on the other side and hurt all over.

Then Benji and I came to a plateau on the mountain with a flowering meadow. A tributary of the river fed into a small, dazzlingly lush pond exploding with shades of green gone extinct in the drought, wildflowers in bloom. An oasis. We walked up to the edge where in the pond, knee deep, a moose chewed lazily at the bog grasses. Such an easy kill, so much meat. I looked down into the cloudy water, and there staring up at me was a person I did not recognize. She had a hard, lean face with skin pulled tight over high cheekbones, and a coarse braid that swung past her shoulder like a jungle vine. She wore a dark, ripped men's t-shirt that fell open at her collarbones exposing her thin, sinewy arms that rippled with muscles. When I gasped, startled, she gasped too. When I flexed my hand up toward my 30-30, she did too. How old this person looked. How weathered and gritty.

Mirrors do not manifest abundantly in nature, and years had passed since I saw any part of myself outside the small disc on the ceramic owl. Even then, I had barely consulted with the mirror since Callie vanished. There was no time for primping, and no piece of my horrid self I cared to see. This person reflected in the water was tough and hard. She looked strong enough to march up a mountain with explosives and a baby, and steady enough to take aim at – and then destroy, harvest, and devour – an animal of any size. When I looked at her, she looked like a person who would attack a grown man, or three. When I looked at her, I felt ready. When I looked at her, I wanted to hoist the Winchester and take aim at the moose in the meadow just to watch it buckle, watch it – so much larger, so much more powerful than me – die. I could never eat so much meat before it rotted with flies. I just wanted to kill it because I could. Benji rustled at my side – so eager for the moose – and I remembered the goat buck. "Easy, boy," I said. "Let him be." And we continued on.

At the other side of the meadow there was a clear trail. Not a narrow, ephemeral trail made by bears and game, but a clear-cut trail, the brush on either side recently swiped by machetes and hacked through by saws. A manmade trail. I knew where it would take us. "Come on, Benji," I said. "We're almost there."

The passing from there was swift. With little weight on my back and an open path to follow, I moved easily. Whereas Dad and I had taken five days to summit the mountain, I would reach its base in less than one.

CHAPTER NINE – *Four Hours Later*

The trees towered and soared overhead as we approached the bottom of the mountain. Here, the river gave life freely and abundantly. Regardless of drought, this was a thriving ecosystem. I felt a pang of jealousy as I crossed the fields of unripe berries and traced animal tracks through the dirt. Timber polluted the landscape. Even the largest of the spruce and hemlock trees were sawed down to the dirt by the jagged and uneven cuts of a handsaw. Sun shone through the canopy here in a way that unnerved me in a forest so close to the sea. This was an engineered landscape. Bird territory.

I saw the potato hills first. They started at the edge of the trees and descended toward the wide-open space of the compound. I had snacked on dried fish and berries for the past five days, but it was wildly insufficient. No amount of restraint could stop me from dropping to my knees in front of the potato hills and digging with my bare hands like a groundhog. The potatoes were small and hard, but I popped them into my mouth, dirt and all, and chewed them until the starches released and relaxed every muscle in my body. Benji took his fill too. I ate until my belly overflowed and I felt nuggets of unchewed potato regurgitating in my throat. The hill was at the edge of a field that stretched on and on like the rice paddies of Vietnam. No one would notice my incursion. Not in time, anyway.

Benji and I hugged the side of the river where the brush was thickest, picking our way through without disturbing a single branch. I kept the potato field in my peripheral vision and gave thanks for the robust and springy vegetation that did not crack or snap under foot. In river brush this choked, I would not see any cabins. I instead listened for voices.

The potatoes transitioned to other crops, still young in the early summer, but doing well. Kale, cabbage, and beets – the same hardy plants I tended. And there, at the transition zone, I heard someone cough. A deep, hacking cough. I pushed away a window in the brambles. A boy. He was crouched over, sowing seeds. Carrots, I guessed. I grabbed Benji by the ruff and stroked his neck while I watched the boy. He was my age, maybe a little younger. Far too small for a cough so loud. Skinny with a thick and fluffy cloud of hair like an angel. They kept the boys with long hair, I thought – though I didn't have much data for these conclusions. And the girls with shaved heads.

Patience pulled me, perfectly quiet, into the deep brush. Dad was at the top of the jökulhlaup, ready for my signal. But my signal would take a while. There was one person we needed, and I had no idea where he was, what his role was, whether he was even alive. The green-eyed boy. I sat down in the brambles and watched, waited. Benji put his chin upon my knee and fell asleep under the gentle strokes of my hand against his fur. I fell asleep too, nestled into a thicket of bendy willows. How much time went by before a voice woke me up, I do not know – the light was lower in the sky, but shadows were short and spoke of daytime.

"Eric!" The voice called. I shot awake, panicked, forgetting where I was, imagining I had been caught, spotted, that the pricks against my back were a chair of nails in which they would torture me until I confessed to Dad and Miles up the glacier. "Eric!"

The boy with the afro worked higher up the hill now, but I could still see him. Straight across from me, through the thicket, was the green-eyed boy. He was taller, broader. But there was no mistaking him. "Eric, time to go in. Come on."

The boy stood up and stretched his arms. His too-small shirt lifted and slash marks crossed his back, light and shiny as welding seams. I reached into the pack for the small jar of liquid Dad prepared. I unscrewed the lid slowly, without a sound, without a single disturbance to the molecules in the air around me. Eric started walking down the hill, stair-stepping over the small plants between the rows. The green-eyed boy stood still for a moment, gazing up at the mountain. He was reflective, lost in his own mind for just a moment. This was it. I grabbed my shoe, and in one swift movement yanked it off my foot and launched it into the air, out of the brush, just downslope of the boy. He whirled around, confused, then moved toward the sound.

I was catlike. Hunting skittish game had honed my speed, reflexes, and cover. I shot out of the brush and grabbed the boy from behind, throwing my chloroform-soaked sleeve over his mouth as he gave two great thrashes, and I pinned it there until he went limp in my arms. I dragged him into the brush without wasting a single moment. The boy named Eric was two hundred feet away and glanced back once – but by then we were gone. He did not even shrug. The absence of his partner, leader, or whoever this was in my arms, did not faze him. How easy it is to pluck someone from the wilderness.

He would revive in minutes, Dad said, if I did not keep a steady application. I set the boy into the brush while Benji sniffed at his pants and feet – bare and calloused as barnacles on a rock. I pulled out my 30-30 and leveled it between his eyes. I did not shake. I did not flinch.

His eyes flickered open as I stood there, counting my breaths six seconds in and six seconds out. He saw the barrel, registered its meaning, and immediately pulled back, crawling away. But I kept the gun in the same place, right between his eyes, and there was nothing but the river behind him.

"Who are you?" I demanded.

He swallowed hard, his breaths rising fast in his chest. He said nothing.

"I said who are you!" I repeated, louder but not too loud. Meaner. "What's your name?"

"A–a—" he stuttered. "Antonio."

"Antonio," I repeated.

"You are Enna," he said. I ground my jaw, displeased by his knowledge. "You saved my life," he continued. "Please don't hurt me now."

"That depends," I said. "Where are they? Where are my mom and sister?"

He did not pause or flinch or even blink. He simply raised his hand, pointing down the hill toward the cabins by the beach. "Over there."

I LOWERED MY GUN. Not all the way. I could shoot him if I needed. But I aimed it away from his head so that it pointed at a slower death. "Why are they here?" I asked.

"I don't really know," Antonio answered, relaxing just a millimeter, still propped on his forearms on the ground. "They make electricity. They are powerful."

I counted my breaths, slow. The insanity of my theory, the utter improbability of it, was confirmed. All those years with Mom, all those years with Callie. And someone else found out before I did. Before Dad did. Someone sinister.

"How many people are here?" I asked.

"Thirty," he said, quickly enough I knew that he too had made plots.

"How many are good?" The question needed no explanation. He had asked me the same thing back on the wooden operating table, looking up at me from his bullet wound. *Are you good*?

"Eighteen."

"Who are bad?"

"The Birds, the three brothers. They have six wives between them. One is with us; she sneaks us food and lets us sing our songs. And three of us, who they kidnapped, they always take their side, they think they were saved by the Birds."

"And you?" I asked.

"I am good."

"How do I know?"

Antonio gave me a long and desperate look, his eyes as green as the alder leaves into which I had him pinned. "I left the bucket at the cove. For you to find."

I relaxed the gun. "I am going to free my Mom and Sister," I said.

"They will find you if you do," he said. "No matter how far you run."

"No," I said. "They won't. Because they will be gone."

"How?"

"Do you trust me?"

"Yes."

"Then I'll tell you. But you have to know. I'm here to save my mom and my sister. I have to be honest with you about that. They're why I am here. But I'll try to get as many of you out as I can, okay? You have to work with me. You have to do everything I say, exactly as I say it."

"Okay."

"Do you really mean that?"

"Yes."

"Even it means you're in incredible danger? You'll still trust me and do what I ask?"

"Yes."

"Do you swear on María Luna?"

He startled at the name. A name that forever circulated in his head and down into his chest like water circling a drain, a name that he could not speak out loud. But he trusted me. "There is nothing you could tell me to do that is worse than what they do," he said. "I swear on María Luna."

"Let's get to work," I said.

WE SAT TOGETHER in the brush and he sketched a map in the bare earth. It was shockingly like what Dad had drawn the year before – but with expanded infrastructure, propelling out in all directions except toward the sea. "The lumber pile," I said. "You are sure it is still right here, by the mouth of the river?"

He gave me a quizzical look that was reassuring,

familiar, in its youth and teenage airs. "Of course I am," he replied. "I live here."

We went through it again and again. The cabin where Mom and Callie were trapped. The mechanisms by which they were tied down. The distance between the lumber pile and their cell. The distance between their cell and the ship – the great wooden Viking ship that we had first seen sail past the cove. Which kids at the compound could run the fastest and could shepherd the others.

Then I gave Antonio the rest of the copper wire from my pack – less than fifty feet left. "You got this?" I asked. "You know what to do?"

"I got it," he said. "I've been waiting a long time for this."

"Okay," I said, looking him in the eyes and marveling at the face of another human being to whom I shared no genetics. What a strange, flimsy species we were. Alien to me now. Soft and fragile.

"What about the girl?" I said. "The girl with appendicitis?"

Antonio looked away from me and down to the ground. "She didn't make it."

"What?" I exclaimed. "But we – but we –"

"Infection, I think," he said. "Her fever got so high. They didn't give her a chance to heal."

This filled me with an unexpected sadness. I had expected to see her face again, there on the ship, as we made our escape. She would show me her scar. We would share our age, our fears, and all the things we mourned in a world that up and quit in our adolescence. But for all of Dad's magic, she was gone.

"What was her name?" I asked.

"Natalie," he answered.

"Let's do this for Natalie," I answered.

"For Natalie," he repeated.

We nodded at each other, almost a bow, and he walked down to the compound.

THE COPPER WIRE came first. Antonio put it in the water, where the river emptied into the ocean on the other side of the Birds' bridge. Across the Qaneqiraluq River, on the Pluto Cove side. The wire would sit, just as it had at Pluto Cove after the spring storm, until the salmon came.

Antonio would find the salmon and initiate the celebration – food, abundant food, fatty, easy food, there for looting. No man can resist a fish easily caught, especially a man surviving in the wilderness. Everyone – Danny, Johnny, and Keith especially – would exalt the miracle of the salmon, would call it divine intervention, and they would be distracted.

Dad and I tested it several times in different locations. The quantity of copper, the proximity to freshwater. It took anywhere from six hours to two days for the salmon to appear. Six hours to wait. But I was good at waiting. I did not need entertainment or distraction. I had a purpose – Mom and Callie down at the compound, Dad and Miles at the top of the mountain. They suffered more than I.

I huddled in the brambles, pulling crops from the edges of the fields and sharing them with Benji. Time would pass, one way or another. I trusted the salmon to come.

The sun dipped to its lowest point on the horizon

before bouncing back up like a rubber ball on a wooden floor. I moved down the river, pushing through the brush, to a place where I could hear commotion and excitement while staying concealed. I fell asleep to the sound of the river rushing by, plunging from under the toe of the jökulhlaup and down the side of the mountain. The flow of the water connected me to Dad and Miles – an artery circulating between us. I saw the shapes of the cabins and knew which one Mom and Callie were in, easily identified by the tangles of wires, emerging from the roof and spreading to the other cabins like branching neurons. I ached, being so close to them. I thought of Miles snug in Dad's arms, with jams and mashes filling his belly, unaware that living and sleeping atop a mountain was no ordinary thing in life. It calmed me. I rested against Benji, and he into me. There was no place more familiar to me than the fur on his belly.

The air had warmed when whoops and hollers jolted me awake. The sounds of elation and unbelievable luck. The salmon had come. Antonio spotted them first and ran back to the compound, right past me, to alert the others. The Birds ran from their cabins, across the bridge, and down to the freshwater zone where the salmon piled against one another, confused and disoriented. Guns fired, just as Dad predicted. Everyone wants to shoot a fish in a barrel. They wasted ammunition just for the joy.

This was my signal. I ran the river's edge, ducking in and out of the swamp grasses along its bank. Benji trotted behind me quietly, seeming to know he could not even wag his tongue. When the bridge came into view, I cut west to the woodpile, following my memory of Antonio's drawing. There it was. I stole a glance across

313

the bridge and saw the three Bird brothers jumping, splashing, and shooting into the water like children at a circus game, throwing fish bodies dead or alive onto the gravel bar with no interest in preserving the meat. This was Christmas and they were little boys tearing open wrapping paper and moving on to the next present before seeing what was inside.

A group of women with long, light hair and long, flowing dresses stood on the bridge, facing away from me and clucked their tongues in mock disapproval but genuine excitement. One asked if there was any paprika left in the pantry. Another replied she would send Girl Four to look. She turned toward the compound, as though she could see Girl Four from the bridge. In profile, her belly was round as a soccer ball anchored to her trunk. I felt a sickness well up in my core. The terms of my plan were simple: us or them. But I had not considered that *them* might include a baby. Another Miles.

I peered to the west, toward the compound. Upriver was the largest of the cabins: Danny Bird's cabin. Its ocean-facing flank was smooth, imposing, and windowless. Instead of an oceanview, a mural covered the siding. I recognized the icon from my own life, from real life, my life Before. The flags waved, the bumper stickers on cars, the patches sewn onto clothing. From the side of our garage the day we fled Anchorage. The single cloud with the piercing lightning bolt. The Cloudburst Crest.

We had suspected. But what did it matter? The Birds were the Birds, LFR or not. But now, here at their compound, hidden and armed, it mattered a lot. This was not me against a family. It was me against a movement,

314

an ideology, a hatred. To fight it, to defeat it, would mean murder. From our first glimmer of the plan back at Pluto Cove, I knew: I would kill human beings en masse. But here, seeing those humans, hearing their voices, I faltered. Nothing was hypothetical now. *Murderer* was a definition of myself too horrific and abstract to reconcile. I was Enna, a kid, a soccer player, a dog owner, a bookworm. Could I take a life to save my sister? My mother? Could I take a life to save Antonio, to avenge Natalie, to claim this river and all its gifts? Could I take a life to extinguish a sect of the LFR, the reason we were at Pluto Cove, the reason my world had unraveled? I took a breath. I looked at Benji, into his inky eyes and felt a seismic shift in my conscience. The answer was yes.

I darted from the brush, across the open gravel – the most exposed I had made myself yet – to a nook in the lumber pile where the logs formed a small alcove like the opening of an igloo. I waited there with Benji for five seconds, then ten. There was no shouting, no one approaching, no indication I had been seen. I made it. I pulled off my backpack and unzipped the pouch, taking out the nine-volt battery and clump of steel wool – our firemaking tools after Callie expended all the matches.

Fire was the great enemy of our time, and I readied to unleash it upon Lamplighter Mountain, our own home. I breathed deeply and closed my eyes. Mom and Callie were fifty yards away. The smoke was my screen to run across the compound – and the smoke was my signal for Dad to detonate. I swiped the wool across the positive end of the battery until it sparked, brighter and brighter, and a splinter of wood ignited. I held the splinter to the lumber pile, willing it to catch before the piece burned my fingers. But this was the age of the Polar Storms. The Pyrocene. The wood begged to be lit on fire. It caught in a swift flush of heat and cackled all around me.

I could not run. Not yet. There needed to be smoke, more smoke. The fire licked up the edges of the pile, and my skin turned warm, then hot, then ablaze. I held out as long as I could before running. I had to tolerate the heat that bore into my skin like hypodermic needles, like animal teeth, like gashes of hot and rusted iron tearing into me. I thought of Joan of Arc and pulled her memory into my bones. She smiled as she burned. I could do this.

Benji whimpered and whined. I pushed him away from me and the fire, but he would not leave my side. He bit and nibbled at my clothes, pulling me from the fire, but I held fast and he stayed.

Finally I could take the heat no longer. From my backpack I pulled out a glass jar sealed with a rag drenched in expired motor oil and hurtled it against the burning timbers where the glass shattered and exploded. Thick black smoke billowed into the air around the oily rag and surged over the beach. This was my moment. "Benji, run!" I yelled. We took off at a dead sprint across the open plain of the gravel beach, toward the cabin with the wires. I wasted no energy to look around, to see if I had been spotted. It didn't matter if I had. Either way, I was going to run as fast as my legs – long and muscular and sure – could take me. My feet plunged into the soft rock, slowing me, but Benji took off fast and set my pace.

I came to the door of the cabin just as someone shouted from the bridge. "Fire! Fire!" came the voices of men. I ripped the door from its handle and stepped into a mechanical room, just as Antonio had said. I tore through the mechanical room to a second, heavier door with a padlock across the opening. I grabbed a metal pipe leaning against the wall – the same kind Mom used to attack Danny Bird, Antonio told me – and knocked the lock off its screws with a dozen unrelenting blows. The door swung open.

There were no windows in this second room. It took a few costly moments for the light to seep in and my eyes to adjust. Before I saw anything – before I could see the partition that separated them from each other, before I could see the thick ropes cuffing their wrists and ankles, before I could see the panels of wires to which they were attached – I heard her voice. "Who's there?"

"Mom!" I screamed, dropping the pipe and running to the direction of her words. "Mom!"

"Enna!" she screamed back, her voice carving ridges and ravines of love and longing into my heart. There was only one voice like hers. And she called my name.

I felt for her in the dark until my arms wrapped around her. Her heartbeat thrummed into mine, the first sound I ever knew, the rushing of her blood, the aliveness of her body, the moment I came into being in the darkness of her belly. "I'm here, Mom," I cried. "I'm here!"

"Baby," she said, sobbing, unable to move her shackled wrists. "My baby."

I spent one more second in the safety of her body, warm and soft to my skin even as a prisoner and slave. Then I rallied. "We have to move fast," I said. "We have to move really fast."

My eyes acclimated to the dark, and I saw a single bulb next to the doorway. I ran to it and patted the wall down for a switch. There was none. I reached up and turned the bulb: it flickered on.

Mom, standing frail and broken, was tied to the wall, bound to a diagram of Delphic, haphazard, electrical wires. On the other side of a plyboard wall was Callie, my Callie, curled up on the floor, her roped hands up and over her face, covering her from the world.

"Callie!" I shouted, running across the room. Her skin was pale as teeth, but it was not the whiteness of death. "Callie!" I grabbed the switchblade out of my back pocket and sawed at the ropes. "Callie, wake up!"

She mumbled, moving her hands across her face. "Callie, it's me," I said, working my way through the arm binds and moving down to her feet. "It's Enna." I pulled off the wires attached to her head by old knit hat, like a paranoid conspiratorialist guarding himself against alien brainwaves, and I scooped her up in my arms.

"Enna?" She asked, groggy, unable to open her eyes. I took her to Mom's side of the partition and set her down on the floor.

"Oh my god, Callie," Mom wept, having been adjacent to – but unable to see or protect – her daughter this whole time. "Callie."

"She's okay, Mom," I said. "She's just weak." I took my blade to Mom's ropes now. They were much thicker. Lines were worn into the wooden floor underneath her like a lion's tracks in a zoo enclosure. She had put up a fight. The blade popped out of its handle halfway through her second wrist and I grabbed the bare blade and kept sawing. Each cut into her ropes was a cut into my hand, but I felt no pain and saw no blood. "Listen, Mom," I said, sweating under the exertion. "As soon as you are out, we are going to run. As fast as we can. Down to the water, down to the boat. The big boat, the ship. Get on the ship. Don't look around. Don't stop for anything. Just run. Got it?"

"What about Callie?" she said. "She can't run."

"I'll carry her," I said. "You are too weak. Don't worry about us. I got it. Just run."

I moved the blade to her ankles and felt an explosive pop in my hand as I severed a tendon. I lost control and sensation in my ring and pinky fingers. But I kept sawing. Until Mom was free.

"Run!" I said. "Run!"

I grabbed Callie and threw her over my shoulders like a gunny sack, her body light and limp. I held her by the backs of her knees with my bleeding right hand, my 30-30 up and cocked in my left hand. "Benji!" I shouted, but he was already there with us, running out of the cabin and down to the beach.

Black smoke hung in the air like a polluted city. The lumber pile had burned like a plane crash and ignited the brush and trees around it. We were awash in thick, shadowy smoke that choked and burned our throats. But it offered us cover. Around us people screamed: the sounds of women shouting for buckets of water, the sounds of men shouting for their slaves. "Where the fuck are they?!" Came Keith's voice from the east. Flames licked up from the river's edge and sparkled along the wrack line where seaweed and driftwood dried at the hightide. It was a war zone: chaotic, incomprehensible, terrifying. It was hell, burning and hot and endless. It was part of the plan.

Mom was slow, so much slower than she had been, but she did not stop. It was 200 yards to the ship. We were closing in on it, the mast was growing in and out of the gusts of smoke that whipped in the air. One hundred yards. Fifty. Callie was getting heavier. My shoulder burned, and my diaphragm collapsed under her weight. But I couldn't stop. Twenty-five yards. Twenty.

"Hey!" someone shouted. "Hey! What the hell?" I did not recognize the voice. I turned toward it for a split second. It was a boy I did not know, tall, strong, and sturdy with a thick crop of brown hair. He was better nourished than Antonio. Better cared for. One of the converts.

I kept moving, pushing Callie higher onto my shoulder as he chased us, unencumbered by weight. "Danny Bird!" he screamed. "Danny Bird! They are here! Enna is here!" He yelled it as though it was expected, as though they had prepared for it.

It went against everything in my body and heart. I raised my 30-30, still running, holding it in my nondominant hand, and took aim. It went off, ripping through the air and the smoke, barreling into his thigh like a wormhole in space into which all other life and light was swallowed. He went down hard and fast, propelled by his own momentum. "Danny Bird!" he screamed more loudly now, frantic, in pain, desperate. "Danny Bird!"

Ten yards. Five yards. There was Antonio, at the dock with his arms outstretched, pulling Mom up onto the planks and hoisting her into the boat. He reached down for Callie and grabbed her off my shoulder, handing her to Mom over the hull. I scooped up Benji, and he leapt from my arms over the side and immediately popped back up to watch for me.

"Are they here?" I asked Antonio.

"They are here," he said.

"Let's go," I said.

I raised my rifle into the air and fired six rounds, one after the other, into the smoke. Antonio rushed to untie the boat from its cleats and two other boys stood in the water, digging their feet into the gravel and pushing at the wooden sides until it gave way to deeper water. I stood there on the dock, gulping for air, urging my heartbeat to quiet so I could hear it. The bomb. Off in the distance, at the top of the mountain.

One seconds. Two seconds. Flames leapt out of the forest all around me now, from the riverbank across the compound, swallowing the cabins and shacks, zipping across the dried jetsam of the beach to the other side and engulfing the trees there too. The world was orange and black, dancing, consuming, disappearing into ash and dust.

There, from the smoke, was a shape. Large and lumbering and fast. Danny Bird. Behind him, running, Johnny and Keith. "Get them!" Danny shouted with the voice of Cesar himself, running into battle leading a thousand men. "Take them or I'll burn the other sides of your disgusting faces!"

That's when I heard it. The pop in the distance. Faint, slight, but unmistakable. The TNT.

"Go!" I shouted to Antonio. "Now!"

I ran and jumped into the boat, toppling onto the deck. Mom and Callie huddled together and I yearned to throw myself on top of them, to bury myself in their arms.

But I grabbed an oar. I had to row.

The other boys were in position. The two pushing the boat off in the water took a running start and grabbed onto the edge to climb up the hull. But one was small. His face was square like a statue that hides within the ruins of a jungle. He ran, he ran, but there was Danny Bird, at the water. He was fast, so fast, faster than any human on this earth. He reached out and grabbed the boy, ripping him down by his shirt collar and pulling him into the water. The boy struggled and splashed. We couldn't stop for him. We could not save him. We had to row.

"Ho!" Antonio shouted, pulling the mast to release the sail. "Ho!"

We rowed. We dug the oars into the water like knives into the flesh of a fallen animal, fast, sharp, desperate. Faster, faster, faster.

But Danny Bird kept going, going into the water until it was up to his knees and then his thighs and then he raised his arms and dove in. He swam. He swam fast, so fast. He was not human at all. He was an animal acclimated to land and sea. He barely came up for air. His kicks launched him through the water like the propeller on a submarine. He was going to catch us. The tide was coming in and slowing us down. From shore Keith and Johnny fired round after round into the boat, shielding their eyes against the smoke, the guns bouncing with their coughs, unable to take aim. We ducked down into the boat while keeping our hands on the oars, but we lost leverage. Holes ripped through the hull like stars exploding in a darkening sky.

Someone screamed. From my crouch, I turned and saw a girl with a bald head, tiny and thin as a mouse, release her oar and grip her forearm. She'd been shot. *She can be saved*, I thought. *Later.* Mom peeled herself away from Callie and belly-crawled toward the wounded girl. Keith Bird shouted unspeakable obscenities from shore as his gun jammed. Johnny Bird ran low in his magazine. We heard the explosion of the ammunition shed as the fire licked at it like a preening cat.

I turned back to look for Danny Bird. He had disappeared into the shadow of the ship. Had he stopped swimming? Had he drowned? I dropped my oar and crawled to the stern, peering out from a crater in the wood carved by bullets. There he was, Danny Bird, there at the bottom, grabbing on to the wooden planks and hauling himself out of the water, climbing up the cracks and grooves like a spider. I looked around the ship, but it was gone – my Winchester. My gun. It was nowhere.

I screamed to Antonio. "We have to stop him!"

"Grab an oar!"

A boy and a girl pulled and tugged at my oar trying to free it from its oarlock – but in their protective crouch could not get it up from the water. They threw all their weight against it, but it would not come free. I looked over and saw the tips of Danny Bird's fingers reaching up to the edge of the boat. His nails dug in like bolts, one after the other. I stood up over the deck, unable to avoid the gunfire, needing to risk it, to risk everything, leaning down to unply his fingers and throw him off the edge before he could pull himself up. But there came Benji.

He leapt up into the wooden rail and with a great snarl, sunk his teeth into Danny Bird's hand. Danny Bird yowled in pain and released his grip, falling back into the water. But with him, attached to his hand, went Benji too.

"Benji!" I screamed until blood curdled in my lungs, hurling my torso over the edge of the boat. "Benji!" He bobbed up with Danny Bird, struggling, fighting, making to swim away. "Benji!!!"

And then it came.

The jökulhlaup. The great flood. The wind came first, rolling down the mountain, accelerating, hypersonic, blowing into us like an explosion and filling the sail. Then came the sound of rushing water: the ripping of trees from their roots and boulders from their perches. Finally, I saw it. A wall of water, biblical, rushing down the ride of the mountain, a rocket in its speed, destroying all in its path, wiping the world clean of drought and sin.

"Brace!" I yelled. "Brace!"

It was going to hit the boat. It was going to launch us up and over, and I prayed to the wind, *Push us out to sea, push us out to sea.*

Closer and closer, faster and faster. It doused the fire and stripped away the burnt skeletons of the cabins like toothpicks under a dinosaur foot. Johnny Bird screamed from the shore, "Flood! Flood!" before it swept him away into a roil of water, bubbles, rocks, and roots. It was a river that ripped the world in half like a piece of paper. It was the atom bomb in New Mexico that blasted a scar into the face of the earth that would never fully heal, splitting time into a before and an after that would never again touch.

Before I closed my eyes to brace for the impact, I looked down at Danny Bird, treading water, watching the approaching river with a look of terror and confusion, begging for mercy. He was just a human after all. I saw my Benji, paddling in the water, looking up at me with big dark eyes. "Benji…" I whispered.

Then I closed my eyes, and the wave hit.

WE DRIFTED ON the boat for a long time, saying nothing. There was nothing in our muscles or brains or hearts to compel us to pick up the oars and paddle on.

When the jökulhlaup hit, it launched the boat up and up and up until the laws of centripetal force required we flip over completely and crash into a pile of splinters and limbs. But the boat did not obey this law. It stayed upright, riding the crest of the wave, and coming down to the trough with a tremendous blow that sent us flying on the deck, landing hard and with great shakes that compressed our vertebrate and squished our bellies. We broke many ribs between us. But those were survivable.

I crawled across the deck to Callie and wrapped her in my arms. I had forgotten how small she was. A child. She fit into my embrace as though she had been built for that space. Mom made her way to us, unsteady on her hands and knees, and wrapped us both in her own arms. Again, as though we had been built specially for that space.

"My girls," she said again and again. "My girls."

We watched the Qaneqiraluq River fade into the distance, great lesions of destroyed earth raking down the mountain like claws. There was nothing left. No structure, no human, no bridge, no trees. Just the mouth of the river where the moon rises.

Eventually Mom, holding my face in both of her hands, looked at me and said what needed to be said, what needed to be acknowledged. "Benji did it for us. It's what he wanted. Our good boy."

At that moment, I disintegrated, losing all connection to my muscles or my bones, falling apart in a way I had not since the very earliest days at Pluto Cove when everything had been nothing but darkness and loneliness, anger and resentment, and the deflated soccer ball. I bawled against Mom like a toddler who had been lost in a crowd. My Benji. My anchor to the world. My best friend.

I cried until I could no longer breathe, and then I sunk down so deep into Mom's chest I had the feeling of her being water and I was the castaway lost at sea. "My Enna," she said. "It's okay to hurt. It's okay to mourn."

And I realized that of all the combinations of words on planet earth, those were the ones I needed to hear the most.

ANTONIO USED THE SAIL to steady us within sight of Lamplighter Mountain while the rest of us slept, rested, or simply let our thoughts glide away like ice skates on a frozen river. Pressure built in the sky and I worked my jaw back and forth to pop my ears. At the same time, my skin grew cool and damp as thick, dark clouds gathered above us. The other kids pressed on their ears, too, taking over-emphasized yawns to work out the pops. The pressure in the atmosphere was plummeting.

Finally, as things did in the era of the Polar Storms, thirst rousted us. All around us was water – saltwater. My tongue was thick and sticky against the roof of my mouth. Callie's saliva was viscous as tar, but I suspected she had already known thirst more dire and would not complain. It would take a long time to undo for her what had been done, a long time to hear her speak in a voice that was her own.

The least damaged of us took the oars and rowed slowly, haltingly, toward the mountain, toward a steep and jagged shore. Antonio fetched a bucket from the hold, and he and I lowered ourselves down the wooden ladder on the starboard. We waded toward land and set out into the trees until we found the trickle of a little creek. I dug away the gravel and moss with the heel of my shoe – the one Antonio retrieved after I hucked it at him – and we set the bucket in the hole to fill with fresh water. Bucket by bucket, we hauled water to the boat. The kids scooped it up into their hands and drank it down like the wine at Cana.

Once everyone had their fill, and our mouths were loosened and elasticity restored to our eyes and skin, we went around the boat and introduced ourselves. Some shook or cried so hard their names were barely understandable. Miguel, Noah, Michelle, Sofia, two Davids, Tyler, Jason, Danay, Liam, Sen, Micah, Eric, Sono, Cyrus, and Diedre – the one with a gunshot wound in her arm.

"Who was the one we lost in the water?" I asked.

"Elian," Antonio answered.

"I'm sorry we couldn't save him," I said.

Antonio shook his head. "You did save him. Even if he didn't live."

The girl named Michelle stood up from her huddle against the side of the boat. She walked over to Mom at the stern and stood in front of her, wordlessly. They looked at each other for several seconds. Then Mom opened her arms wide and gestured the girl in. Michelle walked into her embrace and Mom pulled in her tight, closing her eyes and whispering into her ear. Then each of the kids stood up, in turn, and gathered around Mom, each desperate for the embrace of a parent long lost. She took each one into her arms. "You're safe now," she said. And it didn't matter if we believed it. It was enough to hear someone speak it. "You're safe now."

The boy named Micah hugged Mom the longest. None of us could see how he had been crying into her shoulder until he pulled away and a long trail of snot jump-roped from Mom's shirt to his nose, swinging between them. His eyes went wide, mortified. No matter where we were or we had endured, we were still teenagers – and embarrassment rules. But Mom knew what to do. She pulled her sleeve over her hand and wiped the snot away from his face. And she started to laugh. Not mockingly. Lovingly. Affectionately.

And we all started to laugh, every single one of us. It cleared out our bodies like wind over the dust in an abandoned house when the window is finally opened. It loosened our necks, our shoulders, our lungs.

It would be a long time before I could reach down in my memories and untangle the moments at Pluto Cove that had been joyous, happy. At the time, it seemed there had been none and never would be. But there had been days early on when Dad was detoxing from his coffee addiction and was gripped by splitting headaches and admonishing Mom for forgetting – in all she thought to pack out to the cove – to bring coffee. She massaged his scalp and kissed the top of his head with a big smile *Now, now Alex.* She said, *Think of this as a way to conquer your vices.* And Dad said, *I don't have any vices!* And Callie and I

328

watched from the kitchen table, giggling.

There were the boxes and bags of second-hand clothes Mom had bought at thrift stores in her rush to prepare for our escape. Clothes she had not looked at before stuffing it into "all you can fit for one dollar" bags. For a long time, she wore a nightshirt, every night, with the print of a body featuring an enormous bosom and cinched waist clad in a pink polka dot bikini. *It fits!* Mom insisted as she donned it night after night. *It fits, is all*! And Dad pulled her in close with a kiss on her neck. *We get it, Lisa.* He said. *You've never looked more beautiful.*

There was the time Benji tussled with a porcupine and lost, coming home with a snout full of quills and whimpering like a child wanting to be held but whose mother is busy cooking. Dad pulled the forceps from his medical kit and said *Guess I'm a veterinarian now*, and tweezed out the quills, one by one. Mom and I held Benji by the trunk to keep him still and calm, and Callie climbed under him and scratched his belly as hard as her little hands could. And poor Benji, his face and pride so wounded, could not conceal his joy at having all four members of his family lavish attention and love at him at one time. Dad stuffed his wagging tongue back into his mouth to access the quills. The next day, Benji pulled the forceps off their perch on the counter and nudged us all back to that same spot next to the fire, dropping the forceps on the ground like a fetching ball. How we laughed; our dog, recreating his medical procedure.

There was Dad as his eyes began to change, and he held his books further and further away from his face. One day, Mom and I walked into the cabin to find Callie holding his book for him while she sat on the coffee table

329

and he squinted down his nose from the couch. *Little closer*, he said. *No, wait, a little further.* And she adjusted the book by painfully small increments from five feet away. Mom and I doubled over in the doorway, gripping our sides. *My old man!* She called out. *My old man!*

And the time I pulled the canned raspberry preserves from the cellar as my lunch and ate them even though they tasted a bit off. Tangy, a little bitter. But I was hungry, and they were sweet. I ate them down and then scraped the jar clean. A few minutes later, I was hiccupping on the porch, watching a Steller's jay eye our chickens and yelling at the Steller's jay. *Hey!* I shouted. *Hey you! You get outta here!* faking a New York accent I had seen in a movie. *Scram now! You!* And Mom came out to assess the commotion and took one look at me and sputtered, *Enna! Are you … are you DRUNK?* I swatted her away like a nuisance fly. *Fuhgeddaboudit*, I said making my mouth big and gesturing wild with my hands. But then I realized she was right, and the two of us fell to the floor of the porch, grimy with dirt and sticky with spruce needles, and laughed until we could not breathe.

For as long as I had dreamed of my exit from Pluto Cove, of stumbling out of the forest and into a new life with a group of people, of survivors, who were full of warmth and light and water, who thrived in a new world of music and fruits and color and children, it had never once occurred to me that we were those people. We were our own rescue. We were the people I had been waiting for.

THE NEXT MORNING was dark with clouds, gray and gravid. Hunger buzzed and stung our bellies like trapped bees. Mom stood at the bow as we rounded the corner into Pluto Cove. There was the cabin, boarded up and dark, sitting in the forest like a part of the ecosystem itself. Clouds hung low and heavy, obscuring the side of the mountain and casting the chimney in a swirl of fog. The creek was swollen like a wound, gushing water, widening its own channel, as the jökulhlaup fed it – slower now, but still a torrent. The beach stood empty, quiet. Mist drifted across the gravel, and the color of our evergreen trees ecstatic against the gray world. It was exactly how I remembered Pluto Cove as a child before the Polar Storms. It was exactly how I remembered Alaska.

"It's still early, Mom," I said, setting down my oar and walking over to her. "It could take them a while to get down the mountain."

She nodded, struggling to convince herself of that.

The rest of the kids rowed us in. Antonio guided them in toward the gravel bar where Mom parked the skiff. An easy anchorage. I felt the drag and crunch of gravel under the hull and knew it was time to climb off, to walk again up to Pluto Cove unsure of what awaited us, of the life we would build. Of all the people who know what that new life entailed – the rebuilding, the subsistence, the hard winters and explosively verdant and prolific summers … and the eventual exodus from Pluto Cove in that Viking ship out into the great world beyond – if anyone knows, it's you. That is the life you have led, the only life you have known. The water of Pluto Cove circulates in your veins. The minerals of its soil built you out of air. The fish in its seas strung the folds of your brain together like strands of lights – and what a beautiful, astonishing brain you have. Like Callie's. Pluto Cove is yours to remember and carry when I am gone.

There, emerging from the fog and forest like a mirage shimmering in the brains of starving explorers, was Dad, walking down the hill alongside the creek, you in his arms.

"Alex!" Mom screamed, jumping from the boat, not bothering with the ladder, landing in a crouch and taking off at a run. It was not a mirage. It was you. Dad the old man, weak and bruised, holding his son, sleeping and peaceful and trusting, wrapped in the furs of a bear.

And trotting behind them, slow and limping, was my creature who had swam, who had walked, who had found his way home, my Benji.

I gasped as my chest filled with sweet, heavy air, with the smell of moss and lichen and fluttering grasses, with the smell of spruce in the towering trees and of life itself, reviving me, working its way into the spaces between my cells, the spaces between the electrons in their orbits, into the air passing through my blood, lifting me up and up and up like a paper lantern into the sky.

"Hey guys," I said, looking back to the seventeen of us who would pioneer this speck of land in the northern latitude of this ailing planet. "We're home."

That is when the sky ripped open. And it began to rain.

A Note From the Author

I am a white woman, and this is a story told from the perspective of a Mexican-American girl. When I started writing this story, I did not know Enna; she was merely fragments of a person who occupied my thoughts. As the story unfolded, I came to understand her background, and wrestled with my place in imagining this story. I have not lived Enna's experiences, but have labored to be accurate, empathetic, and true. There are aspects of Enna that I cannot represent, but I strive to honor her story and her identity here in these pages.

ACKNOWLEDGEMENTS

Thank you to the Dena'ina people on whose land I was born. Thank you to the Alutiiq people whose land inspired this story.

Thank you to Alena Gerlek, the other half of my orange. My original frenemy and forever best friend. You are a beautiful tropical fish, a noble land-mermaid, a talented, brilliant, powerful muskox. Thank you, ox.

Thank you to the women in my life: Rachel, Emily, Sarah, Michelle, Eva, Jessica, Virginie, Luz, Alix, Jill, Julie, Alisha, Anaely, Alyse, Alanna, Meg, Melissa, Kate, Grace, Aileen, Laura, Jen, and so many more. They make every day Galentine's Day.

Thank you to the men in my life, who are fewer but just as cherished: Nick, Will, Bradford, Bear, Daniel, Mark, and Lucus. And Vikram Patel ... without for you I would have turned into a belltower monster and been eaten by my own cats.

Thank you to my editor, Sarah Westin, whose coffeehouse chats with me were among my last social moments of 2020, but whose voice continued to echo each time I attempted a quarantine rewrite.

Thank you to my "old" (former) boss, David Nyman, for setting the bar impossibly high for all other bosses to follow.

Thank you to the crew and all the storytellers at Arctic Entries whose courage and unrelenting, unpaid work make Anchorage a wonderful place to live.

Thank you to my family in-state, down south, and abroad – those who I call family by DNA and those I lucked into. A special note to my uncle-dad, Tommy, who knows every feature of the terrain described in this story and who has vanquished every grizzly bear I've encountered, both real and imagined. If cancer were a disease that could be defeated by force of will and physical strength, Tommy would have every advantage. But it's not, and so I ask for your hope.

Thank you to Eva Saulitis, whose poetry and essays taught me that a love for this big, wild place can translate into words and activism.

Thank you to the teachers at Summit High School, a group of adults more caring, imaginative, and encouraging than any I could make from scratch. Fifteen years later (and with no grades or college admissions on the line), I only have ever-increasing love for you.

Thank you to my coworkers at the NICU who remind me every day that there is nothing more powerful in a crisis than a group of dedicated, whip-smart women moving together. My fourth-grade self, wearing an oversized *Girl Power* t-shirt, was always just waiting to meet you.

I could thank people forever. But, if I could thank only one person, it'd be Matt Faust. Somehow both my sail and my anchor, he can navigate any landscape, tie any knot, can correctly pronounce the word *jökulhlaup* in swoony Icelandic, and shovels the driveway for any snow accumulation exceeding ¼ inch. He is the bearded, intellectual mountain man I dreamed of while listening to Jewel's debut cassette tape on my bedroom floor.

ABOUT THE AUTHOR

Arran was born
in Alaska,
raised in Alaska,
and currently lives in
Alaska.
Though she's tried on
a few homes
in other states
and continents,
she only ever goes in a circle.

WORKS REFERENCED

Alcott, Louisa May. Little Women. Melbourne, London, Baltimore: Penguin Books, 1953.

Anderson, Hans Christian. The Little Match Girl. Milwaukee: G. Stevens, 1987.

Auerbach, Paul S., Howard A. Donner, and Eric A. Weiss. Field Guide to Wilderness Medicine, Second Edition. Maryland Heights: Mosby, 2003.

Beowulf: A New Verse Translation. Translated by Seamus Heaney. Norton, 2000.

Chaucer, Geoffrey, and Jill Mann. The Canterbury Tales. London: Penguin, 2005.

Dewdney, Anna. Llama Llama Red Pajama. New York: Viking Books for Young Readers, 2005.

Eliot, T.S. The Waste Land. New York: Penguin, 1998.

Feynman, Richard P. Six Easy Pieces: Essentials of Physics Explained by Its Most Brilliant Teacher Richard P. Feynman. Addison-Wesley Publishing, 1994.

Gregory, Phillippa. The Constant Princess. Knox: Center Point Publishing, 2006.

Leroux, Gaston. The Phantom of the Opera. New York: Barnes & Noble, 1992.

Lowry, Lois. The Giver. New York: Laurel Leaf, 1993.

Morrison, Toni. Beloved: A Novel. New York: Knopf, 1987.

Ovid and Allen Mandelbaum. The Metamorphoses of Ovid. New York: Harcourt Brace, 1993.

Saint-Exupéry, Antoine de, Antoine de Saint-Exupéry, and Katherine Woods. The Little Prince. 1943.

Wilder, Laura Ingalls. Little House on the Prairie. New York: HarperCollins, 1992.

THE KITTIWAKE CLAN

Book Two of the Polar Storm series.
Coming at you, someday.